REMNANTS

by

Stan Poel

HERITAGE BEACON

F I C T I O N

REMNANTS BY STAN POEL
Published by Heritage Beacon Fiction
an imprint of Lighthouse Publishing of the Carolinas
2333 Barton Oaks Dr., Raleigh, NC 27614

ISBN: 978-1-946016-39-3
Copyright © 2018 by Stan Poel
Cover design by Elaina Lee
Interior design by AtriTex Technologies P Ltd

Available in print from your local bookstore, online, or from the publisher at:
ShopLPC.com

For more information on this book and the author visit: http://stanpoel.com/

Brought to you by the creative team at Lighthouse Publishing of the Carolinas (LPCBooks.com):
Eddie Jones, Ann Tatlock, Shonda Savage, Tom Threadgill, Brian Cross, Elaina Lee

Library of Congress Cataloging-in-Publication Data
Poel, Stan.
Remnants / Stan Poel 1st ed.

Printed in the United States of America

Dedication

For the Jan Atsma family, who sheltered Dutch Jews on their farm in the Netherlands. They represent the courageous Dutchmen who protected their neighbors, risking everything with no expectation of reward or recognition.

ACKNOWLEDGMENTS

I thank God for giving me stories to tell and blessing me with both the capacity to write and a fantastic support system that compensates for my shortcomings.

Number one in my support system, in my writing and in every other aspect of my life, is my wonderful wife, Wilma. She was the first to read my drafts and provided invaluable insights, along with tremendous patience and encouragement.

I owe much to the great publishing team at Lighthouse Publishing of the Carolinas. A special thanks to the two editors who led me every step of the way to publication. Tom Threadgill is a master at bringing life to characters. Ann Tatlock has been the ideal managing editor. I have greatly appreciated her kindness and guidance.

I must recognize my faithful critique partners: Barbara Allison, Mary Hamilton, Scott Hamilton, Victoria Kendig, Linda LaRoque, Jan Matlock, Jane Strickland, and Betty Willis. We became friends as we grew together. Watch for their names. Some are already published. I hope they all reach that goal.

A special thanks goes to Chris Fabiszewski and Jane Strickland for their valuable insights after careful study of the entire manuscript. They were wonderful.

CHAPTER ONE

6 May 1940
Nijkerk, Netherlands

A speeding airplane flashed low overhead and shattered the quiet air. The wooden bucket slipped from Jenny's grasp, and she dropped to her knees. A nearby flock of hens exploded into a flapping and screeching panic, raising a cloud of dust and white feathers in the fenced chicken yard. She blinked her eyes open just in time to catch the shape of the single-engine plane disappearing over the trees. Exhaust fumes from the low-flying craft drifted to the ground and pushed aside the earthy scents of the farm.

Jenny ignored her terrified flock and studied the sky where the plane disappeared. *The Germans have come.*

A few billowing cumulus clouds greeted her. Nothing more.

She stood and brushed off the dust. The hens returned to pecking and scratching the dirt. A half-minute later, her heart rate spiked at the sound of an airplane in the distance. *He's back.*

The plane appeared over the trees, flying directly toward her.

Her anxious gaze scanned her surroundings, desperately searching for safety. The nearby chicken coop offered refuge from view, but no protection from guns or bombs. She dropped to her knees again and gritted her teeth.

The aircraft cruised past, slower this time, an orange triangle proudly displayed on the plane. Its wings dipped a few times.

1

Tension drained from her body as the craft disappeared in the distance. She turned to her flock. "You girls just relax. It wasn't a German attack at all. It was one of our planes. I bet it was that crazy DeVries kid showing off." She picked up her pail. "Alec is playing war hero with nobody to fight."

The door to the farmhouse opened, and her mother stepped outside. "What's the racket out here, Jenny?"

"I think it was just that DeVries boy, Mama. The one who became a pilot. I think he was trying to impress me."

A smile appeared on the older woman's face. "Did he succeed?"

"Maybe. But only a little. Mostly, he made me mad when he scared my chickens."

"Don't be too hard on him, dear. He will make someone a good husband when he grows up a bit."

Her mother stepped back inside, and Jenny rolled her eyes before turning to her little flock. "Last thing I need right now is a husband. I have things to accomplish, but not on a farm and not just as some guy's housewife." She dumped the remainder of the chicken feed from her bucket and moved toward the gate. "Now, if you sweet girls will excuse me, I have laundry to do."

Jenny closed the gate to the chicken yard and strode to the barn attached to the back of the farmhouse. Using a hand pump, she filled two wooden buckets with water and attached them to the ends of a yoke. She groaned as she hoisted the contraption onto her shoulders, then toted the buckets outside and emptied their contents into the wood-fired water heater. After stoking the flames, she returned for additional water.

Minutes later, she carried hot water back into the barn and filled two large wooden tubs. She added soap to one, tossed soiled clothing into the mix, and proceeded to stir the contents with a wooden paddle. When done, she rinsed the clothes in the second tub.

A full hour later, she carried a wicker basket filled with clean, wet laundry to the outdoor clothesline. The clip-clop of a pair of large horses echoed as her father guided the family wagon into the farmyard. He slowed to a stop beside her.

"Nicolaas left word at the store that he was coming home today and bringing a friend with him." As he paused, the horses jerked the wagon forward, and he yanked the reins. "These boys always get a burst of energy when we head for the barn. So, everything all right here, Jen?"

"We did have a little excitement, Papa. A Dutch plane buzzed the farm. Probably Alec DeVries."

His eyes crinkled into a smile. "Sounds like him. Those young pilots do have some fun when they are training." A frown appeared. "But things may get more serious for them soon."

"Maybe he's just wasting good Dutch fuel preparing for a war that won't happen."

"Maybe so." He snapped the reins, and the horses pulled the wagon into the barn.

She lifted the wet, faded apron her mother had worn as long as Jenny could remember, pinned it to the clothesline, and paused. Was war coming? *Papa is worried. Mama too.*

A clattering sound caught her attention, and she peeked between the hanging garments. Two men on bicycles rattled along the quiet farm road and turned into the DeHaans' driveway, then rested their bikes against the house.

Jenny returned a wave from the taller of the two, her brother Nicolaas. She looked down at herself, wearing dirty men's slacks and a too-large man's work shirt. *A visitor and I'm looking like this.* She shrugged. *Maybe he's not cute.*

As the young men approached, she waited, hands on her hips. "So, the schoolboy returns. I'm glad you're here. There's real work to be done." She tucked a loose strand of her long hair behind her ear and grinned. "Hello, brother." She took Nic's hand, pulled him to herself, and gave him a firm hug.

She turned to the other man. He actually was fairly cute. Slim. Beautiful brown eyes. "I'm Jenny. Who are you?" She gripped his hand and gave it a firm shake.

He blinked and gazed somewhere over her shoulder. "I'm Marten. Um, you have a strong handshake."

"And your hand is about as soft as a baby's butt. Do you ever work?"

Marten blinked again. "Well, um, not the kind of work you do, but I would like to try."

Jenny studied him, head to foot, then turned to her brother. "This guy might be all right, Nic." She shrugged. "We'll see." She grinned at Marten. "Actually, my brother has told me a lot about you. It's nice to meet you."

He responded with a weak smile.

Nic glanced at the clothes hanging on the line and shifting in the breeze. "Must be laundry day."

"Sure is. Every Monday, week after week after week."

"Well," Nic said. "I guess we'll go inside and check on Mama. See you when you're done, Jen."

As the men headed for the house, Marten turned and locked gazes with her for only a second before hurrying after Nic. Jenny watched him all the way to the house. Something about that guy. Attractive but vulnerable. Even strong in his own way. *I need to find out more.* She rushed to finish her chores.

Near noon, with the week's laundry finally complete, Jenny hurried into the kitchen. Her brother and his friend were already seated at the table.

Her mother stood at the stove, giving the meal one last inspection. "You're just in time for dinner, sweetheart." She placed a lid on a pot and wiped her hands on her apron. "I hope you like simple farm food, Marten."

"I'm sure I will, Mrs. DeHaan."

"Good. You boys might want to wash up. Albert will be on time for dinner."

"The schedule on the farm is a bit different," Nic said. "The day here starts at about four o'clock with feeding the animals and milking. That's every day. Dairy cattle don't take any time off. We come in for breakfast at eight. Then we have a big dinner at noon and a big supper at the end of the day. We work hard around here, and we eat well, thanks to Mama."

Marten looked around. "I guess we should wash up then."

Jenny pointed at the hand pump at the sink. "Water is right here in the kitchen." She nodded her head toward the back door. "Toilet is outside."

The back door opened, and Father appeared. He pulled off his cap, revealing his thick blond hair. His deeply lined and tanned face spoke of his many years working outdoors.

He strode across the room and shook the hand of the young visitor. "You must be Marten." The voice was deep and gentle. "A real pleasure to meet you. From what I hear, you have been a big help to Nicolaas at the university. I'm Albert DeHaan."

"It is a pleasure to meet you too, sir. I have been anxious to visit."

Father gave Nic a quick, strong hug. "Can you stay the night, son?"

"We can't, Papa. Sorry. We were off today but have classes tomorrow. I just needed to pick up a book I left on my last visit, and I thought Marten would like to see the farm."

Mother set a serving dish on the table. "All right, everybody. Let's eat before the food gets cold."

A simple Dutch dinner of pork chops, potatoes, vegetables, and home-baked bread topped with farm-fresh butter covered the large kitchen table. The family gathered around it, and while they held hands, Albert said a short prayer: "Bless us, oh Lord, and these thy gifts which we are about to receive from thy bounty." After a quick pause, he continued, "And protect our family and our peaceful country from war. Amen."

"Do you think the Germans are coming, Papa?" Nic asked.

Albert studied his wife's frowning face. "Probably not, but they did invade Denmark and Norway last month. That does concern me, Emma."

She picked up a serving dish and passed it to her husband. "Let's not talk of such things at the table."

Marten paused to observe the family loading their plates. His gaze met Jenny's, and she stifled a smile. "Better eat up. When it's gone, it's gone."

Mother frowned. "You take your time, Marten. Believe me; there is plenty."

He looked back at Jenny, and she winked.

When the dishes were almost bare, and no one seemed to want more, Nic, still holding his knife and fork, rested his forearms on the edge of the table. "Does it look good for this season, Father?"

"It does. The animals are healthy. We should get enough calves and piglets. And if we can avoid a late frost, the fruit should be good. So, how about school, son? Are you getting all your work done while you're holding down that job?"

"Working in the print shop does slow my education, but I am learning a lot too. And I even have time for fun."

Jenny sliced the last of her meat. "Must be nice. Here I am, nineteen years old, stuck on the farm while my brother, barely a year older, goes to college."

As a tense pause settled over the room, she continued, "I'm still determined to go to university. I learned English and German at our school, and I'm ready after spending this past year working on the farm. And I've already applied to Utrecht."

Papa stopped loading tobacco into his pipe. "I'm proud of your spirit, Jenny. I was happy when you applied, and I hope you find a way to go. I am sorry we have no money to pay for your university. What little we have to offer must go to Nicolaas since he will be a breadwinner one day."

She set her knife and fork on her plate, looked down, and gritted her teeth.

"There are other girls at school, Jen," Nic said. "They have jobs. You could get one. Uncle Jake and Aunt Cora said you could stay with them."

"You would fit right in," Marten added.

His bright expression encouraged her. "If you don't mind hanging around with a first-year student," she said. "A girl with ideas of her own."

"Hey, this is university," Marten said. "It's all about ideas, learning new things, and making new friends. Are you thinking of a career as a teacher or a nurse?"

Typical man. She glared at him. "A doctor, actually."

She winced at the pained expression on their visitor's face. "Sorry I popped off like that. I get a little intense sometimes."

Marten's face softened. "No problem." He paused for a moment. "Say, Jen, next weekend Nicolaas is going with me to my home in The Hague. We are going with my father to an Ajax soccer game. Would you like to come with us?"

"Sounds good." She turned to her father. "Can you spare me for a couple days, Papa?"

He smiled and nodded.

"I can ride back as far as Nijkerk with you this afternoon," Jenny said. "We can talk more."

Mama stood and retrieved a dish from the counter. "How about some *appeltaart* before you kids leave?" Almost faster than they could respond, she placed a slice in front of Marten, along with a bowl of whipped cream.

He smiled up at her. "The Americans call this pie. Yours looks better." He held his fork poised over the dessert. "I'm glad I had a chance to visit your family today. I love your farm. Nijkerk is a nice town too. This morning I got a quick tour as we passed through. Nicolaas showed me his old school and your church."

Papa smoothed a generous helping of whipped cream on the appeltaart. "Which church do you attend?"

"The Sephardic synagogue in The Hague."

Mama gasped and brought her hands to her cheeks. "Oh, my."

The conversation froze.

Nic cast a nervous glance at Marten. "What's the problem, Mother?"

"What's the problem? The problem is I just fed the boy some pork. That was not good. I am so sorry, Marten." She studied the dessert dish in her hand. "It's a bit late on the pork, but is the appeltaart all right?"

"It's fine, Mrs. DeHaan. My family is very relaxed about the food thing. We never require kosher when we visit non-Jewish friends, or even when we eat in restaurants. Frankly, I like pork, especially bacon."

7

Three bikes rattled along the unpaved road on the half-mile ride into Nijkerk, passing small farms on each side.

"I love the quiet out here," Marten said. "Not a car in sight. Much different from the city."

Jenny pulled alongside him. "What's it like in The Hague? I've never been there."

"Just another town. I'll show you all around." He paused for a moment. "So you want to be a doctor, Jen. Me too, maybe. What made you decide on that?"

"Well, it's like this. The thought of spending my life feeding chickens or being a housewife doesn't work for me. Don't get me wrong. I plan to settle down and have a bunch of kids, but not right now. I need to strive for something—something hard and meaningful. I have mountains to climb. Know what I mean?"

"Maybe you should head for Switzerland to climb your mountains, Jen," Nic said with a chuckle. "This country is flat as Mama's kitchen table."

"Oh, you know what I mean. I need a big challenge, something to fire me up. And I like helping people, especially kids. Medical school seems perfect."

"Do you have a backup plan?" Marten asked.

"Nope. Don't need one. I plan to succeed."

The three friends rolled into the small town of Nijkerk.

"Let's get a Coca-Cola at Vander Molen's store," Nic suggested.

"I'll meet you there," Jenny said. "I need to pick up the mail." They stopped in front of the store, and she crossed the street to the post office.

She pulled out the one envelope waiting in the box, and her heart leaped. In bold letters, the return address shouted at her: "University of Utrecht." With trembling fingers, she ripped open the envelope and read it aloud. "Dear Miss DeHaan. We are pleased to inform you"—she gasped and began again— "We are pleased to inform you that you are accepted as a student of the University of Utrecht."

"Yes, yes, yes!" Her words echoed around the room. The wide-eyed postmaster gaped at her.

"I'm in, Jake."

"In what?"

She ran for the door and shouted over her shoulder. "In university."

She burst through the post office door and ran toward Marten and her brother, waving the letter as she went. "I'm in. Utrecht accepted me." She hugged the beaming friends.

"Marten, about that trip to The Hague on the weekend. I think I need to postpone it. I need to see about a job in Utrecht."

CHAPTER TWO

9 May 1940
Utrecht, Netherlands

Marten set his coffee cup on the table and leaned back while the server refilled it.

"Why did you want to meet your driver on the far side of campus?" Nic asked. "Couldn't he just pick us up at our house?"

"He could, but I told him to meet us here. I don't like attracting that kind of attention around our friends, though Karl seems to enjoy showing off the car well enough."

Nic lifted a bagel. "Karl? Is he a Dutchman?"

"German, actually, and I think he loves our German car more than he loves his fatherland."

"Does his family live here?"

"No, they're in Germany. Karl lived here for a couple years after the last war when people there were going hungry. The Netherlands cared for many of the children from Germany and Austria. He was one of them. Karl must have liked it here. He came back last year."

Marten straightened in his chair and pointed down the street. "He's coming."

A large black car with a black canvas top rolled toward them. Sunlight flashed off its chrome bumpers and headlamps.

"I see what you mean about all the attention. That thing does make a statement. Looks really expensive."

Marten hurried toward the street. "I don't know what it cost. Probably a lot." He waved at the approaching car. The vehicle slowed, and its large tires crunched to a stop on the pavement. The deep hum of the powerful engine ceased, and the driver appeared in his chauffeur uniform, complete with black suit and tie, white shirt, and military-style cap.

Marten rushed toward the rear door, but Karl got there first. He opened the door smartly and stood at attention. "Good morning, Mr. Demeester."

Marten dove past him and slid across the smooth leather seat. The guy did it again. Made a big show in front of everybody. *He knows I hate that.*

Karl turned his attention to the second passenger. "Good morning, Mr. DeHaan."

Nic tossed his old satchel onto the seat and followed it into the car.

Marten slumped and waited for the driver to take his position behind the wheel. "Okay, Karl. Enough of the show. Let's go."

"Sorry, sir. Just following orders."

Marten checked Karl's face in the rearview mirror. Just a hint of a smirk. Everybody liked the guy, even the other staff, but there were those little things. *Why does he keep doing that stuff?*

"Well, I'd say we did get everyone's attention back there," Nic said. "I can see how it's embarrassing for you."

"Happens every time. It's even worse when Father puts the top down. Then there's no place for me to hide."

"The driver addressed me by name."

"He has been briefed well. Father is really quite good with details."

"Is this Karl's only job?"

"He also maintains the car and takes care of our landscaping."

In a few minutes, they left Utrecht behind and entered the Dutch countryside. "This will be a new experience for me," Nic said. "I have never visited The Hague, or anywhere else west of Utrecht, to be honest with you."

"It has its good points, I guess, but, believe it or not, I really like your farm. Do you think I could work there sometime?"

"That would be great. My family likes you."

"I'm not sure about your sister, and I sure didn't help matters with some of my comments, like that nurse thing. I thought she might come over the table at me."

That brought a chuckle from the other side of the back seat. "Don't worry about that. Trust me. She likes you. The guys she doesn't like, she just ignores and doesn't waste her time on them."

"So what is the best way for me to treat her?"

"Keep doing what you're doing."

Nic slid his hand across the smooth leather seat. "You never mentioned that your family is rich. Why not?"

"I want to make my own way."

"Interesting. I never had to face that kind of decision. Do you have servants?"

"We do have a butler, who also helps my father manage his business. And we have three maids, who are also cooks."

"Does your father travel a lot in his work?"

"Sure does. He imports a lot of different things, puts them in his warehouses, and then sells them all over the world. And he has taken my brother and me on many trips. His favorite place is America. He's been there at least a dozen times and insists that we speak English in our home. A large part of his business is importing their goods. He even used an American design when he built our house, including large bathrooms."

Nic cranked the window down a bit, then back up again. "Have you ever driven this car?"

"I have, and just between you and me, even though it's a big luxury car that rolls gently down the road when Karl drives, it can really charge if you push it."

"I'm guessing that you have pushed it."

"Maybe a little too hard. I am required to have Karl with me when I drive. One time I got going so fast that I thought he was going to have some kind of seizure. It is the only time he has shouted at me. Probably a good thing he did. I do appreciate that he never told Father about it." He paused for a few seconds. "Maybe I'm not always consistent in my positions in life. Money can be fun sometimes."

"Hey, nobody's perfect."

An hour after leaving Utrecht, they glided through the Demeesters' neighborhood in The Hague. Homes in this area stood alone, each surrounded by manicured lawns and colorful gardens.

The car rolled slowly up the driveway and passed a flower garden filled with yellow daffodils. With a slight squeak of the brakes, the car stopped at the wide sidewalk leading to a heavy, arched door. Karl immediately jumped out, but before the chauffeur could open the rear doors for his passengers, Marten made a fast exit and hurried toward the house. "Come on, Nic."

Before they reached the front door, it swung wide to reveal a tall man wearing pinstriped trousers and a long black coat. Expressionless, he nodded. "Good morning, sir."

Ignoring the formality, Marten jabbed the sober butler in the ribs with an index finger. "Good to see you, Desmond."

A hint of a smile tugged on the mouth of the perfectly groomed butler. He stood aside and held the large oak door for the two young men. Bright sunlight shined through an arched transom window and sparkled among the teardrop crystals of a giant chandelier. Straight ahead, a wide carpeted stairway rose to a landing where it divided, the two sides continuing to the upper floor. Nic took a couple of steps into the house, stopped, and studied a large landscape of the Dutch countryside. "Wow. What a beautiful picture."

"Hey, there are more in the drawing room. I'll show you." Marten led the way to a large paneled room with tall windows overlooking the flower garden. Paintings adorned every wall.

They moved in silence from one painting to the next. Finally, they stopped in front of the smallest painting in the room, an oil on canvas about eighty centimeters wide. "This one is really nice. Who painted it?"

A bass voice filled the room. "Ah, you have excellent taste, young man."

Marten's father stood in the doorway. He wore a tailored, three-piece suit. His dark hair and short, well-trimmed beard framed a kind expression. "A man named Johannes Vermeer painted that picture. It was done in the 1600s." He gave the visitor a firm handshake. "I am Reinaar Demeester. I expect you are Nicolaas DeHaan."

"Yes, sir."

"I have been looking forward to meeting you. Marten has spoken very highly of you."

"You have so many nice paintings, Mr. Demeester. This one is especially beautiful. So real and alive."

Father's smile revealed perfect teeth. "It is my favorite. The first Demeester to come to this country from Portugal arrived here in 1620. He became acquainted with Vermeer when the painter was quite poor. We think he acquired this painting directly from the artist. It has been in our family since that time, and I hope it stays in our family for many more generations."

The clicking of heels on the hardwood floor in the hallway interrupted the conversation. A lady about the same age as Marten's father entered the drawing room. Light-brown hair curled just above her shoulders, and her yellow shirtwaist dress matched the daffodils in the garden outside. She wrapped her arms around her son. It was not the quick hug the young man had received from his father. It was a long, firm, eyes closed, motherly kind of embrace. "Now, son, please introduce me to our guest."

"Mother, this is my friend, Nicolaas. Nic, this is my mother, Francien Demeester."

She offered a gentle hand. "Nicolaas, I have been anxious to meet you."

The conversation ceased abruptly when the giant front door slammed shut and the sound of running feet filled the hallway. Into the room burst a boy wearing a soccer uniform with a bright orange jersey. The dirt on the clothing and his knees and arms told of a recent adventure. Without slowing, the youngster dove into Marten who, after a startled grunt, grappled with the intruder. After allowing the little guy a few seconds of apparent success, the larger combatant pinned the smaller one to the floor. Their eyes met. "You'll have to do some growing before you can take me down, little brother."

The smiling boy looked at the visitor. "I'm Joran."

"I'm Nic. Your big brother told me that you are ten."

"Ten, but I'll be eleven in two months."

Mother glanced at the grandfather clock. "It is almost five o'clock. I think it would be a good idea to introduce our guest to his room. Then you boys can get cleaned up and relax before dinner. I will ask the staff to have the food ready at six."

As they left the room, Joran called after them. "Hey, Nic, maybe tonight we can play my new Monopoly game, okay?"

"I hope so. I would like that." Nic paused. "What's Monopoly?"

"A great new game Father brought me from New York last week."

At six o'clock, Marten led Nic into the dining room. Five settings of blue-and-white Delft china graced the white tablecloth. Father, wearing an open-neck dress shirt, seated Mother at the long oak table.

Marten made a sweeping gesture over the table. "Grab a seat, Nic."

The lady of the house smiled. "Yes, do select a chair, Nicolaas. You are the special guest."

After they were seated, Father gazed at the one empty place and shrugged. "He'll be here soon."

Footsteps clattered across the hardwood floor, echoed through the hallway, and burst into the elegant dining room. Joran appeared and paused for a moment before hurrying to the one lonely setting and plopping into the chair. "Good evening, everyone."

Father, with a hint of a smile, nodded to his son. "Thank you for joining us, Joran."

The boy's voice bubbled with enthusiasm. "I am happy to be here." He turned to Nic. "I hope you are enjoying yourself."

"I am. I look forward to that game you talked about."

"I think you'll like it. Father said everyone in America is playing it."

"They are indeed," the older man said. "In addition to our own, I have given several copies to friends. Based on their assessment, I may begin importing the game for sale in Europe." He glanced at the butler, who stood observing the family from the doorway, and nodded. Desmond disappeared and in less than a minute, followed the maids as they brought the food to the table.

With the meal in place, all eyes turned to Father. "Jewish people have many prayers for various situations, Nicolaas. Even prayers over specific foods. In our family, we have simplified things a bit. We normally have one blessing that we use at our family dinners. We call it the *HaMotzi*. I will add a rough translation. You are welcome to join us."

Nic closed his eyes and bowed his head.

Father's deep voice echoed off the walls. "*Barukh atah Adonai Elohaynu melekh ha-olam ha-motzi lechem min ha-aretz.* Blessed are You, Lord, our God, King of the Universe who brings forth bread from the earth."

In unison, the Demeester family said, "Amen."

Nic hastily responded, "Amen."

Joran reached slowly for the nearest serving bowl but froze when his mother frowned.

"We wait until our guest serves himself," she said, "and it might be helpful if we first told him about the food. You may do that, Marten."

Marten scanned the table. "Okay. Our wonderful staff—with mother's guidance—has prepared a variety of things for us. First, there is a nice salad. Then, we have roasted chicken and stuffed

17

peppers." He pointed to a plate filled with skewered tidbits of brown, green, white, and red morsels. "Those are lamb kabobs. My favorite."

He paused while he studied the table.

"You're doing well, son," said his mother. "Keep going."

"Okay. We also have *farfel*, which is toasted pasta dough." He lifted a lid. "This is *kugel*; it's a kind of noodle pudding." He looked at his mother. "I don't know what's for dessert."

"For dessert, we have *rugelach*, pastries filled with raisins. Or you might like the almond bread cookies."

"May we dip the cookies in coffee, Mother?" Joran asked.

"Yes, with the permission of our guest."

Nic winked at the boy. "I would like that."

Joran leaned over and nudged their visitor with his elbow. "I think I'm going to like this guy."

After dinner, as they enjoyed dessert and coffee, Father leaned back in his chair. "So, Nicolaas, what are you studying at the university?"

"I'm taking mostly business classes. I work part-time at a print shop in Utrecht to pay for my studies."

"And what kind of business interests you?"

"Retail, I think, probably clothing. Everybody needs clothes."

"Indeed. In the future, if things go well, I will want to talk more about this. Who knows? Perhaps we can work together."

"In your opinion, what is the business outlook for Holland right now?" asked Nic. "Are you concerned about the recent, um, activity to the east?"

"An excellent question, and a topic that Desmond and I have studied rather extensively of late. The Germans are causing a great deal of stress around the world right now. However, in spite of the threats they pose to other countries, we must focus on the unique situation in the Netherlands. During the last great war, we maintained our neutrality."

The older man took a sip of coffee and set the cup back in its saucer. "While there are still uncertainties about our current situation,

I hope Germany will consider our neutrality as supportive of their goals. However, having said that, we are very actively working to prepare for all eventualities."

He pulled a pocket watch from his vest. The gold chain drooped as he extended it. With a practiced flick of his thumb, he snapped open the watch cover and glanced at the old timepiece. "I would like to move our conversation to the drawing room. I am anxious to turn on the radio. The Germans have promised not to invade Holland if we observe neutrality. The German Führer is expected to give a speech tonight. It would be good to hear him confirm that promise."

Joran slid his chair back. "I'll get the radio warmed up." At his father's nod, he hurried from the room.

After finishing their coffee, the group walked to the drawing room. Joran sat on the floor and turned the dials on a large console radio. After a minute of listening to a cacophony of voices and music as the dial spun, he settled on a German-speaking voice.

"You've got it," Father said.

The shrill voice of Adolf Hitler filled the quiet room. Marten listened carefully and studied the expressions of those around him. The audience in the room, all fluent in German, sat expressionless, seeming to hang on every word coming through the radio. The words were those Marten hoped to hear, yet they left him nervous. The tone was not right. The room felt violated somehow.

When the short speech concluded, Joran was first to speak. "He said he will respect the neutrality of Holland. What does that mean, Papa?"

"He promised that he won't attack our country, son. He's going to leave us alone. While we can't rely on the man's word, continued neutrality does offer advantages to Germany, so perhaps he will leave us alone, at least for a while."

"So, there won't be a war?" asked Joran.

"Let's hope not. Please turn off the radio, and we can discuss it."

With Joran's turn of the black knob, the radio went silent, and everyone's attention turned to Father.

"We heard some encouraging words just now. However, we are faced with uncertainties, and we must prepare to deal with them. Since we are in the import and export business, our assets consist largely of warehouses full of products that we sell around the world. Desmond and I are working very hard to sell off these things. Although we stand to lose some money in the transactions, we feel we are subject to much greater losses if war comes to our country and to our trading partners. Unfortunately, these things will take time, but Hitler's comments are encouraging."

Marten studied his parents' mannerisms. Father's calm confidence seemed absent. The fidgeting, running his fingers through his hair. That was unusual. Mother sat in silence, studying her hands and twisting her ring. They were very worried and covering for the benefit of their children. It was working with Joran but not for Marten. Life was not the same.

Joran stood. "Enough serious talk. How about a game of Monopoly? You ready, Nic?"

"I am."

"Marten, you up for it?"

"Sure. Why not? Let's go, little brother."

Reinaar gradually emerged from a deep sleep. Moonlight stole through a crack in the drapes and provided the only illumination in the dark bedroom. He clicked the bedside lamp on to check his watch. Three o'clock. He turned off the light and settled back on his pillow. Francien's slow, gentle breathing was the only noise. Then, another sound reached him. The hum of distant airplane engines.

Now wide awake, he got up and dressed quietly. Francien continued her slow breathing as he eased out of the room and hurried down the stairs and out the front door. The Hague was noiseless other than the steady drone of airplanes passing high overhead.

He searched the sky. The moonlight outlined an armada of airplanes moving east to west. "Hundreds of them," he whispered. Where were they going? To England? Could this be the attack the British feared? *God help them.*

When the last of the planes had passed, he returned to the house and crept to the kitchen. As he opened the door, the light from the hallway partially illuminated the large, quiet room. Sliding his hand along the wall just inside the door, he located the switch and flooded the area with bright light.

He opened and closed several cabinets until he located a coffee percolator. After studying the parts for a few seconds, he successfully assembled the unit. From the tap, he added what he estimated to be a couple of cups of water, then opened a can of ground coffee, paused momentarily, shrugged, and filled the basket to the top. His project complete, he placed the unit on a stove burner and set the flame.

The sound and scent of percolating coffee gradually filled the room. He stood, arms folded, and watched the hot liquid splashing inside the little glass top of the gurgling coffeemaker. After searching the cabinets, he found a suitable cup and saucer. Carefully carrying the steaming coffee, he moved through the darkened house to his study and sat at his desk. The first sip—the strongest he'd tasted in recent memory—forced a frown, but he continued to drink as he reviewed documents.

Suddenly, a clap of thunder jolted him. He stood, rigid, looking straight ahead, listening. *Could it really be thunder? With a clear sky?* Then several more cracks in quick succession. The house shook. *No, not thunder.* "Bombs."

He tossed the pen and papers onto the desk and ran through the darkened house toward the front door. Marten's voice reached him from the staircase.

"Father, what's that noise?"

"Bombs!"

Marten ran down the staircase and joined his father outside. Moments later, Joran appeared, wearing pajamas like his brother.

Nicolaas followed, in the clothes from the night before. Finally, Francien, dressed in her robe, completed the gathering.

They stood close together, speechless, as the sounds of explosions rumbled through the now wakened city and repeated flashes lit the dark sky.

"Will the bombs come here?" asked Joran.

"It sounds like they are falling outside the city, at least for now." The wail of sirens began, first one, then a chorus.

"About forty-five minutes ago," Reinaar said, "a huge armada of airplanes flew over, heading west. At the time, I thought they were German planes going to England. Now I think they were just trying to trick us. They went out over the sea and turned around. Germany is attacking Holland. Hitler lied to us last night."

"Let's go up on the roof and look," Marten said.

Reinaar was about to answer, but his wife interrupted. "These children are going with me to the cellar." Her voice had a commanding tone, but a quiver hid just below the surface.

"I will join you when I can," Reinaar said. "I need to see what is happening. If the bombing gets closer, I will hurry downstairs. Marten, please collect everyone and take them with you. Send Desmond to me."

Francien nodded and rushed for the front door. Without any argument, all the young people followed into the house.

A few minutes later, Reinaar and Desmond eased themselves through the attic window and onto the roof of the house. This position allowed a panoramic view of The Hague. Reinaar scanned the proud old city. It appeared to sleep, but surely its people were being shocked awake into a new, terrifying reality.

In the growing morning sunlight, airplanes appeared, diving from high in the sky. When near the ground, they leveled off, guns flashing and chattering. While these small planes flew wild patterns, larger planes made straight runs over two areas north and south of the city. As they passed their target, a path of exploding bombs followed them.

Reinaar pulled a pack of American Camels from his pocket. Holding one between his lips, he lit a match. His trembling fingers refused to light the cigarette. He blew out the match and tossed it and the unlit cigarette off the roof toward the flower garden below. Hitler lied. The little monster put them all to sleep and then he unleashed his killers. So many airplanes. *We have no chance.*

Lights around the neighborhood came alive. People gathered outside their homes. Next door, a man appeared on his roof. He and Reinaar exchanged a weak wave.

"What is going on?" Desmond asked. "What are they doing to us?"

Reinaar pointed at the battle to their south. "It looks like that attack is right where the Ypenburg airfield is located, just outside The Hague, toward Delft."

At that moment, during a pause between explosions, several small planes appeared, apparently taking off from the location of the attack. An aerial dogfight followed that carried the planes up high into the sky.

"I was right," Reinaar said. "That is Ypenburg. We have fighter planes down there, but not many." He watched for several minutes as the nimble Dutch planes darted around the sky, attacking the invaders. "Those brave Dutch pilots are probably no older than Marten. It makes my heart ache. We will most likely watch those boys die today."

The anti-aircraft guns came alive, their tracer bullets chasing the intruding aircraft, catching some and bringing them down.

When the men turned their attention to the north side of The Hague, the unfolding scene was very similar to the attack at Ypenburg to the south. Multiple bomb blasts lit the sky. The sharp cracks of the explosions echoed through The Hague. "It looks like we are losing our young men up there also," Reinaar said.

"Do we have an airfield there, like the one in Ypenburg?"

"It's a new one at Valkenburg, west of Leiden. I've been there. The field isn't operational yet. I'm not sure the soil there would hold the weight of an airplane."

"Look," Desmond said, pointing to the west, toward the sea. "Two of our planes are coming down. It looks like they are landing."

"That must be the small airfield at Ockenburg. It is out near the dunes, on this side of the village of Poeldijk. My guess is that our boys ran out of ammunition. Thank God. Maybe they will survive this catastrophe."

Shortly after the Dutch planes landed at Ockenburg, a group of German fighters directed their attack routines toward that airfield.

Then, a change. The attack ceased, and the German aircraft flew off in various directions. Black smoke rose from bomb-damaged areas. Emergency sirens continued their warnings.

"Is it over?" whispered Desmond.

"I have no idea." Reinaar sat on the roof and leaned against the wall of his house. With quivering fingers, he lit a cigarette, successfully this time. Now that the Germans bombed the airfields, would they decide to hit the city next? His own house? Not just a house. It was, until minutes ago, his fortress, his haven, the gathering place for family love. Now it was a fragile box waiting to be destroyed.

"No, it can't be over, my friend. This is a major attack. There is no way a bit of Dutch resistance will make them run off."

"But the planes are gone, sir."

Reinaar looked to the sky out over the sea. "Not gone. They're still out there, just waiting for some reason." Scattered airplanes dotted the western sky above the gentle swells of the North Sea.

A new sound brought both men to their feet. The steady drone of airplane engines coming from the east. "Those planes sound different from the others. They sound like rotary engines. Like passenger airplanes."

Desmond pointed east over the neighboring rooftops. "There they are." A large group of dots, close together, gradually grew into a formation of airplanes. The cluster split to their left and right, moving to the north and south of The Hague.

"I know those planes," Reinaar said. "They are Junkers, Ju52 models. I have traveled on them. Lufthansa uses them. Unfortunately, I am sure we aren't dealing with Lufthansa today."

The two men stood silently as the slow-moving aircraft lumbered past Ypenburg airfield.

"What is that?" Desmond pointed as a trail of white objects followed each of the airplanes."

"Parachutes. They are dropping soldiers out of the sky. The Germans aren't content to let their ground army fight through our defenses. They are hopping right over them."

Some of the planes passed Ypenburg and moved on to Ockenburg and discharged their paratroops in that area.

"What next, Mr. Demeester?"

"Don't know. Since they're putting soldiers on the ground, the bombing at the airports must be finished. They might or might not bomb the city next. Probably not with soldiers moving in." He hesitated for a couple of seconds. "But now we are faced with the possibility of combat inside The Hague if our defenses collapse." He slowly shook his head. "I have no idea what to do or where to go to be really safe, Desmond."

Marten appeared at the open window. "The explosions stopped, Father. Is it over?"

"No, son. The bombing has stopped for now, but the Germans are now putting soldiers on the ground."

"Everyone is in the cellar now, except for Karl. He was not in his room."

"Gone?"

"Yes, sir. I noticed that his personal things are also gone. It's not like him to leave the house without telling us. I'm concerned."

"I'm concerned too. Very concerned." Reinaar's heart sank. Faithful Karl ran off right when he was needed most. Maybe the young German was not so faithful after all.

"May I come out and watch with you?"

"I think that might be all right for a few minutes. It's quiet at the moment."

A Heinkel bomber, flying slowly and about a hundred meters above the ground, passed in front of them, close enough to see the helmets of the pilots. As the twin-engine plane cruised past, it banked slightly left. The bold swastika painted on its tail left no doubt of its ownership.

"They're looking for something," Marten said.

Having reached a commercial area of the city, the bomber took on a straight-and-level posture. Doors on its belly swung open. Torpedo-like objects fell from the plane. As the Heinkel lumbered off toward the sea, the bombs tumbled silently downward. The men on the roof gazed as the bombs plummeted toward the buildings resting peacefully in their path. They pierced the roofs, then a millisecond later, the structures erupted. The shock wave slapped the men's faces and left their ears ringing. Pieces of rubble arched skyward, and a cloud of dust rose above the ruins. They continued to stare as flames appeared in the rubble.

Marten's voice broke. "What is that place, Father?"

Reinaar paused for a moment and then peered into his son's frightened eyes. In words just loud enough to be heard, he said, "That was the New Alexander Barracks, where military recruits live. I am afraid there are many dead and injured young boys in those barracks, boys just like you."

A confusing mixture of sorrow, fear, and anger stirred Reinaar's mind. His heart pounded on his ribcage. Tears escaped from the corners of his eyes. He turned away from his son and blinked them away.

"Maybe I should go back to the cellar," Marten said.

Reinaar gathered himself and nodded. The boy ducked back into the house.

The bomb blasts paused. Heinkel bombers gathered and departed toward their bases in Germany, leaving the Messerschmitts to continue their diving attacks. Scattered small arms fire continued from the direction of the three airfields. The civil defense horns continued to duel with the sirens of emergency vehicles.

Reinaar gazed at the smoke rising in the distance. "Go ahead and tell the family they can come upstairs for now, Desmond."

In a few minutes, his family had moved upstairs to the attic. Marten, Nicolaas, and Desmond came out on the roof. Francien and Joran stood inside the window while the young boy begged without success to go outside.

Reinaar approached Francien and hugged her. "They hit the barracks hard. There were over a hundred young recruits in the building. Most must be dead, the rest nearly so. Those Germans knew exactly where to go to kill our young soldiers."

Francien's muscles tightened. "What else do they know?"

"Probably a great deal, I'm afraid. They have friends hiding among us, perhaps more than we realize. Even Karl may be one of them."

"They're coming back!" Marten shouted. A fleet of airplanes approached from the east. The drone of their engines grew steadily louder. "What are they?"

"It sounds like more Junkers," Reinaar said.

As the planes passed, no parachutes emerged. Instead, the aircraft began circling the city and soon began an organized descent toward all three airports.

"No parachutes," Reinaar said. "They are trying to land a fleet of transports."

"Bringing in supplies?" Desmond asked.

"No. Can't be. They don't control the area yet." Reinaar sat on the roof and rubbed his temples. "I know what's happening. Those planes are full of soldiers. The bombing and strafing, along with the paratroops, was all done to kill our defenders. Now they are bringing an army in here on airplanes."

Suddenly, the areas around the airfields came alive with the rapid fire of chattering machine guns and the louder, sharp cracks of the anti-aircraft weapons.

Reinaar stood and gazed at the airports in the distance. "I might be wrong. Maybe our boys aren't quite as defeated as I feared."

The heavy defensive fire had a dramatic effect at Ypenburg. One by one, the transports made their slow approaches, only to be destroyed by gunfire as they touched down. Other planes, cruising above the conflict and waiting for a landing opportunity, became victims before they reached the battle. Dutch anti-aircraft batteries, using tracer rounds, found multiple targets. Some burst into flames in flight and became falling torches. Others lost control and fell to the ground, engines screaming.

Marten squinted toward the airfields at Ockenburg to the west and Valkenburg to the north. He watched one and then the other. "Look at the other two airfields. I see transports coming down, but they seem to be staying down. Nobody is taking off to allow others to land."

"They are probably getting torn to pieces," Reinaar said, "and clogging up the runways."

"I think you are right, Mr. Demeester," Desmond said. "Look out there by the sea. I see transports coming down out there. It looks like they are landing on the beach."

"Reinaar, I need to know something," Francien said. "Those bombs that fell. They sounded very close. They frighten me terribly. How far away are they?"

"The Germans dropped their bombs on the three airfields, all outside the city. Because of their power, they sounded much closer. The only bombs inside the city were directed at the barracks. They were carefully targeted. I believe the Germans want to preserve our city. They want to use it."

"I want my family to come inside now," Francien said. Her tone commanded attention. "Desmond, please arrange for breakfast in the dining room as usual." She paused, staring straight ahead for a few seconds. "And I'd like all the staff to dine with us. Tell them to fix anything they want."

Desmond took just a moment to study her face. "Yes, madam."

"And one other thing. Tell them there is no need to dress in their uniforms."

Accompanied by the sounds of gunfire in the distance, the group moved quietly to the main floor of the Demeester home.

Nicolaas approached Reinaar. "Mr. Demeester, may I speak to you for a minute?"

"Certainly, Nicolaas."

"I'm worried about my family, sir. I am sure the war won't be limited to The Hague. The German army must be rushing through the country. I think I should try to get back to my family on the farm."

"And your farm is outside Nijkerk, right?"

"Yes, sir."

A deep wrinkle etched Reinaar's forehead. "I wish we could drive you, but there are German troops all around The Hague. They would love to have a large Mercedes in their possession. You will be much safer on a bicycle. You may take one of ours."

Reinaar clutched the young man's shoulders. "The land army will move swiftly from the German border. You must hurry."

CHAPTER THREE

10 May 1940
DeHaan Farm

A sharp knock echoed through the DeHaan farmhouse. Jenny closed her book and peeked out her bedroom window. Gray exhaust curled out of the tailpipe of a black sedan with police markings on the front door. She bounded down the stairs and passed through the kitchen. "I'll get it, Mama. Looks like Chief Atsma's car."

Her mother looked up from the stove. "Invite him in for coffee. I'll call your father."

The police chief of Nijkerk stood at the front door in his crisp uniform, complete with a pistol in a hip holster. He removed his cap, and his voice was deep and urgent. "I must speak to your father, Jenny."

She swung the door fully open. "Sure. Come in."

As they entered the kitchen, Jenny's father opened the back door. "Morning, Chief." He pulled back a chair. "Coffee?"

"Can't, Albert. We got the call this morning."

"The call?"

"The alert that the German army is coming across the border. A full invasion. They are also conducting an airborne attack on The Hague."

Jenny's mouth sagged. She blinked. "Papa. Nic and Marten are at The Hague."

Her mother set a serving dish on the table with a clatter. "Are they dropping bombs on the city?"

"Doesn't look like it, Emma. Reports are that they are bombing all around the city, not much inside. We think they want to capture The Hague. Probably figure if they capture the queen and the government, the country will fold up quickly."

"What about the land army?" Jenny asked.

"The Germans are moving fast. Not much to stop them until they get to the Grebbe Line. That's where the army will stop them. It's the only good place, really, with all the water barriers and the fortifications."

Jenny looked from her father to mother. "And we are on the wrong side of the line. The German side. What happens to us?"

"Geography wasn't good to us," said her father.

"That's why I'm here," Atsma said. "Nijkerk and Hoevelaken are being evacuated to Harderwijk and Putten."

"Hold on, Chief." Mama's voice had an edge that Jenny had never heard. "The Germans will be everywhere. Why are we safer in Putten?"

"The Dutch guns in Amersfoort can reach Nijkerk, Emma," Atsma said.

She slumped into her chair. Papa took a seat and held her hand. "We can stay with my brother at their farm, Em. Only until things calm down here. Then we'll come back."

Atsma glanced at his watch. "I have to go. Let me know if I can help you."

With that, the policeman hurried off, leaving a stunned DeHaan family.

"Well, let's get packed," Jenny said. "We can't just sit here and have the Germans trample us."

"Sit, child," said her mother. "Food's on the table. We need it. How long do we have, Albert?"

"We should leave as soon as we can pack, dear. I have no idea when they will come."

Jenny joined them at the table, not the least bit hungry, and shoveled food onto her plate. Now what? Just accepted to school and now everything was turned upside down. Would the school be closed, even blown up? And her farm, her family. What about them? *Everything is wrong.*

She scraped back her chair. "Sorry, Mama. I can't eat. Can hardly think. I need to feed my animals. We can't take the chickens. Can't take the hogs. What a mess."

She started to stand and sagged back onto her chair. Her brother, her best friend, was out there somewhere.

Mother seemed to read her mind. "My son is in danger, Albert."

"He's probably on his way home right now, Em. He'll be fine."

Nicolaas pedaled out of The Hague and entered the countryside north of the city. The rich palette of a Dutch spring welcomed him. Vast fields of multicolored tulips basked in the sunshine. Above the fields, blue sky with scattered cumulous clouds complemented the fields of color. He inhaled the soothing, fragrant air.

A low-flying Messerschmitt, coming from behind, roared past him, engine screaming. He and his bike fell to the ground. He looked up to see the plane bank slightly to the left and fire its cannons at a target somewhere west of the highway. After the plane disappeared, the smell of its lingering exhaust overpowered the scent of flowers.

Calm returned, and Nicolaas moved on. After a peaceful ride of about ten minutes, a vehicle approached, traveling from the direction of The Hague. He pulled well off the right side of the highway, stopped, and looked back. As the large black sedan neared, he raised a hand in greeting. The driver stared straight ahead, both hands tight to the wheel.

About fifty meters ahead, four armed men wearing German uniforms appeared from a stand of trees and pushed a small farm cart into the road in the path of the approaching car. The soldiers held up their hands, palms facing the approaching vehicle. The sedan's brake lights lit, and it slowed. Near the roadblock, the lights went dark; the car veered away from the cart and toward the soldiers. The engine roared, and a slight puff of smoke emerged from the tailpipe. The soldiers jumped behind the shelter of the cart, scrambling to ready their weapons. One man raised a submachine gun. As the car passed him, the small gun chattered. The vehicle slowly rolled to a stop with the gunmen close behind, guns raised. While three men aimed their guns into the car, the fourth eased the driver's door open. The soldiers conferred briefly, dragged a limp body from the sedan, and dumped it in the nearby ditch.

Nicolaas watched in stunned silence as the four men pushed the cart from the road. Three of them entered the car quickly and slammed their doors. The fourth man opened the driver's door, turned toward Nic, and stared at him. After a few seconds, he climbed inside and drove north.

He rode to the scene of the attack. The cart stood near the right side of the motorway. The body of the driver lay among tall weeds on the left side. Nicolaas pulled the weeds aside to check for signs of life. The massive chest wounds and lifeless eyes left no doubt. He scrambled back to the road, lifted his bike, and forced his weak legs to peddle. The poor man. Suddenly dead. Driving down the road, probably going home, just like him. "The world has gone mad."

Nicolaas continued on, scanning ahead for any signs of German soldiers. Traffic was very light. No cars approached from the north, but several cars reached him from the direction of The Hague. He flagged down every driver and urged them to reverse course. After hearing his story, the first two drivers turned back.

The third was different. As the vehicle approached, Nicolaas offered a sweeping wave with both hands. The sleek, two-seater DKW with a gleaming white-and-black color scheme signaled its deceleration with a crisp shift to a lower gear. It glided to a halt, and the window slid down, revealing a Dutch army officer.

The man frowned. "What?" he demanded.

"There are Germans ahead and they—"

"I must go." The window rolled upward. With a roar of the engine and a squeal from the rear tires, the shiny, little sports car sped away.

Nic gazed as the car accelerated through the gears and disappeared to the north. "I hope I don't see you again today. Those Germans would love your car."

He traveled without incident until he came within sight of the Haagsche Schouw Bridge at the Old Rhine River. On the near side of the bridge, a large truck and a few parked cars blocked the road, and a small group of German soldiers manned the roadblock.

He stopped and studied the scene. What now? Go back? Germans were back there too. Would these men hurt him, a kid on a bicycle? Not likely.

He mounted the bike and advanced. As he approached the barricade, the Germans watched him until he was within fifty meters. At that point, one of the soldiers aimed his submachine gun directly at Nicolaas.

He skidded the bike to a stop and raised both hands. The grim-faced soldier beckoned him to proceed and followed Nic's movement with the muzzle of the gun.

With knees trembling, he struggled to pedal the bike. It wobbled as he approached the roadblock. Another soldier approached. Nicolaas looked for a weapon, saw none, and his tension eased. He stared at the ground and waited.

The man barked, "*Was machst du hier?*"

What am I doing here? He searched for the right response. "I must go to Leiden," he said in fluent German. "I attend the university there. May I please pass?"

A hint of a smile appeared on the tanned face. "We are in the middle of a war here, boy."

Nicolaas managed to return the smile. "And I hope you are successful, sir. We will be your partners soon."

For a tense moment, he waited for a response. Finally, it came. "Let the boy pass." He dismissed him with a careless wave, turned his back, and walked away.

Still weak in the knees, Nicolaas urged his bike to a shaky start. After he passed the parked truck, he glanced back. Under that vehicle, two men lay behind a heavy machine gun pointed directly at his back. He increased his pace. He stopped and stared ahead. Parked on the shoulder of the road, a very familiar-looking, two-seater DKW—with gleaming white-and-black paint—sat empty. Its brand-new appearance was marred by only one thing: multiple bullet punctures in the driver's door. *I warned the guy.* Nicolaas fixed his eyes on the far side of the bridge and pushed the pedals as hard as he could manage.

Jenny placed a box into the back of the wagon and returned to the house. Her mother met her at the door with another box.

"What's in this one, Mama?"

"Pictures, letters, my Bible. Precious things. Breaks my heart, Jen. I must leave much behind, and it may be gone when we return." Her eyes glistened with tears. "This should not be. I have lived in this house since I married your father. Our life is here."

Jenny took the box, set it down, and hugged her mother. "We'll be fine, Mama. You'll see. The Germans may not come this way. The sounds of the guns are far to the south."

"Where are your books?"

Jenny nodded toward the wagon. "In one of those boxes up there."

Father appeared. "Cows are milked. I wish Nicolaas was here with us."

Mother rubbed her hands together. "I am worried about that boy."

"Nic is probably just fine, Emma," Father said. "Chief Atsma said the Germans are trying to capture The Hague, not destroy it. He said most bombs are falling outside the city."

Emma put her hands on her hips. "Yes, he said *most.* Most isn't good enough, Albert. There is still danger."

"He's surely on his way home, Mama," Jenny said. "He wants to be here with us, don't you think?"

"Well, I will just pray until I see his face."

"How will we manage the cattle, Papa?"

"You can lead two, and I'll lead two. Emma will drive the wagon with the other two cows tied on. It's only five kilometers to Uncle Abel's farm. Travel will be slow, but we can make it by dark."

Her father looked up the road. "Sure wish I could see Nic coming."

The family continued the packing and loading process for another half hour.

Papa harnessed the two horses and met Jenny and Emma in the front room. "We must leave soon."

They added a few more food items to the picnic basket.

Suddenly, the door banged open, and Nicolaas appeared. He leaned on the doorframe, face drawn and pale.

Jenny's mother gasped, ran to him, and hugged him. "I have been so worried. What happened to you?"

"I'll tell you later. I am just glad to be home, Mama."

Father wrapped an arm around his son's shoulders. "We are going to your Uncle Abel's place where we will be safer. You can ride in the wagon until you feel better. We can handle the cattle."

"No. I'll help with that. I can do it. What about the hogs and chickens?"

"I gave them a lot of food," Jenny said. "I hope we are back soon."

Minutes later, the DeHaan family left their farm. Artillery fire rumbled in the distance. Jenny turned to look at her home. It stood quiet and strong, its possessions and memories locked inside.

Would it be that way when she saw it again?

CHAPTER FOUR

11 May 1940
The Hague

Marten knocked on the study door. It opened and revealed the weary face of his father. His sleeves were rolled up, and the corners of his tired-looking eyes crinkled into a gentle smile.

"Can I help you with anything, Father?"

"Come in, son. Desmond and I have been working for hours. Maybe you can give us a fresh perspective."

Marten joined them at a worktable covered with folders. The drawers of a nearby file cabinet stood open.

Father crushed a cigarette into an overflowing ashtray. "Well, Marten, it is obvious that the German invasion cut our methodical planning short." He waved across the cluttered table. "Look at this mess."

"Have you heard news of the fighting?"

"Although our people suffered yesterday, we have reason for some encouragement. The Germans failed in their attack on The Hague. Their airborne assault was a disaster for them. There are, we estimate, a couple of hundred German transport planes destroyed or disabled. They are lying in the polders, the airfields, and even on the beaches. The remaining German forces around The Hague are scattered and unorganized. They attacked three airfields near us. We counterattacked and took control of all three.

Our queen is safe, and the government is intact. Throughout the day yesterday, our soldiers were heroic."

He lit another cigarette and took a deep draw. "But we must not deceive ourselves. Our successes yesterday will only inflame Hitler. The sad reality is that the Germans are going to take over our country. Have no illusions about that."

Marten clenched his jaw. "I have none. Hitler has proven he cannot be trusted."

Father picked up a folder, sighed, then tossed it back onto the table. "I have always tried to be analytical and cautious in all my financial decisions. I'm afraid I now don't enjoy the luxury of slow deliberation." He turned to Desmond. "What is your opinion?"

Desmond laid his arms on the pile of folders in front of him. "We have converted a lot of assets into cash, but we still have warehouses full of products. You are facing the possibility of huge losses if the Germans take it all from you."

Marten's father nodded, and the hands of the usually composed businessman betrayed a slight tremor as he ran his knuckles across his short beard. "But there is a chance the Germans will treat our country well. They always have, and it would be to their benefit. Your thoughts, Marten?"

"Where is all the money?"

"Some in banks. Much of it is right in this house, in various currencies, mostly in very large bills."

"We could conceal it. Bury it somewhere," Marten said. "The DeHaan farm would be a great place to hide it. Those are people we can trust."

"A good idea," said Father. "I don't think you noticed, but we have already moved the Vermeer painting. It's in the art museum in Amsterdam, carefully hidden in storage. We replaced it with a very good, but inexpensive, painting. Francien and I must decide together what to do with our other artworks."

He went to the window and stared outside. After a long moment, while Marten and Desmond waited in silence, he returned to the table and sat heavily in his chair. "Let's get down to the real issue here. We are Jews. Our Gentile neighbors may be able to retain their assets with the Germans in control. But it is different for us. Based on reports out of Poland and from the stories of German Jews who have fled to the Netherlands, our assets—and our very lives—are very much at risk." He waved at the pile of folders on the table. "I'm being a fool. I am clinging desperately to things that are slipping through my greedy fingers."

"I think we should go," Marten said. "The money, the stuff. It doesn't matter now. We need to leave this place. We could do very well in England or America. It will be difficult, especially for Mother, but we need to get out."

"Yes," his father said. "I must talk to Francien. There is no more time."

Francien stood alone in the drawing room and studied a floral still life. So beautiful. What was Rachel Ruysch thinking when she painted this picture those many years ago? Was her life peaceful?

Reinaar approached and placed his arm gently around her back. She leaned her head on his shoulder and closed her eyes. "This painting has a special place in my heart. I have admired it since I was a little girl. My mother kept it in her bedroom."

"You have a wonderful collection, dear, and a beautiful home."

Tears welled, and she pushed her face into her husband's chest and felt his embrace. "And I have a wonderful family. What is going to happen to us, Reinaar? All those airplanes and bombs."

He took his wife's hand and led her to the couch. "Let's sit and talk."

She sat close to her husband and gripped his warm hand. "Reinaar, I am afraid—terribly afraid—like never before in my life."

His voice was calm, soothing. "I am afraid too. The danger is real."

They sat in silence for a long moment until the rumble of distant explosions intruded. Her body stiffened.

Reinaar pulled her close. "I have never seriously considered leaving Holland until now. I hate to even think about it, but it looks like we need to find a place that is safe for us. Somewhere the Nazis can't reach us."

She pulled away and looked at him through teary eyes. "Leave Holland? But our soldiers have driven off those Germans. They shot down all those airplanes and captured all those invaders. I heard you say we are trying to find space to hold two thousand Germans. Is that not right?"

"Yes, you are correct. But I fear our defenses are simply not capable of withstanding the German army very long. They are too large and powerful."

"And if we just run off, how will we live?"

"I have turned many of our assets to cash, Francien. We can take it with us."

She looked around the room. "We have lived here so long. My children grew up here. My art is here. More than that, my heart is here. If we leave, some German will take everything. Can't we just wait? Maybe the Germans will treat us well. The Netherlands has always been a good neighbor."

"Yes, dear, but this is no longer about being a good neighbor."

After sitting in silence for a long moment, she stood and shook her head. "No, it isn't. It's about being a Jew. And here I am prattling on about these, these *things*. I am trying to hide from reality. I went to see the rabbi this morning, Reinaar, while you were working in your study."

He arched his eyebrows. "What did he say?"

"He was very concerned. He has close relationships with many Jews who have come here from Germany. He heard their stories." She twisted the ring on her finger. "The rabbi said he believes that Hitler will not simply dominate the Jews, he will eliminate them."

She waved her hand. "I have been blinded by my love for all the things I have. My house, my art, my clothes. What use is any of it without my family? I have been so very wrong. We must leave. Take our family and go somewhere safe."

She sniffed and wiped her tears with the back of her hand. "But how? How are we going to escape this place? Are there any safe roads left?"

Reinaar stood and pulled her close. "Let's find Marten and discuss our plans with him. Whatever we do, we must do it quickly."

Marten sat at a table on the garden patio, for years his favorite place to think. The warm sun and cool breeze played on his face. Beautiful yellow garden flowers surrounded him. A rumble in the distance pushed his pleasant thoughts aside. His chest tightened.

His parents stepped out of the house and approached his table.

"May we join you, son?" his father asked.

"Sure. I'm just sitting here thinking."

His parents held hands and sat close together.

"Francien and I have decided that we must leave Holland."

A tear slid down his mother's cheek. She rested a gentle hand on Marten's arm. "It will be so very hard, but we must find a place where our family will be safe. I know that now."

"How, Father? How do we get out?"

"Evacuation by air is almost impossible. We have seen how the Germans attacked the three airfields around The Hague. Those locations are now littered with the hulks of German transports and are likely to be the sites of battle. In addition, I have learned that Schiphol airport in Amsterdam has been bombed."

"Can we drive out somehow?"

"There is nowhere we can travel by train or car. Germany is east, and I have received word that the Nazis are attacking Belgium to the south. North and west is nothing but sea. Still dangerous but our only option, it would seem."

Marten leaned forward and tapped his finger on the table. "So, we escape by sea. I know of three places that might work: the shipping channel from Amsterdam, the channel serving Rotterdam, or the harbor of Scheveningen."

"There's fighting between here and Amsterdam," his father said. "The other two options may still be open. The challenge is to locate a suitable vessel that can carry us to England. Communication is very bad right now."

"Let me explore, Father. I can take my bike. The Scheveningen harbor is only fifteen minutes away, and I could ride to the Rotterdam channel in a couple of hours."

His parents exchanged a glance, and after a long pause, Francien sighed. "The thought of you out there terrifies me, but, right now, *everything* terrifies me. Please be careful, son. I will pray the entire time you are gone."

Marten stood. "It will be dark soon. Too dangerous to travel at night. I'll leave first thing in the morning."

CHAPTER FIVE

12 May 1940
The Hague

The next morning, Marten departed for the harbor at Scheveningen, the small fishing village near The Hague. The leather bag secured to the rear fender of his bike held a supply of sandwiches, toiletries, and a set of binoculars, all lovingly packed by his mother. He turned onto Fishing Harbor Road and stopped at the first inner harbor. It seemed intact, untouched by the German invasion. Numerous fishing boats clung to the pier and bobbed gently in the breeze.

"Hey, Marten! Is that you?" The shout came from somewhere to his right.

He scanned the harbor area. A concrete pier lined three sides of the fisherman's inner haven, providing mooring and shelter for boats. The southern side opened to the larger, outer harbor, then to the sea. In this dense scene of fishing boats and equipment, about a hundred men moved about or stood in small groups. Most ignored Marten, but one individual waved to him from the deck of a fishing boat moored near the end of a long dock.

Marten returned the wave and hurried toward the man. He threaded his way through the cluttered pier, listening to fragments of conversations, all related to war rather than fishing or weather.

The man waiting for him strode to the edge of his boat and with little effort cleared the three-foot gap to the concrete. His face and arms were tanned, his hair sun-bleached. He grasped Marten's hand. "Marten Demeester, my old friend. I thought that was you. I recognized the leather bag on the back of your bike. Never saw another one like it. Hey, what's it been, six years, eight?"

The man's name jumped into Marten's mind. "Orin DeVries, good to see you too. I think I last saw you in elementary school. One day you were just gone. Whatever happened to you?"

"We moved out. Papa got a great job down in Hook of Holland. He runs a pilot boat, taking ships from the sea into Rotterdam."

"So what brings you back to the docks in Scheveningen?"

Orin pointed at the nearby boat. "I'm a deckhand. It's not much, but it's better than sitting on the front porch doing nothing."

"Do you stay around here?"

"When I'm working. I go home to Hook of Holland as much as I can."

"What's going on here, Orin? The place looks normal, except that everybody is just standing around."

"From what I hear, the fishermen are all planning to stay in harbor. These old guys aren't dumb. Stupid fishermen die young, know what I mean? The open water is no place to be right now. Some hotshot Messerschmitt pilot will think you're on your way to England. Wouldn't end well, I'll tell you that."

"Has anybody tried it?"

"Nobody. There's been a steady stream of Jews down here, all trying to pay fishermen for the trip, but nobody has agreed to go, not for any kind of money."

Marten's stomach churned. "I think we have a big problem."

"What?"

"My family may need to leave the country too. I'm scouting around to see if we can manage that."

"You're Jewish?"

"Yes."

Orin shrugged. "Didn't know. Didn't matter, I guess." A deep frown pulled his eyebrows together. "I guess it does now. So what are you going to do?"

Marten gazed around at the quiet boats and idle fishermen. "The sea is our only way out. And now, it looks like I'm wasting my time here in Scheveningen. That only leaves the channel out of Rotterdam."

"Might be a possibility. I want to get down there myself as soon as it's safe to go. My cousin is on his way from there. He called me early this morning. Should be here soon. We'll know more then."

The two boarded the boat and waited, accompanied by the sounds of constant surf and a chorus of seabirds hunting stray bits of fish in the harbor.

For an hour, Marten scanned the harbor area, frequently checking his watch. The sun was midway up the eastern sky. The day was wasting away. There were a lot of miles and maybe a lot of Germans between here and Hook of Holland. *Where is that guy?* He stood. "I can't wait any longer. I've got to get going."

Orin pointed at a bike entering the harbor. "Wait. Here he is."

They jumped to the dock, and Orin ran to the man and gave him a crushing hug. "I'm sure glad to see you, Dirk. I was afraid some German got you."

"Glad to be here myself, I'll tell you that. We got us a war, little cousin, and your family is worried—about them and you."

"My friend here, Marten, and I want to get down there. Is it safe?"

"The road is clear; at least it was for me. The Germans who were hiding in the woods near the Ockenburg airfield are gone. Must have run off last night."

"So we have a clear path all the way to Hook of Holland?" Marten asked

"Looks like. But things are wild down in Hook. There is still fighting going on. Believe it or not, there are even some British warships there."

Marten's heart jumped. "I want to go there."

"I'll go with you," Orin said. "I think I need to be with my family."

The friends pedaled out of the Scheveningen harbor. About thirty minutes later, they passed a quiet Ockenburg airfield. They stopped at the woods between Ockenburg and Loosduinen. "This is where our guys had the Germans trapped," Orin said. "They're gone now."

"We hope."

They approached a group of Dutch soldiers. Marten stopped near the man who appeared to be in charge. "Where did the Germans go?"

The tired looking sergeant shrugged. "I'm sure they are trying to link up with their friends. Probably went east, maybe south. Who knows? I'm just glad they're not here. I thought we were going to have a bad fight. It's never good to fight somebody stuck in a corner, that's for sure. Where are you guys going?"

"Down to The Hook. My family lives there," Orin said.

The soldier frowned. "I hope they're well. Our boys have some Germans cornered in the woods down there too. You better watch yourself."

"What route should we follow?" Orin asked.

The soldier paused for a moment. "Just stay close to the beach. Go through Monster."

"Thanks," said Marten. "Good luck to you guys."

The tired looking soldier nodded. "A bit of advice for you guys. Take it slow, and keep your eyes open. You barge in on some unhappy Germans, and it might not end well, that I can tell you."

At about four o'clock, they arrived at the small village of Gravenzande, a few miles from Hook of Holland. Anxious people crowded the normally quiet streets. The two approached a small group of men.

"What's happening at Hook?" Orin asked.

A sharp blast from the Hook area sent a shock wave that slapped Marten's face and left his ears ringing.

"Pretty wild, right?" said a wide-eyed young man. "They turned those big coastal guns away from the sea. They're firing flat over the village at the Staalduinse woods. Some Germans are hiding in there, poor devils."

"And not only that," another teenager said, "a British destroyer in the waterway was blasting broadsides at those woods. I'm guessing those Germans are real sorry they came along." Nervous laughter erupted in the small group.

A deep frown etched Orin's face. "My family is down there." He sped off with Marten close behind. Leaving the village of Gravenzande, outside the village, they had a clear view to the south across the flat landscape. The three coastal guns were indeed aimed inland. To the left of the town, the Staalduinse woods stood quiet.

They stopped at a small group of people approaching from the direction of Hook. It appeared to be a family of four, with the father pulling a handcart piled high with belongings.

"What's going on?" Orin asked the older man.

"The British are here, but the Germans are also around."

"How many British?"

"Not many yet. About a hundred came on the first day of the invasion. Today a couple of destroyers pulled into the harbor and more men got off. They're moving into town. We think we will be safest in Gravenzande, out of the line of fire."

The boys sped off and soon rolled into Hook of Holland, where the British were unloading a variety of military equipment and supplies onto the docks. While small groups of soldiers trudged into town, villagers were in the process of moving out.

They hurried through the town, pedaling hard until they approached the DeVries home at the eastern edge of the village, near the Rotterdam waterway and about a mile from the Staalduinse woods.

A man wearing a black, short-brimmed sailor's cap emerged from the house, carrying a wooden box. He peered at the young men, set the box into a handcart, and hurried their way. He embraced Orin. "I am sure glad to see you, son. Your mother has been worried sick."

"Papa, this is my friend, Marten. He's from The Hague. We came down together."

The man gripped his hand. "I'm Niels DeVries."

"What are you doing, Papa?"

"We're leaving as soon as we can load up. Going to my sister's place in Gravenzande. If it gets too bad, we'll go up to my brother in The Hague."

"It's pretty quiet right now, Papa."

"Won't be for long, I'm afraid."

Orin rushed inside the house. His father turned a quizzical look at Marten. "Why have you come here? Doesn't seem like the place to be right now."

"My family needs to leave. I'm looking for a boat out of here."

"But I have heard that The Hague is not directly under attack. Leaving may be more dangerous than staying."

"But we're Jewish, Mr. DeVries."

The man hesitated for a moment. "I see. Then you have other concerns."

Orin, along with a woman and a teenage girl, emerged from the house with armloads of belongings. With only a glance at Marten, they handed the items to Niels and hurried back into the house.

Mr. DeVries positioned the belongings on the cart. "As you can see, Marten, Hook of Holland is far from peaceful. We still have woods full of Germans over there. And now the British have landed. Don't know just why. There aren't enough of them to beat the Germans. Maybe they plan to evacuate their own people. Problem is they are going to attract a bunch of Germans, and our little village will get wiped out in the process." He opened his pocket watch. "We need to get going. Coming with us?"

"I need to scout things out, Mr. DeVries. May I sleep on your front porch tonight? I expect you will want to lock—"

The man waved him off. "You're welcome to stay inside. Forget the lock. It wouldn't stop the Germans."

A short time later, Marten stood on the front porch of the DeVries home as the owners departed, perhaps for the last time.

After enjoying the generous meal Mrs. DeVries left for him, he moved to the swing on the front porch and watched the boats pass in the shipping channel. Except for the sounds of distant gunfire, quiet had settled on Hook of Holland.

When the sun touched the waters of the sea in the west, he moved inside and sought the comfort of the couch. In a few minutes, he was fast asleep.

CHAPTER SIX

13 May 1940
Hook of Holland

A warm feeling on his face gently melted the fog of sleep. Marten eased his stiff body to a seated position and looked around. Sun poured through an east window of the quiet house. He stretched, then stepped out onto the front porch. Ships, trailing black smoke from their stacks, glided along the Rotterdam channel. If only the Demeesters could find a place on one of them.

Minutes later, he rode west toward the village.

When he arrived at the harbor, the British were busy. Two passenger carriers, *Canterbury* and *Maid of Orleans*, disgorged men and supplies onto the pier. Hundreds of soldiers already stood there, along with crates of all sizes. What was the goal of all this? If the British intended to take on the Germans, they would need a larger force.

Farther on, he encountered a man with a horse-drawn cart selling produce to a few British troops. His quiet mare stretched her neck to nearby grass. "Don't recognize you, boy. You live around here?"

"I'm from The Hague. Down here looking for a ride to England."

The man lifted his hat and ran his fingers through his thick gray hair. "Don't see that happening, young man, unless you can

53

get a ride on one of those steamers." He nodded in the direction of *Canterbury* and *Maid of Orleans*. "Other than those two vessels, the only thing moving out of here are the British warships. There are some of those around, but they don't seem to be in the business of carrying civilians."

"Maybe if we work fast we can hitch a ride on one of the steamers. They must have plenty of room."

The farmer lifted an apple from his cart and bit into it. "Well, lad, I believe you're a little late on that one. Take a look." As they stood watching the activity on the pier, crewmen freed the heavy bow and stern lines attached to the *Maid of Orleans*.

Marten pointed at the other steamer. "Now they are freeing her up too."

With smoke pouring from their stacks, the ships cleared the harbor and headed for open water.

The farmer pulled two apples from a box on his cart and tossed them to Marten. "These are for your ride home. I suggest you go soon. This is no place for a young man like—"

The sound of airplane engines interrupted their conversation. Two Messerschmitt fighters approached from the direction of Rotterdam, flying low above the ship channel. One continued straight on toward the group of steamers and destroyers that had just departed. The other made a slight turn to its right and brought Hook of Holland—and a wide-eyed Marten Demeester–directly into its path.

He ran toward a low stone wall about ten feet away. As he had done many times on the soccer field, he made a headfirst dive, cleared the wall, and landed with a huge grunt on the hard earth. With his nose pushed tight to the ground, the aroma of rich Dutch soil filled his nostrils. The air was filled with the chatter of large machine guns and the ringing of bullets bouncing off hard targets. The plane shrieked low overhead, and an eerie quiet crept back into the village. Marten lay perfectly still and allowed the silence to reach inside him and slow his raging heart.

Renewed sounds of men and machines encouraged him to raise himself. He lifted his head over the top of the wall. Fruits and vegetables were scattered everywhere. The farmer's cart was overturned, apparently rolled not by bullets but by the thrashing of the panicked horse that lay on its side, kicking the air. But where was the farmer? He didn't have time to get far. Marten stood and got his answer. The man who was speaking to him seconds before lay still, body shredded, on the opposite side of the stone wall that had sheltered Marten.

Knees weak, he sat on the wall. The vegetable cart trembled, along with the last twitches of the dying horse. His bicycle stood alone on its kickstand, amazingly intact. He approached his bike, stopped, and looked back at the body. He must leave, but to abandon that man, lying in the dirt with no dignity, was not right. He picked up a jacket that had fallen from the cart and draped it over the face of the farmer. He must do more. Mother would pray. Pray what? *The Mourner's Kaddish.*

Groping to get the words right, the sound right, Marten bowed his head and recited the small part he remembered. "*Yit'gadal v'yit'kadash sh'mei raba.* May His great Name grow exalted and sanctified. Amen."

He rose slowly, walked to his bike, and rode away.

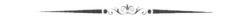

Marten encountered squads of soldiers preparing defenses, and he passed small family groups rushing from the village. The steamers were gone, but the area was dense with British soldiers and British destroyers. To what end? He had to learn more.

He selected a wooded area off the flight path of the German planes where he could observe the activities in the port. With the bike hidden in the brush, he pulled out his binoculars, sat on the soft ground, and nibbled an apple.

He froze with a mouthful of fruit. A long caravan of vehicles drove directly onto the pier and pulled to a stop. Marten flung the half-eaten apple behind him and focused his binoculars.

The activity was concentrated on one vehicle in the middle of the caravan. A group of men in suits gathered outside the car.

One man opened the rear door and stood at attention. A female passenger emerged.

Marten straightened and squinted into the binoculars. An officer in naval uniform bowed to the woman. His hand jerked. "It's Queen Wilhelmina."

The officer escorted the queen to one of the destroyers moored to the pier. Well-dressed men, assisted by British soldiers and sailors, carried boxes and chests from the motorcade onto the destroyer. Smoke rose from the stack of that ship and another beside it. Within minutes, these two British warships, one carrying the Queen of the Netherlands, steamed out of the harbor and headed for open sea.

The motorcade drove away, and the British military returned to their work. Marten eased back to the ground to see if anything else happened. He didn't have long to wait.

Another motorcade arrived on the pier. This one was a mixture of armored cars, motorcycles, and taxis. Vehicle doors opened, and well-dressed civilians emerged. A man from an armored car approached two figures who appeared to be British commanders. After conferring for a few minutes, the commanders gestured to the waiting crowd. They responded by unloading suitcases and trunks from the parked taxis. Who were these people? The Hague was crowded with people from all over the world. Probably British. Could that be the sole purpose of these Brits being here: to evacuate their people?

He slid the binoculars into the case and jumped to his feet. *I have to get word to Father.* He rode hard in the direction of The Hague.

Marten rolled into the darkened driveway of the Demeester home. He rushed in and found his parents in the dining room, then paused to catch his breath. "Our best hope is the British. Hook of Holland is crawling with Brits. There must be a thousand of them down there—with their ships."

"Is it some kind of invasion?" Reinaar asked.

"Don't think so. They would need a much larger force to stop the German army. I think they are here to evacuate people. I saw the queen leave today."

Francien gasped. "The queen left?"

"She's gone. I saw her board the ship. It steamed out to sea."

Father leaned forward, arms on the table. "What else, son?"

"Another motorcade arrived with a crowd of people. I couldn't tell who they were. They had lots of baggage. It looked like they were on their way out too. I didn't wait to watch them leave. Maybe the evacuation is not finished. Maybe we can join them."

"I will check on it immediately. Good work. I'm proud of you."

CHAPTER SEVEN

14 May 1940
The Hague

A gentle hand squeezed Marten's shoulder. "Sorry to wake you, darling, but I must." He opened his eyes. The voice belonged to the angel who had roused him from sleep thousands of times, always with a kind and gentle tone.

"What time is it, Mother?"

"Eleven o'clock."

Marten jolted upright. "It's late. What's happening? Any news?"

"Your father just got off the phone with his friends in government. They said we could board a British ship at Hook of Holland this afternoon if conditions are favorable. We must finish packing now. Please come down quickly." She patted his arm and hurried out.

After lying still, brain racing for a few seconds, he threw off his bed covers and jumped up. He raced down the stairs, still buttoning his shirt, and found his father in his study. "What's happening?"

"We have a chance to leave the country today, Marten. That group you saw yesterday was a mix of government officials, mostly Dutch and British. They got out on a British ship. I was able to contact a Dutch minister who missed that opportunity. I got approval to take our family out with him. Things are fairly unstable down there right now, so nothing is certain. I was told to be there at three o'clock."

"Can we be ready, Father?"

"We must."

Joran appeared. "What can I take, Papa?"

"Each of us can take one small suitcase, son. Choose very carefully."

"When we come back, will my things still be here?"

His father looked away from the boy. "I hope so."

Joran blinked. "I must go pack." With that, he turned and left.

"What about the staff?" Marten asked.

"I have met with each one to explain the circumstances and to give them a generous severance payment. I think they will be fine. They are not Jewish, and all have family in Holland. It was a sad scene for all of us, especially your mother."

Desmond appeared at the door. "The staff have all departed, Mr. Demeester."

"Then pack your bags, Desmond. You're coming with us."

"Sir? You said only family could go."

Reinaar smiled. "I told them you are my nephew but like a son to me."

"Yes, sir. I must pack a few things."

At one o'clock, they gathered for a quick lunch of sandwiches, prepared and served by Desmond. Their bags waited at the front door.

The phone in the hallway rang.

"May I answer that, Mr. Demeester?" Desmond asked.

"Please."

After a very brief conversation, Desmond returned. A deep frown creased his forehead.

"It's Mr. Van Kampen. He said he must speak to you. He said it's urgent."

Marten bit his lip as his father's deep voice echoed from the hallway. "This is Reinaar Demeester." A short pause. "When?" A longer pause. His father's voice came back, barely audible. "Our prayers are with them. With all of us. God be with you and your family."

Reinaar returned and slumped into his chair. "The Germans. They bombed Rotterdam."

"How bad?" Desmond and Marten said in unison.

"Very bad. The center of the city is rubble. It's so bad that they now have a firestorm. We have lost thousands of our countrymen."

Francien gripped the arms of her chair. "What about us?"

"We can't go down there now. It's far too dangerous."

After a few moments of silence, Joran spoke. "What are we going to do, Papa?"

"I don't have an answer right now, son. I just don't know."

Chapter Eight

17 May 1940
On the road from Putten to Nijkerk

Jenny stopped and stroked the nose of her tired cow. "Not much farther, Margreet. We're almost to Nijkerk, then a short walk to the farm, and you'll get milked." And after a week with her aunt and uncle, she'd be back in her home, with her books and her mama's cooking. The scent of homemade bread played in her mind.

The cow stood rigid until Jenny gave a slight tug on the leash. The animal snorted and swished her tail while Jenny waited. Finally, the cow eased into motion and followed the family procession.

They pulled alongside Nic and his two cattle. "Pretty quiet around here," she said. "The farms all seem okay. No damage."

"They do look good. Maybe there wasn't too much fighting on this end of the defensive line. We'll have a better idea when we get into town. It's closer to the big Dutch guns."

Nic glanced at his father. "Papa was awfully anxious to get back home, Jen."

"Me, too." Her hens hadn't been fed in a week. They must be starving. Same for the poor hogs.

"I hope everything's okay," Nic said. "I heard the Germans came through Nijkerk. Anything could have happened in town."

"If they're still there, surely they got word of the surrender. No more fighting. We should be safe, right?"

Ahead of them, a dust cloud announced the arrival of a motor vehicle.

"Oh, great," Nic said. "Probably Germans."

Their mother, sitting beside her husband in the wagon, turned and looked back at them, frowning and biting her lip.

"Let's just keep going, Mama," Jenny said. "The fighting is over. They won't bother us."

"I hope you're right," muttered Nic. "We may be the first Dutch to return to Nijkerk after the evacuation."

Father pulled the wagon to the edge of the road to allow the approaching vehicle room to pass. The German Kübelwagen stopped beside them, its canvas top rolled back, exposing four uniformed soldiers. The two officers in the back seat turned their expressionless faces toward the family but said nothing.

The young driver spoke for the Germans. "*Wohin gehst du?*"

Father turned to Nic for an answer.

"He wants to know where we're going," Nic said. He then answered the question in perfect German. "To our farm."

The backseat passenger nearest them dismissed the family with a lazy wave and muttered something to the driver. The Kübelwagen sped away.

She gritted her teeth. *No. We can't have this. It's our country.* "Did you see that, Papa? Those people think they own this place."

Father didn't turn his head. He snapped the reins and scolded the horses. "Up, boys."

The wagon jolted into motion.

When they entered Nijkerk, it was not the same town they'd left only days before. No Dutchmen were visible. Most buildings stood intact, but others had been reduced to wreckage.

The wagon stopped beside the rubble of what had been the Vander Molen's store. Jenny's tug on the leashes weakened. Her shoulders sagged. "We were just here a few days ago, Nic." She pointed at the charred remains of the front door. "I was standing right there, all excited about my letter from the university. Mr. Vander Molen came out and hugged me."

Father stared at the wreckage for a long moment. "I spoke to Jake Vander Molen yesterday when I was in Harderwijk. He didn't know about this. So sad." He turned his tired eyes to Jenny. "But they are strong people. They will rebuild, and we will help."

Jenny's mother looked from the ruins to another destroyed building across the street. "Why did the Germans blow up these two places and not the others nearby?"

"Hard to tell," Albert said. "It may have been our own guns. That's what happens in battle."

They continued slowly along Kolkstraat. Approaching the town hall, Albert pulled the team to a halt. A small group of German soldiers stood outside the front door, eyeing the arrivals. One flipped his cigarette to the ground, turned, and entered the building.

"So, they already took over city government," Jenny whispered.

Another man in the group scowled at the DeHaans. He pointed at them and gestured for them to pass. "*Weitermachen.*"

Needing no translation, Albert flicked the reins, and the wagon moved ahead.

The family passed the idle soldiers. No words were spoken by either group.

The family trudged in silence through town. Entering farm country, they picked up the pace. Even the animals seemed to find more energy as they neared their home.

When they entered the long driveway of their farm, Albert relaxed the reins. The horses needed no guidance or encouragement. They surged forward.

The farmhouse stood tall and proud. The attached barn waited peacefully for its owners. Brother and sister released their cattle, and the animals trotted toward their pasture.

Jenny ran ahead toward the house with Nic close beside. When she had a clear view of the home's entrance, she jolted to a stop.

The door stood wide open. A cat strolled out, saw the approaching humans, and bolted into the tall grass nearby.

Jenny swung around to her brother. "Papa locked that door. I saw him."

"Me too."

Father was helping her mother scramble down from the wagon. Not waiting, Jenny ran into the house and saw nothing unusual in the front room. Good. She rushed to the kitchen and gasped. Unwashed pots, pans, and dishes filled the sink. Cigarette butts and chicken bones littered the floor. The smell of spoiled food twisted her face.

Her parents appeared and stood frozen at the kitchen door.

"Oh, no," were the only words mother managed before she collapsed into the nearest chair.

Jenny ran upstairs to her bedroom. The odor of old sweat met her at the door. Bed covers cluttered the floor. Crumpled, soiled sheets partially covered the mattress.

Her jaw tightened. *Somebody, some filthy somebody violated my bed.*

An open book rested on her nightstand. *I forgot one.* She moved closer. A borrowed textbook had eluded her hasty packing. On the book, a fly roamed around a greasy, half-eaten chicken bone.

Fighting the nausea that stirred inside her, she clattered down the stairs.

She raced out the back door into the barn and called behind her as she ran. "I'll check the animals."

She stopped at the hog pen, her mouth dropped open, and she grasped the fence post to support her weak knees. The smell of death filled her nostrils. The adult hogs and piglets lay dead, all covered with blood and dotted with bullet holes. One large sow showed signs of a botched attempt at butchering. She waved away the flies that buzzed about her head.

Her hand went to her mouth. Somewhere inside, anger was brewing but unable to overcome her shock.

She moved toward the chicken coop but stopped short. The still, white forms of dead hens lay silent in the dirt. "Oh, my sweet girls. What did they do to my little friends?"

Her feeble legs carried her to the barn where Nic was feeding the horses.

She walked up behind him and tapped his shoulder. When he turned to face her, she embraced him and sobbed into his chest. "They destroyed my animals. They violated my home—and my dreams. What kind of ... why would they ..."

Nic squeezed her tightly and told her it would be okay.

They both knew he was lying.

CHAPTER NINE

28 November 1940
Utrecht

Jenny DeHaan sat alone at a small table in the corner of the coffee shop. So much change in her life. Her family, traumatized by the invasion, had returned to a measure of normalcy. Mama had cleansed the house of any visible signs of the German intrusion, but the memories still lingered. Surely they would fade with time. And she was in the school of her dreams. Hope survived.

She peered at the dark, cold world outside. Dutch winter had arrived. Pedestrians wore warm coats and caps. Trees held only a few stubborn brown leaves.

In the warm café, all the other tables stood empty. Her open chemistry textbook rested atop her closed biology text. Kitchen sounds told her the cook was hard at work in the back room.

A bell attached to the front door of the café jingled. Nic entered, along with a quick rush of cold winter air. He strode to her table. "Glad to see you working so hard, young lady. If you expect me to call you 'Doctor DeHaan' one day, you have a lot of books to read."

"Trust me on this. The doctor thing *will* happen. Nothing is going to keep me from it. And speaking of tests, I have a chemistry exam tomorrow, and I'm not nearly ready for it."

She leaned closer to her brother and lowered her voice. "Looks like you have been working hard too, but not at school. You might want to hide that ink."

Nicolaas slipped his hands, fingers stained with printer's ink, into his jacket pockets. "No need to whisper, Jen. We are among friends."

The proprietor, a large man, tall and wide, approached the table with a towel draped over his arm.

"Good morning, Kees," Nic said. "This is my sister, Jenny. You can speak freely. She's good. Do you think you can have that story ready for me tomorrow?"

"No problem. It will be done. Great to meet you, Jenny. Sorry I was so quiet earlier. I'm sure you understand."

Jenny nodded at the balding, middle-aged man. "I do. Caution is our best asset." She turned to her brother. "So, how is the newspaper doing?"

Nic pulled his ink-stained hands from his pockets. "Circulation is better than I expected. We printed a thousand last night. People are hungry for news that isn't censored by the Germans." He nodded at Kees. "This guy is our best writer. Still getting your information from the BBC?"

The big man refilled Jenny's coffee cup. "Yes, along with our own Radio Orange. It's carried on BBC every night at nine o'clock."

Jenny eased the steaming cup to her lips and sipped. "Then you are getting the real news of the world? What's happening?"

Kees pulled out a chair. It creaked under his heavy frame. "The news isn't all that good. The Germans failed in their air war with Britain, but things are largely going well for the Nazis. America is staying out of it, and the Brits are pretty much doing all the fighting. The future is a big question right now."

"We just need to keep up what we are doing," Nic said. "Resist the Nazis. If America gets involved, we'll beat them and get on with our lives. I was really inspired by Marten's father. I'm anxious for you to meet him, Jen. He is a role model for me right now. He made a fortune working hard, and I will too."

"Won't the Germans just loot all our national resources?" she asked.

"Let's hope that is the worst they do. I am worried about the Demeester family and all our Jewish countrymen. My newspaper is my mission right now. It is something I can do to oppose the Germans without getting into the fighting."

Jenny tapped her pencil on her open textbook. "I'm in a kind of wait-and-see position right now. Until I figure out what to do about all this occupation business, I am focused on my schoolwork. I can't walk away from that." She grinned. "There is one thing I do enjoy. When I walk down the street, these young German soldiers often smile and make comments, sometimes nice and sometimes not. Either way, I totally ignore them, like they don't exist. It drives them crazy."

Kees gazed out the window at the passing pedestrians. "I get a lot of soldiers in here. Some are really bad guys, but a few are very polite kids who seem like they got caught up in something they don't want." He scraped his chair back. "Everybody needs to make tough choices. When somebody carries a gun, I react to what they do, not what they say."

"Where is all this going, Nic?" asked Jenny. "The Germans aren't causing as much trouble as we expected."

"They are proceeding very carefully and quietly so far. They're putting their claws into our country. Besides that, they are cultivating a large group of Dutch traitors to work for them."

She narrowed her eyes. Her own countrymen helping the enemy. What kind of person does something like that? *Their time will come.* "I don't understand why anyone would help the Germans."

"Many think the Nazis are unstoppable, and they want to be with the winners," Nic said. "They see an opportunity to get ahead. I'm afraid those people may be our greatest enemies since they know the country so well. What is frightening is that we often don't know friend from foe."

The little bell attached to the front door jingled. Marten Demeester entered and strode to the table.

"Marten, this is Kees," Nic said. "He's with us."

They shook hands, and Marten pulled up a chair, then looked from Nic to Jenny. "We have problems. Last month, the Germans hit us with the Aryan declarations. You knew about that, didn't you?"

Jenny leaned forward. "Yes. All the government employees, including teachers, were ordered to sign a paper indicating whether they were Jewish or non-Jewish."

"Exactly. A lot of people were upset, but in the end, most complied, except the Jews who fled here from Germany. Well, something else happened last month. The Germans ordered the registration of Jewish-owned businesses. It should have been obvious at that point the Nazis were just clearly identifying their enemy, or more accurately, their victims."

Marten slapped the table hard enough to rattle Jenny's coffee cup. "It finally happened. I knew it would, and so did my father. They have decreed that all Jewish government workers, including professors and teachers, be removed from their positions."

Jenny straightened in her chair. "I have a Jewish professor. Everybody loves him."

"You *had* a Jewish professor," Marten said. "All around the country, little kids are coming to school and learning their teachers are gone. The really important point here is that this is not the end, in spite of what a lot of people are saying. I am convinced that the Germans won't stop until they remove every Jew from the Netherlands."

Jenny held her breath as she gazed on Marten's glare. "Remove to where?"

"Who knows?" Marten stood and paced the floor. "There is talk about sending Jews to work camps. Can you imagine such a thing? My father and mother in a work camp. I expect that they will first take all our possessions."

"What should we do?" asked Nicolaas.

"Some people aren't sitting still. The students at Delft College and Leiden University had a strike to support their professors who were tossed out."

Jenny scooped up her open chemistry textbook, slammed it shut, and tossed it onto the table. "Let's do it!"

Marten held up his hand. "Not so fast, Jen. Yesterday, the Germans closed both schools."

She looked down. "Oh. That might be a waste of our time."

"I think you are right," Marten said. "We need to oppose these people, but we need to be smart about it."

CHAPTER TEN

11 February 1941
Utrecht

Jenny found Marten and Nic sitting on a bench at the Utrecht railway station and sat between them. The scent of burning coal hung in the chilled winter air. Shrill whistles and the persistent chugs of steam locomotives echoed around the brick and steel world. Multiple platforms hummed with activity as hundreds of passengers hurried toward their destinations. A steady stream of trains, some powered by electric locomotives but most powered by steam, moved in and out of the place.

"Sorry I'm a little late," she said.

Marten checked his watch. "No problem. We're fine, Jen. I'm anxious for you to see our Amsterdam house. My parents are still at our place in The Hague, but I expect they will move to Amsterdam soon. The Hague is full of Germans now. Not a good place for a wealthy Jew. We'll do better in Amsterdam. After I go to the registration office, I'll take you two out for dinner."

A large black locomotive directly in front of them drew her attention. A fireman shoveled coal into the firebox, and the big engine responded by pushing generous amounts of heavy smoke from its stack. The growing energy of the iron beast announced itself with creaks and hisses.

Nic pointed at a white feather of steam escaping from the safety valve on top of the engine. "She's powered up and ready to go."

The engineer sat tall in his command seat, framed by the large open window at the rear of the engine. He reached up and pulled on a cable hanging from the ceiling. The steam whistle responded with two shrill blasts. Water vapor rushed out both sides of the engine, escaping from the area around the front wheels. The cloud raced across the platform and enveloped the young observers.

Jenny waved her hand in a vain attempt to keep the cloud from her face. "Why do they do that?"

"Just clearing the water out of the cylinders," Marten said. "Bad for the pistons."

She rolled her eyes. "Wonderful."

The old locomotive, now pouring a mix of acrid, black smoke and steam from its stack, strained to pull the mass of the train into motion. The huge drive wheels edged forward. A sequence of metallic clanks rose down the length of the train as the couplers between cars pulled tight. Then, with a quick puff of exhaust from its stack, the locomotive released its first sharp *chug*. With the gradually increasing speed of the rolling train, the chugs came closer together. In half a minute, the determined locomotive won the battle, and the train cleared the platform. As the staccato of chugs faded in the distance, out of sight, the train seemed to voice its goodbye with an extended wail from its steam whistle.

"I know we're changing to electric locomotives," said Nic, "but I still love those old steam engines."

"Me too," echoed Marten.

Jenny shrugged and shook her head. "Must be some kind of guy thing. I just want to get where I'm going. What type of train do we take to Amsterdam, Marten?"

"You'll like it. It's electric, clean and quiet."

"That will work for me." Jenny looked around the platform. "It's finally quiet enough to talk. What is going on in this place?

We're under German occupation. These people are acting like it's business as usual."

"Right now it *is* business as usual," Marten said. "In some ways, even better than normal. My father said that the depression has finally eased, partly because the Germans are buying lots of stuff from us. In spite of our losses during the invasion, business is up right now. Some people are happy the way things are."

A wry smile crept onto Nic's face. "Sounds too good to be true."

Marten nodded. "Father says it is all part of German plans. They are being very careful to keep things calm and keep money in people's pockets. But it will change. You'll see. First, they will buy from us, but later they will steal from us to fuel their war machine, like all conquerors throughout history."

A vendor approached, pushing his three-wheeled cart on the brick platform. Martin bought some rolls with cheese and carried them to his friends. "This should keep us going until we get to my house."

Jenny reached out for her share. "Thanks. I'm starv—"

Marten jumped to his feet. "Here comes our train."

An electric train glided to a stop.

"Would you look at that," Marten said. "Most of the cars are crowded with travelers." He pointed at the two cars in front. "Except those two are empty." Both carriages displayed signs in their windows reading *nur für Wehrmacht*. "Isn't that just great? Reserved for German soldiers."

The three friends boarded an available car. Marten slid into a seat beside Jenny, while Nic sat directly behind them.

When the train passed the outskirts of Utrecht and entered farm country, Jenny turned to Marten. "Tell me more about this registration business."

"The Germans have ordered that all Jews must register. This could be really bad. The Germans will be able to do anything they want with Dutch Jews."

"Then don't do it. Don't walk into their trap."

"Not that simple. For one thing, our culture is very detailed. Nobody in the Netherlands is anonymous. We are all on the books somewhere. The Germans will be able to find us in time. Besides, the penalty for noncompliance is five years in prison and confiscation of property. Even though I am technically on my own, the Germans could use my violation to take my parents' property. So I decided to go in and fill out the papers."

About an hour after leaving the Utrecht railway station, the train glided to a stop at Amsterdam Centraal. The three college students stepped out and strolled along the platform. They ignored a group of somber German soldiers.

"What's the plan from here, Marten?" asked Nic.

"Our home is in South Amsterdam, in the Beethovenstraat area. Tram line twenty-four will get us there. I intended to walk home so I could give you a tour of the Jewish Quarter, but I think we should avoid that until I can find out how things are going."

"What's the problem?" asked Jenny.

"We've been having big problems with the NSB."

"NSB?"

"The Dutch Nazi party, our former friends and neighbors who have joined the invaders. I think they may be as dangerous as the Germans. They know too much, and they are willing to do anything to please their bosses."

"What have they been doing?" asked Nic.

Marten raised his hand. "Hang on a minute." He led the way to a quiet bench. "Now we can talk. We must be careful what we say in public. Sometimes the NSB are in uniform, sometimes not. Anyway, they have been causing a lot of problems in the Jewish Quarter. Gangs of thugs are roaming the Quarter, harassing people, even ransacking their homes."

"And the Germans aren't doing anything about it?" Jenny asked.

"Nothing. They are being very sly, letting their goons cause all the problems."

Jenny turned toward Marten. "Why aren't the Jews doing anything about it? I'd fight the bums."

Marten grinned. "I do believe you would. And I think you will, in your own way. To answer your question, the Jews *are* fighting back. They are forming their own gangs. There have already been a few big fights. Right now, I don't want to walk through that area with the two of you. With this enemy, everyone needs to pick their own battles."

Marten looked into the distance. "Here comes our tram."

After a twenty-minute ride, they got off the tram on Beethovenstraat and made the short walk to Chopinstraat, a quiet residential street of modest, connected homes. Marten walked to the front door, key in hand. "Well, this is it. Nobody home except one or two of the maids, and possibly Desmond. He stays here when he is working in Amsterdam."

Marten led the group inside. "Hey, anybody here?"

A female voice answered from somewhere out of sight. "Oh, young Mr. Demeester. You are here." A gray-haired lady in a maid's uniform appeared at the top of the stairs. She held the rail and descended quickly. When she reached the ground floor, she stopped and smiled.

Marten set his bag on the floor and strode to the woman. He pulled her to himself and hugged her. When he released her, she looked up, face flushed, blinking at Marten. "Oh, my goodness, Mr. Demeester, you have never hugged me before."

"The world is changing, Hanna. It's time for us to show our affection for people. We don't know what tomorrow will bring."

"Thank you, sir. You make me very happy."

"Anybody else here, Hanna?"

"Desmond is out somewhere. He said he is working on a project."

"These are my university friends, Jenny and Nicolaas. They will probably stay with us for a couple of days."

"Wonderful. I have not been nearly busy enough. I will get their rooms ready and plan for lunch and dinner. What would you like to eat?"

"Just simple sandwiches for lunch, Hanna. I need to go to the registry office this afternoon. No need to fix dinner. I'm going to take my friends out on the town."

After lunch, while Jenny and Nicolaas strolled around Beethovenstraat, Marten boarded the tram into town. About ten minutes later, he entered the Plantage neighborhood in the Jewish Quarter.

The tram rumbled along Plantage Middenlaan and stopped directly in front of the Hollandsche Schouwburg theater. Marten stepped out and paused to look at the façade. How many times had he attended concerts here? Thirty? Fifty? Wonderful performances of the great masters, performed by orchestras that included fine Jewish musicians. He pictured himself sitting in the back, observing Jewish high society, dressed in their best. What would the future bring to this great place? Already the Germans had prohibited Jews from the cinemas. When would they be banned from the theater?

As the tram behind him pulled away, Martin turned and viewed the scene across the street from the old theater. The registration office, normally a quiet building, easy to ignore, was now a hub of activity. Long lines of people stretched down the sidewalks. As Marten walked past the crowd on his way to the end of the line, only a few sober faces made eye contact with him. Most ignored him, their faces expressionless.

Marten stopped at the end of the queue, turned toward his destination, and looked at his watch. How long would this take? Should he leave? The Germans would have him in their grasp. No. He must stay. He would do what he was told and hope for the best. He would wait and see, just like all the other Jews in this line.

After a couple of hours of slow movement, Marten reached the door and entered the building. Officials sat behind long tables, deeply involved in the process of gathering and filing detailed information about every Jew who entered. A bored-looking man, without comment or eye contact, handed several sheets of paper to Marten. He took the forms to a vacant spot at another table, filled them out, handed them to the first available extended hand, and walked out. He hurried to a waiting tram at the Schouwburg and climbed aboard.

Tram Fourteen carried mostly Jewish passengers, having just completed their duty at the registration office. Most sat in silence and gazed out the side windows. Was it creeping hopelessness that subdued the passengers? He glared at the road ahead. *Not me. Never.*

At Spui Square, he transferred to another tram. This one carried a diverse group of citizens. He found a vacant aisle seat, sat, drew a deep breath, and exhaled slowly. Home would be very welcome. He closed his eyes. The passenger chatter and rhythmical clacking of the tram wheels hummed in his ears. At the next stop, an elderly blonde lady boarded and stood in the aisle near Marten. He tapped her arm lightly. "Would you like my seat?"

"No, thank you. I have been sitting all day. I should stand."

Marten returned to idly watching the passing scenery. After a few minutes, his eyelids grew heavy, and his chin slowly drifted toward his chest.

"Hey, you!"

Marten jolted awake. He met the angry eyes of a young man about his age.

"Yes, you," continued the man. "You look like a Jew. Am I right?"

"No, I mean yes." Marten gulped. His heart pounded.

"What right does a dirty Jew have sitting while this Aryan woman must stand? Get up, Jew—now!"

Everyone in the car turned to witness the confrontation.

"Wait a minute," said the woman. "This young man did offer me his seat. I told him I preferred to stand."

The man persisted. "No matter. He needs to get up."

Marten's eyes narrowed. His pulse pounded in his neck, and his jaw clamped shut. He looked up. The tram was slowing for the next stop, and the man had shifted his attention to the world outside.

Marten jumped to his feet. Before the man could react, Marten slammed a tight fist into the side of his chin. His head jerked toward his shoulder and, with a slow groan, he collapsed like a puppet whose strings were severed. The watching passengers gaped at the groaning heap of humanity in the aisle.

As the tram squeaked to a stop, the lady smiled. "I believe this is your stop, young man."

Marten stepped over the semiconscious thug and rushed down the aisle. He whisked past the conductor who had turned his back to Marten and seemed to be studying his watch. The tram continued on its way, and Marten quickly found a nice, quiet coffee shop for a temporary haven.

When he finally opened the door of the house on Chopinstraat, Jenny greeted him. "How did it go, Marten?"

"There are good people in Amsterdam, Jenny. I even met a nice tram conductor this afternoon. Also a sweet little lady who I hope to see again. The future may not be as bleak as I thought."

Chapter Eleven

11 February 1941
Amsterdam

Later that afternoon, bright sun warmed Jenny's face as she entered the Jewish Quarter of Amsterdam with Marten and Nic. Shops stood open. People bustled from store to store. Children played in the streets. Life was good. But, as they walked, the place didn't feel quite right. Tension was written on the quiet faces of the adults. People avoided eye contact. A strange unease hung in the air.

Marten led them to a small café. "Here we are. Nothing special, but I love the food. I hope you're okay with more kosher."

"Kosher is great," Jenny said. "Could we eat inside? Looks like a nice little place."

They selected a table inside, and the proprietor approached, his face drawn, a towel draped over his arm. "Hello, Marten. Good to see you and your friends."

Marten frowned. "You look troubled, Bernard."

"We have a problem. The NSB is getting bolder by the day. At this moment, things are fairly quiet, but last night a gang of them came down the street and drove people out of their way. They even went into some people's homes and took whatever they wanted. The police did nothing. I locked my door, turned off the lights, sat here, and prayed. They left me alone."

They sat without words for a moment.

Bernard clapped his hands. "Enough bad talk. How about some spicy *bazargan*? I made it this morning, so it's well-blended. It's my special tonight."

"Sounds perfect," Marten said.

Bernard disappeared into the kitchen. Jenny turned to Marten and whispered, "What did we just order?"

"It's a cereal food, mainly wheat, but it has lots of spices and nuts. He serves it with braided egg bread."

Five minutes later, Bernard set a pan in the center of the table and lifted the lid. Jenny leaned forward and inhaled the rich scent of lemon juice, onion, and garlic. Her eyes closed, and a gentle smile spread over her face. *This could turn into a nice evening.*

Noises from the street shattered the pleasant mood.

Nic straightened in his chair, and his eyes narrowed. "Is that singing?"

Bernard wiped his hands on a towel as he hurried to the window. "The goons are back."

The singing faded, and shouts began.

Chairs scraped across the wood floor as the three friends abandoned their dinner and rushed out the front door. To their left, about a block away, a loud mob of men wearing black uniforms marched toward the café.

Bernard waved the three toward the door. "This gang is worse than the one yesterday. You must come inside now."

"Not yet," Marten said. He studied the approaching men. "There must be a hundred of them."

Ahead of the advancing mob, people on both sides of the street retreated into nearby buildings and pulled the shades on the windows.

An elderly man leaned on his cane and struggled to reach a door held open by an elderly woman. One of the marchers caught up with him, yanked the cane from his hand, and clubbed him on the head. With blood running down his face and onto his suit, the gray-haired gentleman crawled through the open door. The thug tossed his cane inside and slammed the door. "Here's your stick, filthy Jew."

Marten lunged forward. "I know that man. He's our friend, Abraham Bergman."

Jenny gripped the hard muscles of Marten's arm and held him back. "No, Marten. There are too many."

Marten's arm relaxed, and he yielded to Jenny's pull, but intense anger lingered in his glaring eyes, and his breath was heavy.

The mob stopped their forward motion. The men, now silent, stared straight ahead. Marten, Nic, and Jenny looked to their right. About a block away, another armed group appeared, all dressed in civilian clothes. Without hesitation, they moved forward. Though they were also silent, their intent was clear. Every man carried some kind of solid object. Most had wooden clubs. Others carried iron bars or steel chains.

"Here come the Jews," Marten said.

A sense of dread gripped Jenny as the three friends stood silent, ignored by two forces that were intent only on each other. Along both sides of the street, gaps in window shades revealed watching eyes.

The groups met directly in front of the café, and violence erupted. Shouts and curses gave voice to a volatile mix of adrenaline-fueled hatred and panic. Few of the combatants emerged unscathed. Blood flowed freely. More than a few arms bent at unusual angles. After a seeming eternity, the two armies had vented their wrath and reached a bloody conclusion. When that moment arrived, the participants paused and surveyed their surroundings. Some men stood and panted. A few sat on the ground. One keeled over and retched.

In the middle of the street, one man in an NSB uniform lay still. Blood flowed from a large, open wound on his head. Another uniformed man knelt by his side. "He's dead!" he shouted. "Koot is dead!" The fallen man then shook violently with a seizure. "Not dead, but hurt real bad," added the kneeling man.

Hurriedly gathering their weapons and their wounded comrades, the Jewish fighters fled. Bernard came out of his café and joined the three students. "I don't know who won that fight, but it's not finished."

As if to confirm Bernard's comment, the man in command of the NSB force pointed to him and yelled, "You! Do you have a phone in there?"

"Yes."

The man strode to his side, club in hand. "Take me to it."

Bernard led the man inside.

Within minutes, an ambulance had removed the unconscious NSB fighter, and calm returned to the Jewish Quarter.

The three friends returned to their table. Their dinner was waiting for them. With quivering hands, Jenny lifted the lid of the pan and brought a spoonful of the bazargan to her mouth. Cold. She laid the spoon on her plate. The taste was gone. Her hunger too. The pleasant mood of the evening was long gone. "Marten, do you think maybe we should just go?"

When the three arrived at the Demeester home, darkness had settled over the neighborhood. They entered a well-lit but quiet house. "It looks like Hanna has already retired to her room," said Marten. "How about some hot chocolate? I can fix it."

Moving to the kitchen, they discovered that Hanna had anticipated their needs. Flaky, almond-filled *banket* awaited them in a covered cake stand. Nic and Jenny nibbled pastries at the table. Marten served hot chocolate.

"What will happen now?" Jenny asked.

"Don't know," Marten said. "The whole thing scares me. Those mobs could go anywhere, even here. I was really proud of the Jewish boys and the fight they put up today, but we can be sure this is not the end of it."

"I'm not a doctor yet, but I think that one guy may die," Jenny said. "His skull may be fractured."

Nic lifted a piece of banket toward his mouth, then lowered it to his plate. "If he dies, the Germans may not be content to let the NSB do their dirty work."

Marten set his mug on the counter hard enough that hot chocolate sloshed over the rim. "Exactly right. In fact, it might be just the excuse they need to crack down on us." He stood. "I'm afraid my head is full of all this stuff. It's been a really tiring day. If you don't mind, I'd like to call it a night."

"Me too," Jenny said. She replaced the lid on the cake stand.

Marten showed his quiet houseguests to their rooms upstairs. "Rest well, my friends."

Jenny entered her room, closed the door, and flipped on the light. A colorful quilt, decorated with Dutch scenes of children wearing wooden shoes, covered the bed. Her bag rested on a rocking chair, apparently deposited by the efficient and thoughtful Hanna. Two walls displayed landscape paintings of the Dutch seashore.

A closed door drew her attention. *Must be a closet.* She opened it. A thick terrycloth robe hung on a brass hook beside a shower. She pictured the outdoor toilet at home and her many Saturday baths in a tub in the kitchen. *I'm sure not on the farm tonight.* She turned on the water, dropped her clothes on the tile floor, climbed into the shower, and lost herself for the next fifteen minutes in steamy, warm comfort.

Relaxed, refreshed, and wrapped in the luxurious white robe, she returned to the bedroom, searched through her bag for a book, and settled into the leather wingback chair beside the bed.

After reading only a few pages, the book drifted to her lap, forgotten. She stared straight ahead, her mind filled with the day's events. Although she felt warm, clean, and comfortable, tension lurked inside. This was not life on the farm or at the university, where she enjoyed structure, love, and predictability. Today she witnessed hatred and chaos.

The image of her new friend crept into mind and brought a gentle smile to her face. Strong, kind Marten. They both wanted to become doctors, healers of people. And today they both witnessed violence. He probably felt the same tension that she was enduring No, he was stronger. *He's probably fast asleep.*

Thoroughly awake now, she stood, went to the closet, and looked inside. Sure enough, there on the floor rested a pair of fluffy bedroom slippers. She left her room and returned to the kitchen on the ground floor. After a brief search for a switch, the room came alive with warm light. Most of the banket pastries remained. She located coffee and a percolator. A few minutes later, she was seated at the table, sipping a steaming cup.

With a slight creak, the door opened. Marten appeared, also dressed in a terrycloth robe. "Hi. I smelled coffee and figured somebody else couldn't sleep."

Jenny blinked and set her cup on the table. "Hi, Marten. You surprised me. I wasn't too sleepy. Made a pot. Hope that's okay."

"Great. No problem. Think I'll have some." He poured a cup and sat.

She carefully lifted her cup and sipped. "Rough day, huh?"

"Worse than that. I can't get it out of my head."

"That's how I feel too."

Marten lifted a pastry from the dish. "Let's talk about something—anything—else. Try to get our minds off what we saw today." He paused for a moment before continuing. "School going okay?"

"Fine, fine. A lot of work, but it's worth it. I'm on my way to reaching my goal of being a doctor."

A slight grin chased away his sober expression. "I remember you talking about that when I visited the farm."

Her cheeks warmed. "I am so sorry about how I acted that day. It was really rude."

"No problem. It seems like a long time ago. A lot has happened since then."

She searched for words. "So you are interested in medicine too. What specialty?"

"Pediatrics."

The room seemed to brighten around Jenny. "Me too. Maybe we can study together sometime."

A frown appeared. "I hope so. Maybe life in Holland will return to normal soon. But I have my doubts about that."

She studied his face, aching to continue the conversation, but came up with nothing but sadness. Life wasn't returning to normal anytime soon, and they both knew it. She sighed. "I think I'm finally ready to get some sleep."

"Me too."

She followed him through the darkened house. In the upstairs hallway, he stopped. "Take my hand, Jen. That little table is hard to see in the dark. I've knocked it over before."

She reached out and grasped his hand lightly. Electricity raced from his hand to her heart.

He stopped at her room. "Well, this is it."

"This is it." She still held his hand. "Uh, Marten. There is something I need to say."

"Yes?"

"On that first day we met, I made a joke about your hands."

"I do remember." His voice was smiling. "Something about how soft they were."

"The truth is that I like the feel of your hand."

Marten squeezed lightly. "Not too soft?"

"Just about right, actually." She reached with her free hand and squeezed Marten's forearm. "And today, when you intended to fight for that elderly man, your arm was strong, hard."

"There is a time to be soft and a time to be hard. It says something about that in one of the Jewish holy writings."

"It says that in the Christian Bible too. Ecclesiastes, I think."

"I'm glad we met downstairs tonight, Jen. This day started off bad, but it ended up pretty good." He leaned over slowly. "Thanks for being my friend."

The first kiss was brief and light, but it ignited a craving for another. The second kiss left her with a light head and weak knees. She'd never had a boyfriend, but suddenly recognized something powerful inside her that demanded more. Warmth spread through her body, but confusion stirred in her brain. Her strict upbringing struggled with a powerful compulsion to fan the flame that had just ignited. Reluctantly, she forced herself to pull back. "Wow, um, that was really, um, really nice." She inhaled. "I think I better go now."

Marten released her slowly. "Okay ... good night." He turned and entered his room across the hall.

Jenny hurried into her room, pressed her back on the closed door, and smiled into the darkness.

Chapter Twelve

12 February 1941
Amsterdam

The next morning, Marten eased awake to a warm, quiet room. He thought briefly of his time with Jenny before other thoughts intruded. The long lines of weary Jews at the registration office. The brawl in the street the night before. Fear pushed aside all pleasurable sensations. He tossed his covers aside and grabbed the same clothes he wore the day before.

After descending to the main floor of the house, he found Desmond at the desk in his father's office.

"Good morning, sir. I was just speaking to your father in The Hague. You just missed his call."

Marten sat in the chair beside the desk. "How are you? I've been wondering where you were."

"I've been working on our hidden apartment project. I got in very late last night after you and your friends went to bed."

"How's it going?"

"My brother Ari and I are making good progress but not as fast as I'd like. We can only use people we totally trust. We have an excellent contractor who has worked with your father for years, but he has other similar projects right now. One of them is for our friend, Otto Frank."

"Then I need to help. Also, maybe my two friends, Nic and Jenny, can join us."

"As a matter of fact, your father and I were just discussing that very thing. He was impressed with your friend, Nicolaas. After doing some checking on the DeHaan family, he decided that we can trust them."

"Okay then. I will ask them to join us."

"When can you all start?"

"I can start today. This must be my priority. I will need to drop my classes at school for a while."

"I would not advise that, sir. I urge you to continue with your schooling. It is important."

Marten wrinkled his forehead. "More important than protecting my family?"

"By continuing your schooling, you *are* protecting your family. Your absence may be noted by our ever-vigilant adversaries, and they may investigate. It is best to avoid that kind of attention."

Marten paused while Desmond's logic settled in his mind. He was right. If his absence was reported to the wrong people, it could be dangerous. "I see your point. I don't like it, but I will continue at school ... for now."

Desmond checked his watch. "Very good, sir. Now, please excuse me. I must make sure we have some breakfast for your guests."

"Something simple, like eggs," Marten said. "Oh, and lots of coffee."

"Eggs in shakshouka?"

"If Hanna is up to it."

Desmond hurried off, and Marten sat in his father's chair. He tapped the desk with a pencil. Every day, school seemed less and less important, but he must stay. And spending time with Jenny both at school and at the apartment would be great. He stuck the pencil in the drawer and rolled back the chair. He'd talk to his friends about helping with the apartment. *Just hope we get it done before it's too late.*

Hanna served a breakfast of poached eggs resting in a tomato sauce, complete with the rich scents of onions and garlic, and added a plate of warm bagels and two carafes of hot coffee. After watching his guests obviously enjoying themselves for a few minutes, Marten set his cup down. "I would like to share a carefully kept family secret with you."

Jenny and Nic both perked up, Jenny with a spoon at her lips and Nic reaching for a bagel.

Marten leaned closer to his friends. "My family is getting more and more concerned about our safety. We have made plans to construct a place where we can hide if necessary. Desmond and his brother, Ari, are working on it now, but we need to get it done as soon as we can."

Jenny set the spoon on her plate and straightened in her chair. "Of course we'll help. Right, Nic?"

"Absolutely. We aren't carpenters, but we picked up a lot of skills on the farm."

"And we can come here on weekends," Jenny added. "No classes."

"Don't you both have weekend jobs?" asked Desmond.

Jenny waved off the question. "We'll take time off until this job is done."

Nic took a bagel from the serving dish. "Can you tell us more about the project?"

"No need for too much detail right now," Desmond said. "We have an ideal place. And please guard this information very carefully. Lives may depend on it."

Marten stood. "We should probably get back to Utrecht. You two are fantastic friends." He focused on Jenny. "It will be great working here with you."

"Yes," she said with a grin. "It will be."

Chapter Thirteen

22 February 1941
Amsterdam

On Saturday of the next week, the three friends returned to Amsterdam. The electric train glided into Centraal station, and Marten led his friends across the platform. A crisp February breeze met them. German soldiers mixed into the crowd of Dutch travelers.

Marten pulled out his wallet. "We should probably get something to eat here. I'm buying. There won't be anything open in the Quarter today. It's the Sabbath."

After a few minutes on a bench, eating and watching the crowds, they set off and soon entered the Jewish District on Jodenbreestraat.

After they passed the German checkpoint and walked a short distance, Jenny stopped. "I had a strange feeling when we passed those German policemen."

Nic smiled. "That's because Germans are strange people, sis."

"No," Marten said. "I noticed it too." He thought for a moment. "Normally, the Orpo stare me down and try to intimidate me. These guys never made eye contact, just looked away and motioned us through. It's like they were hiding something. Strange ... and a bit troubling."

They continued on.

"I see what you mean about the shops," said Nic. "The Jews take their Sabbath seriously. This place is really dead."

"It will be a lot different tomorrow," responded Marten. "On Sunday, the Gentiles descend on the Quarter and business booms."

In the middle of the next block, Marten's heart jumped, and he stopped short. "We have a problem. Listen."

Distant sounds, completely foreign to the Jewish Sabbath, violated the normally peaceful setting. Shouts. Screams. Hysterical barking of dogs. The source of the commotion was somewhere around the next corner.

As they approached the intersection, they edged forward, holding close to the bricks of the last building in the block. As they passed the door, it swung open. A gray-headed man dressed in a black wool cassock beckoned them. "Children, you must come inside." Something about the urgency in his voice and fear on his face pulled the three young people like a powerful magnet. Without any hesitation, they hurried into the building. The door slammed shut. "You must go no further, children. Terrible things are happening on Jonas Daniel Meijer Square."

"What is it, Father?" asked Marten.

Jenny frowned. "Father?"

"I am Father DeYoung, the parish priest here at Saint Anthony's." The old priest eyed the frown on the young visitor's face. "Yes, child, a Catholic church right here in the Jewish district."

Father DeYoung studied Marten's face. "Are you Jewish, son?"

Marten nodded.

"Then you must stay here until this horrible event is finished. I have been watching as the Germans, hundreds of them, have been snatching people, young Jewish men like you, off the streets and right out of their homes. They have them gathered together over at Meijer Square."

Anger swept over Marten. "I must see this."

"Then follow me," the old man said. "We can watch from the tower."

The group climbed the stairs on the southeast corner of Saint Anthony's and lined up at the arched opening facing the square. "Keep low," Father DeYoung said. "We don't need the Orpo raiding our church today."

"Oh, no," whispered Marten as he stared at the spectacle below. Hundreds of uniformed officers maintained firm control of hundreds of young men in civilian clothes. The captives formed a long line. They squatted and held their hands high in the air. As they watched, one man's hands drifted down to his shoulders. He forced them up only to have them drop again. A Nazi officer strode to him and raised his rifle, barrel toward the sky. He then brought the butt of the weapon down on the victim's head. The man collapsed to the ground and lay still. Neighboring captives pushed their arms higher. Some other men, overcome with fatigue from squatting, fell to their knees and received the same rifle butt reward.

Jenny turned to the priest. "Father DeYoung, what is happening here? What did those boys do to deserve this?"

"They were simply in the wrong place at the wrong time. I think it is all the result of the violence we have seen here lately. The Germans are telling us that opposition will not be tolerated. I am afraid there isn't much we can do to stop them."

Marten tensed. "Not true, Father. We can't just become sheep to the slaughter. We must find a way to stop these people."

"Perhaps so, but fighting today would not be smart. Am I right?"

Marten nodded and turned back to the scene on the square. "I am really worried about my friends, Desmond and Ari. We were to meet them here today."

Squatting beside his brother, Desmond stared straight ahead, fighting the temptation to glance left at an approaching officer with a large, frenetic dog. When they reached a position directly in front of him, the officer relaxed the leash enough for the dog to snarl and snap inches from his face. Desmond held his gaze on a distant tree until the animal's hot breath and saliva hit his face, forcing him to flinch. He closed his eyes, awaiting a bite. It never came. Instead, the man and dog left him and passed Ari.

Hysterical barking and snapping pulled Desmond's gaze to his right. The man beside Ari had slipped to his knees, and the animal was attacking. The unfortunate victim raised his arm in defense, but the dog clamped his jaws on the exposed arm and shook it wildly. Blood flowed from the lacerated limb and spread over the snout of the snarling dog.

The officer calmly allowed the mauling to continue for a few seconds. He then jerked the leash. The dog released its jaws from the man's arm and licked the blood from its nose. The German, without comment, continued along the line of squatting men. The injured man groaned and crawled back to his position and slowly forced his thin arms up toward the sky, one draining blood onto his jacket.

Desmond's arms and legs started to tremble and spasm. How much longer could he last? Another minute, maybe two? A line of trucks rolled into the square. They were large vehicles with open, canvas-covered cargo areas. The trucks rolled to a stop in a line.

A German officer, holding tightly to the leash of his lunging dog, shouted the command to load the Jews. *"Laden Sie die Juden."*

Hundreds of Orpo men jumped into action. With shouts, kicks, and crushing blows from rifle butts and truncheons, they set upon the young Jews. The captives, legs and arms numb from their prolonged poses, had difficulty standing and walking and could offer only weak defense from the blows. One young man made the mistake of looking into the eyes of a young German. A fist smashed directly into his face, shattering his spectacles.

Desmond and Ari followed the group toward the trucks, moving toward the middle of the pack to avoid the assault. Waiting his turn to climb into the back of the truck, Desmond exercised his leg muscles to regain his strength. The man in front of him was not so prepared. He put one foot on the bumper of the truck and attempted to lift himself, but failed. As he fell back to the road, a German kicked him on the back of his head. He lay still on the ground. Other Jews lifted his unconscious body onto the truck. Desmond, assisted by his younger brother, climbed aboard and took a seat at the back of the vehicle.

In the open, arched window of Saint Anthony's church tower, Marten, along with Jenny, Nic, and Father DeYoung, watched in silence as the scene on the square unfolded. The trucks stood idle, slight trails of smoke drifting from their exhaust stacks as their engines rumbled. When the entire caravan was loaded with young Jews, the long procession began moving.

Jenny turned to the priest. "Where are they taking them, Father?"

"I don't know, child, but I am very afraid for them. Three or four hundred innocent young men, probably taken as a lesson to us to never oppose the German empire."

Marten's anger rose. "A lesson lost on me."

"And me," added Jenny.

"Look!" Marten pointed at one of the trucks as the convoy rolled directly past Saint Anthony's church. "It's Desmond in that truck. I'm sure of it. And it looks like Ari beside him."

From the back of the rolling truck, Desmond looked toward them. He made a slight wave with the hand that was extended outside the vehicle. An observant German rewarded his gesture with a sharp truncheon blow. Desmond jolted, turned away from his friends, and put his hand to his head.

The three young college students, along with the gray-headed priest, stood in silence and gazed at Jonas Daniel Meijer Square as the sound of trucks faded in the distance. The old priest slowly performed the sign of the cross and whispered, "God's chosen people."

"Are they going to put them in jail somewhere?" asked Jenny.

Father DeYoung placed a frail hand on Jenny's shoulder. "I expect so, young lady." He straightened his body slowly and scanned his audience. "I think the immediate danger outside has passed for now. It might be best for you young people to go to your homes now. I think I should spend some time in prayer. May God go with you."

The three friends left the church and stopped on the sidewalk outside. Marten's gaze was pulled to Meijer Square. It stood empty and quiet under the black clouds of February. The Germans had gone, their malicious assignment accomplished. The locals had not ventured out. As oak tree skeletons stood guard, brown leaves skittered across the lifeless square, pushed by the cold winter wind.

"Evil is hanging over that place," Marten said. He shifted his gaze to his friends. "I need to get home and call my father. We must get Desmond and Ari released."

"Can we go with you?" asked Nic. "We still want to help you with the new place you are building."

"Thanks, but right now, Desmond's arrest will interrupt that process. After these latest developments, I need to leave the university and give my full attention to protecting my family and my people. Anyway, it won't be long before Jews are shut out of the schools. I suggest that you and Jenny return to school."

Jenny tugged Marten's sleeve, drawing his eyes to hers. "Would you call me soon, Marten?"

A slight smile appeared. "Be sure of it."

Chapter Fourteen

March 1941
The DeHaan Farm

Albert DeHaan pulled off his boots, their soles heavy with a generous coating of mud. He set them in a tray outside the back door and hung his wool coat on a hook. He opened the door, and the warm kitchen air, heavy with the aroma of a hot meal, pulled him forward.

"Cold day, Emma," he mumbled, glancing at his wife's back as she worked at kneading a large ball of dough. A variety of ingredients and cooking implements cluttered her workspace under a window overlooking the garden.

"Spring is coming, Albert." Her hands paused as she gazed out the window. "I can see green shoots from here."

"Maybe, but winter has not given in yet. Shall I touch you with my cold fingers to prove it?"

Emma betrayed a slight smile. "Your choice, sweetheart, but your fun would distract me from the dessert I'm working on. Might not turn out well for you."

"Then I believe I will keep my hands to myself, at least for now."

He eased his tired body into his usual place at the kitchen table. Emma wiped her flour-covered palms onto her generous apron and brought a steaming cup of coffee to her husband.

The sound of a turning latch on the large front door announced visitors. Their voices quickly identified them. "Mama, Papa, we're home." Jenny and Nicolaas strode into the kitchen. Albert rose and met them with warm hugs.

"Good timing," Emma said. "Dinner's ready."

The two children promptly sat and attacked the home-cooked meal. After a few minutes, Albert leaned forward. "As happy as I am to see you young rascals, I think there might be more to your surprise visit than a desire for your mother's cooking. Especially coming in the middle of the week."

"Actually, you are right, Father," Nicolaas said. "So much has happened. Not all good. Your children need some wisdom from their parents."

"Well now. There's a comment I haven't heard before. Emma, I believe your children have passed from adolescence to adulthood."

Emma's eyes narrowed, and her gaze shifted from Nicolaas to Jenny. "You two aren't in some kind of trouble, are you? We have been hearing about lots of unrest due to those Germans. I think you should leave those people alone."

"It's not as simple as that," Nicolaas said. "We were in Amsterdam with Marten when the Germans made that raid in the Jewish District. They grabbed hundreds of Jewish people, young men who just happened to be there, and loaded them in trucks. They are now being held somewhere. Our friends Desmond Aaronson and his brother were with them. They are fine men who did nothing against the Germans."

Emma slid her chair back, moved to the window, and spoke while she looked out the window. "I am sure they will release them soon. You children must not get involved in things like this. I want my family to be safe."

"We will be safe, Mama," Nicolaas said. "I will watch out for Jenny. We just think we should do something. The things that are happening ... it's just not right."

"You may have come at a good time," Albert said. "The men of our church are meeting this afternoon to discuss the problems with the Germans. I may learn some things I can share with you."

"Can we come?" Jenny asked.

"The consistory is all men, Jenny. It might be best if you stayed—"

"Papa, that's not right. I have things to say."

Albert leaned back in his chair. This was a dilemma. A male-dominated church. An independent-minded daughter. Critical issues to resolve. An immediate decision was needed.

"Come with us, Jenny." He hesitated for a moment. "Try to be careful what you say."

"Will you come, Mama?" Jenny asked.

"I think it might be best for me to stay home … this time. Maybe next time."

The three DeHaans rode bicycles the short distance from their farm to the *Gereformeerde Kerken,* the Reformed Church of Nijkerk. When they arrived, numerous bikes, several horse-drawn wagons, and one car were gathered near the old church.

Jenny's father led the family into the building and removed his hat. He nodded to several men before leading his children to one of the wooden pews near the front.

The sanctuary hummed with conversation as additional members arrived. Finally, when about a dozen men were seated, the pastor, Pieter Jansen, closed the church doors. As he walked down the center aisle with his well-worn Bible in hand, the room quieted.

Standing at the pulpit, the pastor offered an opening prayer. When finished, he addressed the group. "Thank you for coming on a weekday. We have concerns that demand our attention. The German invaders are tightening their grip on our land. We need to resolve how we, as a church, will respond."

Gerrit Van Dijk, a store owner, stood. "Things really have not been too bad under the Germans. As a matter of fact, business is good, and the German soldiers haven't caused any trouble in town."

This comment stimulated a hum of conversation that quickly grew in intensity.

Pastor Jansen gestured for quiet. He glanced at the DeHaan family. "Certainly, the invasion was a very bad time for us. We all agree on that. Then, for a time, most of the occupiers were careful to respect our people. But now I am getting reports of mistreatment of Dutch citizens."

Jenny stood. "Pastor Jansen, if I could say something, things are getting bad in Amsterdam. Nic and I have seen what the Germans are really like. They grabbed people on the street, hundreds of innocent people, and beat them with clubs. They threw them into trucks and took them away."

"That stuff hasn't happened here," Van Dijk said.

Jenny shot an angry look at the man. "Don't let those Germans fool you. It is just beginning." She glared at the stunned gathering. "Wake up, people!"

Van Dijk smirked. "I think we should all act like grown-ups here."

Jenny's temper erupted like fuel had been thrown on a fire. *He has no idea what the Germans are capable of.* Her heart pulsed in her neck, and she opened her mouth to speak, but Nic grabbed her arm. She plunked down in the pew and shot him an irate glance.

Van Dijk sat back in his seat and folded his arms. "All I got to say."

"We clearly have a variety of opinions," the pastor said. "That's why we are here. Let's see if we can sort them out and come to an understanding of what we, as Christians, must do. The Bible should be our guide. What does Scripture have for us?"

Willem Bakker, a deacon and middle-aged farmer, stood. "We are taught to obey those in authority over us. Doesn't that mean we must obey the Germans?"

Jacob De Jong, a gray-haired elder of the church, got up and faced Bakker. "I believe that our only legitimate government is our Queen, not the German invaders. We owe them nothing."

Bakker turned to Jenny. "Those people in Amsterdam who got beaten by the Germans. They were Jews, right?"

Jenny's anger boiled again, and she shot to her feet in spite of Nic's firm hand on her arm. "Yes, they were Jews. What difference does that make? They are people. One of them is our friend."

Bakker continued, "I am not defending those Germans. What they did wasn't right. But we do need to remember that the Jews are descendants of those who crucified Christ."

Jenny's arms trembled in spite of her firm grip on the wooden pew. She searched for a response.

Elder De Jong stood. He first gave Jenny a kind, reassuring look, then turned to Bakker. "Think of this, Willem. Jesus and all his followers were Jews. So, there may have been a descendant of Peter, or another of the disciples, in the group that was attacked in Amsterdam. Perhaps we should deal with our neighbors as they are today, and according to Holy Scripture, these Jews are definitely our neighbors." His words hung in the air for a minute before De Jong continued, "Also, Jesus said that what we do for the least of these, we do unto him."

Van Dijk broke the silence. "I think we all agree on one thing. We are responsible to care for our families. If we oppose these Nazis, we put our families in danger. Seems to me that what we should do is mind our own business and let the Lord deal with these Germans."

Pastor Jansen rested his Bible on the podium and gestured toward Jenny's father. "Albert DeHaan is not one to impose his beliefs on others, but I expect he does have feelings about this matter. Could you share with us, Albert?"

Father slowly stood and studied the room full of familiar faces. "I'm just a common man with very little education. I have heard many opinions tonight. I also read the Bible a lot, and I try to do what it tells me. I pray often. It's not hard when you work the fields all day. So, in spite of what you all say, I am going to pray, then be still and listen to that voice deep inside me. I know it's the Lord talking to me. Then I will know what I must do. It may not be the smart thing or the easy thing, but it will be the right thing. The Lord demands nothing more, nor nothing less."

As the sun touched the trees on the western horizon, the DeHaans turned their bikes into the long driveway of the family farm. Their milk cows raised their heads and trotted in the direction of the barn.

"I'll take care of those girls," Nic said. "It looks like they are anxious to unload their milk."

"Tell them I'm sorry we are a bit late," called Father.

Jenny led the way through the front door, stopped, and inhaled deeply. The scent of almond pulled her toward the kitchen. "Smells like Mama was busy while we were gone."

Sure enough, her mother stood over a plate, cutting a pastry log into short pieces. She smiled at Jenny. "How about some banket?"

Jenny looked around the room. All evidence of the baking process was gone. The sink was empty, and the countertops were clear. "I wish you had saved the clean-up for me, Mama."

"I needed to do that. I was doing too much thinking. A baking project calms me. Let's enjoy the banket before we talk about your meeting at the church."

After the family emptied the plate of their favorite pastry, Jenny began to clear the table. Her mother raised a hand. "Later, child. Now it's time to talk."

Her father loaded his old pipe and lit the contents. Smoke drifted to the ceiling. Watching this routine and smelling the tobacco brought soothing memories to Jenny.

"There was a lot of talk about the invaders," Father said. "Some said we should work against them. Some said we should submit. Most said nothing."

"And what did you say, Albert?"

"I said I would do the right thing."

Mother frowned. "That worries me. What does that mean? What exactly are you—we—going to do?"

Her father set his pipe on his ashtray, reached across the table, and rested his large, rough hand on his wife's arm. "I think we need to take each day, pray a lot, and do what we feel led to do."

She pulled her arm free. "I know you, Albert DeHaan. You're likely to do very dangerous things to stop those Germans." She paused for a few seconds. "And what about the children? What will you permit them to do?"

Smoke from Father's ignored pipe curled toward the ceiling. Silence filled the room. He looked down at his hands. After a long pause, his steady gaze met his wife's moist eyes, then those of each of his children. "Nicolaas and Jenny are grown. We have done all we can to teach them right from wrong. For years, we have told them they are responsible for what they do. Now we must allow them their freedom. They must make their own decisions."

Her mother stood, gathered some dishes, and placed them in the sink. She paused for a long moment and turned to face her family. "You children and your father are my life. I need you. Please be careful."

Jenny pushed back her chair and rushed to her mother. She pressed her cheek into her hair and hugged her. "I love you, Mama."

"We won't disappoint you, Mama," said Nic. "Or you, Father."

Their mother laughed weakly in her tears. "And, Nicolaas, I want you to watch out for your sister. She may be grown, but she does run off a bit sometimes."

Chapter Fifteen

19 June 1941
The Hague

Colonel Ernst Schmidt leaned back in his leather chair and rested his gleaming boots on top of his desk. A light breeze wafted through the open window behind him and brushed his neck gently. He inhaled the cool, fresh air, his telephone braced between his shoulder and closely shaved chin. As the phone crackled to life, he dropped his feet to the hardwood floor and swung his chair toward the open window.

"Good morning, my darling. I am calling from Holland. I'm sitting in the Binnenhof, a complex of government buildings that we now control. Believe me, my dear, this is the greatest opportunity of my lifetime. The Gestapo is our path to a secure future."

"Ernst, my brother, Derrik, is still being held."

"We both know his arrest was all his own doing. He should not have attended that union meeting. Nevertheless, I will try to intervene when I can. Be patient. These things take time." He swung around and rolled the heavy chair close to the desk. "Enough of such talk on the telephone, Gerda. We must think of ourselves in times like these. We have been loyal Germans, and we will remain so. Our future is bright indeed."

"And what is your job? Can you at least tell me that?"

He stood and walked to the window, carrying the rotary phone the length of its cord. "I have achieved a position in the Office of Jewish Affairs, led by Adolf Eichmann. Your mail may go to Section IV B4. It will reach me here in The Hague."

"And what's happening with those Jews, Ernst?"

"Nothing you need be concerned about, my dear. Our leaders will make those decisions. They will give the orders, and I will obey, like any good soldier."

He returned to his seat at the desk, then opened a drawer and pulled out a framed picture, a family portrait of himself, his wife, and their young son. "Enough about me. How is Hans? It has been too long. I miss that boy. How are his lessons going?"

"His teacher says he could be a great violinist. I wish you were here to listen to him."

"Perhaps soon, my dear."

A gentle knock on the door wiped away Schmidt's pleasant mood. "I must go." He clicked the phone to its cradle and turned his attention to the closed door. His voice lowered and sharpened. "Yes."

The door opened, and a young secretary appeared. "Colonel Schmidt, your next appointment is here."

He slid the family picture to his drawer. "Show him in."

The blonde woman nodded and left.

A tall young man walked through the door. Schmidt studied his tan face, freshly trimmed light brown hair, and his casual and clean clothing.

After looking down at Schmidt's desk for a few seconds, the visitor looked up, made brief eye contact with the colonel, then glanced back at the desk.

Schmidt stood. "You are Karl Müller, yes?"

"I am Karl Müller, Herr Schmidt. Thank you for seeing me."

"And you are seeking employment here. That is correct?"

"Yes, sir."

"Then let's get to it. And before I ask you any questions, I will share two things with you." He tapped the manila folder in his hand. "First, I already know many things about you. And second, it would be a very big mistake to lie to me. You are in the office of the German Gestapo." He paused for a moment to allow the comment to take effect, then pointed at the leather chair facing his desk. "Sit."

Karl eased into the chair and folded his hands.

"Tell me, Karl Müller, why should I hire you?"

"I am a loyal German, sir. I also have lived in the Netherlands for several years, so I know the country, and I know the people. I think I could help you."

Schmidt tapped the folder. "You approached our military during the invasion. They report that you provided much helpful information."

"I did my best, Herr Schmidt."

He raised the volume. "*Colonel* Schmidt."

"Colonel. I'm sorry."

"I represent the Office of Jewish Affairs, Müller. Tell me what you know about Jews."

"For the last two years, I have worked for a Jewish family here in The Hague."

Schmidt straightened in his chair. "And did you like them?"

"They did treat me fairly." Karl paused, frowning. "I can't say that I liked them, but I needed work. A man needs to eat, you understand?"

Schmidt stood and walked to the window, his back to Karl. "I can imagine a time when there are no Jews around, when only Germans are in control. That would be a beautiful world." He turned slowly and scrutinized the man before him. "Don't you think, Karl Müller?"

"Yes, I do think so, Colonel Schmidt."

"Now, think about this, Karl Müller. Your job here would be to help us deal with the Jewish problem, or perhaps I should say, the Jewish *problems*, for there are many. The Führer has taught us that the Jews are responsible for much of Germany's problems. They really are a cancer afflicting our people. They, along with other undesirables, are detrimental to our efforts. I believe they must be separated from the master race. We must be free of their corrosive effect."

"Will we send them elsewhere?"

Schmidt shrugged. "That is not for us to decide, Müller. It will be our responsibility to follow the orders of our superiors, whatever they may be. He paused for a few seconds. "Does that trouble you?"

Karl tried to maintain eye contact but blinked and looked down.

Schmidt sat down at his desk and tapped the blotter with his large, gold ring. "I see from your hesitance that you have concerns. The Führer, and those of us who are loyal to him, have a great vision for the future. A vision for a society run by a superior race. To reach that point, inferior beings must be removed. It is simple science, Müller. Darwin has explained everything."

"I have heard of Darwin, Colonel Schmidt."

"I am sure you have known some Jews who seemed very human, as have I. But they were, in fact, abnormal. Jews generally appear to be fully human, but when you see the harm they have done, you realize that they fall far short. Understand?"

"I think so."

"We all want to do what is right. Sometimes it is difficult to discern right from wrong. Each must decide. I have decided to follow my leaders in achieving our new great society. I think my decision will serve me well."

Schmidt leaned back in his chair. "Now, Karl Müller. What is your decision? Will you commit to join us, or will you walk away from this opportunity?"

Karl sat up tall. Unblinking, he responded, "I will join you, Colonel Schmidt."

A slight smile turned the lips of Schmidt. "You may have a future in our great organization, young man, if you do your job well. Let me begin with a name you recognize. Adolf Eichmann is the head of our Section. My supervisor is Willi Zopf who works directly for Eichmann. You see, of course, I am in a good position to advance myself. You will also have the opportunity to advance yourself."

"You can count on me, Colonel Schmidt."

"Excellent. Now, let me explain your job. It is really quite simple. You will do anything I tell you to do. If you follow my orders, you will be richly rewarded. My best people have their own houses, even their own automobiles, all formerly owned by those who were a detriment to the German Reich. Your initial task is to provide me with information. You are in an excellent position to find out certain things about the people in this country. I would like to know who may be helpful to our cause, and who may be a danger to us. With your background, you could even infiltrate Resistance organizations. I have great hopes for you, Müller, and high expectations."

"Thank you, Colonel Schmidt."

"Let us be very clear on something. I intend to succeed in my position. As an officer of the Gestapo, I have unlimited power of arrest. If you endanger my position by disloyalty or failure, you are subject to the same punishment that is given to those Jews. Do I make myself clear?"

"Yes, Colonel Schmidt."

"And you still choose to work for me?"

"Yes, sir."

"Be here tomorrow morning at eight sharp, and we will begin."

Karl stood and moved toward the door.

"Oh, one more question," Schmidt said. "That Jew who employed you, what is his name?"

"Reinaar Demeester. He lives right here in The Hague."

At seven thirty the next morning, Karl Müller stepped off the tram. The ancient buildings of the historic Binnenhof complex loomed ahead of him. When he arrived at the arched entrance gate, he joined a small group of people who were patiently enduring the security screening by four uniformed SS men.

When Karl finally reached the head of the line, a young guard, standing erect in his crisp, new uniform, raised his chin just enough to peer down his nose at Karl. He extended his hand, palm up. The youthful tone of his voice confirmed his immaturity, but it had a practiced edge. "Papers."

Karl offered his identification and watched as the soldier studied the document.

"Purpose of your visit?"

"I am here to see Colonel Ernst Schmidt. He is expecting me."

"Wait here." The guard stepped away, examined documents on a clipboard, and returned. "Follow me." He led Karl to the Gestapo section and into Ernst Schmidt's outer office. A smile appeared on his face when he approached the secretary. "Good morning, Gretchen. This is Karl Müller to see Colonel Schmidt."

Gretchen returned the smile. "We are expecting him, Hans."

The guard turned to leave, stopped, and looked back at Gretchen. "See you later maybe?"

Gretchen stared at her typewriter. "Perhaps sometime, Hans."

Hans glared at Karl, and his face hardened. He snapped the heels of his boots together and strode from the room.

For a few minutes, Karl sat, rigid, on the front edge of a hard visitor's chair. His tight shoulder muscles throbbed, and his thoughts raced.

He checked the clock. Exactly eight o'clock. Ernst Schmidt strode into the room wearing his gray uniform, similar to the SS, except for a plain, black collar patch and green shoulder boards. The bright sun, streaming through the tall windows, flashed off his black boots.

The secretary stopped her typing. "Good morning, Colonel Schmidt."

Schmidt brushed past the woman without looking at her. "It *will* be a good day for us, Gretchen. I will make sure of that." He stopped and turned to Karl, pulled his pocket watch from his vest. "On time. You passed your first test, Müller. There will be more. Follow me."

Karl jumped to his feet, followed Schmidt into his office, and took a seat facing the desk.

The colonel eased his tall, muscular frame into the chair behind his desk. He leaned back and rested his elbows on the padded arms of his chair. "Tell me, Müller. What strikes you most about my behavior?"

Karl blinked a few times, swallowed, and paused, his brain racing in search of the correct answer. Finally, he braved a response. "I think it's your eyes, Colonel Schmidt. They are very powerful."

Schmidt leaned forward and slapped both hands on the leather blotter of his desk. "Exactly. Very good, Müller. Your eyes are your best tool. You must use them well in two ways. First, you must develop a piercing stare that can burn into the brain of your victim. I can easily make most Jews cower with a look." A wry smile appeared. "It is quite enjoyable, actually."

Karl studied Schmidt's eyes and quickly shifted his focus to the clock on the wall. "I need to work on that, Colonel Schmidt."

"Indeed. Now the second thing. When you interrogate someone, you must observe their reactions carefully. Fear is easy to see, but it tells you little." He shrugged. "We are Gestapo. Everyone is afraid of us. You must learn to ask the right questions and look closely for lies. Sometimes, people are nervous beyond the circumstances. Or, they may appear too calm. But mostly you must study their eyes carefully. With practice, the skill will come to you. Even if the lips lie, the eyes will reveal the truth." Schmidt grinned. "It is almost an art. Any questions, Müller?"

"Just one thing, Colonel Schmidt. You are wearing a uniform. The Gestapo in Germany has a reputation for wearing civilian clothes."

Schmidt responded with a practiced, humorless laugh. "Ah yes, the black leather coat and the fedora, along with the Gestapo strut, guaranteed to strike terror into the hearts of any German, guilty or not. I have seen people lose all control of their bodies right there in front of me. Now we have taken our polished skills to the occupied countries. Here, I prefer to wear my uniform. I would hate to have my own soldiers shoot me, thinking I am one of the Resistance."

Schmidt continued in a quiet, deliberate voice. "Since I can quite easily instill fear in people, I don't need to be overly aggressive. I usually approach my targets in a very calm manner. No need to exert myself. You understand?"

Karl nodded.

Ernst Schmidt rolled his chair back from the desk and stood. "Enough talk for now, Müller. Report back here tomorrow. I expect you to have interesting things to tell me about your neighbors in this fine city, especially those Demeesters you know so well."

Chapter Sixteen

15 July 1941
The Hague

Joran pushed away his dessert plate, the sweet, flaky rugelach roll untouched, and tossed his napkin onto the linen tablecloth. The roiling tension inside him spoiled any lingering hunger.

A frown creased his mother's smooth forehead. "It has chocolate filling. Your favorite."

"I'm worried about Desmond. When is he coming home, Father?"

"We just don't know, Joran. The Germans give us only little bits of news. Desmond is in prison, along with all the young men who were taken from Meijer Square. We are told the group was moved from Buchenwald to Mauthausen."

"Where is that?"

"Buchenwald is a prison in Germany. Mauthausen is in Austria."

Joran sat tall in his seat, and his voice took on the urgency that was rising in him. "Wait a minute. You said those places are prisons. That's where they put bad people. Desmond is a good person."

His mother laid a gentle hand on his arm. "Desmond is a very good person. We love him and want him back in our house. Sometimes bad people put good people in prison. That's what is happening here. Some bad people have come to our country."

Joran gazed out the dining room window and processed her words. "We are good people, aren't we, Mama?"

Mother looked to his father for the answer.

"Yes, son, we are good people, and we are taking steps to protect our family. When the Germans arrested Desmond, I think they wanted to show the Dutch that they are in charge. Our country is quiet right now. They may release Desmond and his friends soon."

Marten, observing his young brother quietly, laid his fork on the dessert plate. "Has anyone heard from those men now that they are in Mauthausen?"

"Not that I know of," Father said. "Many people have sent letters and packages to the prisoners, but we get nothing but silence in return. Apparently, the Germans are keeping them isolated."

Joran slid back his chair. "May I be excused, Papa? I would like to go to my room now."

His father exchanged a quick glance with his mother, then nodded. "Certainly."

Reinaar felt an ache deep inside as Joran left the room, the boy's normal, bouncing gait missing.

Marten turned to Francien. "Joran has changed while I have been staying in Amsterdam. Is he doing a lot of reading, alone in his room?"

"I think he prefers the book world to the real world now. It started in April when all the restaurants posted the *Für Juden Verboten* signs. Suddenly, there was a sense of separation between him and his friends. Then last month when the Germans closed the beaches and parks to Jews, he started spending most of his time in the house. I'm glad you came to visit, Marten. It is good for him."

"What is he reading?"

"Some adventure books about American teenagers. I think they call them *Hardy Boys*." Francien smiled for the first time that day. "Joran loves all things American. It is good for him at this point."

Marten looked at his father. "I sense that you know more about Desmond than you shared with Joran."

Reinaar stood and walked to the window. His gaze rested on the brightly colored flower garden while his thoughts were a tangle of concerns. He turned back to his family. "I am fearful for Desmond. The Germans have notified the Council of numerous fatalities among our men at Mauthausen. It seems, according to the Nazis, that more than a few have died trying to escape. Enough of them to raise very serious questions about Germany's candor and the nature of that facility."

The deep frown returned to Francien's face. "And the list of illnesses they report sounds like the index of a medical manual. It defies credibility that a group of healthy young men is dying as they describe."

After a thoughtful pause, Reinaar changed the subject. "So, are you taking good care of the house in Amsterdam, son?"

"Sure am. And our building project at the Bramer factory is also going well. The apartment should be quite comfortable. Do you think you may be joining me at our Amsterdam house soon, Father?"

"Possibly. We continue to prepare for that. Most of our valuable things are now there. Are you enjoying the artworks?"

"Very much. And the substitutes you put in the drawing room here are really quite nice."

Francien gazed out the window. "I dearly love this house and all our friends here, but our home in Amsterdam is also comfortable." She eased her chair back. "If you gentlemen would excuse me, I need to sort through some things."

Marten and Reinaar stood as Francien left the room.

"Mother moves a little slower than usual," observed Marten.

"I probably do, as well. Let's go to my office. I need to give you something."

Once inside the office, Reinaar closed the door and emptied the contents of an envelope onto his desk. He handed an identity card to Marten. "This is your alternate identity. Your new name is Dirck Meijer. This is the work of the best Dutch forger I could find. My contacts in government selected the name of a man, non-Jewish of course, who was killed, along with his entire family, in the bombing of Rotterdam."

Marten slowly examined the card. "Perfect. It's exactly like my government ID. And just in time. The Germans have announced that all Jewish IDs have the large letter *J*. Does Joran have one also?"

"Joran is now known as Joran Elzinga. Sadly, that young man and his family also died in Rotterdam. On the amended government records, you both survived the bombing."

"Do you and mother also have false identities?"

"We do indeed. They may become useful in difficult situations."

"And business? Are you still able to operate?"

"Fortunately, before I lost Desmond, we had sold off much of our assets. The import business remains, but it is much reduced in scope. I am hopeful that the Germans will allow it to continue since they stand to benefit from it."

"Have they shown an interest in your business?"

"More than that. The Germans have assigned a Nazi supervisor. He is nothing but a Dutch collaborator with eyes to taking my company from me. He took an office near mine where he can observe everything."

The ringing of the doorbell ended their discussion.

"I'll get it," Marten said.

Reinaar swiveled his chair around and gazed out the window, his mind focused on his many worries. He was vaguely aware of the front door opening.

He snapped upright as an unfamiliar voice with quiet intensity spoke in German. "I want the head of the house."

Reinaar's pulse throbbed in his neck as he rose slowly from his chair, listening, his mind racing through the possibilities awaiting him.

The German voice came back, with a tone of controlled anger. "Now, boy."

Marten finally responded. "Yes, sir."

The voice, now calm and detached, added, "I want the entire household right here, right now."

The sound of Marten's running footsteps filled the hallway. Reinaar met him at his office door. His son's wide eyes spoke for him.

"Get the others," Reinaar said.

As Marten clattered up the stairs toward his mother and brother, Reinaar walked to the open front door. Three men stood outside, watching his approach. In front was a tall man wearing a long black coat made of smooth, soft leather. A black fedora covered his head. His face betrayed no expression, but his cold, piercing eyes gripped Reinaar's attention, sending a jolt to the pit of his stomach. Reinaar glanced at the man's companions, two young men about Marten's age in crisp, gray uniforms. Both stood silently behind their leader, their right hands resting on leather belt holsters that revealed pistols.

Reinaar gathered himself and, in perfect German, began the discussion. "Good morning. I am Reinaar Demeester. How may I help you?"

"Does your family speak German?"

"*Ja.*"

"Very good. We will continue in my language. My name is Schmidt. I represent *Geheime Staatspolizei.* Many call us simply Gestapo." He reached into the pocket of his coat and withdrew a silver-colored identification disk, flashed it, and returned it to his pocket. "We have an extremely efficient operation, Herr Demeester. I know a great deal about you, perhaps more than you imagine."

Francien, Marten, and Joran gathered in the foyer close behind Reinaar, their faces pale and blank, jaws tight. Joran pulled close to his mother and wrapped his arm around her back.

Schmidt shifted his steady gaze from one family member to the next, lingering long enough to make fixed eye contact, starting with the youngest and ending with the father. Reinaar blinked away the feeling that the German's eyes reached deep into his mind.

Having achieved the full attention of his audience, Schmidt continued, "According to our records, Herr Demeester, you and your wife are Jews, as are all your parents. And according to the man assigned to supervise the operation of your business, Willem Barkman, you have been a successful businessman for many years, as was your father." He paused, and a slight smile curled his lips. "You look a bit surprised by my words. Yes, Barkman works for us. Anyway, he also tells us that you own, in addition to this beautiful home, a house in Amsterdam? Is my information correct?"

Reinaar sensed his family's close attention. What else did these people know? How did Karl play into all this? He responded in a calm, clear voice. "That information is correct."

"Very good. You are a prudent man. I am not surprised by your business success. Well, I am sure you are aware that, since your country has come under the authority of the German Reich, a substantial number of our personnel have taken up residence in your fine city. I am here to determine if your residence may prove to be suitable for one of our senior leaders. My assistants and I will tour your home."

The Demeester family stood in stunned silence.

Schmidt looked at them for a few seconds. Speaking softly, he continued, "I don't mean at a time that is convenient." His voice changed to a shout. "I mean right now!"

The Demeesters jumped aside and opened a path into the foyer. Schmidt strode into the house, followed closely by the uniformed soldiers. "You Jews will stay right here. I can find my way quite nicely. Sergeant Becker will keep you company." The young sergeant, face expressionless, pulled the Luger pistol from his holster and held it at his side.

As the shocked family watched, Schmidt and the other soldier climbed the staircase to the second floor. The sounds of doors opening and closing and the crunch of German boots on hardwood traced the path of the uninvited visitors. After about five minutes, the two men descended the stairs and proceeded to tour the main floor. When they reached the kitchen, a scream erupted, followed by an angry response from the Gestapo officer. *"Halt die Klappe."* Silence returned to the kitchen.

After an inspection of about ten minutes, the men joined the Demeesters under the large chandelier in the spacious foyer.

The two soldiers stepped back, making way for Schmidt to enjoy the full focus of the family. "I find this house to be suited for our purposes. May I assume, Herr Demeester, that you are willing to make it available to the German Reich?"

Reinaar shifted his gaze from Schmidt to his family, then back to Schmidt. In his deep, clear voice, he responded, "I recognize the authority you hold, Herr Schmidt, as a representative of the German Reich. This house will serve your government well, as it has served my family for many years."

Schmidt paused for a moment. "You are indeed a prudent man, Herr Demeester. My report will show that you were most cooperative. Perhaps your generosity will benefit you in the future."

The Nazi started toward the front door, then stopped and turned back to the stunned family. "Today is Tuesday. We will return on Friday to begin our occupancy. You will be out of the house prior to that day. I expect we will find all the furniture and all the artworks in place when we arrive." He strode out the door, closely followed by the two soldiers. Without looking back, they entered their black sedan and motored away.

Joran stood, hands hanging at his sides, chin on his chest, biting his upper lip. Francien got onto her knees and pulled him close. They clung to each other and wept.

Marten, face red, body rigid, glared at his father. "You gave them our house without a word of protest. Are you crazy? Surely you could have appealed his action."

Reinaar reached out to his son, held his shoulders gently, and looked into his eyes. "Marten, I want you to think carefully about what you witnessed here today. Not all battles are won. We must recognize when we are in a situation where success is not possible. A lost battle does not mean that a war is lost. If your goal is to overcome an opponent, it is always best to hide your true feelings and your plans. Finally, don't underestimate that man. There is evil inside him, consuming whatever good that remains."

CHAPTER SEVENTEEN

14 December 1941
Utrecht

The little bell on the door jingled, and Jenny DeHaan entered the warmth of the Barreto Café, along with a rush of cold December air. Near the window, a group of diners paused for a moment to take a look at the newcomer. Jenny's eyes settled on her brother at a back table. She joined him.

"Hi, Nic. Marten not here yet?"

"Not yet, but he said to meet him here. I guess he knows what he's doing."

"Good. I hope he's okay."

The bell rang again as the door swung open, and Marten appeared. The customers showed only mild interest until Jenny jumped from her seat and embraced him with a hug strong enough to generate a grunt.

A smiling Marten returned the embrace. "Hey. Easy. It's only me."

"I missed you."

Marten grasped Nic's hand, and the three friends took seats.

"A lot has happened since we saw you last," Nic said.

"For sure." Marten leaned forward, prompting his friends to do the same. In a quiet voice he said, "Before you start using names, mine is now Dirck Meijer,"

Nic grinned. "Can you prove that?"

Marten patted his pocket. "No problem. Father has many friends. The guy who made my ID has the skills to print his own money."

Jenny shrugged. "So, it's Dirck then. That's going to be an adjustment, but a rose by any other name ... you know the rest."

Nic rolled his eyes. "My sister has been gathering a lot of ideas at school, not all related to becoming a doctor."

Kees Veltkamp approached. "Ah, my good friends and favorite customers, all with a pocketful of tips."

"You seem awfully cheerful," Jenny said.

Kees took a long pause and waited while the noisy group of students vacated the place. "I suspect those kids may be NSB. I take their money and listen to what they say, but I'm careful what I say."

"What are you so happy about?" asked Jenny.

"I heard good things on the BBC a few days ago. The Americans declared war on Germany. News doesn't get much better than that."

Nic clapped his hands. "Fantastic. Now I have the headline on our next newsletter."

Kees pulled out a pencil and small tablet. "Now, what can I get you folks today?"

"Coffee, please," said Marten. "Why don't you just bring a carafe of the stuff?"

With a cordial nod, the proud café owner departed to the kitchen.

Marten folded his arms and looked from Jenny to Nic. "The news isn't all good, I'm afraid. We need to enjoy our coffee and everything else we love. I have the feeling the Germans are going to put the squeeze on all of us real soon. They already have on the Jews."

"What's happening?" Jenny asked. "Start with Desmond. How is he doing?"

Marten shook his head slowly. "We lost Desmond."

"Lost him? You mean ..."

"We got the news last week, Jen. The Germans notified the Jewish Council that both Desmond and his brother died in an accident while working at the granite quarry at Mauthausen."

Kees appeared with a steaming pitcher and a plate of banket. "It's on the house today, folks." The scent of almond and fresh coffee rose from the table but did not erase the grim faces.

"Thanks," Marten said without a smile.

Jenny sat upright. "I don't believe it for a minute, that German report about Desmond. It was no accident."

Kees pulled up a chair and sat down. "I've heard reports from my Resistance friends. Since those men got to Mauthausen, the Germans have been slowly releasing reports of numerous deaths from various causes. I expect they are all dead by now."

Marten leaned back in his chair, face calm but voice strong. "Now we know. We know what is happening here. For a while the Germans were quiet. They let the NSB collaborators do their dirty work. But, when they snatched those innocent men, they exposed themselves." He tapped a finger on the table. "It's clear to me now. Since all the Jews are registered, the Germans can easily find them. First, they identify them. Then they will isolate them. Then they will remove them. And finally, they will eliminate them."

Discussion stopped. For a minute, a gloomy silence settled on the room except for the sounds of chattering pedestrians passing the café.

Jenny spoke. "How is your family?"

Marten drew a long breath. "A lot has happened. They have moved to our house in Amsterdam. The Nazis have taken over our home in The Hague. A few Gestapo agents just showed up one day, took a little tour, and told us they were taking over the house and all the contents. We had only a couple of days to take our clothes and personal things. Father saw all this coming. He had already moved his important papers to Amsterdam. He now has a place where he hides the car and a supply of petrol."

Marten glanced at his watch. "I should get going."

They stood and moved toward the door.

Nic checked the clock on the wall. "Me too. I'm late for work." He shook Marten's hand, gave Jenny a quick hug, and hurried out the door.

Jenny lingered. "Do you have to leave so soon?"

"I wish I could stay longer, Jen. I've missed you. There is so much going on. None of it as pleasant as being here with you, believe me, but it's stuff that must be done."

"Dangerous stuff?"

"Sometimes."

She pulled him to herself, pressed her face into his chest. If she could only protect him, keep him just like he was. But she couldn't. She had to let him go.

They walked out the door.

She turned to him and poked his chest. "You be careful, mister," she scolded.

He pulled her close and kissed her.

She held the kiss until the tears began. Blinking, she held his hands for a brief moment, then turned and ran away, not looking back.

CHAPTER EIGHTEEN

23 May 1942 - Saturday
Amsterdam

While Jenny's gaze rested on the beauty of springtime Holland as it passed her train window, her thoughts focused on Marten. Was he safe? Was he thinking of her?

The train slowed and glided to a stop at Amsterdam Centraal station. She and Nic exited and took a tram to the southern part of the city. They walked to Chopinstraat, a quiet residential street of modest, connected homes, and stopped mid-block at the Demeester home.

"Too bad you didn't have a chance to see their house in The Hague," Nic said. "It was really incredible."

"This one looks great to me. Even if I become a doctor, I'll be lucky to have a place like this." She ignored the brass knocker and tapped sharply on the door with her knuckles.

The door swung open, and a middle-aged man appeared. He had a full head of dark hair and a short, well-trimmed beard. Smile lines marked the corners of his warm, brown eyes. A yellow star, large as a teacup saucer, dominated the left side of his chest, creating a jarring contrast to the impeccably tailored three-piece suit. She forced her focus back to the man's face.

"You must be Jenny," the man said. "I am Reinaar Demeester. I have heard so much about you that I feel like you are part of the family. And I must say, you are even more beautiful than I expected."

A gentle warmth spread across Jenny's face. "And you are even more charming than I expected." They embraced briefly.

The man shook Nic's hand. "Do come in, both of you. Dinner is almost ready."

Marten appeared and, without any preliminaries, hugged Jenny. He let his right hand linger on her shoulder. "Hi, Nic."

A middle-aged woman descended the stairs, wearing a light-blue shirtwaist dress and matching suede pumps. No yellow star. "Oh, wonderful. They're here." She hurried directly to Jenny and embraced her.

The faint essence of rose-scented perfume tickled Jenny's nose. No way she'd ever be able to afford something like that.

Marten's mother extended a gentle hand. "My goodness. What a beautiful young woman. I am beginning to understand why Marten has spoken so often of you. It's a pleasure to meet you, Jenny."

"It's nice to meet you too, Mrs. Demeester. I have heard great things about you and your whole family."

The sound of cello music filled the brief pause in the conversation. "That's Joran," said Mrs. Demeester. "His cello has captivated him in recent months." She paused, and her expression darkened. "It all happened while the public schools have been closed to Jewish children. Mr. Feinberg is his teacher in both academics and music. He has become almost part of our family."

"Joran has made stunning progress in playing the instrument," added Mr. Demeester. "And it seems to be therapeutic for him."

"May I go see him?" asked Jenny.

Mrs. Demeester smiled. "Certainly. Let's all go. I think he would like that."

Jenny followed the sound of the music and stopped at the door of the drawing room. Joran sat with his cello, facing the window, his back to the door. He seemed lost in his music, unaware of his audience.

She knocked gently. "Joran?"

The boy stopped playing and turned a solemn face.

She spoke in a quiet voice. "Hi, Joran. I'm Jenny." He started to rise. "No, no, please don't get up. I would like to hear more." She approached the boy. "Nicolaas is my brother."

"Oh, hi, Jenny. Marten talks a lot about you. Do you like cello music?"

"Love it. The sound is beautiful, no, better than that. The best word I can think of to describe it is *delicious*. What are you playing?"

"Suite Number One of Bach's six suites for unaccompanied cello. Bach lived in Germany a very long time ago. Things were different then. Do you play?"

"I wish. We could never afford an instrument or lessons. But now that I'm at the university, I can listen to it. I fell in love with cello when I heard Jaap Spaanderman play with the Royal Concertgebouw Orchestra. Were you there to hear that performance?"

Joran's shoulders sagged. "We can't go there any longer. We mostly stay right here."

"I'm sorry." Jenny looked to Reinaar for a comment.

"The Germans have taken a number of steps to segregate the Jews from the rest of the Dutch. Many of these you may not have heard of. The Nazi directives are sent through the Jewish Council. One of them, effective last September, said that Jews are forbidden to take part in public gatherings or use public facilities intended for relaxation, recreation, and education. That included concerts, parks, sporting events, and much more."

Marten spoke, a hard edge to his voice. "You see? They are isolating us. Tell them the rest, Father. Start with that yellow monster on your suit."

The corners of Reinaar's eyes crinkled slightly, and he tapped the yellow star on his chest. "Attractive, don't you think?"

"Oh, Reinaar, please." Mrs. Demeester's voice carried a tinge of anger. "Sometimes your humor is not appropriate. I would rather stay in this house for the rest of the war than wear one of those."

The appearance of the family cook broke the tension. "Dinner is served, ma'am."

Joran brightened. "We are eating American, right, Hanna?"

"Yes, Joran. I hope I did it right."

The family gathered in the dining room. A white linen tablecloth and fine china graced the table.

As soon as Mr. Demeester concluded the prayer, Joran spoke. "This is great. Hamburgers, *frieten*, and Coca-Cola served in the bottle. Now this is how I like to wrap up the Sabbath, Mama."

She shrugged. "Not exactly like I grew up, but times change. I guess I need to loosen up a bit."

Joran peered into a small silver pitcher. "What's the red stuff, Father?"

"Well, the Americans don't put mayo on their frieten. They use tomato ketchup instead. And, instead of frieten, they call them French fries. I believe Hanna got it exactly right. This looks just like the burgers and fries I ate in New York a couple of years ago."

Joran cautiously swiped a tan, crisp potato stick through the red sauce and devoured it. "Not bad, but mayo is better." He took a big swallow of his drink, tapped his fist on his chest, burped, and grinned widely. His mother rolled her eyes and bit down on her smile.

"How is our supply of Coca-Cola, Father?" Marten asked.

"It's on the table in front of you. We probably won't have more until after the war."

"Very soon, I hope," added his wife.

"How is your business going, Mr. Demeester?" asked Nic. "Have the Germans interfered with your operations?"

All traces of humor fled from his face. "Thank you for your concern, Nicolaas. As a matter of fact, much has happened, very little of it good. The Germans have assigned a supervisor for me, who, unfortunately for us, happens to be an excellent accountant.

Tragically, I lost Desmond before we could move our assets and cover our tracks. This allowed my German supervisor to get control of much of our wealth."

This comment drew a sigh from his wife and a deep frown from Marten.

"Then, the Nazis took some steps that have proven to be quite disastrous. First, they established a new branch of the venerable Lippmann and Rosenthal Bank. Then they issued two catastrophic directives. The first one came down last August. It required that all full Jews deposit all their cash and checks in the new bank branch. First, this requirement applied to more wealthy Jews. However, this directive now applies to even poor Dutch Jews."

The man took a sip of his Coca-Cola and returned the bottle gently to the linen tablecloth. He drew a long breath and exhaled slowly while he watched all the sober faces. "Well, a couple of days ago, the other shoe fell. The Nazis dictated that before the end of June, Jews must hand over all their valuables. This means gold, silver, art, everything. After that time, no Jew may hold more than two hundred guilders." He paused for a moment and stole a glance at his wife. "They will have impoverished us."

A stunned silence filled the room. Then Marten spoke, anger boiling in his deliberate words. "That's not all. Tell them about the relocations, Father."

His father shifted his calm, steady gaze from Nic to Jenny. "The Germans are now in the process of herding Jews from the provinces into Amsterdam. It began in Zaandam in January. Jews got notice that they had only a few days to leave their homes. They could take only what they could carry. When they left, their homes were sealed. Dutch Jews were ordered to move to Amsterdam. Non-Dutch Jews were taken to Westerbork."

Jenny frowned and bit her bottom lip before speaking. "What is Westerbork?"

"It's a camp up north. It was originally established to help Jewish refugees coming to the Netherlands from Germany. Dutch Jews helped sponsor it."

Marten leaned forward, eyes narrow. "The writing is all over the wall. It is becoming painfully obvious what is happening. They first ordered us to register, and like dumb sheep, we all complied. They order us to wear those ugly yellow stars so we stand out like naked people in a crowd. And, the way things are going, we *will* be naked. They are stripping us of everything. I fully expect they will ship us all to Westerbork, and we won't stop there."

A heavy silence hung over his words. Finally, Nic spoke. "Marten, when I spoke to you on the phone, you said there was a topic we needed to discuss today."

"Yes. I learned this week the Gestapo has concerns that ministers are nurturing opposition among their congregations."

"Many are doing so," Nic said. "That is what they *should* be doing."

"I agree, and I respect them greatly," Marten said. "Those ministers are also taking great risks right now. The Gestapo is watching them very closely, and there are NSB collaborators in the churches spying on the preachers and the church members. They have their eyes on one man in particular. He is a *Gereformeerde Kerk* pastor in Amsterdam. Since you are members of a Gereformeerde Kerk, I thought you might be acquainted with him. His name is Visser."

Jenny's eyes widened. "That would be Henk Visser. I know him. His daughter Julia is one of my best friends at the university."

"Well, the Gestapo is hanging on his every word, from what my contacts tell me. Someone, maybe you, Jenny, could send him a message to watch his words carefully. The Gestapo may try to make an example of him. Dachau is not a nice place to be sent."

Jenny stood. "If I may be excused, Mr. Demeester, I would like to go to their home now. I need to warn them before Dominie Visser takes the pulpit tomorrow morning."

"Of course. Be careful. Gestapo may be watching."

"I think they have meetings at the church on Saturday evenings. I can blend into the group and maybe get a chance to speak to Dominie Visser or Julia."

Jenny stepped off the tram and blended into a group of young people who were taking advantage of the warm spring weather to socialize before curfew at dark. After walking a couple of blocks, she maintained her casual gait as the old stone church came into view. An eerie feeling crept over her, a vague sense of someone, somewhere, holding her in their gaze. She forced herself to continue her momentum. She was only feet from the front entrance when the large oak door opened and six or eight young people emerged. They turned to walk down the street, away from her. She recognized her friend Julia among the group. Seemingly unaware of Jenny, the girl continued an animated discussion with her friends. Jenny began to raise her hand, preparing to greet her friend, but stopped. *Can't do that. Not now.*

After the last person in the group passed, Jenny slipped inside and closed the door behind her. She proceeded down the well-lit hallway and checked the nameplates on the doors. The doors on the right led to the sanctuary. Those on the left all looked like offices and meeting rooms. Near the end of the hallway, she found an office marked *Dominie.* A man's voice, reciting a quiet monologue, seeped through the closed door. Should she knock or wait for the talk to end? "He's preaching to himself," she whispered before tapping lightly.

The sound of a heavy chair dragging on the hardwood floor replaced the words. The door opened, and a middle-aged man appeared, dressed in casual clothes, his face expressionless, and his eyes tired. He peered at Jenny. "Yes, child. Can I help you?"

"I must speak to you, Dominie Visser."

The door opened wide. "Of course. How can I help you?"

"I am Jenny DeHaan. I am a friend of Julia."

"Julia was here only moments ago. I'm afraid you just missed her. Perhaps if you hurry ..."

Jenny shook her head and raised a hand. "I saw her leaving, but I didn't speak to her. I need to speak to you in private."

Pastor Visser paused for a moment and examined Jenny's eyes before beckoning her to enter. "Come in, child. Please have a seat."

He returned to the chair behind his desk, and Jenny sat in a leather side chair.

"I apologize if I am intruding."

"Not at all. I am practicing tomorrow's sermon. I always test it out on these four walls." The corners of his bright eyes crinkled into a smile. "They make a very receptive audience."

He leaned forward and spoke in a calm, quiet voice. "While my loud preaching reaches the hallway, our discussion will be private. And, if you wish, Jenny, I will keep confidential anything you say."

She straightened in her chair. "Dominie Visser, I must warn you about something. Word has come to me that the Gestapo is becoming concerned about ministers and priests undermining their efforts to control the Netherlands."

The pastor rested his arms on the desk. "Yes, they are concerned. Right now, the voices from the pulpit are quite influential. Churches in this country are filling up. It seems that when people feel threatened, they seek divine help. I hope their attendance doesn't end when the war is over."

Agitation stirred inside Jenny. "But there's more. I have learned that you *personally* are being targeted."

"May I ask the source of this information?"

"I am sorry, Dominie. I must protect my source. We are learning the Nazis have extreme methods of getting information from even the most courageous of people."

"I understand, and I recognize you are brave in being here tonight. Please tell me what I need to know."

Jenny studied Dominie Visser's face. The eyes betrayed a hint of fear. "I am afraid there are informers in your congregation. We think the Gestapo is fully aware of all your sermons and all your publications. They must consider you a threat, and they are looking for justification to arrest you. You need to expect them at your worship service tomorrow."

The pastor leaned back in his chair, made steeples of his fingers, and studied them. "I am not surprised. They have counseled me on two occasions already. They quite bluntly told me that my job is limited to providing spiritual support to my church members and that any involvement in political matters will not be tolerated."

He grew silent, looked past Jenny, and appeared to study something on the wall. After inhaling deeply and allowing his lungs to slowly deflate, he lowered his hands to his desk blotter and posed a question, more to himself than to his visitor. "What am I to do? If I constrain myself, I will be safe, and I can continue to minister to my congregation. They need comfort. They need reassurance of eventual deliverance, in this life or the next." He paused for a long moment. "But, there is an evil, right here in our country, and I must oppose it."

The minister's old chair creaked as he rocked slowly, his eyes closed and head bowed. After about a minute, his eyes opened, and a gentle smile appeared on his face. He gathered the written notes from the desk blotter and slid them into the center drawer of his desk. "That sermon can wait for another day. I need to start over, and I still don't know what I will say. It is going to be a long, prayerful night."

He stood and gave Jenny a warm handshake. "Thank you for your visit and for your guidance."

The next morning, three well-dressed young adults entered the old church at a quarter after ten, early enough to observe the arrival of all worshipers and visitors. The pocket of Marten's tailored suit held a precious document, complete with a photograph identifying him as Dirck Meijer. Nic, in a suit he had borrowed from Marten, compensated for his slightly larger waist size by ignoring the front buttons of his jacket. Jenny wore a white blouse and plaid skirt, tailored by her Aunt Cora. Inside the door, an usher gave each a bulletin which outlined the order of worship.

They sat in the back pew and casually observed the worshipers as they filed into the sanctuary. At a quarter to eleven, Marten pressed his elbow to Jenny's arm, just hard enough to get her attention. She turned slowly and followed his gaze. Two men in dark suits entered from the street. An usher greeted them with a smile and a bulletin. They accepted without smiles or comments, then separated and both selected aisle seats near the back of the sanctuary.

Jenny looked back at Marten, and he nodded ever so slightly. She turned to Nic, tapped his leg, and leaned toward him. Her brother tilted his ear toward her. "They're here," she whispered.

Pastor Visser entered, clad in a black robe. He sat in the large pulpit chair and looked over the congregation as the organist finished the introductory music. He stood and approached the lectern. An air of silent attention captured the sanctuary, broken only by a cough somewhere in the room. When the pastor made his customary welcoming comments and invited worshipers to greet each other, the tension seemed to drain from the room. Jenny was perhaps the only person to ignore those around her as she studied the two strangers. Neither turned to greet their neighbors but did shake the hands that were offered to them.

The congregation took their seats and settled into what began as a typical worship service including songs, prayers, recitation of church creeds, and the offering. When the collection plate circulated, the two strangers passed it without contributing.

The last item in the order of worship was the sermon. Pastor Visser approached the lectern and located a passage in the large pulpit Bible. A palpable silence settled over the room. The elderly lady in front of Jenny, whose head had been drooped in sleep at the end of the long prayer, stirred and straightened in her seat.

Dominie Visser took a long moment to scan the congregation. "This is the first time in my ministry in this church that every pew is filled. While I am pleased with your decision to be here today, I am also concerned, as I am sure you are, about the circumstances that brought about the recent upsurge in church attendance. Everyone in our country has been profoundly affected by recent events. Many of you have shared with me your fears and your uncertainty about how you should now live your lives.

"The authorities in our country have forbidden priests and ministers from any involvement in politics. Therefore, today I will not discuss matters of politics or international relations. Instead, we will give careful attention to our inspired Scripture. I have faith that, if you open your hearts and minds, the Holy Spirit will speak to your hearts. In that way, each and every person here, regardless of your personal background or religious affiliation, can apply those Scriptures to their own lives." Visser tapped the large Bible. "This book has for many years provided guidance to God's people. We are going to review two passages today, one from the Old Testament and one from the New.

"I invite you to take your Bible, or use the pew Bible in front of you, and turn to the Old Testament book of Daniel." The sound of turning pages filled the pastor's pause. The two strangers sat rigidly. When quiet returned, the congregation looked to the speaker.

Dominie Visser reviewed the account recorded in the book of Daniel. "The empire of Babylon, under King Nebuchadnezzar, conquered the Jewish nation and took many of the Jews into exile. From this group, the king selected a few of the best and brightest Jews to be educated and assimilated into Babylonian culture. Daniel and his three friends, Shadrach, Meshach, and Abednego, experienced great success in this process until their strongly held values conflicted with those of the Babylonians.

"King Nebuchadnezzar built a ninety-foot-tall golden statue. All the citizens were ordered to worship this statue when special music played. Anyone who failed to comply would be burned alive. Someone reported to the king that Daniel's friends failed to bow to the golden statue. They were ordered to report to the king, and Nebuchadnezzar gave them a test. He said the music would play, and if they bowed to the statue, everything would be fine. If they failed to worship his statue, they would be thrown into a blazing furnace."

Pastor Visser paused and looked around at his congregation. "There you have it. Three young men who have everything, power, money, security, everything any young man could imagine. All they had to do was play the king's game. Just bow down and act like they were worshiping the silly statue. Just do it and move on. No problem.

"But these young men did the unthinkable. They refused, right there in the presence of the king of Babylon. They believed that their God would protect them. Now, look with me at verse eighteen of chapter three. 'But even if he does not, we want you to know, O king, that we will not serve your gods or worship the image of gold you have set up.'

"These young men were willing to give up everything, even their lives, to do the right thing." The preacher went silent as he looked around the room. His pause lasted perhaps a half minute. To Jenny, it seemed much longer.

Finally, the pastor continued, "How far are we willing to go to do the right thing?"

Dominie Visser turned the pages of his pulpit Bible. "Now let's look in our New Testament for guidance. How should we implement our commitment to do the right thing? I believe the answer lies in chapter twenty-five of the book of Matthew, verses thirty-four through forty. In this passage, Jesus is teaching his disciples that all people will ultimately face a judgment based on their faithfulness. He talks of separating people into groups, the righteous on his right and unrighteous on his left. Listen to his words.

> "'Then the King will say to those on his right, "Come, you who are blessed by my Father; take your inheritance, the kingdom prepared for you since the creation of the world. For I was hungry and you gave me something to eat, I was thirsty and you gave me something to drink, I was a stranger and you invited me in, I needed clothes and you clothed me, I was sick and you looked after me, I was in prison and you came to visit me."
>
> "'Then the righteous will answer him, "Lord, when did we see you hungry and feed you, or

140

thirsty and give you something to drink? When did we see you a stranger and invite you in, or needing clothes and clothe you? When did we see you sick or in prison and go to visit you?"

"'The King will reply, "Truly I tell you, whatever you did for one of the least of these brothers and sisters of mine, you did for me.'""

Pastor Visser closed the pulpit Bible gently and made a slow visual examination of the silent audience. "There you have it. We come faithfully to this building to worship and pray. That is easy. We also profess to be followers of Jesus Christ. We claim to follow his teachings. Words come easy, do they not? But words are empty if they are not demonstrated by action. And what are the actions that are required? Simple. We should, no, we *must* serve those in need. And who are they? Look into your heart. Look around you. Ask yourself who is suffering? Who is helpless? You will find the answer. Your conscience will shout it to you if you will only listen. Your very soul depends on your response."

Dominie Visser did not deliver his normal benediction. He stepped down from the pulpit and stopped in front of the altar, facing the congregation. "Go now. Open your hearts and serve all those in need." He strode down the center aisle toward the front door. The only sound in the room was the swishing of his robe and the creak of the old hardwood floor.

Jenny, Marten, and Nic stepped to the side aisle and pretended to have a discussion. The worshipers moved soberly to the exits. Several members were tearful. A few huddled in guarded discussion. About half of the worshipers filed past the pastor. Their greetings were warm but brief.

The two strangers met, spoke briefly, and waited.

With the sanctuary mostly empty, the two men approached the pastor at the door. He greeted them. "Good morning. I am Henk Visser. Welcome to our church." He offered his hand.

Both men ignored the extended hand. One, older than his companion, spoke in German, loud enough to be heard throughout the sanctuary. "We represent the German Reich. We are *Geheime Staatspolizei*, also known as Gestapo." He reached into the pocket of his coat and withdrew an identification disk, flashed it, and returned it to his pocket. "I trust you speak German."

Pastor Visser maintained a calm facial expression, except for few quick blinks of his eyes. *"Ja. Ich spreche Deutsch."*

The man lifted his chin and continued in German, "Well, preacher, you seemed to have a definite impact on your flock. They left here with sober expressions on their faces. I have not been to many church services, but my recollection is that such events were generally pleasant. People left with smiles. I didn't see that today. Tell me this, if you had delivered this sermon a few years ago, would the reaction have been, should we say, a bit more casual?"

"We are in difficult times."

The man brushed aside Visser's comment with a sweep of his hand. *"Ja, ja.* We all have problems. I want to know more about the story you told, the improbable one about the three Jews who disobeyed their king. You seemed quite fond of that tale. Did it come from Jewish literature?"

"The story is included in the Hebrew Bible and the Christian Bible."

"Let's get right to the heart of the matter, preacher. I sensed a Jewish tone to your sermon. Were you including Jews in your comments about people in need? Were you encouraging your members to help Jews?"

Jenny, Marten, and Nic stood rigidly, their eyes glued to Pastor Visser, waiting for his response.

Dominie Visser turned his gaze from the Gestapo officers. He scanned the sanctuary, now empty except for his accusers and the three young people in the side aisle. His gaze settled on Jenny. Their eyes locked. The tension drained from his face, and just a hint of a smile graced his lips. He turned back to the Nazis.

"If I am true to my faith, I must show love to all people. I must dedicate myself to helping people who are suffering, *all people* without regard to nationality, race, or religion. If an officer of the

German Reich is suffering, I must help him." He paused. "And, if Jewish people are suffering, I must help them."

"And you feel that you must advise your church members to support Jews. Yes?"

Pastor Visser nodded. "Yes."

"We are finished here, Visser. You are coming with us."

Jenny, Marten, and Nic stood in stunned silence as the two Gestapo agents marched the robed pastor out the front door. The silence was broken by the sounds of car doors slamming, followed by the departure of the vehicle.

The three friends moved to the street and watched until the lone black car disappeared into the heart of Amsterdam."

"That was terrible," Nic said.

"Yes, terrible," Marten said. "But also beautiful. That man knew in his heart what he must do. He also knew the cost. Yet he did it anyway. It was the greatest thing a man could ever do. He just offered his life for others ... for me."

Jenny nodded and grasped Marten's hand in her own. "For all of us. He made his choice. And now what will we do?"

CHAPTER NINETEEN

6 August 1942
Utrecht

The mid-morning summer sun streamed through the open window. The heat of August had settled on Holland. Jenny's focus wandered away from the textbook in front of her and toward a boat gliding along a nearby Utrecht canal. Thoughts of life as a doctor played in her mind. Then the sight of a pair of German soldiers on the street pushed her pleasant thoughts aside. Her nagging worry returned. Where was Marten? Was he safe?

A gentle knock jolted her attention back to the small upstairs room in the home of Uncle Jake and Aunt Cora. "Yes?"

The door edged open, and Aunt Cora appeared. "Sorry to intrude in your studying, but you have a phone call." The smile on her face hinted at what was to follow. "It's that young man you've been talking about."

Jenny jumped up so fast that her chair fell over backward. "Oops, sorry." She bent to right the chair.

"Just go, child. I'll get the chair."

Jenny rushed toward the door. "Thanks, Aunt Cora."

"Take your time, dear. Don't fall down the stairs. I think he'll wait."

The phone waited on a small desk in the front room. Jenny grabbed the receiver. "Hi, Marten. I am so glad you called. I've missed you." Her heart pounded as she hoped for an excited response.

Instead, his voice was sober and strained. "Hi, Jenny. I have been thinking of you too, but I'm afraid I don't have much room for happy thoughts. Things are getting bad in Amsterdam."

"Oh ..." Jenny held the receiver to her ear and moved to a nearby chair.

"The Germans are starting to force the Jews out of Holland on a big scale. We are in the middle of a massive raid right now. They are pulling Jews out of their homes. Even grabbing them off the street. They're dragging everyone to the *Zentralstelle.*"

"What's Zentralstelle?"

"Central Office, Jen. It's the central office for Jewish emigration. That's where the Germans are running their deportation operation. They took over a couple of school buildings on Euterpestraat. It's only a few blocks from our house."

"Is your family okay?"

"Yes, for now. There are only a few Jews in our neighborhood, but the Jewish Quarter is in a real turmoil right now. The Nazis are brutal, and they are getting plenty of help from the NSB. In a way, those collaborator kids are worse than the Germans. They hurl insults while the soldiers do their work. The whole thing is heartbreaking. Old people, kids, they don't care. They just want Jewish bodies. They have trains to fill."

Jenny paced the floor within the length of the phone cord. "Where are you now?"

"I'm on a pay phone. They disconnected our home phone a couple of weeks ago."

Her volume rose. "So they know where you live?"

"Don't worry, Jen. We are being very careful. Father has contacts in the Dutch police who will let us know if they plan to raid our area ... I hope."

"But you are out on the street. They could grab you out of the phone booth."

"Relax, Jen." Confidence filled his voice. "I'm not standing here with a yellow star on my chest. Besides, the ID I'm carrying says I'm Dirck Meijer. I'll be fine. I would be happier right now if I were blue-eyed and blonde like you, but I am what I am."

His confidence calmed her. "And I like you just like you are. When Aunt Cora told me it was you on the phone, I thought my heart would pop out of my chest."

"Thanks, Jen. I really do want to see you." A slight pause. "Holding you right now would be good. Really good."

"There goes my heart again. Wow, the things you do to me." Her focus came back to the task at hand. "What can I do to help you, Marten?"

"That's why I called." His tone was sober again. "Is Nic still involved with the underground newspaper?"

"Very much so. We are careful to hide it from our parents. If they knew the danger, I expect Papa would lock him up."

"The truth needs to get out. In his own way, Nic is a soldier in our army. A terrible thing is happening here. Many Jews are clinging to the hope that they are going to work camps. Even my mother thinks the Jews will be spared since the Germans need workers. But it's all a fraud. They are going to kill them all. Everyone needs to know, the Dutch people and everyone outside Holland. I would like Nic to come here. Today if possible. He needs to see what's happening."

"Where should we go? I'm coming too."

The phone crackled as Marten paused. "I wish you wouldn't. It's not safe, but I have a feeling you are coming regardless."

"You're right about that. It's about time I find my place in this war."

He sighed. "Okay. Take the train to Amsterdam and then use tramline twenty-four. That's the same one you used when you came to our house on Chopinstraat. Get off at Euterpestraat and go west. The Zentralstelle is in the third block. The Germans took over the two schools on each side of the street."

"Got it. Where can we go to watch everything?"

"There is a family living in the building on *Rubensstraat* at the intersection of *Euterpestraat*, the first door from the corner. The name is Vanden Brand. Their place has a good view of the Zentralstelle rat's nest. They expect you. Tell them Fritz sent you."

"Fritz?"

"Fritz. Just say it."

"Okay. What is Mr. Vanden Brand's role?"

"I can't tell you that."

"Oops. Sorry."

"Let's just say he is a friend of ours."

"I wish I could see you when we come."

"Me too, but I can't plan to meet you. I'll try to see you soon."

"Okay. Bye." She slowly hung up the phone. *I love you.* The words echoed in her head. "I should have said it," she whispered.

Two hours later, a warm breeze flowed through the open windows of the tram and whisked the faces of Jenny and Nic. They sat side-by-side, gazing out the window as the city of Amsterdam passed by. The passengers of the half-filled streetcar were unusually quiet. As the tram plied its way through the old city, the prominent sound was the clicking of the wheels on the rails.

Nic turned to his sister. "See anything different today?"

"Sure do. There aren't many Jews on the street. No yellow stars."

"Exactly. Word of the raids must have spread quickly. The Jews of Amsterdam are doing their best to disappear."

She nudged her brother. "Look." She pointed down a side street. Uniformed men were loading people, all wearing the yellow star, into the back of a large military-type truck. "That is what people are hiding from." One elderly woman struggled to get into the truck. An old man on the ground and a young man in the truck helped her climb while a uniformed soldier prodded her with a truncheon.

The tram rolled on. It crossed the North Amstel canal and came to a stop at Euterpestraat. The siblings got off the tram and headed west. After walking only one short block, they stopped and gaped at the scene ahead of them. Hundreds of people, maybe a thousand, appeared to cover the entire area between two large buildings on opposite sides of the street. Several military trucks were lined up, disgorging their human cargo. Uniformed men formed a cordon around the crowd.

"We can't walk through that chaos," Nicolaas said.

"Let's walk around the block."

They circled around the area until a smooth-faced German soldier about their age confronted them with his standard command. "*Papiere.*"

The two produced their identity documents. The man studied the IDs and gave them back. He lifted his chin and peered down his nose at the two locals. "*Was machst du hier?*"

Jenny generated her best puzzled expression. *What am I doing here? I live here, you jerk.* Although she understood his German, Jenny responded in Dutch. "We are staying with our uncle." She pointed ahead to the building on the corner.

The soldier frowned and scolded in his language. "Speak German."

With a well-practiced 'I know nothing' look, Jenny shook her head and shrugged. Nic studied his shoes.

After a slight pause, the young soldier dismissed his two clueless detainees with a lazy wave. They proceeded to the building described by Marten and escaped the mob scene.

They knocked on the apartment door. It opened, and an older man appeared. His steady gaze went immediately to the eyes of his visitors, first Jenny, then Nic. "May I help you?" His voice was deep, calm.

Nicolaas responded. "I am Nicolaas DeHaan. This is my sister, Jenny. We are looking for Mr. Vanden Brand. Fritz sent us."

The man smiled. "Ah, yes. Fritz. Good man. I am Rik Vanden Brand. Please, call me Rik, and this is my wife, Lettie. Please come in."

Lettie Vanden Brand welcomed the guests to her table with tea and crisp, spicy cookies shaped like windmills. "I hope you don't mind *Sinterklaas* cookies in August."

"We eat them all year," Jenny said. She dipped a cookie into her tea.

Rik pulled a paper from his nearby rolltop desk and tossed it onto the table in front of Nic. At the top of the sheet, in bold letters, was the name, *Free Netherlands*. "Does this look familiar?"

Nic placed his hands on the table and spread his fingers, still bearing ink stains. "I wrote part of that issue. We still use mimeograph, but we hope to go with typeset before long."

"Well, you do good work, Nicolaas. I helped get that paper started back in August of 1940, very soon after occupation. I'm glad the work goes on." He got up, walked to the window, and looked at the scene outside. "There is your next story. It's a big one."

Nic and Jenny joined him at the window, an ideal location to grasp the extent of the tragedy. The German Reich had commandeered the two former schools. The building on the south side of Euterpestraat proudly displayed, in sharply angled letters, the black flag with the dreaded *SS*. Around both buildings were several large Swastika flags.

"There must be a thousand yellow stars down there," Nic said.

"I would say closer to two thousand and growing," Rik said. As they watched, more trucks arrived, and people of all ages climbed out. The number of soldiers, police, and NSB helpers was ample to control and confine the mass of prisoners.

"What happens next, Rik?" asked Jenny.

"I don't expect they are gathering all these people only to let them go their way. Most or all of these people will be shipped out to Westerbork in the north. That seems to be the place where Jews are held temporarily before shipment east. The camp is certainly large enough to accommodate this many people … and more."

As the Vanden Brands and their young guests watched from their third-floor window, the Germans and their eager assistants continued to add to the mass of captured Jews until darkness descended on the city. The harsh reality became clear. Two thousand captive people would spend the night in the courtyard of Zentralstelle, all within walking distance of their now-empty homes.

Lettie broke the depressed silence. "Perhaps we should pull the blackout curtains and have some supper."

"And it is far too late in the day for our guests to return to Utrecht," added Rik. "We don't have rooms or beds for you in our small place, but the davenport will be good for Jenny, and perhaps Nicolaas might survive the rug. It's fairly soft."

"Actually, I think I should take the rug," Jenny said. "It won't bother me. I even enjoy sleeping on the ground, under the stars."

Nic turned to his hostess with a shrug. "My sister never avoids a challenge."

"Jenny may be a person for our time," Rik said.

Very early the next morning, sleep released its hold on Jenny with some reluctance. Her first sensation was the contrast of a soft pillow and a hardwood floor. In a few brief seconds, full awareness came to her. A crack of light broke through a slit in the drapes, enough for her to find her way to the bathroom. Her thoughtful host had left all the wake-up necessities, including toothbrushes. A couple of minutes later, she peered from the apartment window. The sun was high enough to see the crowd of prisoners in the courtyard below, some moving around, others still lying on the ground without cover. Uniformed soldiers and police stood by. Surely they were fresh replacements from those of the previous day.

Soon, her brother and the Vanden Brands joined Jenny at the observation post. The quiet vigil began.

Rik pointed. "There he is." A uniformed man stood outside the door that led to the crowded courtyard. The reaction of both the captors and the victims made it clear that the newcomer was someone of significance. Other uniforms quickly gravitated to him. He lit a cigarette and scanned the crowd of prisoners. Activity in the courtyard ceased, and all attention turned to the man of the hour.

"Who is that?" whispered Jenny.

"Ferdinand Hugo Aus der Fünten. He is in charge of this nasty affair. I think it's his job to get the Jews out of our country."

Jenny leaned close to the glass. "He doesn't seem to be very comfortable with his job. He's already on his third cigarette, and he can't seem to stand still." Aus der Fünten's nervous movements notwithstanding, he clearly had control of the operation. His every gesture generated an instant response from his subordinates. "Now what's he up to?"

The agitated SS man strutted and gestured with both hands. In response, his underlings organized a tight line of about twenty prisoners. He moved to the head of the line, and his entourage took position behind him.

Then the process began. The first person, a middle-aged gentleman in suit and tie, stood rigidly before the Nazi. Although Jenny could not hear the conversation due to the glass and distance that separated them, the process was clear. Aus der Fünten held out his hand, palm up. The prisoner produced his papers. The German's verdict was a wordless wave of the hand. In this case, he waved to the right. The man was goaded to a newly forming group within the courtyard. The next prisoner, a young woman, followed the same procedure, except the German's gesture was to the left. She was allowed to leave the confinement area. Moments later, she hurried in the direction of the Jewish Quarter. She did not look back.

"Why was she excluded? asked Nicolaas.

"I suspect her papers showed that, for some reason, she is exempt," Rik said.

"So she may survive all this?"

"For now."

The process dragged on. Aus der Fünten took regular breaks. He would simply turn and disappear into his headquarters, leaving a line of people to suffer in their anxiety. By eleven o'clock, a large number of Jews stood waiting, either in the slowly shrinking group of those waiting sentence or in the growing group of those who had been sentenced to an uncertain fate.

"They seem to be freeing a fair number, Rik," Jenny said.

"Yes. My guess is that this group exceeds the capacity of the train they have waiting. They are thinning the herd. I do hope the Jews who are escaping today do not leave too hopeful. The trains will keep running until they are no longer needed."

Nic turned to his sister. "I think I have seen enough, Jen. I have my story. Now I need to report it."

She turned her back on the window. "And I don't really want to wait until the trucks leave here for the train station. Seeing that happen to Desmond was enough for me."

With thanks to their new friends and allies, Jenny and Nic left the Zentralstelle and walked quickly toward the tram stop.

CHAPTER TWENTY

7 August 1942
Amsterdam

Jenny and Nic boarded the tram and proceeded north on Beethovenstraat. They sat near the front of the lead carriage. Jenny's mind churned with thoughts of the unfolding tragedy she had just witnessed. She sat in silence beside a similarly quiet Nic as the tram rolled along. The only sounds in the car were the creaking and rattling of the old vehicle, the clacking of the steel wheels on the rails, and the hum of the persistent electric motor.

She studied the people around her. This car had no yellow-star passengers, nobody who looked like they had come from the Zentralstelle nightmare. They appeared to be a typical tramload of everyday Dutchmen. Except the tone was not ordinary. These people were somber, distant. The news of the mass arrest must have spread. The Nazis had declared that neighbors and friends were different, unacceptable. The oppressors were dragging away these undesirables and driving them into a holding pen. A large group of Dutch people, assimilated for hundreds of years into the fabric of a tolerant society, were being torn from the tapestry. Had the evil of Nazism begun to erode the minds of the Dutch?

She nudged her brother. "What about the Demeesters? I hope they're okay."

Nic put his arm around her shoulders. "Don't give up, Jen. That family is careful and smart. They also have lots of contacts and lots of money. They will find a way out of any trouble they get into."

"I hope so. It just seems like everything is going crazy, and we can't do anything about it. I saw that Aus der Fünten guy strutting around, deciding who would die and who would walk away." She leaned closer and whispered, "If I had a gun, I think I could have shot him."

Nic responded with a gentle pat on his sister's shoulder as the tram rolled on.

After a minute of silence, she gripped her brother's arm. "What about *our* family?"

"What do you mean?"

"We are concerned about our Jewish friends and neighbors for good reason. But think about it. It is obvious that the Germans are capable of really bad things. Why should we expect them to limit their evil to the Jews? They already violated our farm. What's to stop them from doing far worse to anyone in Holland?"

The old streetcar slowed to a stop at Amsterdam Centraal Station, and Nic turned to his sister. "While we are waiting for the train to Utrecht, we could take another tram through the area where Jews live. I would like to report the conditions there. Do you feel up to it?"

"Sure. If we are going to fight these people, we need to know everything that's happening."

The tram crossed the Amstel river and passed Saint Anthony's Catholic Church on their left and Meijer Square on their right. "So much has happened since we saw Desmond arrested here," said Nic. "I hope Father DeYoung is okay."

"Stop!" shouted Jenny. The startled operator brought the tram to a quick halt.

A shaken Nic turned to his sister. "What?"

Without responding, she bolted out the door and onto the sidewalk, then ran across the street and down a narrow lane that followed the canal.

A girl who appeared to be about three years old stood alone in front of a house with a shattered front door. Her arms hung loosely at her sides. Jenny ran to the girl, knelt, grasped the child's shoulders gently, and peered into her expressionless eyes. She pulled the girl to her chest. "It's okay, sweetheart. It's okay." The child was silent.

Nic disappeared into the house. In a few minutes, he returned and shook his head. "Gone."

After several minutes of Jenny's gentle whispers, the little girl sniffled and spoke her first words, just above a whisper. "I want my mama."

"Where is she?"

"I woke up from my nap. There was lots of shouting. Then they took Mama and Papa away."

Jenny sat on the concrete and wrapped the little body in her arms. The girl's parents must have been at the Zentralstelle selection and were probably loaded on a transport. This child was all alone in the world. No, not alone. *She has me.* "Don't you worry, sweetheart. Everything is going to be okay. What's your name?"

"Aniek."

"Our house is starting to feel like a home again, Albert." Emma set her coffee cup on the kitchen table. "It's been a couple of years since those invaders came into our home and dirtied everything. I thought the place would never feel clean again. The memory is still there, but each day it fades a little more. I'm almost comfortable again, except when I am alone. When you are in the fields, I watch you sometimes, wishing you were here with me. And the children. I worry about them all day long."

"The worry follows me around the farm also, dear. Wherever they are, I'm sure they think of us too. They are good kids. I'm proud of them."

The front door opened. "Hello?" It was Jenny's voice.

Emma's heart leaped. After a quick glance at Albert's bright expression, she rushed to the front room—and stopped in her tracks. Her mouth hung open. Jenny and Nicolaas stood close together. A small child was fast asleep on Jenny's shoulder.

Emma scrutinized the serious expressions on her children's faces. "Whose child is this?"

"She was wandering on the streets of Amsterdam, Mama. Abandoned." Jenny pressed her cheek to the girl's hair. "A raid swept through. They took her parents, but they missed her."

"She's Jewish?"

"*Ja.*"

"Oh, Lord help us. The danger. We shouldn't keep her here. If the Germans catch us, we will all be arrested. Our family ... we must protect our family. Isn't there someplace else?"

"I couldn't leave her, Mama. I had to help her."

Albert joined the group. Emma, trembling, rushed to his embrace.

The little girl yawned and struggled to awaken. She blinked a few times, scanned the room with confused eyes, and finally set her gaze on Albert. She opened her arms to him. Jenny placed the child on the floor, and she rushed to him.

Albert went to his knees and embraced her. The girl immediately stroked Albert's beard. "I believe I remind you of your father." His voice was calm and soothing.

"I want my mama."

"Are you hungry?"

"And thirsty."

"And what is your name?"

"Aniek."

Emma blinked. Her tight shoulders softened a bit. "My mother's name was Aniek." She looked at Jenny. "The child is here now. We must meet her needs today. Tomorrow, well, tomorrow we will see." Emma joined her husband down at the child's level. "Aniek, would you like some chicken soup?"

"And some milk?"

"*Ja*, milk. Let's go to the kitchen and get some supper." The child extended her hand timidly, and Emma grasped it. The feel of that small, soft hand raced directly to Emma's heart. Her entire body relaxed, and her mind sharpened in an instant. She looked up at the startled expressions on her children's faces. Tears filled her eyes. Embracing the girl, she turned to her husband. "Whatever was I thinking? Lord, forgive me. We must look after this child of God."

Jenny woke from a deep sleep and struggled to orient herself. The realization crept into her brain that she was on the couch in the darkened front room of the DeHaan farmhouse. The lights from the kitchen allowed her to see the wall clock. Five thirty. She found her mother and father in the kitchen.

"Sorry to wake you, Jenny," her father said. "We know how tired you are. Cows needed milking, just like any other day."

"I hope Aniek didn't keep you awake."

Her mother's face sparkled with the radiance of a new grandmother. "Once I put her down on your bed, I never heard anything more from her. I would have heard. I got a lot of practice when you were her age. What's your plan for today?"

"I need to go back to Amsterdam to Aniek's house. Not everyone in that raid was transported. The Germans released some people. Maybe Aniek's family went back home. Is Nic still sleeping? I thought he might like to go with me."

"He already went out," her father said. "He said he had work to do in Utrecht. Something about a writing project he was working on."

Jenny nodded and pictured her brother at work on his printing press. "Oh, okay. I can go alone. No problem."

Her mother's face stiffened. "I want you to be careful, young lady."

"I'll be fine, Mama. I'm more Aryan-looking than many of those Germans. They won't bother me."

"Think again, young lady. Those young men may bother you because you *are* Aryan-looking. Very good-looking."

Jenny felt her cheek warm just slightly. "I will be extra careful, Mama."

"And, Jenny, if there are other children, bring them. But remember that we can only care for a few at a time. Perhaps there are others who will join us."

Albert took a last sip of his coffee and set the cup on the table. "We can also take in adults, but they might need to sleep in the hay." He picked up his pipe. "Can you fit this new role into your university schedule?"

"I've decided to drop all my classes, Papa. School can wait. It just doesn't seem very important right now."

At half-past twelve, Jenny was back in Amsterdam. A truck sat in front of the home where she had found Aniek. Painted on the side of the attached trailer, in large letters, were the words *A PULS*. Who and what was A PULS? Whoever it was owned at least one big truck and trailer.

Jenny hurried down the street lined with houses on her left and the canal on her right. The homes were all silent, a few with doors standing wide open, exposing their lifeless interiors. She had left the vibrancy of Amsterdam and entered a different world. A sense of vulnerability and uncertainty gripped her, like an evil force had sucked the life from the neighborhood. When she approached the Puls moving van, two men carrying a chest of drawers emerged from the house. One of the drawers hung slightly open, exposing neatly folded clothing. "Someone is moving?" asked Jenny.

The men set the chest on the sidewalk near the ramp that led into the trailer. One of the men smiled. "They moved, sure did."

The other added, "Left in a hurry. Food on the table. Cold now."

"Any idea where they went?"

"We wouldn't know about that. Mr. Puls just gives us a list, and we go load our truck. We don't leave anything. We take everything to the warehouse. As far as the Jews ..." He shrugged. "They are probably in Westerbork by now." The man lifted his end of the chest, and his partner did the same. "That's all we know. We have work to do."

Jenny watched the men disappear into the trailer. She peered through the open front door of the house. The room inside was bare. With no clear plan in mind, she turned and walked toward a tram stop. As she passed a house, a few doors from Aniek's home, the front door edged open, and a hand beckoned to her. A female voice said, *"Kom hier."*

Jenny frowned and drew closer to the door. The hand beckoned again, this time with greater urgency.

Jenny looked back at the Puls truck to ensure she was not being watched, then entered the house. She found a nervous couple in their sixties or seventies.

The woman shut the door. "Thank you. Thank you. We saw you, my husband and I, we saw you take that child yesterday. The Germans came. They blocked off the street, both ends. Then they went to the houses. All the houses. Some were already empty from the last raid. We were hiding, and they missed us. Later we came out. We saw that child on the street. We were afraid to go out; I was shaking, but my husband said he must help her. I finally said he could go, but then you came, like an angel, before he went out. You came and took the child." Tears flowed down the woman's cheeks as she embraced Jenny.

With a calming hand on the woman's shoulder, the husband spoke up. "What became of the child?"

"Aniek will be fine. I will find a place for her. Do you know what happened to her family?"

The man frowned. "They have not returned. Two raids, and nobody on our street has returned. Maybe they were killed. Probably they were transported to Westerbork. The trains, they wait at the Amsterdam Station. Then they go to Westerbork." He paused. "Who knows? Maybe they escaped."

"They did not escape, Herman." Anger filled the woman's voice. "You are dreaming. The Germans have dogs. They have guns and clubs. No. They did not escape."

"And what will you do?" asked Jenny.

Herman brightened a bit. "We are moving to our son's flat. He is a member of the Jewish Council. The Council is trying to work with the Germans. He has an exemption."

The Puls moving van rolled past the window, and Jenny turned to the couple. "I hope all goes well for you and your son."

"One thing more to tell you," Herman said. "There is an orphanage nearby. Number 171 on the next street." He laid a gentle hand on his wife's shoulder. "Agnes helps there sometimes."

"It is a good place," Agnes said. "Maybe you could take that little girl there."

Jenny put her face near the front window and looked up and down the street. "It looks safe. I'll go there now." She shook Herman's hand and hugged Agnes. "Be safe. God bless you."

She found the orphanage without difficulty and knocked.

The door edged open. "Yes?" A young woman greeted her with a timid smile.

"I am Jenny DeHaan. A little girl needs help. May I come in?"

The young woman, about twenty years old, invited her in. "I am Anna. Rebekka Frank is the principal. She is out right now. I am new here, but please tell me your concern."

"Yesterday I found a child abandoned. Her parents were taken in a raid, and I just now visited their home. A Puls crew was removing their belongings. I want to help her."

"If the Puls people have come, the family has been transported. Puls works closely with the Gestapo."

"Can you accept her?"

"I am afraid that would not be wise. The Gestapo knows all about our children. Some of our girls are German refugees. I am very fearful they will export our children to the camps. If we anger them, that will surely happen."

Jenny's eyes widened. "Surely not the orphan children."

"I fear it. I feel that the child you found would be much safer in hiding if you can find a place for her. I wish all these children could go into hiding, but the Gestapo visit us. They have records. If any children disappear, the rest will suffer."

A familiar feeling of anger swelled inside Jenny. "Yes. The Germans always retaliate. I have seen it. A friend of mine was in that group they snatched from Meijer Square and sent to Mauthausen. He died there."

Anna's eyes welled. "My brother was in that group." Her reaction prompted tears in Jenny's eyes. They embraced for a long moment.

Anna suddenly pushed Jenny back. Her face paled. "Oh, no. I have said too much. I don't really know you. You could be anybody—even one of them. You just looked so good." The tears returned. "Please don't report me," she begged.

Jenny embraced the sobbing woman. "Do not worry, Anna. I will never betray you, and I will do everything in my power to protect the children. I swear it on my life."

Getting off the train in Nijkerk, Jenny had a plan. She hurried to the local police station and strode up to the desk. The young Dutch officer, eyes tracking her from the front door to his desk, looked up and smiled. "*Goedemorgen,* Jenny."

"*Ja, goedemorgen aan u, Jake.*" Jenny was off to a good start. She and Jake had been school and church friends. "Is the captain free?"

"I will check." Jake disappeared down a hallway and returned in a few seconds. "He's available. Last office on the right. Door's open."

Jenny approached the door. The sign outside read *Captain Atsma.*

"Jenny DeHaan. Come in here." Captain Atsma's deep bass voice filled the small police station.

She approached and shook the smiling man's hand.

"Jenny, it's good to see you. I haven't seen you in church for a while. You're not one of those backsliders, are you?"

"Oh, no, sir. I have been spending most of my time in Utrecht. I work most weekdays, and I study a lot getting ready for the fall semester."

"I understand. Went to school there myself. Learned a lot. Had a lot of fun too." He paused. "Now, what can I do for you?"

"May I close the door?"

The captain's face went sober. He nodded.

She closed the door and followed the captain's gesture to a side chair. "Captain, I am hoping you can help me. I respect you because of your leadership in the church."

Captain Atsma, face expressionless, nodded again.

Jenny leaned forward in her chair. "Captain, I found a little girl abandoned on the streets of Amsterdam. I took her home. I need to find a home for her. Can you help?"

"A Jewish child?"

"Yes."

The captain's frowning eyes pierced into Jenny's. "Are you crazy, girl?" His voice was quiet, deliberate. "I am a police officer. I enforce the law. You come in here urging me to break the law. I have a job and a family to protect. You think you know me. You think you know a lot of people. You barge ahead and say things that could get you and your family killed. You are being foolish. Very foolish. I could report you."

Jenny turned her gaze to the hardwood floor, her face burning, heart pounding. She started to rise, knees trembling.

"Sit down, Jenny." The captain's voice had softened. "I have more to say."

She collapsed into the wooden chair, her brain reeling. "What?"

Atsma leaned forward and rested his arms on his desk. "I'm sorry I frightened you. I had to do that. I'm one of the best friends you have right now, but you need to learn an important lesson. You must be very careful who you talk to and what you say. Suspect everyone of being collaborators unless you are sure they are not.

That includes Dutch police officers. Some are good, some are bad. The most dangerous are those who are skilled at pretending to be what they are not. Remember what I am telling you. If you make a mistake, it could cost the lives of many people, as well as your own."

The police chief's chair squeaked as he leaned back. "Another thing. Gestapo people are skillful at getting information. I have heard stories, and I do not doubt their accuracy. Anyone can be broken. So, for our success, nobody should know more than what is critical for them to do their job. Many of your Resistance contacts will use false names. You should also. When you interact with people out of our group, your name will be Greta. Got it?"

A slight smile crept onto Jenny's face. "Greta. Got it."

"Where is the child now?"

"With my parents. Mother is quite taken with Aniek."

"They know the circumstances?"

"They do."

"I'm not surprised. They are fine people. There are other good people in our church and our community. You will learn about a few of them. There are others who I don't trust. Be wary."

Captain Atsma stood. "I want you to go home now. Tell your parents of our conversation. I will speak to my contacts. If possible, I think you should stay at the farm until we make arrangements for Aniek. We will notify you as soon as we can."

"Yes, sir."

"And one more thing, young lady. I have known you since you were born, and I love you like my own child. I am proud of you, but remember what I said here today. One misplaced word to the wrong person could get us all killed."

CHAPTER TWENTY-ONE

21 August 1942
Nijkerk

Jenny and her father parked their bikes in front of the Gereformeerde Kerk and walked directly into the unlocked front door of the old church. They proceeded through the darkened sanctuary and stopped at a door marked *Consistorie*. Father knocked.

"*Kom aub.*" Jenny recognized the kind voice of Pastor Pieter Jansen. They entered a room that was just large enough to accommodate a heavy, dark-stained table and eight matching chairs, along with two bookcases that framed the single window. Pastor Jansen sat at the head of the table. "Ah, Deacon DeHaan, please come in. And our special guest, Jenny DeHaan. Brother Atsma has been telling me great things about you."

Seated on the right side of the table, Captain Klaas Atsma smiled and nodded. Jenny took a seat beside her father. This should be a good meeting. She held her father and her minister in the highest regard, and now Captain Atsma had entered that elite category.

Pastor Jansen leaned forward and rested his folded hands on the table. He glanced at Jenny's father and Chief Atsma, then rested his gaze on Jenny. "Well, it seems Jenny has graduated from the ranks of our church's children. She is not only an adult member, but also in a very special group. I want to commend you for acting courageously on behalf of our Jewish neighbors. To my knowledge, you are the first young person in our congregation to do so, but I pray not the last. And I must commend you, brother Albert. Jenny's maturity is surely evidence of your nurturing."

The corners of Father's eyes crinkled. "Perhaps my prayers made up for my many failings."

Jenny reached over and gave her father a one-armed hug.

Jansen straightened in his seat and gently patted the edge of the table. "For the last couple of weeks, Captain Atsma and I have been working to find others who will support this effort. As you all know, we must be deliberate, enlisting only those who we know to be true to our cause." He turned to the policeman. "Comments, Klaas?"

"Specific to your new little friend, Aniek, I think we have located an excellent placement for her, a family with other children who live in a rather remote area."

Jenny beamed. "Wonderful." She paused for a moment. "I'm afraid Mama may have trouble giving her up. That child sparked something in her."

Captain Atsma nodded with a smile. "Little ones do that. I have five grandchildren. But we must be objective about these things. Your family is stereotypical Aryan, blond and blue-eyed, the whole thing. Aniek does have an appearance that distrustful Germans would suspect as being Jewish. I think it might be best to place her in a setting where she will blend better. We have found such a location."

Atsma pushed a piece of paper across the table. "Here are directions to the farm." He then passed them a page from a magazine, torn roughly in half. "Show them this. They have the other half."

At nine o'clock the next morning, a solitary bicycle rolled along Nykererstraat, the road between Nijkerk and Putten. Jenny

DeHaan carried her young passenger on the bike's crossbar. A bright sun climbed in the clear blue sky and promised a warm day in central Holland. A light breeze drifted over the open fields and offered welcome relief.

Aniek, facing sideways and cradled by Jenny's strong arms, had a firm hold on the handlebars. After about ten minutes of silence, she made her first comment. "I want to stay at your house."

"I know, sweetheart, and I like having you there, but I want you to be in a safe place until your mama comes back. I will come to visit you."

A couple of miles east of Nijkerk, just past the waterway that led to Schuitenbeek, Jenny turned into a hard-packed dirt drive. It led to a farmhouse much like her own. She eased Aniek from the bike and approached the home, holding the child's hand and walking at her pace.

The door opened, and a young woman in her mid-thirties appeared. At her side, partly lost in her mother's skirt, peeked a little girl about Aniek's age. The children stared at each other.

"Good morning. I am Greta, and this young lady is Aniek. I think you might have the other half of this." Jenny held out the torn magazine page.

The woman's deep frown faded. She reached into the pocket of her apron and produced a matching torn page. "I am Sophie, and this is Hanna."

Happiness sparkled inside Jenny. "These girls look like sisters."

Sophie crouched to Aniek's level and gently took both of her hands. "Perhaps the story should be that they are cousins." She turned to her daughter. "Would you like to show Aniek your room and your dolls?"

Hanna held out her hand. Aniek took it and looked up at Jenny, who nodded her encouragement. The girls trotted away. Jenny called after them, "I'll see you soon, Aniek."

Without looking back, the girl responded, "Okay. Bye."

Sophie started to follow the children, then turned back to Jenny. "I have several children and a husband. The ration coupons don't go far enough. Is there some way you could bring us more coupons?"

"I cannot promise, but I will try."

"Thank you. And please pray that I receive only friendly visitors."

Jenny drew her lips into a thin line. "That is my prayer for all of us."

Chapter Twenty-Two

9 October 1942
Nijkerk

Marten Demeester, better known on the streets of Holland and confirmed by the ID in his possession as Dirck Meijer, sat alone at an outside table at a small restaurant on Kolkstraat. He nibbled a sandwich, vaguely aware of the taste. He studied the building across the street. The town hall was a two-story brick building with shuttered windows. Its steep, tiled roof had three chimneys, each neatly topped with a pagoda-shaped cap. To his left, boats bobbed gently in the small harbor, waiting patiently to move down the channel to the open waters of the Ijsselmeer.

He checked his watch. Twelve noon. As expected, the door to the town hall opened, and workers poured out. Many walked in his direction. He gulped the last of his sandwich, vacated his table for the newcomers, and crossed the street to the building. A leather satchel bag hung from his shoulder.

Inside the door, a framed building directory welcomed him. The distribution office was in room 201. *This is too easy.* He located the stairs and started up. Footsteps echoed in the stairway above him. He stopped. Were they German or Dutch? Should he leave or stay? It sounded like women's heels. Sure enough, two young women appeared, gave him a cheerful hello, and went their way. He exhaled slowly and continued his mission.

The door to 201 was closed. He pulled out a large red kerchief and tied it behind his head, covering his face below the eyes. He paused, inhaled, pushed the door open, strode into the room, and scanned the area. A single clerk, sitting behind a large desk, looked up. Behind his wire-rimmed spectacles, his eyes widened. Rigid and wordless, he stared at Marten. The nameplate on the desk read *Vander Wey.*

Marten approached the counter between them and pulled a short-barreled revolver from his pocket. "Believe me, I don't want to hurt you," he said in Dutch. "People need to eat. You have coupons." He tossed the satchel onto the desk, and it slid into the man's chest. "Fill it quickly."

The man pushed his chair back, stood, and rushed to the file cabinet behind him. He stuffed sheets of ration coupons into the bag until it bulged. He hurried to the counter, set the bag in front of Marten, and peered at the door. "You need to hurry."

Marten blinked. "What?"

"They are coming."

"Who is coming?"

"Inspectors are coming. They check our records. I'm waiting for them."

"Germans?"

"SS. You must go."

Marten relaxed his grip on the gun and pointed it away from the clerk. "Thanks, my friend."

The door opened, and Marten swung around, his pistol raised. He pointed the gun at two shocked men, an SS Captain and a Dutch police officer.

"Come in and shut the door," Marten said. The SS man closed the door and turned to face Marten. While guarding the newcomers, Marten reached his hand behind him and beckoned to the clerk. "Come forward and join these men." The clerk quickly complied.

Marten tipped the barrel of his gun toward the ceiling. "Hands up." His voice had an authority that surprised and emboldened him. He quickly assessed the faces of his new hostages. The police officer, face pale and tight, betrayed his fear. The German's gaze was steady and cold. Marten aimed his gun at the bridge of the man's nose, "Listen carefully. I lost a dear friend. Killed by the SS. I would prefer to kill you, but if you don't resist me, I may let you live. Face the wall."

The German blinked slowly and deliberately, then eased around, exposing his back.

"Lean forward, hands on the wall. Good boy. Now, slide your feet back toward me." The German moved his feet back. He was now off-balance, weight on the wall.

Marten pointed the gun at the cop. "Do as he did." The officer leaned into the wall.

Marten glanced at the clerk. "Bring me two trash cans." He trained the gun on the two men and listened as the clerk retrieved a pair of cans from nearby desks. "Dump the stuff out." Papers and the other miscellaneous trash of a busy office fell to the floor. "Now, put those cans over the heads of those two." The clerk edged his hand upward and gingerly lifted the Nazi's hat and replaced it with a can. Some pencil shavings drifted onto the man's shoulders. Next, the policeman suffered the same indignity. That done, Marten lowered his weapon. Tension drained from the clerk's face.

"I need a duffel bag or a laundry bag. Something large. Get it."

In moments, the man produced a cotton bag with a drawstring at the top. "Good job. Go stand with the others."

Marten checked the clock on the wall, then back to his captives. "Okay, SS man, take off your clothes and don't let the can fall off your head. Start with the gun belt."

The leather belt holding a Luger pistol clattered to the floor. Then, balancing on one foot at a time, he pulled off his boots. About a minute later, the formerly proud German officer stood in his underwear, fists clenched.

Marten rapped the man's new helmet with the barrel of his gun. "Now, lean on the wall again, big boy."

The man complied.

Marten pointed at the bag. "Okay, put the uniform in there. Skip the boots." The clerk obeyed, then looked up and tapped his wristwatch—three insistent taps. Marten frowned, studied the man's face, and nodded. He pulled a roll of white adhesive tape from his jacket pocket and handed it to the clerk. "I want you to wrap the wrists of these men." He jabbed the barrel of his gun into the ribs of the German. The man jerked. "Ease yourself back from the wall. Good boy. Now slowly bring both hands behind your back."

The clerk tore off a strip of tape and wound it around the Nazi's wrists. They repeated the process with the Dutch policeman.

The clerk touched his watch again. Marten nodded again. "Now turn and face me, both of you. Okay, clerk, now tape their mouths shut." With one hand, the clerk lifted the overturned trash cans and, with the other hand, pushed tape over their mouths. This left both officers bound and gagged, displaying old trash cans as helmets.

Now Marten turned to the clerk with a smile. His voice was still firm. "Hold out your hands." Marten taped his wrists and mouth.

He checked the clock on the office wall. 12:50. He grabbed the cotton bag and his leather satchel and ran to the door. As he opened it, voices filled the front stairway. Marten ran toward the steps at the back of the building and hurried down. He paused at the first landing. The voices were casual, loud, and unalarmed. He pulled off his mask and walked normally down the remainder of the stairs and out the back door, an everyday Dutchman with places to go.

The Kommandant stood rigid, muscles tight with rage. A draft of air tickled his bare legs. Smells inside the waste can filled his nostrils. Pencil shavings, paper, ink, and decaying things he could not identify. New sounds echoed inside his unwelcome helmet. A door opened, relaxed office workers entered the room, chatting and laughing. Then shocked silence. In his mind, the Captain pictured the young ladies gawking at him, mouths hanging open. He did his best to shout his favorite German curses. The words sounded hollow and weak inside the can. A hand gingerly lifted his steel covering. He glared into the wide eyes of a woman. She pulled the tape slowly from his mouth. As the tape peeled free, the German exploded. "*Ich möchte jetzt kleidung!*"

The woman gasped. "He wants clothes. Oh, Lord, help us. He's a German."

The SS man inhaled. Before he could shout again, another clerk, already heading for the door, responded in German. "I will bring clothes."

Another woman added, "We need the police. I'll get Captain Atsma." She fled out of the room.

The German raised his bound wrists and shook them at his audience. "*Befreien Sie meine Hände.*" A secretary obediently freed his hands.

The Nazi strode to the nearest telephone and spun the rotary dial, got a wrong number, cursed, and dialed again, slower this time. He paced the floor to the extent of the phone cord while he waited for an answer. He then shouted orders into the phone and slammed the abused instrument into its cradle.

Within a couple of minutes, Captain Atsma entered the room with a Dutch policeman's uniform in hand. His smooth gait and calm bearing brought some peace to the room. "I think this will fit, Kommandant. I will personally lead the investigation of this crime. In addition, beginning today, we will assign an officer to protect this office from further attacks."

The German studied the policeman's face. The anger and embarrassment eased just a bit. "*Danke schön.*"

Captain Atsma raised a strong, straight-arm Nazi salute. "*Bitte schön. Heil Hitler.*"

CHAPTER TWENTY-THREE

16 October 1942
Barreto Café, Utrecht

Standing in the dark alley, Marten tapped on the back door of Barreto Café. The door cracked open, light flooded out of the bright kitchen, and the frowning face of Kees Veltkamp appeared. A broad smile broke out on his clean-shaven face. "Ah, yes. My favorite villain." The door swung open, and Marten joined him inside.

"You open for breakfast? I'm starving."

His friend glanced at the clock on the wall. "It's six o'clock. But for you, I am always open. Looks like you're making a delivery."

Marten set his bulging leather satchel on the counter. "I have a whole load of ration coupons for Jenny, plus a bonus. I am now the proud owner of an SS officer's uniform, complete with Luger pistol."

"Where did all this come from?"

"Nijkerk. Right in Jenny's hometown."

The man wiped his flour-covered hands onto a towel and flipped it over his shoulder. He opened the satchel and examined the contents. "Good work, young man. I assume you have a good story to go with all this."

"An SS captain interrupted my work. He donated the clothes and the gun."

"I trust that the captain is still among the living?"

"He was very much alive when I left him. Good thing. If I had killed him, I'm afraid Nijkerk would be rubble by now."

"So, you are saying you left an SS captain standing there naked?"

"Not completely. When I last saw him, he was in his underwear, tied up, with a trash can for a helmet."

The deep laugh matched the man's large frame. He turned to his stove and lit a burner. "Well, my friend, you deserve a free breakfast."

Marten scanned the well-stocked shelves. "It looks like you are still able to get the food supplies you need."

"No problem. My German customers are quite happy. I guess they want to keep me in business. Looks like I'll keep my phone too. They like to use it, and it is amazing, the things I learn from their conversations."

"Well, keep up the good work."

Kees looked up from his sizzling frying pan. "How is Jenny? I haven't seen her lately."

"I've missed her too. I left word with her aunt that I would be here."

A few minutes later, Kees brought fried eggs, bacon, and steaming coffee to his table. He paused. "Oops. I keep forgetting you're a Jew. Sorry about the bacon."

Marten waved him off and lifted a crisp slice. "I don't worry about the small stuff. I have my hands full with bigger things."

The bell on the front door jingled, and Jenny walked in. Kees waved to her, then pointed at Marten's breakfast. "Want some of this, Jen?"

"Yes, please. A plateful. I grew up on a farm." She leaned over and planted a light kiss on Marten's cheek, pulled back a chair, and sat down with a mischievous grin.

The café owner cleared his throat and wiped his hands on his towel. "Be right back." He winked at Marten and disappeared into the kitchen.

"So, Mr. Dirck Meijer, assuming that name is still correct, what is the purpose of this meeting, besides to attract your admirers?"

"I have a surprise for you."

"Not jewelry, I hope. I don't wear the stuff." She paused for a moment. "Well, from you I think I'd wear it."

"Not jewelry. Better. Ration coupons. A whole bunch of them."

Jenny clapped her hands and gave Marten a swat on the shoulder. "Good man."

Kees set a full plate of bacon and eggs in front of Jenny and took a seat with them.

She attacked her breakfast for half a minute. "How is your family doing, Marten?"

He lowered his fork. "Okay, for now. The authorities have left them alone in the Amsterdam house. They're very concerned, though, and have started shifting things to the apartment. They even got the Vermeer from museum storage, and I took it to the hidden place. Joran hates staying at home. He's twelve now and feels like his life is escaping him. A visiting teacher just can't compare with being with friends at school."

He tossed his used napkin onto his empty plate. "It's getting bad at the Schouwburg. A once great theater, now nothing but a holding pen for Jews."

Kees slapped the table. A rare frown creased his forehead. "And it's run by another Jew. Can you believe that? Walter Süskind runs the operation. The place is full of Jews, ripped from a normal life, waiting to go to Westerbork."

The man scraped his chair back and strode to the front window of the café. Sunlight was just beginning to bring life to the street and the canal outside. Fall color was emerging on the trees. He returned to the table. "I have been speaking to some of my partners in Amsterdam. We are making plans to take him out."

Marten raised a hand, palm facing his angry friend. "No. Stop. You've got it wrong. Süskind is one of us."

Kees ran his fingers through his thinning hair. "But our people have seen the man hanging around, drinking with Aus der Fünten, the engineer of all the deportations."

"Exactly. He's playing the man like my brother plays a cello. When the Nazi is drunk, the books are changed, and the Jews are getting away."

"What is happening to the children at the Schouwburg?" Jenny asked.

Marten tapped an index finger on the table. "You need to hear this, Jen. Across from the Schouwburg is a nursery that the Germans have taken over. They are housing the children there. I know some people who work in the place."

Jenny leaned forward. "Are you saying it's possible to get kids out of there?"

"Maybe."

"But how?"

"I'm working on that."

She grabbed his hand and squeezed hard. "We have to save them, Marten. We have to."

CHAPTER TWENTY-FOUR

30 October 1942
Amsterdam

The tram glided down Plantage Middenlaan and eased to a stop in front of the Hollandsche Schouwburg theater. Marten Demeester emerged into the cool but sunny autumn morning. As he stepped onto the sidewalk, he pulled a black hat from under his jacket and placed it on his head with the distinctive NSB markings clearly displayed. He waited for the tram to depart and crossed the street to the Huize Henriëtte Nursery. Without hesitation, he jerked open the door and strode inside.

Silence gripped the place as all eyes turned to the newcomer. Marten pulled the hat from his head. "Sorry about the cap. I wanted to look like a friend of the Germans at the Schouwburg." A frowning older woman, who appeared to be the one in charge, stepped forward. "Yes, sir. How may I help you?"

Marten pulled a magazine page, torn roughly in half, from his shirt pocket and handed it to the woman. "I am Smit. I think you are expecting me."

The frown disappeared, and the woman's eyes sparkled. "Yes, as a matter of fact, Mr. Smit, we have been waiting for you. I am Klara. Your package is being prepared, but there has been a change in plans."

"Oh?"

"You were expecting a toddler. Unfortunately, that child was taken last night. He and his family were transported to the train station. But we have another child, an infant, probably scheduled for transport in a day or two. Right now, you are her only hope."

Marten's confidence faded a bit. "I don't know much about infants."

"She is a very good child, Mr. Smit. Very quiet. Her name is Tessa. We have bottles prepared. We gave her a tiny amount of antihistamine. She may sleep all the way to Utrecht."

"But how do I leave without being noticed?"

"We have a nice suitcase, all soft inside with vent holes so you can board the tram without being conspicuous. But if you don't think you can—"

"No. We must try. It is a short train ride to Utrecht. Capable women will meet me there."

"Good. The child is ready. Herr Süskind has secured the parents' permission and corrected the records. First, we must wait until the tram returns. It will block the view of any Germans at the Schouwburg and allow you to leave quickly."

"While we wait, may I use your phone?"

"Certainly."

Marten got through to Barreto Café in Utrecht. "Kees, is Jenny there?" A pause. "Change in plans. Tell her to meet me at the station." He hung up.

A couple of minutes later, one of the nurses rushed into the room. "The tram is coming. We must hurry." She returned to the front door.

In seconds, Klara appeared with a medium-sized leather suitcase. "Just the right size for Tessa. We have plenty to pick from. We put holes along the seams."

Marten grasped the handle of the case and strode to the front door, his heart racing and his lungs dragging in volumes of air.

The door burst open. "Now. Go."

Marten walked into the sunshine. The door closed behind him. Perfect timing. The tram glided to a stop directly in front of him. He boarded and peeked at the operator. *Was that a wink?* The man said nothing but waited until Marten took a seat before he eased into motion. Only a half dozen passengers occupied the car. They were all gazing at the group of German soldiers in front of the Schouwburg. One woman muttered, "The place is jammed with Jews, our neighbors." Her companion quickly shushed her and eyed Marten with a frown.

Marten sat in the back of the tram carriage. Tessa was perfectly quiet on the short trip to the Amsterdam train station. The train to Utrecht stood at the platform. Marten rushed aboard and took an isolated seat.

He looked around to ensure privacy and opened the case. His tension eased at the sight of the sleeping infant. Two nursing bottles rested at her feet. Marten eased his hands under Tessa, lifted her out, and cradled her in his arms. After withdrawing the bottles, he closed the case and shoved it under the seat.

The waiting passengers ahead of him seemed to ignore him. A woman boarded and selected a seat across the aisle. As the train glided out of the station, she turned to Marten with a smile. "You look like a proud papa."

Marten studied the woman's face, tried to read her motives. She looked like many ladies in his church at home. Good people. Or was she a really skilled collaborator?

He forced his best friendly face. "A nervous papa. Tessa's mama is sick. I am taking her to my sister in Utrecht. I hope she keeps sleeping."

The woman nodded with a slight smile and turned her attention to the passing scenery.

The fifteen-minute ride to Hilversum seemed longer as Marten spent most of his time gazing at Tessa and hoping she would not wake up. At the Hilversum stop, a few people left and a few boarded. Among the newcomers were two German soldiers. The train jolted as it started to move. Tessa's eyes opened, and she began to cry. Attention in the car turned to the disruption.

Marten pulled out one of the bottles and inserted it at the source of the screaming. Silence for a few minutes. Then the crying returned.

The woman across the aisle took the seat beside Marten and, without words, held out her hands. Marten hastened to give her the child.

"She needs to burp," she whispered. The lady resolved the problem with a few well-placed pats and peace returned to the carriage.

"I am Naomi. Who are you?"

"Dirck. Dirck Meijer. This is Tessa. I sure appreciate your help."

"I thought you might."

"Pardon me?"

Naomi leaned over and whispered into Marten's ear. "I saw you run out of the nursery at the Schouwburg with that." She pointed at the suitcase on the floor. "I was riding in the carriage behind yours. And since this baby doesn't look anything like you, and you don't have a clue how to care for her, I have no doubt that you just rescued her."

Marten's cheeks warmed, and his heart pounded. "Are you going to turn me in?"

"Turn you in? Certainly not. Relax. I'm a friend of Walter Süskind. I know what's happening here, and you obviously need some help. Also, my children are grown. We will take Tessa if you need a place for her. We can handle one more."

The train rolled into the crowded station in Utrecht. Jenny stood on the platform, scanning the train cars as they passed.

Marten waved, and she ran in his direction. She stopped a couple of feet in front of him. "Aren't you supposed to have a package with you?"

"I want you to meet our new friends, Naomi and Tessa."

A gentle smile erased the frown on Jenny's face as she gazed at the sleeping child snuggled in the woman's arms. "You two seem like a good fit."

The gleam in Naomi's eyes settled the matter.

Jenny's frown returned. "You need to see Kees at Barreto. There's a new problem. I will help with Tessa. You need to go. Now."

Marten jerked open the door of Barreto Café. The lunchtime crowd turned as one toward him. He blinked and forced himself to slow down and reclaim his anonymity. The patrons turned back to their companions. Kees, serving a corner table, nodded his head toward the back. Marten walked to the kitchen and found Nic there.

"I just got here too," said Nic. "Kees told me to get over here."

"What's going on?"

"Don't know."

Kees entered the kitchen and closed the door. "I got word from my friends in Amsterdam. A raid is planned for tonight in the area where your parents live, Marten. What street do they live on?"

"Chopinstraat."

"Not good. It's in the target area. Do you want me to help you?"

Marten's jaw tightened. "Maybe. Let me think."

Kees returned to his customers.

Marten gazed out the back window while Nic stood by his side. "Do you still have that suit at your apartment?"

"Sure," Nic said. "The hat and overcoat too. A guy from my church gave it to me, but it's old. Why?"

"You could pass for Gestapo. Will you help me?"

Nic's cheeks paled. "Um, I don't know. I would like to, but—"

"You can do this, Nic. I need you."

"I don't think I could use a gun."

"You won't have to. Just be there and look evil."

"Okay, I'll try."

Marten grabbed his friend's shoulders. "This has to work, Nic. My family's lives may depend on it."

CHAPTER TWENTY-FIVE

30 October 1942
Amsterdam

The music eased to a gentle conclusion, and the resting cello allowed silence to fill the room. The bow in Joran's gentle hand seemed to have a life of its own as it rose from the instrument. He opened his eyes, inhaled, and straightened up in his chair.

"It's beautiful, Joran. Peaceful. What is the name of that piece?"

Joran blinked and turned to face his father. "Oh, Papa, I didn't know you were there. It is *The Swan* by Saint-Saëns. My favorite."

"His name sounds French," Father said with a hint of a smile. "That's good. My taste in music is definitely not German these days."

Joran carefully placed the cello in the stand beside his chair. "I am really glad to have my music. Evenings in a house behind blackout curtains would be hard without my cello. Do you think it would be okay for me to go outside the back door for a few minutes if we turn out the lights in the kitchen?"

"Surely."

Joran opened the back door and stepped into the cool, fresh air. A solitary cricket greeted him. Due to all the neighbors' compliance with blackout regulations, a thin crescent moon provided the only light. He inhaled the scents of flowers that hid in the darkness.

Groping for a seat, he located a concrete bench near the door. Thin clouds drifted past the moon.

The sounds of distant truck engines caught his attention. Nothing unusual. Probably military at this time of night, traveling on Beethovenstraat. Then the trucks' behavior changed. The steady pull of the engines ceased, replaced by the squeak of brakes. The vehicles seemed to come to rest somewhere on the street in front of the Demeester house. Doors slammed. Silence returned for a few moments, and then German voices disrupted the quiet. He jumped to his feet and listened.

When the sound of barking dogs joined the voices, Joran rushed to the house, stumbled, caught himself, yanked open the door, and slammed it closed as he ran through the kitchen. As he passed the dining room, he looked inside. The table was set for dinner, but his parents were absent. He rushed to the front room. Father and Mother were embracing in the middle of the room, eyes closed.

Joran jolted to a stop and caught his breath. "You heard?"

Father looked up, a deep line etched between his brows. "Yes. It looks like a raid."

Joran's lungs forced him to take short, quick breaths. "Can we run, Papa?"

"No. I looked outside. They have both ends of the street blocked off."

"So we are stuck?"

"Maybe not. I know lots of people. We might be able to buy our way out of this."

"Can I go upstairs to watch?"

"We will go with you," said his mother.

Standing in Joran's dark room, they opened the blackout curtain. In the dim light provided only by a few trucks with taped-over headlamps, human figures, along with more than a few dogs on leashes, waited at roadblocks at both ends of the block.

"More lights coming," Joran said as he gazed at the roadblock at Schubertstraat.

"Looks like some kind of high-level German staff car," whispered Father. "This is not good."

The vehicle stopped at the roadblock, the lights from its large headlamps reduced to small dots. After some kind of exchange with the men at the roadblock, the car proceeded. It glided along Chopinstraat and eased to a stop directly in front of the Demeester home. Two figures emerged and slammed the doors. Darkness shrouded the vehicle. The three Demeesters leaned close to the glass, searching for information.

"Where did they go?" Mother asked.

The deadbolt lock on the front door came alive with a sharp clack. The heavy oak door broke its seal and squeaked open. Joran held his breath. His father's large hand gripped his shoulder. On the other side, his mother's body trembled.

"They have a key," Father whispered. "Karl has a key. He's the one who betrayed us."

A familiar voice from the front door filled the silence in the house. "Father, Mother, Joran, come quickly."

Mother's trembling stopped. She took a sharp breath. "Marten. It's Marten." She led the way, her slippered feet barely touching the stairs as she hurried. She embraced Marten in his SS captain's uniform.

Father studied the young man dressed in the black overcoat with a fedora pulled low on his forehead. The man lifted his hat, revealing the young face of Nicolaas DeHaan.

Father embraced him. "Never hugged a Gestapo goon before."

"We need to go," Marten commanded.

Joran appeared, holding his cello case. "Can I take it?"

Marten paused for just a moment. "We'll get it. Let's go. Everybody remember that you're being arrested. Act like it in case someone turns the lights on us."

The SS officer and Gestapo agent emerged with their captives. The big car idled peacefully in the darkness, unimpressed with all the drama. Both adults displayed appropriate resistance. The boy followed. When they were inside the Mercedes, the Gestapo man returned to the house and emerged with his personal prize, Joran's cello.

The car's engine roared to life, and its headlamps illuminated the group of Nazi officials working the raid to the east. They made a quick turn-about and headed west.

To the left, the Demeester house sat quiet, empty. The vehicle eased to a stop at the roadblock. A German soldier edged to the closed window, stopped, leaned to the side, and examined the dark interior. The window rolled down, exposing the SS captain at the wheel. The young sergeant jolted to a position of rigid attention. "*Ja, Haupsturmführer.*"

Marten glared at him until the young man blinked, then allowed his face to soften into a slight smile. "Just a few Jews on their way to a new home, Sergeant."

The young man stood rigidly, eyes focused somewhere over the roof of the car. He raised a straight-armed Nazi salute. "Heil Hitler."

Marten lifted a lazy forearm toward the windshield. "*Ja, ja.*" He rolled up the window, and the Mercedes rolled through the roadblock. Audible sighs complemented the hum of the car's engine. The Demeester family rode in silence along the quiet streets of Amsterdam until they were creeping along Van Limburg Stirumstaat. Joran, holding his mother's hand, spoke for the first time since they left their home. "Papa, I'm really afraid. Where are we going?"

"Do you remember when I took you to my warehouse near the waterfront?"

"When we went down and looked at all the ships in the port?"

"That's it. We are almost to that part of the city."

"Are we going to live in our warehouse?"

"Not there. I'm afraid that would not be safe. However, I have a dear friend, Mr. Bramer, who owns a factory near our warehouse. He has converted an area at the back of his building into a home for us. A hidden place that almost nobody knows about."

"Does it have windows so I can see outside? I like to see outside."

"No windows, only solid brick walls, but it will be okay, Joran. We have a doorway that opens to the roof. We can go out there at night, get plenty of fresh air, and look at the stars."

Joran released his mother's hand and sat up in the seat. "I wish I had a telescope to see the stars."

"You do. It's waiting for you in our new place."

Joran eased back in the soft leather seat. "I think I might like this place, Mama."

His mother gripped his hand again. "I hope so, son. I hope so."

The Mercedes turned onto the dark and deserted Van Beuningenstraat. Nic, sitting in the front and still wearing his fedora, turned to the back seat.

Mother raised her free hand. "Nicolaas, dear, would you please remove the hat now? That Gestapo costume is altogether too realistic."

Nic snatched off the black hat. "Sorry."

"Much better. Now I see the Nicolaas whom I know and love."

Marten guided the Mercedes to the alley behind the industrial buildings fronting Van Beuningenstraat. He stopped at a large nondescript structure, then hopped out and raised a large sliding door, exposing a room large enough to accommodate the vehicle. He pulled inside and turned off the engine.

"We are going to live here, Father?" asked Joran.

"This is just a place to hide the car. I own this place, but Desmond carefully hid that fact in our records. I hope to secure the Mercedes here, perhaps until the Germans leave. We will be staying a couple of doors down. I'll show you." He pulled a flashlight from the glove box, and the family moved to the darkened alley. The light sent a thin beam ahead of the group. Joran gripped his mother's hand, her skin moist in spite of the cool night air.

As they passed one building, a violent metallic clattering erupted from a collection of metal cans. The group froze. The flashlight beam danced up and down for a moment, then swung slowly to the sound. A large garbage can toppled to the ground, renewing the clatter, and a black cat bounded to the cobblestones and raced into the darkness.

Joran, heart pounding, tightened the grip on his mother's hand. "I think we should go inside soon."

They skulked past several more buildings, finally stopping at one whose appearance differed little from the others. Father led the way up the stairs to the loading dock and shined the light on the name on the entry door: *Bramer Fine Lederwaren*. He slid a key into the lock and stepped inside. Upon entering the building, he scanned the room with his flashlight and saw multiple cardboard boxes on pallets.

"I do like the smell of leather," Mother said.

Father continued to examine the room. "Herr Bramer does a thriving business. Those shiny black boots that Marten is wearing at this moment may have been manufactured right here."

"You mean he does business with the Nazis, Father?" Marten's voice carried an edge.

"Indeed, but his profits are a great benefit to the Resistance. I would say it is a definite net gain to our cause. Also, if he maintains his operation until the Germans are gone, our place will be secure."

Father moved to a large wooden shelving unit, removed some dusty books, and pulled a tiny switch. The unit swung neatly away from the wall and revealed a small room containing a narrow stairway. He led the family upstairs to the apartment door.

"Welcome, everyone, to the Demeester residence."

A black sedan approached the darkened roadblock on Chopinstraat. The narrow beam of its modified headlamps cut through the darkness and exposed the small group of uniformed men gathered beside an army truck. With a slight squeak of brakes, the car came to an abrupt stop. The apparent leader of the group approached the vehicle. Using his flashlight, he scanned the interior, exposing the five occupants. The flashlight beam settled on the black collar patch of the driver's gray uniform. The torch abruptly went dark, and the guard snapped to rigid attention.

Ernst Schmidt swung the door open, striking the stiff guard, who jumped back and resumed his tight stance. Schmidt jumped from the vehicle. "Are you in charge here, Lieutenant?"

The young officer's voice cracked. *"Jawohl. Oberst."*

"Have you started the sweep yet?"

"No, sir. I was told to wait for Colonel Schmidt."

"You are now looking at him. Let's get to work. I am particularly interested in one house on the left side of the street. Do you have people covering the back side of the street?"

"Jawohl."

"Very good. We can begin then."

"One thing I should mention, sir ..."

Schmidt paused and turned to the tense lieutenant. "Spit it out."

"About thirty minutes ago, an SS captain and a man in a suit, he looked like Gestapo, came here. They went to a house in mid-block and then left again."

"Which house?"

"I don't know, sir. It was very dark. I'm sorry."

Schmidt stood silent. Anger stirred inside him, and his jaw clamped tight. Did somebody in the SS interrupt his operation? Crickets chirped somewhere in the darkness. After taking a deep breath, he moved closer to the lieutenant and jabbed a stiff index finger into the man's chest. His voice emerged, deep and slow. "Someone was here? And I wasn't immediately told?"

The man's stumbling speech betrayed his fear. "The driver was SS. The car was a big Mercedes like the generals use. It happened very fast. I thought—"

Schmidt jumped into the vehicle, slammed the door, gripped the wheel, revved the engine, and roared down Chopinstraat.

He jerked to a stop in front of the Demeester residence, then strode toward the front door, followed closely by two uniformed subordinates. Taking up the rear was Karl Müller. A man in a suit remained in the car.

Karl hurried beside Schmidt. "Colonel, I'm wondering about that car."

"I am too, Müller. Only our top officers use those. I don't understand it. We must have some kind of communication problem."

"There is something else, Colonel. It also sounds like a car I drove for the Demeesters, a big black Mercedes. Do you think someone may have rescued them with their own car?"

Schmidt stormed up to the house and yanked the door open. Bright light flooded out. He rushed inside, gun drawn. His subordinates all pulled weapons out and followed.

He paused in the foyer. The peaceful house offered neither welcome nor resistance, only silence. Schmidt rushed through the ground floor, aiming his weapon into empty rooms as he moved. When he reached the back door, he stopped, lowered his gun, and faced his men. He looked at one sergeant and jerked his thumb toward the back door. "Get out there and check out the yard. The rest of you scour this place."

Schmidt moved to the dining room, adrenaline fading and anger growing. A sparkling chandelier added a touch of life to the deserted room. Clean place settings, complete with folded napkins, graced the abandoned table. Serving dishes waited, full and undisturbed. He touched the side of a covered dish. Still warm. He paced the room, tapping the baton on his open, gloved hand, ears tuned to the ongoing search upstairs. In only a few minutes, his men returned with the report he expected. The house was deserted.

Schmidt slapped his baton on the table, rattling the dishes. "Müller was right. They jumped through our net." He brought down the baton again, shattering a delicate cup. "That rescue took careful planning. Obviously, they were warned of the raid." He pointed his baton at Karl. "And what does that mean, Müller?"

Karl, eyes wide, blinked. "There is a leak somewhere, Colonel. Reinaar Demeester has many contacts. He probably knows the top Resistance people, and they have lots of listening ears out there."

"And we obviously have loose lips somewhere, undoubtedly among our NSB amateurs. Perhaps we should shoot a few of them to tighten their faces. And we need to follow up on that car." Schmidt paced for a moment, stopped, and turned to Karl. "Now think, Müller. What will these Jews do next?"

"They only have the two houses as far as I know, but they have lots of money to spend. I think they might still try to escape the country. Reinaar Demeester can buy his way anywhere."

"Now we need Barkman," said Schmidt. "Go out to the car and get him, Müller."

When Karl returned with Willem Barkman, Schmidt was sitting at the head of the dining table. Having regained his composure, he was spreading a piece of bread with butter. He pointed at a chair. "Sit."

While Barkman seated himself, Schmidt took a sip of coffee and set the cup in its saucer. "Okay, your turn, Barkman. We missed them." He shrugged. "Gone somewhere." He lifted his baton and pointed it at the startled accountant. "We assigned you to take over Reinaar Demeester's businesses. Now, earn your big salary. Help us out here. What's your assessment?"

Barkman straightened himself in his chair and pushed his spectacles up on his nose. "It's clear to me now that Demeester sold off many of his assets before the occupation. He may have sent some assets out of the country, but with the sudden invasion, he didn't have much time. From our records, we do know that he did not turn in much money or all their artworks. I expect he has hidden most, perhaps all, of his wealth somewhere in Holland."

Schmidt examined the paintings lining the walls. "There is a lot of the art in this house and in their house in The Hague." He turned to Karl. "You spent a lot of time in both places, Müller. Is there anything out of place?"

"Well, I didn't pay much attention to their pictures."

Schmidt rolled his eyes.

Karl cleared his throat. "But there may be some pieces missing."

Schmidt raised his chin. "Tell me more."

"There was one picture that they seemed to like best. It wasn't very big, but it was real pretty, almost like a photograph."

"And the artist was ..."

"Meer something."

Schmidt leaned back in his chair. The adrenaline returned. "Vermeer?"

"That's it. Vermeer. They showed it off to lots of people. I don't see it here."

Schmidt's agitation grew. He rose and strutted around the room, tapping his open hand with the baton. He stopped and swung around to face his wide-eyed subordinates. "And I didn't see it in the house in The Hague. I would recognize a Vermeer." Schmidt slapped the table with his baton another time. "Put out a top-level alert for these people. Watch all the trains, all the borders. Barkman, I want you to scour all the paperwork in this house. There must be clues about their plans. I want them caught." A pleasant thought popped into Schmidt's head. "I want to personally deliver that Vermeer to the Führer."

Schmidt turned to Karl, and the scowl returned. "And we must find that car, Müller. I want a full description of it so we can put out the alert to all our people."

CHAPTER TWENTY-SIX

5 March 1943
Amsterdam

Standing in the darkened interior of the dress shop, Marten turned his wristwatch to catch light from outside. "They should be here any minute." He and Jenny edged to the large front window. Their footsteps on the hardwood floor and the rustle of their clothes echoed around the cavernous room, empty but for a few bare display racks.

They leaned near the glass and peeked south on Plantage Kerklaan. "We should hear them coming," said Marten. "It will be a group of about ten kids and a couple of nurses. We must be ready to pull the door open as they pass."

Jenny pressed her hand to her sternum. "My heart's trying to get out of my chest."

"Mine too." Marten's voice sounded calm, but his pounding heart and oxygen-hungry lungs seemed to be struggling for control.

"Should we be in here, Marten? Who owns this place?"

"The Goldbaum family. They ran this place for twenty years, maybe more. The Nazis dragged them out. Then they hauled out all their inventory. I expect some collaborator will take over soon."

"And this is going to work, right?" Her tone revealed her alarm.

"No problem. It's all set. Süskind deleted the boy from the Schouwburg records. The parents have given permission. The nurses are the bravest people in the world. They won't fail us. Our target is about ten, blond hair, name is Max. He looks downright Aryan. Is the host family good, Jen?"

"The best. They are in Friesland. We have lots of solid people there. This boy will fit in nicely. Does he know what's happening?"

"I hope so. The nurses should have him prepared." Marten paused, raised his hand, and listened. "They're coming. Let's move to the door."

He grasped her hand and noticed a slight tremor and a moist palm. He gripped the door handle and tensed, listening to the chatter of approaching children. An adult voice brought order. "Let's all stay together now, children. Gretchen, please catch up. That's right, sweetheart. Look, children, a bird in that tree. Can you hear it singing?"

A child's voice came alive. "Can we take a long walk today, Miss Clara, like yesterday?"

"All the way around the block, dear. Just like yesterday if everyone behaves. That includes you, Hein. Please don't pester Max. You need to act like a good friend."

The group came into view. A uniformed nurse led the procession. Another took up the rear. As they neared the dress shop, the lead nurse pulled a white handkerchief from her pocket and touched it to her face. About ten feet from the front door, she let it drift to the sidewalk.

"Miss Clara, you dropped something."

"Leave it, child. Keep walking."

"But—"

"Hein, do as I say."

"Yes, Miss Clara."

Marten released the door handle and stepped back. "Called off."

Jenny clutched his arm. "What's wrong?"

"Don't know, but she shut it down."

The group passed the store. Their voices continued. "I wish Tina was here, Miss Clara. She is my best friend."

"Yes, I know, Willa. She had to leave last night. She and her family took a trip."

"Where did they go?"

"I don't know. To another place. Perhaps a nice new home."

The voices faded as the procession walked to the north.

"What's going on, Marten?"

Gazing out the window, he nodded. "Look. There's our problem." A *Kubelwagen* staff car crept past the window, moving in the same direction as the group of children. "Clara saw that they were being watched. Good thing. We will live to fight another day. Looks like we are done here now. Let's grab a tram. I would like to see what's going on at our house."

"Okay. So you are now Dirck Meijer. Is that still the name in your pocket?"

"Yes. Still a good ID. I also have an exemption certificate. Believe it or not, I'm a farmer from Gelderland, essential to the mission of the Reich. No German factories for me."

"Nice touch, Dirck."

They emerged from the Goldbaum shop, blended with the passing pedestrians, and strolled south on Plantage Kerklaan, arm-in-arm, maintaining a practiced friendly chatter. When they reached the end of the block, they turned right and stopped in front of the Schouwburg Theater, directly across from the nursery. Marten held Jenny's hand as two uniformed Germans passed.

After about ten minutes, the sound of children's chatter drew their attention. Coming from the west, the nurses and their charges were returning from their adventure. As they neared the front door of the building, Clara Van Dyke, still leading the procession, looked up and met Marten's gaze. Simultaneously, they nodded slightly. Clara and her group disappeared into the building.

Marten and Jenny left the area on the next tram. Within a few minutes, it rolled to a halt near the Amstel River. Jenny leaned up to the tram window. "What's going on here?"

Marten's chest tightened. "This isn't good, Jen. We need to get off."

He jumped out of the carriage, and Jenny followed. Uniformed men lined the sidewalk in front of a building on Amstel Street. A group of civilians confronted them with gestures and shouts. Marten and Jenny stepped aside as several military trucks rolled past. The vehicles forced a path through the protestors and stopped in front of the facility.

Marten, jaw tight, took a few quick steps forward. "That's the Jewish boys' orphanage. I know that place. My mother volunteered there when I was little. My friend Samuel grew up there and still works there."

The large front door of the orphanage swung open. Marten tensed. "Oh, no. It's happening, and we're too late."

A line of boys poured out of the building, herded by men in uniforms. The children's startled faces turned side-to-side as they took in the chaotic scene. Their ages appeared to range from three- and four-year-olds to teenagers. Several of the oldest boys carried toddlers.

Marten stiffened and pointed to a young man walking in the line of children. "Jenny, it's my friend, Samuel Kops."

The young man approached a truck, assisted several small boys into the vehicle, and joined them in the canvas-covered cargo area.

The loading process went on until the line of children ended.

With rumbles and puffs of smoke from exhaust pipes, the trucks came alive. They crept down Amstel Street. The crowd at the orphanage stood in tearful, stunned silence as the caravan turned a corner and disappeared into the city. The large orphanage door hung wide open, exposing the emptiness of the place to the relatives and friends outside whose hearts were also empty.

Marten looked into Jenny's moist eyes. With arms that felt heavy, he pulled her to himself. "We're too late. We just lost a hundred kids."

Jenny's face pressed into his chest close to his pounding heart. Her words were weak, almost a whisper. "Surely they won't kill children, Marten."

He drew a deep breath and blinked away the tears in his eyes. "The unthinkable is becoming our reality, Jenny. They just hauled a hundred little kids out of an orphanage. They aren't planning to send them to a work camp someplace."

A tram rolled to a stop beside them.

"Let's get out of here, Jen, before I start screaming."

Marten gazed over the driver's shoulder, vaguely aware of the passing scene as the tram cruised south. Rattles and creaks of the old streetcar roamed at the far edge of his consciousness, while fears and frustrations formed an unending loop in his mind.

Marten reached over and took Jenny's hand. "I like being with you, Jen." He turned and looked into her eyes. "Maybe when this terrible war is over ..."

A Kübelwagen staff car, spare tire bolted to its hood, cruised past the tram carriage. The canvas top was rolled back, exposing the two occupants. The driver wore a German officer's uniform, and the lone passenger wore civilian clothes.

Marten stared at the vehicle. "I know those guys."

"Who are they?"

He ignored the question, his attention riveted to the car as it proceeded ahead of them. The vehicle made a left turn at the next intersection.

Jenny tugged at Marten's sleeve. "Marten, who was that?"

"Karl. It was Karl Müller. He was our driver when we lived in The Hague. He disappeared at the start of the German invasion. The other guy looked like Gestapo. He seemed familiar too, but I can't remember his—no, wait—now I remember. It was Schmidt, the Gestapo devil who kicked us out of our house in The Hague. And now they're only a couple blocks from our new place."

"And you think they have their hands on the Amsterdam house too?"

"We need to find out."

"But should we go near there?"

"I have to. Maybe you should wait for me someplace."

"I'm coming."

They exited the tram and assumed their boyfriend-girlfriend pose, walking arm-in-arm and chatting but constantly scanning for trouble. They strolled south on Schubertstraat and stopped just before entering the intersection with Chopinstraat. Marten edged forward until he could peek around the corner of the building.

Directly in front of the Demeester house, a Kübelwagen sat unoccupied. The door of the house opened, and two men emerged.

Marten jerked back and started walking away from the intersection. "Let's go."

She hurried to catch up with him as he strode toward the tram stop. "What did you see?"

"Not good. It was definitely Karl and Schmidt together. Can you believe it? This is not good, that's for sure."

"They took over your house. That's disgusting."

"Worse than that. It means the Gestapo has access to a lot of information about my family. For one thing, my old buddy Karl, who treated me like a brother, knows way too much. And besides that, I expect they unleashed Willem Barkman in the house."

"Who's he?"

"The guy who was appointed as my father's business supervisor. His job was to ensure all our assets ended up in the hands of the German empire. Father was in the process of hiding our stuff in various places, but the invasion surprised him. Anyway, Barkman is a smart devil. I'm afraid the raid might have caught Father by surprise. He may have left something in the house that Barkman can use."

They boarded the next tram and headed into downtown Amsterdam. For a few minutes, Marten sat in silence, his brain racing. He turned to Jenny. "Do you think we could move my family?"

"I think so. We are developing a good network. I know of places in the farm country of Friesland that would be safe and comfortable. We have some Calvinist families up there who are rock-solid loyal to the cause. I also know of some Catholic families down in the Maastricht area that are equally reliable. There are good people all over this country."

"Is your family still involved?"

"Very much. I know they would do everything possible. We have a steady stream of guests who pass through our place. The problem is that our house is pretty small. Most of our visitors are short-term, and they stay in our barn."

Marten paused. "It might be hard to convince my parents to leave the apartment, especially Mother. I need to talk to them tonight."

At ten o'clock, Marten Demeester edged his way through the industrial area of Amsterdam. Under blackout conditions, the only light came from the sliver of a moon and the blanket of stars hanging over the city. Because of the curfew, only he and some feral cats braved the deserted streets in the warehouse and factory district of the historic city, at least as far as he could tell. He pictured Jenny, back on the farm by now, probably sitting outdoors, violating curfew and feeling good about it.

Reaching the loading dock at the back of the Bramer leatherworks, he slid his key into the lock and entered the building. After carefully easing the door closed, he found himself in a totally dark room. By edging a toe ahead of himself on the floor and extending both hands into the darkness in front of his face, he worked his way through the collection of boxes and pallets. When he reached the wall, he slid his hands to his left until he located a large wooden shelving unit. He slid his hand behind the dusty books and found the latch. With a click, the bookcase swung away from the wall. He entered the space and pulled the bookcase until it clicked into position.

He climbed the stairs to the apartment door, pulled a key from his pocket, but returned it. It would be bad to shock his parents.

Better use the bell. He slid his hand along the doorframe. When he felt a small doorbell button, he pressed twice, paused, then once more. He stood and waited in the darkness.

About ten seconds later, he heard a faint tap, barely audible, from behind the door. It was one sound among the many creaks and groans common to the centuries-old structure, but just what he was expecting. "Papa, it's me," he whispered.

The door opened. His father appeared and pulled his son to himself. They stepped into the apartment, windowless but tastefully decorated with oil paintings on every wall.

A Chopin sonata filled the softly lit space, then stopped in mid-stanza. Joran looked up, his face mirroring the peaceful music. A slight smile appeared. "About time you came home, big brother. Mama has been worried half to death."

Mother appeared from the kitchen, wiping her hands on a dish towel. "And your brother mentioned your name a few times too."

Marten hugged his mother, then moved over to Joran who was still seated, the bow in one hand and the neck of the cello in the other. "You're getting pretty good with that thing, big guy."

"Well, there isn't much else to do these days. Sometimes I think I'll go bonkers."

"*Bonkers?* Where did that word come from?"

"The BBC, I think. We listen to it every day." Joran rested the cello against its stand, then approached his brother and hugged him.

Marten held his brother by the shoulders, looked down at the boy's feet, then up at the top of his head. "Oh, no. This is bad. My little brother is tall as I am ... without shoes."

"And get this, Marten. I'm thirteen. I still have more growing to do. And with the way Mother is feeding me, I may be taller than Father before long."

"We have missed you these weeks, son," Mother said. "I really have worried about you. Where have you been staying?"

"Mostly around Amsterdam with friends. I do move around some." Martin let the topic fall as he moved to the sink and poured a glass of water. "So you are doing okay without the staff, Mother?"

"I'm afraid our kosher lifestyle has suffered, but we do fine. We have a large supply of canned goods. I find that working in the kitchen settles my mind."

"Judging from Joran's size, he isn't suffering from malnutrition."

Mother pulled out one of the chairs at the table and sat. She pointed at the vacant seat beside her. "Come sit down. Would you like some soup?"

"Very much."

The family gathered in the small, simple kitchen, around a table for four. A single pot resting on a hot pad functioned as the serving dish. The place settings were Delft china but accompanied only by a single spoon, knife, and fork. Two opened cans rested on the counter beside the stove.

"Do you think we could afford a bottle of wine for our special guest?" Father asked.

Mother smiled. "I managed to save one bottle of Château Lafite-Rothschild. I dare say that it has never been served with canned soup, but now may be just the right occasion. A better time may never come."

"Even for me?" asked Joran

His mother shrugged. "Why not, but only a small glass."

Marten took a sip. "Remember it well, Joran. I expect even the Führer can't get his hands on wine like this."

Marten leaned back in his chair and surveyed the scene. "I am looking at something that even four years ago I could not have imagined. My family, gathered around a simple table, no tablecloth, eating canned vegetable soup prepared by my mother and sipping Château Lafite from crystal glasses, all in a room with no windows. Unbelievable."

Mother lowered her glass to the table. "And the joy doesn't come from the wine."

Silence dominated for a few moments before Father looked across the table and met Marten's gaze. "I sense that you have other things on your mind, son. More than you have shared."

Marten drew a deep breath. "I saw things today that shocked me. First, I saw the Nazis take away all the boys from the Jewish orphanage. They just loaded them on trucks and left the place standing empty."

Mother gasped. "Oh, the children." Her eyes went to a blank stare, and her face paled.

"Sorry, Mama, but there's more I must tell you. I saw Karl today. He was riding in a German military car with Schmidt, that Gestapo agent. It was down in our neighborhood. We—Jenny and I—went down to Chopinstraat. They were there, at our house."

Father eased his glass to the table while staring at the wall. He blinked and looked around at his family. "I have long suspected it. Now I know for sure. We are faced with an alliance of Karl and the Gestapo. In addition, that little nest of villains includes Willem Barkman. He is a quiet man, but brilliant and, I think, quite treacherous."

Mother began to lift her glass, but her hand trembled, and she lowered it to the table. "What are you saying, Reinaar?"

He frowned and rubbed his chin with the back of his hand. "I am trying to remember what paperwork is left in the house. Individually, those men are not a great concern, but, taken together, I am afraid they could pose a grave threat to our safety."

Joran's eyes widened. "But how, Papa? Nobody knows we are here. Only Nic and Jenny. They won't tell."

"I am sure you are right, son. And add Mr. Bramer to that list. He would never tell either. He is risking his life for us." Father paused again. "Right now, I can't think of how they could discover us. We have been very careful ... yet ..."

Joran stood up and leaned over the table toward his father. "Let's go somewhere else."

"There is no other place." His mother's voice was almost a whisper.

"Jenny could find a place, Mama," said Marten. "She is involved with people all over Holland. They are very successful. Nobody has been arrested."

"No. This is our home now. I am sure we are safer right here. We will stay."

Marten leaned forward, arms resting on the table. "I have another idea. Joran, with his light hair and blue eyes, could easily pass for Aryan. With his good ID, he would be perfectly safe anywhere in the country. Jenny said he would be very welcome in their home."

"Could I go to school?"

"Of course, and work on a farm."

"Horses? I would like to ride a horse."

"They have two horses," said Marten. "And cows."

"And maybe I could take my cello."

Mother raised her hand. "Wait. Not so fast. You are talking about splitting our family."

"Only until it's safe," Marten said. "This war can't last much longer."

The family sat in silence for a few moments. Then Father spoke. "Perhaps we should consider this, Francien. If we change our minds, we can bring him back. Marten is right. Joran could move about the country in safety."

A tear slipped down Mother's pale cheek. "Just for a short time."

CHAPTER TWENTY-SEVEN

10 March 1943

Jenny DeHaan stepped off the tram in the factory warehouse district of Amsterdam, near the seaport on the North Sea Channel. The area bustled in spite of the war, but the tone was different from her previous visits. Today, the Germans were an inescapable presence. Military trucks approached and departed from loading docks. "They come empty and leave full," she muttered. Roughly dressed workmen moved among the busy facilities.

An army truck approached from the rear. She continued to stroll, attempting to duplicate her many walks on the university campus. Her hairstyle and bright spring dress were carefully selected to portray a young Dutch office worker. As she anticipated, a young male voice came from the passenger window of the rumbling vehicle. "*Nizza kleid, junge Frau.*"

Jenny maintained her pace. *Nice dress, young woman.* That comment sounded harmless enough. She turned to face the caller. "*Danke.*" She suppressed a smile as she studied the smooth cheeks under the helmet.

With a squeak of brakes, the truck stopped and a new voice, deeper and older, came from somewhere in the vehicle. "*Schöne beine.*"

Heat rose in Jenny's cheeks. *Nice legs indeed, you big fool.* The truck crept along beside her, its engine idling, and its large wheels crunching on the pavement. She looked ahead. The sign on the next building read *Bramer Fine Lederwaren*. She quickened her pace, eyes trained on the door. As her hand grasped the handle, the voice returned. "Auf Wiedersehen."

Jenny yanked the door open and stepped inside. The delicious scent of leather welcomed her. The place hummed with activity. Some men were cutting large sheets of tanned leather into usable pieces. Skilled workers, mostly middle-aged men, ran the stitching machines that produced the final products. Young workers, men and women, carried materials to the machine operators and toted away finished products. Missing were the common consumer products like handbags. Now the finished products consisted of boots, heavy belts, and pistol holsters. Two German soldiers leaned on the wall, silently observing the operation.

She scanned the large room. In the rear part of the building, an open stairway led from the tall production area to a second level overlooking the workspace. She spotted a sign on the upper level that identified the office. As she strode through the factory toward the office, several workers looked up, smiled or nodded, and returned to their work. Before reaching the stairs, she stole a glance at the stone-faced soldiers.

On the office door, another Dutch sign: *Welkom*. She entered without knocking. Inside, the sound of typing ceased. An elderly couple, seated at two large desks at the back of the room, looked up at her. The woman smiled, her hands hovering over the typewriter keys.

The man was first to speak. "Yes, child. How may we help you?"

"I am Jenny DeHaan. I am here about a job."

Expressionless, the elderly man peered over his half-spectacles. "I am Herman Bramer. I own this facility. What type of job interests you, young lady?"

"I have the skills for many jobs, but marketing is my specialty. I do well at placing products where they are most productive."

The man leaned back in his chair. "I assume you have references you could share with me?"

"I am not sure if he is still in business, but I know the owner of Demeester Importers. I am certain he would speak highly of me."

She detected a slight sparkle in the man's eyes.

"I have met Reinaar Demeester," he said. "Nice gentleman. Nice family. In fact, one son is about your age."

Jenny searched for the right words. "Yes. Marten." She looked deeply into the man's eyes and nodded slightly before she continued. "As a matter of fact, it was Marten who urged me to speak to you. He said that you and I shared many interests. He seemed quite sure I would fit perfectly into your organization."

The tension seemed to drain from Bramer's weathered face. He reached across his desk and grasped her hand. "It is an honor to meet you. This is my wife, Antje."

The woman smiled. She was about to speak when her phone rang, and she turned her attention to the caller.

Mr. Bramer stood and beckoned to Jenny. "Please come into my office. We can discuss your marketing ideas."

They retreated to an inner office, and Bramer closed the door. "Thank you for your caution, young lady. That is a critical trait these days. I expect you are here regarding a certain young man."

"Yes. Joran. I am planning to make him a guest in our home."

"Excellent. While I am confident in the family's safety, he could use some outside experiences. He feels very confined here. Quite normal for a young man his age."

"May I speak openly with your wife?"

"Absolutely. Antje and I work together."

Bramer pulled a gold pocket watch from his vest, glanced at it, snapped the cover shut, and slid the timepiece back into its small pocket. "Here is my tentative plan. It is now three thirty. The Demeesters are prepared for your arrival. My workers will depart at four. The soldiers should leave soon thereafter. At four thirty, the factory next door will empty. That would be the ideal time for you and Joran to blend into the departing crowd. Sound good?"

"Perfect."

Herman opened the closet door behind his desk. In back was a bookcase which he pulled open. It turned on its hinges, revealing another door.

Francien stood at the sink, hands immersed in soapy water. Behind her at the kitchen table, Reinaar and Joran were deeply engaged in a chess game, a daily activity since their arrival in the hidden apartment. She placed the last plate in the drying rack and pulled the drain plug. In the relative silence of draining dishwater and the creak of chairs, her mind roamed the past. The opulence of the old days, joy on the faces of her small children, holding them close when they hurt. Her tight face relaxed.

"Checkmate." Joran's excited voice filled the place.

Suspense hung in the air, waiting for the father's response.

It came in the form of a deep laugh, the first Francien had heard since the move. "I have done too well. The student has defeated the master. Joran, I am proud of you."

The sound of a buzzer echoed through the small apartment.

Renewed tension gripped Francien's chest. Was it Herman bringing supplies? News maybe? Or was it a raid? She waited, staring at the blank wall in front of her.

Leaving the chess pieces in place, father and son moved to the door adjoining the office of Herman Bramer. Reinaar drew back the door, exposing the expectant faces of Herman and Jenny, both standing in the small storage closet. They entered the apartment quietly, and Reinaar eased the door closed behind them.

With privacy restored, Reinaar welcomed the guests. "Ah, Herman, my friend, you have brought the most beautiful young lady I have seen in some time, with the exception of my lovely wife, of course." He hugged her.

Jenny looked up at Joran. "Oh, my goodness. The last time I saw you I was taller than you."

"There isn't much to do these days. I just spend my time eating my mother's good cooking, playing the cello, and growing. Can I go outdoors at the farm? Out into the sun?"

"More than that. My father needs a strong young man to help run the farm. You are just what he needs."

Joran brightened. "How about the cello. Can I bring it?"

"I don't see why not."

Francien observed in silence from the kitchen door.

"Is it okay, Mama?"

Francien leaned into the doorframe and blinked at the tears. It was not okay. She might never see him again. But he must survive. She managed a weak smile. "It will be okay, Joran, but just for a while, until this war is over. Then we will come and get you. You'll see."

Herman checked his pocket watch. "My employees are now departing. It would be best if Jenny and Joran left the building when the employees next door are leaving. They will blend quite well into the crowd. With your permission, Francien, we should move to the front door soon."

Francien pulled Jorah tightly to herself and looked at Herman through a flood of tears. "I will get his suitcase."

"I have a suggestion," said Herman. "I could arrange for his personal items to be delivered to the DeHaan home. It would not draw the attention of the authorities. A young man and his cello, walking with his sister, will not be a problem."

"Thank you, my friend," Reinaar said. "And I have one more thing to ask of you. In addition to the suitcase with his belongings, I have another one full of cash that needs to go to Jenny's home as well. I am hopeful they will hide it for us until after the war."

"Absolutely," Jenny said. "Joran and I will bury the money as soon as we get it."

"Certainly. I will deliver both cases today," Herman said without hesitation.

"There is a third suitcase. A bit smaller, but also full of cash. It is for you, Herman, to do with as you see fit."

The man nodded. "It will be put to good use."

Reinaar handed the identification documents to his son. "For the next few months, until we can safely bring you back home, your name is Joran Elzinga."

"Right. Elzinga. I will remember."

Reinaar clutched his son to himself and kissed the top of the boy's head. "We will come when we can."

CHAPTER TWENTY-EIGHT

28 April 1943
Amsterdam

Colonel Ernst Schmidt slumped in the leather wingback chair in the drawing room of the former Demeester home, now his personal residence. He planted one gleaming boot on the slightly dusty coffee table and rested the other on the Oriental rug.

Footsteps echoed in the hall. Willem Barkman appeared in the doorway, gazing over his half-eye reading glasses.

Schmidt flipped open a carved wood humidor on the coffee table and gestured to it with a lazy open hand. "Cigar, Barkman? They're Cuban. The Jew left plenty behind."

"Thank you. No."

Schmidt pointed to a matching wingback chair a few feet away. "Okay then, sit. Let's talk."

The accountant, frown lines between his eyebrows deepening, eased himself into the chair and eyed the Gestapo colonel.

Schmidt prolonged the suspense by slowly preparing a long cigar using a small guillotine cutter left behind by the previous occupants. After lighting it, he blew a smoke ring toward the ceiling. "All right, Herr Barkman, you have pored over the Jew's paperwork full-time since we raided this place. It's been two weeks, plus a couple of days. Frankly, my patience is wearing a bit thin."

He paused until the nervous man made full eye contact. "Now, tell me what you know."

Barkman's bald head took on an increased sheen with the appearance of perspiration. "Demeester was very good. He hid his tracks well. It's a shame that his accountant is not available. We could learn a lot from him. He is dead, is he not?"

Schmidt shrugged. "Dead and gone. Suffered an unfortunate fall at Mauthausen, I am told." He tapped some cigar ashes into a ceramic vase resting on a nearby table. "Proceed."

"Well, his lifestyle indicates strongly that he had far more resources than I am able to locate. I think he has funds hidden away, and I don't believe we will find them without his, uh, cooperation."

Schmidt placed both boots on the floor and leaned over the table. His eyes bored into those of the accountant. "Then tell me where he is."

"As a matter of fact, I discovered something interesting yesterday."

"Enlighten me."

Barkman swallowed. "On one of the many innocuous documents in his wastebasket, I found a small, scribbled note. On it was written 'call Bramer.'"

"That's it?"

"There was no phone number. However, when I searched through Demeester's listing of contacts, I found a listing for Bramer Fine Lederwaren. It's in the warehouse district. We are doing a lot of business with them. I can't find any evidence of business dealings between Demeester and that operation for months. The note just popped up. I'm curious about it."

A smile crept onto the face of Ernst Schmidt. "I believe I will pay them a visit."

Colonel Ernst Schmidt, accompanied by Karl Müller, entered the front door of Herman Bramer's factory, took a few steps forward, and stopped. Wearing his gray uniform, similar to the SS except for a plain black collar patch and green shoulder boards, Schmidt lifted his chin, put his hands on his hips, and waited for the expected reaction.

Workmen who noticed his arrival glanced up, then quickly gave full attention to their tasks. Two young Wehrmacht soldiers, a lieutenant and a sergeant, rushed to him, snapped a sharp Nazi salute, and stood at attention.

Schmidt frowned at the soldiers. "What is your job here?"

The lieutenant responded without losing his rigid pose. "We are ensuring that the work here meets German standards, Colonel."

"And you know the facility well?"

"We have both worked here for over a month, sir."

"Good. You will be assisting me today. Follow me." Schmidt strode to the factory office with the young men in tow. The workers seemed to ignore them as they passed.

When Schmidt reached the office door, he turned to his two new assistants. "Wait right here." He opened the office door, walked inside, and stopped. After completing a quick scan of the room, he turned his attention to the elderly man facing him. He detected fear in the man's eyes and posture.

Schmidt continued to study the man as he waited for a response.

The man blinked, cleared his throat, and looked down at his hands. "May I help you, sir?"

"My name is Schmidt. I represent *Geheime Staatspolizei*. Most call us Gestapo. Who are you?"

"I am Herman Bramer." He swallowed with difficulty. "I own this facility."

"Well, Herr Bramer, I believe you can help me." He paused to allow tension to grow. "What do you know about Reinaar Demeester?"

The words hit the old man like an electric shock. His head jerked. He blinked, and his eyes widened. Color drained from his cheeks.

With a well-developed air of supreme confidence and total domination, Schmidt stood erect, folded his arms, and studied the stress on the old man's face.

Bramer held his blinking gaze somewhere over Schmidt's shoulder. The jaw muscles on his lined cheeks swelled as his pale lips pressed together. A slight tremor gripped his frail body.

The experienced interrogator waited patiently.

Bramer blinked several times and drew a deep breath. "I have known Herr Demeester for a number of years. He purchased many of my products for further sale. I have not seen him for a couple of months now."

"Do you know his family, his living arrangements?"

"We had only a business relationship. I know he owned at least two residences. I had no social associations with him or his family. They are Jewish, and I am Calvinist."

Schmidt raised his gloved hand and eased Bramer's chin into alignment with his own and waited until their eyes locked. He looked deeply into those eyes, searching for panic. He found it.

The colonel turned to the empty desk. "Who works here?"

"My wife, Antje. We run the business together. She is at home right now."

Schmidt rolled back the chair behind Antje's desk, sat, and rested his gleaming boots on the desktop. "Herr Bramer, I have reached a conclusion." He stroked his smooth-shaven chin and paused for a few seconds. "I have no doubt you are lying to me."

Beads of perspiration appeared among the few remaining hairs on the top of Bramer's head. "No, sir."

Schmidt held up a gloved hand. "Oh, but you are, in fact, lying. You see, Herr Bramer, I am very good at my job. The secret to my success is that I read people's actions and their eyes." He tapped a gloved index finger below his eye. "Your eyes reveal truths that are hidden in your words. You were shocked when I appeared, no surprise there, but you were shattered when I mentioned Reinaar Demeester's name. Yes, you are indeed lying to me."

"But I told you the truth, sir. I have associated with Demeester in my business, but nothing recently. I am fearful because you are Gestapo. Everyone is afraid of Gestapo."

Schmidt dismissed the comment with a wave of the back of his hand. "It's decision time, Bramer. I want to find Reinaar Demeester. Tell me where he is."

"I don't know where he is."

Schmidt paused while the tension in the room grew. "That picture on your desk there. Who are those people?"

"That is my family. My wife, my daughter, and my grandchildren."

Ernst Schmidt felt a smile growing on his lip. He reached and pulled the desk phone to himself, then pulled off his gloves and dialed a number. While waiting for a response, he studied Bramer's puzzled expression.

"Colonel Weber, Schmidt here. Would it be possible for you to send me a package from your satellite facility? Yes, one of those. For interrogation purposes. Good. I'll send an assistant. His name is Müller. He will arrive shortly."

He replaced the phone and walked to the door. Karl and the two soldiers, sitting in nearby chairs, jumped to their feet. Schmidt frowned. "Müller, take the car to Schouwburg and ask for Colonel Weber. He has a package for you. Bring it here."

Schmidt closed the door and looked at Bramer. The old man's face was pale and drawn. The German pulled out a cigarette. "Now we wait."

Thirty minutes later, an exhausted Herman Bramer sat at his desk, sustained by the adrenaline coursing through his aged body. What evil device were they bringing? Surely to wring the truth from him. *He's going to torture me. I will not talk. Better for an old man to die.* If only he could warn his family. A sharp knock jolted him. He gripped the arms of his chair.

Ernst Schmidt dropped a half-burned cigarette on the floor, alongside three other butts, and crushed it with his heel. "Enter."

Karl Müller walked into the room, carrying a small boy in his arms. The child appeared to be about three years old with sandy-colored, well-trimmed hair. He wore a white shirt and short, black pants with suspenders. With one arm draped around Karl's neck, the child scanned the room. He seemed relaxed, curious about the new surroundings. The boy leaned his head on Karl's shoulder.

"The boy seems taken with you, Müller," said Schmidt.

Karl grinned. "Guess so. I have a nephew his age. They even look a bit alike."

A deep frown pulled at Schmidt's eyebrows. His voice took on an edge. "Time to make an important distinction, Müller. Your nephew is Aryan. This creature, even if he has some Aryan features, is a documented Jew." He pointed to a worktable near the two desks. "Put it there." Karl placed the child in a chair at the table. Schmidt pointed toward the factory area. "Before you sit, Müller, go out there and get a hammer, a heavy one."

The little boy turned his full, silent attention to Schmidt. The German glared at the child for a moment, then turned and looked at a puzzled Herman Bramer.

Karl returned in less than a minute, carrying a two-pound sledgehammer. "Like this?"

"Exactly." Schmidt smiled at the little boy. "What is your name?"

The child grinned. "Alec."

Schmidt turned to Herman Bramer. A deep frown replaced the smile. "Herr Bramer, I am accustomed to getting what I want. Fortunately, I am in a position to achieve my goals with few restrictions. It is clear to me that you have information I need. It is also clear you are quite resolved to withhold that information. So, here is what we are going to do. I will ask you a question, and you will answer. If your answer does not satisfy me, Müller here is going to break the boy's arm with that hammer. Then I will ask you the question again. If you lie, we continue the process." He shrugged. "I guess until the child dies."

Schmidt paused and studied the faces in the room. Karl's eyes were wide, and his mouth hung slightly open. The child sat, perfectly quiet, seeming to absorb Schmidt's every word without comprehending. Herman felt an ache below his pounding heart.

Schmidt turned to Herman, waited until he had eye contact, and continued, "If necessary, we will get more small Jews. There are plenty more where this one came from. We will go through the same thing all over again." He paused while his words drove a nail into Herman's heart. "I trust that you fully comprehend what is happening here, Bramer."

The objects in the room began to drift in front of Herman. Vague spots appeared. The sound of Schmidt's voice began to fade.

He felt Schmidt's hand shaking him by the shoulder. "Don't leave us now, Herr Bramer. You wouldn't want to sleep through the excitement, would you?"

Herman gripped the arms of his chair and clenched his jaws. His perception cleared.

The Nazi leaned back in his chair, lifted his boots onto the desk, and folded his arms. "Let us begin. Herr Bramer. Where are the Demeesters hiding?"

Panic enveloped Herman. Despite being clamped to the chair, his hands trembled. He cleared his throat and forced a barely audible response. "I can't tell you what I don't know. Please don't hurt the child."

Schmidt turned to Karl. "You know what to do, Müller."

Karl's wide eyes blinked several times. His breath came in short gasps. "Um ..."

"Müller, your future with the German Reich will be decided here and now. It's easy. Just hold the Jew's hand so he can't move. Then smash his arm."

Karl held the boy's tiny hand, extended it over the table, and slowly lifted the sledge. He held it high above the table, closed his eyes, and brought it down hard. The sound of the impact, mixed with the child's scream, echoed around the room.

Schmidt jumped to his feet with such force that he drove his rolling desk chair into the wall behind him. "You missed, you fool! All you did was scare the Jew."

A dent the size of the hammer's head, located a couple of inches from the boy's forearm, gave silent testimony to Karl's failure.

"You know those camps where all the Jews are going, Müller?"

"Yes, Colonel Schmidt."

"Should you fail again, I'm going to send you to one of those places. Do it right this time."

Alec's crying stopped. Sniffling, he studied Karl's movements.

Karl lifted the hammer slowly, held it high, and clamped his jaws tight. From somewhere deep in his chest, a growl rose. The hammer began its descent.

"Stop!" Herman Bramer's shout filled the room. His head drooped toward his chest. "Please stop," he murmured.

Karl arrested the hammer's fall just in time to gently tap the tabletop beside the child's quivering arm.

Schmidt turned to Herman and spoke in a quiet voice, almost a whisper. "You may tell me now, Herr Bramer. Where are they?"

"They have a hidden apartment, directly behind me." Strength drained from Herman's body, leaving him weak almost to the point of paralysis.

The colonel stood and tapped the wall behind Herman. "Very nice. A solid brick wall. I expect that the occupants didn't even hear what just happened on our side. Nevertheless, we must act quickly."

Schmidt sat on the edge of Herman's desk. He lifted the telephone receiver and dialed a number. Twisting the phone cord around his left index finger, he brought the receiver to his smiling face. "This is Schmidt. I need a police transport vehicle at Bramer Fine Lederwaren on Van Beuningenstraat. We have an arrest to make. This is priority one. Don't delay. I also want two Gestapo investigators for a search."

Schmidt stood. "Well now, Herr Bramer, gather your strength, and show me the entrance to your little hideaway."

Francien Demeester set her knitting on her lap and peered over the top of her bifocals. Reinaar was sitting on the couch across the small room, reading a book. Two small tabletop lamps provided the only light. She smiled. "Look at us, Reinaar. You are wearing a suit and tie. I am wearing my favorite dress and high heels. We really don't need to do that."

"Somehow, it helps me feel normal, dear."

"I suppose you're right." Francien returned to her knitting for a few moments, then glanced at a family portrait on the wall. "I find myself constantly thinking about the children. I wish I could hold them in my arms right now."

Reinaar looked up from his book. "The same for me. I remember how our house in The Hague was always so full of sound and life. Things have changed a great deal in a short time."

Francien sighed. "I worry a great deal about Marten. I fear that he is involved in dangerous things. Things he is not sharing with us. And Joran ... there is something about the youngest one. I miss him immensely." She paused for a moment. "But I don't fear for him. He will do well with the DeHaan family. I do hope he retains his Jewish—"

The click of a key in a lock grasped Francien's attention. "Marten?"

"It's the other door," said Reinaar, rising from his chair. "It must be Herman."

Ernst Schmidt strolled out of the shadows, followed by two men in German army uniforms. A Luger pistol hung loosely in Schmidt's right hand. "So the Demeesters have found a new home. How nice." He tightened his grip on the pistol and aimed it at Reinaar's chest. "Get up slowly and keep your hands where I can see them. You are now the property of the German Reich."

Francien's raging heart drove her pulse up into her neck, and her lungs demanded air in giant gulps. The people and objects in the room started to drift lazily in front of her. She attempted to stand. Her body refused. She felt Reinaar's strong hands on her arm and around her shoulders, giving her the strength to get up. Cradled by her husband, her mind cleared, and her vision returned.

A second SS officer and two men in dark suits entered the small apartment, followed by Karl Müller. He approached Schmidt. "The van is waiting outside."

"Karl?" Reinaar said. "I suspected but didn't want to believe. What did we do that turned you against us? Were we not kind? Did we not treat you as family?"

Karl looked at him for a brief second before his gaze dropped to the floor.

Colonel Schmidt checked his wristwatch. He turned to the SS soldier at his side. "Load them in the van immediately. We still have time to deliver these Jews to the train before today's departure for Westerbork. Leave a man behind to watch Bramer. Don't let him near a phone."

With Reinaar's strong arms supporting Francien, they made their way out of the apartment. As they passed Karl Müller, his gaze was fixed on the floor.

Ernst Schmidt watched the soldiers escort their prisoners from the apartment. Karl Müller and two Gestapo men remained with him. "These Jews are, or should I say, were, very rich. I am convinced that we have not discovered most of their wealth. We need to turn this place upside down. They must have valuables hidden here."

The men went to work. In only a few minutes, Karl Müller spoke up. "I found something." Karl had his hand on a small oil painting that depicted a Dutch scene with windmills and spring flowers. He pulled on the left side of the picture, and it swung away from the wall. "There's a safe behind this thing."

One of the Gestapo men hurried up with a medical stethoscope. "No problem." In a few minutes, he opened the safe.

Schmidt laid out the contents on the kitchen table. "Jewels and cash, and lots of it. I knew we would find it." He then swept the contents into a leather briefcase.

"I guess Demeester isn't so smart after all," said Karl. "That safe wasn't difficult to find."

"Perhaps," said Schmidt. "Or he simply offered these things to us, thinking we would stop looking. No, I think there is more."

Thirty minutes of additional searching revealed nothing new.

Schmidt turned to one of his lieutenants. "All right, that's it. We are done here." He lifted the briefcase from the table. "I'll take this case back to headquarters. You arrange for the artwork to be taken to the warehouse. They must be valuable." He paused. "Except for that little one covering the safe. It looks modern, maybe even a family painting. I wouldn't want that to go to the Führer. The furniture is also junk. They can throw it out."

"What about the old man? He's still sitting in his office, cuffed to his chair."

Schmidt paused for a moment, then shrugged. "Take him out in the street and shoot him. It might discourage other Dutchmen from sheltering Jews."

The group left the apartment and entered the factory office. Schmidt brushed past Herman without a glance. Approaching the door, a picture on the wall caught his attention. He stopped and examined it. The Bramer family, with Herman at its center, looked back at him. A young boy, about seven or eight, smiled into the camera. He was resting a hand on his grandfather's shoulder and cradling a violin under the other arm. Schmidt leaned closer and examined the blond hair, the smile, the eyes. A vague discomfort crept into his mind. Then it hit him. *He looks like my Hans.* Yes, that was it.

With a quick look at the exhausted old man handcuffed to his chair, Schmidt forced his military bearing back to the surface and turned to his lieutenants. "This factory is vital to the Reich. We need Herr Bramer's services here. Release him."

Chapter Twenty-Nine

28 April 1943

Francien gazed out the train window. A colorful scene of lush meadows, green trees, and fields of multicolored spring flowers glided past. The view took the edge off her gnawing tension. Abruptly, the scene changed as they slowed and passed through a village. Life outside the window seemed in utter contrast with her world in the locked car. On both sides of the rolling train, people hurried in various directions. Only a few turned to look, surely unaware that a few of the cars contained special passengers.

One man sitting on a bench offered a casual wave. A young couple strolled arm-in-arm, eyes only for each other. Children, in view of their teacher, played outside their village school. Their laughing and shouting briefly pierced the steel and glass walls of the carriage. Then, the village was gone, and peaceful farm fields reappeared. A man leading a dairy cow into his barn paused for a moment to watch them pass.

Francien shifted her gaze to her husband, whose focus was also riveted on the passing scene. "I never fully appreciated the beauty of Holland."

Reinaar, without speaking, lifted her hand and gave it a gentle squeeze.

For several minutes, she gazed out the window and listened to the rhythmic clicking of the wheels and the chugging of the locomotive as it mindlessly carried its captive passengers to an unknown future. Francien felt a bond with the other people in the carriage. All carried the yellow-star label of Jew. All had tight faces and tired eyes. *We're all the same, with the same fate.*

The train rolled to a stop at the Amersfoort station. While the captive Jews remained locked in their compartments, some of the free passengers embarked from the train. Others boarded. The locomotive returned to work, pulling its load into motion with escalating chugs.

Francien glanced at the bolt on the compartment door. "Where exactly is Westerbork?"

"Way up in the northeast part of the country, in Drenthe province. It's a really isolated place. I was there once. Back in 1939, German Jewish refugees were assisted there. Now the SS owns it."

After a while, the chugging of the locomotive eased, the train slowed, and the squealing brakes dragged it to a stop in another small town.

"This is Nijkerk," said Reinaar. "The DeHaan farm is somewhere nearby."

Francien gripped his hand and put her nose to the window. "Joran. He's here?" She looked again at the bolt on the door. An ache took hold of her chest. "I miss him so much it hurts me inside." An image of her son, tan and strong and standing in a sunny farmer's field, filled her mind. "But this is a pretty place. It's peaceful. And Jenny is nice. Joran will be fine here, right?"

Reinaar squeezed her hand. "He will be fine."

The train chugged back to life and rolled on.

At Hooghalen, the cars carrying the Jewish captives were separated from the train and routed to a separate rail. "This would be the line taking us to Westerbork," said Reinaar.

After a five-kilometer trip through the Drenthe moorland, a camp appeared, surrounded by electrified barbed-wire fence complete with guard towers. A gate swung open, and the train crept into the enclosure and squeaked to a stop.

"What a dreary place," said Francien. "Just a collection of ugly wooden buildings, all lined in rows. The streets are no more than dirt."

"And the people," Reinaar said. "Their faces. Tight, afraid. No smiles anywhere. There is a blanket of fear hanging over this place."

"And we are adding our own fear to the poisonous atmosphere."

Men wearing green coveralls and military caps appeared. One unlocked the compartment and opened the door without comment.

Reinaar and Francien stepped out. A low overcast sky hung over them. Several hundred people, all wearing yellow stars, exited the train and stood outside, waiting.

"The guards don't look like SS," said Francien. "They are wearing the yellow stars, just like ours."

"I've heard about them," said Reinaar. "They are the OD, *Ordedienst,* the Jewish police force here in the camp. They work for the SS. The Germans are the puppeteers pulling the strings. These guys are on the end of the strings. Maybe they think they can climb those strings to safety."

The guards, with a cold, detached courtesy, ushered the crowd into a large nearby building that bore the name *Transportaufnahme.*

"Ah, the reception department. Looks like we register here," said Reinaar with a wry smile. "Just like a fine hotel."

Inside, the trainload of arrivals endured the tedious process of visiting several stations, guided by unsmiling and often rude OD men. After waiting patiently in lines and completing numerous forms, Reinaar and Francien came to yet another station. The man behind this desk peered up, met Francien's eyes, and brightened. "Mr. and Mrs. Demeester, it is good to see you both." He paused for a moment while he looked all around. His face became sober, and his voice lowered. "Actually, I am truly sorry we are meeting in these circumstances."

There in front of Francien sat a familiar and friendly face, the first since their arrest. Jacob Siegel, a childhood friend and synagogue member. The room somehow brightened. Her body gathered strength. Her husband's face took on some color.

"I did not realize you had been brought here, Jacob," said Reinaar. "How is your family?"

"Unfortunately, they are here with me, my wife and two children. We have been here for six months."

Reinaar leaned closer. "And, if I may ask, what is your role here?"

"I am a member of the Antragstelle department. We are authorized to apply for exemptions for the prisoners here."

Francien's heart jumped. "What kind of exemptions?"

"From deportation to the other camps. Almost every Tuesday a train leaves here loaded with people."

"Then what?"

"We do not know, Francien. However, the possibility of transport causes much anxiety in the camp."

"And who makes the assignments for transport?" asked Reinaar.

"The camp commandant receives an order to deliver a specific number of persons on that week's transport. The Jewish leadership, appointed by the SS, then makes the assignments."

A deep frown etched Reinaar's forehead. "I expect the process you describe causes a great deal of tension among the Germans' guests."

"There are many desperate people here. Things get especially uncomfortable in the camp on Mondays of every week. Today is Wednesday. Relief is in the air. It fades as the week passes."

Reinaar's voice lowered. "Can you help us, Jacob? It appears you may be our only hope in this awful place."

"We explore all possibilities, Reinaar. Tell me if there are any circumstances we can use to plead your case."

"I am a very successful businessman with expertise in accounting. Francien is a qualified nurse. We could provide some benefit here."

"Good. You both have valuable skills. I will record these things."

Jacob then studied the records related to the Demeesters. His eager expression faded. A furrow appeared between his brows. "Oh. This is a problem."

Francien's face grew limp. Her shoulders sagged. "What problem?"

He looked at her over his wire-rimmed spectacles. "This report indicates you were arrested while hiding in Amsterdam. You have been assigned to the punishment barracks."

Francien leaned over the table, her hands trembling. "What does that mean?"

"Your activities will be tightly controlled. It has three barracks and is ringed with its own barbed wire fence."

Reinaar put his arm around Francien's shoulder and pulled her gently to himself. "And what impact will this assignment have on future transports?"

Jacob responded while looking down at the papers. "I am sorry. I don't know. Final transport assignments are out of my control." He finally looked up at Reinaar. "But we always do our best to help." He turned and nodded at the waiting OD escort, who stood tall in his green coveralls with arms folded. Then, he added the Demeester file to the stack on his desk and shifted his gaze to the next person in line.

The OD man, expressionless, beckoned to the Demeesters and headed for the door, his charges closely in tow. The sky had darkened, and light rain fell. Their OD escort quickened the pace. "We have one more stop before I take you to your barracks."

Francien, still wearing the high-heeled shoes that she wore when arrested, struggled to keep up. The dirt road was turning to mud, and her stylish shoes were becoming a detriment to her. She gripped Reinaar's arm for support.

The officer stopped and waited for them to catch up. "I have a suggestion for you. We are going to the quarantine barracks. Some vultures from Lippmann Rosenthal will be taking your valuables. If you want to keep any of your jewelry, I can hold them for you. I will return them when we leave." He studied Reinaar's open suit coat. "Except for that gold pocket watch. I'll keep it for myself, as my commission." He then turned to Francien. "I suggest we hide your best rings and hand over the others, along with your necklace. We must satisfy the thieves with something. I will also keep the pin in your hair."

Anger rose inside Francien. Her jaw tightened. "That pin came from my mother, and her mother."

The man shrugged. "Fine. I'll return that to you as well. I'm not greedy. Oh, one more thing. Put most of your cash in your shoe for now."

The three of them scanned the area. Reinaar and Francien removed their most-treasured items and handed them to the officer. Reinaar quickly pulled most of the cash from his wallet and stuffed it into his shoe.

They entered the building and joined the line of other new arrivals. Their escort held back and watched the process. Francien drew close to her husband and lowered her voice. "Do you think that man will return our things?"

"Probably not." He nodded at the well-dressed men behind the first table. Their suits were free of yellow stars. "But these vultures will definitely not give them back."

When their turn came, things happened as their escort promised. The two officials, expressionless, sat behind the heavy wooden table with a metal lockbox and a logbook. The man, his pen poised over the book, glanced at the wall clock, then, with a bored expression, looked up at Reinaar. "We must have all your valuables, cash, jewelry, everything of value. Don't be concerned. We will keep careful documentation and return the items at the appropriate time. It is all for your security. There are many people staying here."

Francien felt anger rising inside her again. She bit her lip and turned to her husband.

Reinaar offered his best professional smile. "Thank you for this service. I am afraid we have only limited jewelry to offer. The men who arrested us relieved us of the best things." He pulled his wallet from the side pocket of his suit and smiled again. "They missed this."

The man accepted the wallet and studied Reinaar for a long moment. Apparently satisfied, he opened the wallet and sorted through the remaining cash and documents. He pulled out a small photograph and handed it to Reinaar. "You won't be needing anything else for a while. We will keep it all for you." He passed the wallet to the man beside him, who proceeded to record the contents in his book.

Reinaar took the small picture of his family and slid it into his pocket.

Their OD escort, seeing that the transaction was complete, approached the Demeesters. "One more stop in this building. The barber."

"Why?" asked Francien.

"You are going to the punishment barracks. Everyone there is specially groomed."

The haircuts lasted only a minute or two. The Jewish barber shaved Reinaar's hair and cut Francien's unmanageably short. She clamped her jaws together and looked at a husband she barely recognized.

Outside the building, the rain had stopped, but the dark overcast sky remained.

Francien stopped and turned to the officer. "I believe we have some unfinished business."

The man kept walking and responded to the trailing Demeesters. "Not yet. Follow me."

Francien glared at Reinaar. He responded with a slight shake of the head.

They left the crowded area, proceeded past several large barracks, and finally stopped. The guard pulled a strip of cloth from his pocket. With his right hand, he offered the cloth to Reinaar. With his left, he dropped something into Reinaar's coat pocket. He clipped the cloth strip, marked with a large letter *S*, to Reinaar's sleeve, then repeated the process with Francien "Beginning now, the letter *S* must be clearly displayed."

"Why the S?" asked Francien with an edge in her voice.

"*Strafkompagnie*. You are assigned to the punishment company for something you have done, whatever that was. I just follow my instructions. Unfortunately, you will not have the same freedoms enjoyed by most guests of the German Reich."

They proceeded to a fenced enclosure at the northeast corner of the camp. Inside, three long wooden barracks waited.

As they approached the entrance gate, Francien stopped and turned to their guard. "Our things?"

"I have them," said Reinaar without stopping. "It's okay."

Francien, frowning, hurried to catch up.

At the gate, a man dressed like their escort met them.

The OD man who had accompanied them since their arrival handed the gate guard a form. "New guests." He then turned his back and walked away.

Chapter Thirty

12 May 1943
Amsterdam

Jenny closed the door and switched off the light. Total darkness filled the classroom of the Teacher College next door to the Schouwburg Nursery. She edged across the room, navigating by touching items of furniture, first the teacher's desk, then a row of students' desks. When she reached the window, she raised the heavy blackout curtain. A full moon illuminated the front of the Schouwburg Theater across the deserted street. She moved a chair to the window and began her vigil.

Ten minutes later, a figure wearing a military hat and uniform appeared in the moonlight, ambling from the nursery toward the theater across the street. He opened the front door, allowing light from inside to escape. The German's long shadow reached into the dark street and evaporated into darkness as he went inside.

The classroom door behind Jenny squeaked open and clicked shut. Footsteps creaked across the darkened room. "It's me, Jen." Nic pulled up a chair beside his sister. "See anything?"

Jenny continued her watch. "A guard crossed the street. That means he just completed his rounds. He shouldn't be back for an hour or so."

"He may not return at all if Süskind's party in the back of the building is successful."

"Hopefully, the place will be run by a bunch of drunk and thoroughly distracted Germans tonight. They also need to watch over a few hundred Jewish prisoners in there. That should keep them busy enough."

At the sound of a light knock, Jenny closed the blackout curtain, and Nic opened the classroom door. A young woman wearing a nurse's uniform appeared, her hand holding a tiny flickering candle. "I'm Lena, from the nursery. Everything is ready for you. Herr Süskind's party for the German staff is in full operation. We have six children prepared with permission from their parents."

They moved to the school administrator's office where Mrs. Zuiderveen, one of the college instructors, waited for them.

"Let's do it just like we planned," said Nic.

Zuiderveen nodded. "We must assume our calls are monitored." She pushed her phone across the desk to Nic.

He dialed a number and returned the phone to the teacher. She listened for a moment. "Mr. Ahrens," she said, "we will need your help tomorrow. A class needs a teacher. Can you come?"

Marten Demeester's voice came from the handset. "I understand. I will be there."

"Very good. We will expect you." Mrs. Zuiderveen set the phone in its cradle.

"Excellent," Jenny said. "Marten will be here shortly. We need to go, Nic. Thanks for your help, Mrs. Zuiderveen."

"I will be praying for your success, children."

Lena led them out the back door of the college. From the moonlit area, she pushed through the hedge into the adjoining garden and entered the back door of the nursery.

After passing through the darkened entryway, they entered a fully equipped children's playroom. Multiple bins filled with stuffed animals and toys for all age groups lined the wall. Several small balls rested in a miniature soccer goal tucked into an isolated corner.

Six sober-faced children sat around a playhouse in the center of the room. Each child held a bulging cloth bag.

Lena smiled. "Children, these nice people are here to take you to new places where you can stay until your parents can bring you back to your own homes."

Jenny knelt beside a small boy, about four years old, who was biting his lip and wiping tears from his face. "Hi, sweetheart. I'm Jenny. What's your name?"

"Max." He frowned. "I want my mommy. I want to go home now."

Jenny smoothed his hair. "We all want that for you, Max, but for a while, you need to stay with new friends, just until your parents can come back. Okay?"

After a pause, the boy responded with a whisper. "Okay."

Nic touched Jenny's shoulder. "We need to move up front."

They proceeded to the reception area in the front of the nursery and entered the director's office. After closing the door and turning off the lights. Nic raised the blackout curtains. The moonlit façade of the Schouwburg faced them, dark and silent.

Jenny leaned close to the glass, peering up the street. "Something's coming."

"A car?"

"Can't tell yet." Jenny studied the lights for a few seconds. "Yes, a car."

The vehicle's headlights, mostly tape-covered, allowed a small beam to escape. It eased to a stop at the curb in front of the nursery. The two flags on the front bumper hung lifeless. The headlights went dark.

"It's him, Nic."

The front door of the theater opened. Light from inside the building flooded the dark street. Jenny caught her breath.

A man in a German army uniform emerged and closed the door, wobbling like his knees were not entirely reliable. He leaned against the building, reached inside his coat, and pulled out a pack of cigarettes. With fumbling fingers, he managed to light one. The ember glowed as he inhaled.

The man pushed himself from the wall and ambled toward the Mercedes. As he neared the car, Marten emerged. The interior lights came alive, revealing Marten's SS uniform. He stood erect and tucked his thumbs into his belt.

The inebriated soldier forced his reluctant body into an erect posture and dropped his cigarette. "Good evening, sir," he managed.

Marten approached the man and jabbed a finger to his chest. "You are a disgrace, you drunken fool. Get back inside. I'll be there shortly."

The soldier turned around, steadied himself, and staggered a few steps, stopping when the theater door swung open again, revealing a German in an officer's uniform. The man closed the door and stood motionless, facing the situation in the street. After pausing for a long moment, he strode toward the two men.

Jenny gasped. "Be careful, Marten," she whispered.

The drunk soldier wavered, turning from one officer to the other.

"Good evening, Colonel," Marten said. "I'm here for Süskind's party."

Without responding, the officer pulled a small flashlight from his pocket and scanned the car, then approached Marten. Using the light, he studied Marten's face and uniform.

Jenny gripped her brother's arm. "He knows."

Jumping back, the German dropped the light and yanked a pistol from his leather holster.

Marten drew his weapon and aimed.

Both guns fired at the same moment. The blast shattered the quiet night air. Both men fell to the ground.

The drunken soldier stood, gaping and rocking side-to-side. With one last look at the dead officer, he gathered himself and forced his drunken body to move toward the theater.

Jenny and Nic bolted from the room and crashed out the front door of the nursery. The smell of gun smoke hung in the air. Marten lay in the street, illuminated by the headlights of the Mercedes. The car's powerful engine purred, unaffected by the unfolding tragedy.

The drunken soldier disappeared into the Schouwburg.

Jenny knelt by her fallen friend. Blood pulsed from his chest. She pressed the wound. "Don't die, Marten. Please don't die," she begged. Warm blood poured over her hand.

Marten attempted to speak. He coughed, and blood ran down his cheek.

Nic pulled off his jacket and pressed it to the wound. The coat quickly went dark with blood.

Marten pointed at Nic. "The money ... buried at the farm." He turned his head and coughed blood. He looked back at Nic and swallowed. "Use it to fight them."

"I will. I promise."

Jenny grasped Marten's hand and held her face close to his. "I love you, Marten."

"I love"—he coughed and squeezed Jenny's hand— "you too, Jen." He coughed several times, still gripping her hand. "Jenny ..."

Tears streamed down Jenny's face. "Yes, Marten."

He gasped for air. "Look after the children."

Through her tears, Jenny watched Marten's chest rise and fall twice, then rest.

She peered deeply into his eyes. His pupils slowly widened as the life in his eyes faded away.

Jenny pulled his silent face to her chest and sobbed. Nic's trembling hand rested on her shoulder. "He's gone, Nic. He left me."

"We must go, Jen. More Germans will come soon."

"And leave him here, lying in the street? No. I'm not going anywhere."

"We must do what we promised him."

She sniffled and drew her arm under her nose. "I can't go on. I'll just die with him."

Nic grasped her arm and pulled her gently but firmly toward the nursery.

Lena, still wearing her white nurse's cap, held the door and beckoned them. "Hurry. Hurry."

A thick fog shrouded Jenny's thoughts. Her heavy legs refused to bear her weight. Relying on Nic's strong arm around her, she moved her feet forward, through the empty playroom and out the back door. She leaned on her brother and focused on moving her feet. She felt the rough leaves of the hedge as her brother forced his way to the college garden.

A voice, hollow and distant, came from the school door. "Quickly children. Come quickly." Jenny blinked and recognized Mrs. Zuiderveen.

The teacher closed the door behind them, grasped Jenny by the shoulders. "Are you hurt, child?"

"No. My friend died out there. He—"

"Up the stairs. Go. They will be coming. We must hide you."

Jenny found a bit of strength and climbed the stairs with her brother's assistance.

Mrs. Zuiderveen led them to an equipment room. She brushed some books from a shelf and opened a hidden door at the back of the bookcase. Nic and Jenny crawled inside.

The small door closed, leaving them in total darkness while the sounds of sirens penetrated their tiny haven.

CHAPTER THIRTY-ONE

19 May 1943
Westerbork Transit Camp

Reinaar admired his wife, still beautiful in spite of roughly cut hair, blue overalls, and wooden clogs on her feet. He reached for her hand and gave it a gentle squeeze.

The reception area of the Westerbork administration building bustled with activity. The Demeesters sat in simple wooden chairs, backs against the wall. Uniformed SS men and their Jewish assistants passed without a hint of recognition.

Francien turned to her husband. "Why did they bring us here?"

"Not for our benefit, I am sure."

A dark-haired man in a nicely tailored suit approached. "Herr Demeester, Frau Demeester, come with me." He turned and walked away.

They exchanged hurried glances and followed him into a nearby office. The man closed the door and motioned them to seats at the conference table. He sat across from them. "My name is Becker. I represent the German Reich. I have the unfortunate responsibility to share some tragic news with you."

Both Demeesters jolted upright in their chairs.

The man's face remained calm and expressionless. "I am sorry to inform you that your son Marten died in an exchange of gunfire with soldiers of the Reich."

The strength evaporated from Reinaar's body. He sank in his chair while his view of the room faded.

Beside him, Francien gasped. She clamped her hand on his arm. "No! You are wrong. You killed someone else, not my son."

Reinaar forced himself upright, studying Becker's face.

Becker's calm demeanor and steady eyes conveyed honesty and maybe a hint of sympathy. He frowned just slightly. "Sadly, I believe I am correct. He was driving a car that we traced to you. Also, he was positively identified."

Reinaar's alertness returned. Anger rose in him. "Identified by whom?"

"I am not permitted to divulge that information."

Reinaar edged to the front of his chair. "You work with a man named Schmidt, do you not?"

Becker's eyes narrowed. He raised his hand, palm forward. Reinaar sat back. Calm returned to Becker's face. "Colonel Schmidt has been removed from this case. We have reason to believe that he made inappropriate use of your resources."

Becker placed his hands on the table. "I want you to know that I understand your loss. I myself have lost a son in the war, and I have taken steps to ensure that your son's body is buried with dignity in the Jewish cemetery."

Francien hugged herself and pressed her face into her husband's shoulder. "I don't want to listen to that man." Reinaar studied his wife's face. Her cheeks were dry, face calm, like she had taken herself to another place.

Becker continued, "I also want to change your status in Westerbork. You have committed no crime except for hiding from the authorities. I have the power to move you out of the punishment barracks and provide you with jobs that will keep you off the transport list."

Reinaar frowned. "There must be more."

"Yes. I must justify my actions with a significant response from you. My analysis leads me to the conclusion that you have control of resources you have not disclosed to the authorities. I am convinced there is money hidden somewhere. Also, I understand you owned a Vermeer painting. We have not located that work."

Becker observed Reinaar for a few seconds. "To justify my favorable actions on your behalf, I will need sufficient information from you to locate these things."

Becker's words seemed to bring Francien back. She sat up in her chair, and her voice came out strong. "Don't tell him anything. We can't trust him. We can't trust any of them."

"We have no choice, dear. It's our only hope. Even without Marten, we must consider our family's future." He studied Becker's expressionless face. "The money is in two locations inside the apartment. There is a wall safe behind a picture." He paused while Becker nodded. "Also, there is a cash box sealed in the wall about five feet to the right of the wall safe."

Becker leaned forward and rested his arms on the table. "Excellent. And the Vermeer?"

"It is also in the apartment. It has been thinly painted over with a contemporary Dutch scene of a windmill. A simple cleaning will expose the original Vermeer."

Becker stood. "I believe we have concluded our meeting. You will return to the punishment barracks until I have confirmed the accuracy of your information." He summoned a guard who led the couple out of the building. They shuffled along in their wooden clogs, Reinaar holding tightly to Francien.

In an officer's suite in the camp, Ernst Schmidt sat alone, perched on the edge of a desk, arms folded. For the third time in the last three minutes, he checked the wall clock.

Becker strode into the office without a knock. Schmidt stood, hooked his thumbs in his gleaming leather belt, and studied Becker's face. Pleased by the man's bright expression, Schmidt's tension eased. "So, how did it go?"

"Quite well, actually. My sense is that he spoke the truth. He confirmed the location of the wall safe, then added new information. There is more cash hidden in a wall."

"Good work, Becker. I thought my plan would work. What about the Vermeer?"

"He said it is hidden there in the apartment, painted over by another picture. He said it could be easily restored."

Schmidt's jaw tightened. He glared at the startled Becker. "Which picture?"

"He said it was covered by a Dutch scene of a windmill."

Schmidt removed a glove, threw it on the desk, and grabbed the desk phone. In his haste, he misdialed on his first attempt but succeeded on the second. He paced to the length of the cord as he waited for a response.

"Krüger, this is Schmidt. Put an immediate guard on the Demeester hiding place. What have you done with the contents?"

"The furniture was all cheap stuff. We trashed it. We locked up the artwork as you ordered."

Schmidt's muscles tightened. "What about that windmill picture?"

"We trashed it along with the furniture."

Schmidt shouted into the phone. "Trashed it! I want that thing, you fool!"

"But you said—"

Schmidt slammed the phone on its cradle.

Becker stood, eyes wide, his face blank like he was searching for words. Finally, he found some. "What about the Demeesters? Should we put them on the next transport to Auschwitz?"

Schmidt looked out the window at the gray Westerbork sky. His rage faded, and he forced himself to process. "No. Keep them here. I'm not done with them yet." He replaced his leather glove, grabbed his ever-present baton, and tapped his open hand a few times. "Reinaar Demeester is a shrewd man. I suspect he only offered us a portion of his money. He must have hidden much more. And there is one more Demeester child out there somewhere. We need to get our hands on him. The father will give us anything to protect that boy."

CHAPTER THIRTY-TWO

27 May 1943
The DeHaan Farm

"She must come out of that room, Albert, or she will sink further." A cloud of flour puffed from the kitchen counter as Emma DeHaan pounded the ball of bread dough. "It's three o'clock, and she has been out only one time to relieve herself. I can't reach her. Could you speak to her?"

Albert studied his wife's tense face. "I will try again."

He knocked softly on the bedroom door. No response. He opened the door a crack. "Jenny? May I come in?"

Silence from the dark room.

He softened his bass voice. "Jenny, sweetheart?"

"Okay, Father."

Albert eased the door open. Light from the hallway illuminated the small bedroom, revealing his daughter covered to her chin by a quilt. He closed the door. A sliver of light appeared through a gap in the window curtain. "May I add some light, Jen?"

"Okay."

Albert opened the curtain. Sunlight flooded the room. Jenny blinked, rose, and then lay back on her pillow. He studied his daughter's face, the pale, hollow cheeks and tired eyes, then sat on the side of the bed and rested his hand on her shoulder. "Could we talk a little bit?"

"Okay."

"It might help if you tell me how you are feeling."

"Like I'm half dead ... and I really wouldn't mind if I were all the way."

"Tell me more."

"My body is so heavy. My mind is so slow. I don't want to do anything at all. I could stay here forever."

Albert lifted Jenny's hand and enveloped it with his own. "And what is your slow mind thinking about?"

"Marten ... always Marten. What he did. What he said. The feel of him. The scent of him. I have a hole in my chest where he was. Will that hole be there forever, Papa?"

"Yes, but it will get smaller as it makes room for other things."

Jenny sat up, and her voice gained strength. "Somehow it was my fault, Papa. Surely I could have done something to keep him alive. Couldn't I?"

Albert plumbed his mind for the right words. They finally came from somewhere inside. He took a slow breath. "Maybe there was something we all could have done, Jenny." He gave her shoulder a gentle pat. "We can never do perfect things. And sometimes things happen that we can't understand. We just do our best and keep moving."

"I loved him, Papa. Did you know that?"

The memories and feelings of young love, long forgotten, captured Albert's mind. "I have been your father for a long time, young lady, and I know things without you telling me. Yes, I knew you loved him. Your mother and I loved him too."

Jenny's eyes widened, and tension shaded her words. "But there's more, Papa. Marten and I came from different worlds, different religions. I want to see him again. Will I?"

Albert paused, searching for an answer to a question that tormented his precious daughter. While he pondered, he gave Jenny's hand repeated gentle pats to encourage her patience.

He drew a deep breath before he responded. "I'm just an old farmer, Jen. I don't know the minds of people, and I surely don't know the mind of God. I only know what is in my heart. My heart tells me that we will see Marten again. My heart tells me that he will be just fine. It is only you—we—who are hurting."

Jenny stared at the ceiling while her father waited. "Thanks, Papa. I feel a little better now." She paused again. "Papa, I think I would like to talk to Joran. Is he nearby?"

Albert smiled. "He's out in the barn. He fell in love with the new calf. I believe I might make a farmer out of that boy. I'll get him." The bed squeaked as he lifted his powerful frame.

Jenny sat up in the bed and watched her dear father stride from the room. She looked out the window at the sun-drenched pasture, then at the mirror on her dresser. A gaunt, pale face with oily, tangled hair stared back at her.

While she was making a vain attempt to get control of her hair, Joran appeared, wearing old clothes that Jenny recognized. "Well, hello, farmer Joran. It looks like Mama saved Nic's old clothes."

"They fit just fine. And I can work almost as hard as Nic." He frowned as he studied Jenny's face. "I hope you're okay."

"I'm a little better. Tell me how you're doing."

Joran sat hard on the bed. The springs creaked, and the tears came. They streamed down his cheeks, onto his plaid shirt. He sniffed several times and leaned toward Jenny.

She pulled him to herself and hugged him while he sobbed.

"My new family is very good to me, and I like the farm." He pulled a handkerchief from his pocket and blew his nose. "But I miss Marten terribly. I wish my mother was here to hug me like you're doing." He tensed and started to pull away. "I'm not being very grown up, am I?"

Jenny pulled him back and held him as his tears and sniffles returned.

After a few moments, Joran calmed, and she relaxed her hug.

He wiped his nose and looked into Jenny's eyes. "I want to talk about Marten. Nic told me how Marten died. He was brave, wasn't he?"

"Yes, he was very brave. And more than that. He loved his family, and he loved the children. He died trying to save the lives of children. That is the greatest love possible, don't you think?"

Joran nodded. "I never had a chance to say goodbye to him. Did you?"

"Yes. I told him I loved him."

"That's good. What did he say?"

"It was hard for him to talk, but he said he loved me too." She paused while Joran continued to study her eyes. "And just before he died, he told me to look after the children."

"Are you going to do that? Don't you think you should do what he said?"

Jenny's clouded mind began to clear. *I must do this.* Of course she would follow Marten's wishes. If only she could get her dull body to function. "I will try, Joran. I will try."

"That's good, Jen." Joran stood. "I need to go back to the barn. Maybe when you feel better, I will introduce you to my new baby calf." He paused at the door and turned back. "Do you think I could be great like my brother?"

"I have no doubt."

Joran sat at the kitchen table with Albert, Emma, and Nic. They held hands and bowed their heads while Albert prayed. "Lord, bless the family in this house. Bless Joran's family where they are. Comfort them and protect them. Thank you for this food and for your love."

After a pause, Joran cleared his throat and spoke. *"Barukh atah Adonai Elohaynu melekh ha-olam ha-motzi lechem min ha-aretz."* Then, with his adolescent voice breaking slightly, he continued, "Blessed are You, Lord, our God, King of the Universe who brings forth bread from the earth."

In unison, the four voices concluded, "Amen."

Albert lifted the lid from the steaming stew and loaded the plates.

The door of Jenny's room squeaked open. "I smell stew and homemade bread. Is there enough for me?"

Nic smiled. "If you hurry."

Jenny took her customary place at the table. A place setting awaited her there.

Her mother slid back her chair, approached Jenny, and kissed her oily hair and whispered, "I love you."

Albert took her plate and loaded it with hot stew and two slices of bread coated with home-churned butter.

"Should we say another blessing?" asked Joran.

Jenny offered a weak smile. "I think we're covered. Your first prayer pulled me out of that cave."

The family ate in silence until the plates were scraped clean. Words were not needed. The love in the air and the nutritious food cleared Jenny's mind and lifted her spirits.

Joran cleared the table, returned to his chair, and turned to Emma.

A broad smile lit up the mother's face. "I believe our adopted son has learned how to hasten the dessert." She placed bowls of strawberries, covered with whipped cream, in front of her family, a double portion for Jenny.

After a few bites of the fruit, she glanced at her brother. "What's happening with the publishing work?"

Nic set down his fork and held up his ink-stained hands. "It goes on. We are reaching a lot of people with the paper, but we have big problems."

"Oh?"

"It all started back in February."

"The university raids?"

"Exactly. When they swept through the Utrecht campus, they grabbed over a hundred students. I was hiding in a closet, and they missed me."

"I remember."

"Well, apparently, the NSB goons learned about that. I lost my anonymity around campus. Then, I ignored the directive to sign the loyalty pledge. The April deadline passed."

Jenny set her spoon into her dish. "So where do we stand right now?"

"Men between eighteen and thirty-five have been ordered to report for work in Germany."

Jenny attempted to run her fingers through her hair, felt the disorder, and brought her hand back to the table. "It looks like it's time for you to go into hiding. Just disappear for a while. There is a lot I can do. I am still free to move around the country."

"There is a big problem with that, Jen. The NSB is watching me. If I disappear, I think they will go after my family. I can't let that happen."

Their parents eyed each other across the table. Emma scraped her chair back from the table. "I can't listen to all this talk. My son going to Germany where bombs are falling. My whole family in danger any way we turn." She went to the sink and pumped water to wash dishes.

Albert inhaled deeply, drummed his rough fingers on the table, and slowly exhaled. "When will you report, Nicolaas?"

"Tomorrow, early. I have considered this carefully, Father. I must remove pressure on the family. When the time is right, I will find a way to return."

Jenny ate the last of her strawberries and pushed back her chair. "I have children to look after."

Chapter Thirty-Three

June 1943
Chelveston, England

The *Barbara Jean* waited at the end of the runway, engines roaring. Inside, bombardier Richard DeGraaf gazed through the plexiglass bubble on the nose of the giant B-17. From his vantage point extending beyond the front of the airplane, nothing obstructed his view. A thousand feet ahead, another Flying Fortress raced toward the end of the steel-matted takeoff strip. Beyond that speeding plane, more than a hundred four-engine heavy bombers, clones of *Barbara Jean*, were gathering somewhere over the English Channel.

Barbara Jean's tight brakes held it in place as the four Wright Cyclone engines throttled up to full power. The big bird vibrated as its power plants roared and their giant propellers bit the air, straining to move the beast.

Thirty seconds after the preceding bomber began its takeoff roll, the pilots, sitting in the flight deck behind and above bombardier DeGraaf, released the brakes, and *Barbara Jean* was free. The vibrations stopped and the airplane, weighed down with almost three thousand gallons of high-octane gasoline and two and a half tons of bombs, entered its takeoff roll.

The heavy machine bounced occasionally as it rolled, gradually getting lighter as its wings gathered lift. DeGraaf, veteran of twenty bombing missions, watched the end of the runway as it raced closer. His muscles tensed. "Come on, sweetheart. Time to fly."

From behind him came the deep voice of the engineer, carried from the flight deck and into the nose section as he called out the airspeed for the pilot. "Ninety ... ninety-five ... ninety-eight ... one hundred."

The plane rose, the end of the runway flashed below them, and the landing gear clunked into the fuselage. A hundred yards farther, blackened wreckage littered the ground. Broken bits of a tail assembly identified it as the remains of a destroyed B-17.

DeGraaf turned and made eye contact with Lieutenant Jones, the navigator, seated at his small desk a few feet behind the bombardier's seat. "We ran long on that take-off, Jonesie. Since we have a good headwind for extra lift, I suspect the gunners loaded some extra fifty-caliber ammunition today."

Jones shrugged. "Can't blame them. A fella really hates to run out of supplies on a business trip."

As it gained altitude, the plane executed a series of turns, working its way to the assembly point of Bombardment Group 351. DeGraaf had an unobstructed view as the major strike force gathered. Each squadron of six aircraft came together and united into the eighteen planes of the Bombardment Group. Once all groups joined, a wing of three hundred Flying Fortresses would head toward their target.

Lieutenant Jones looked up from his navigational charts. "I have mixed feelings about sitting behind a hotdog bombardier, DeGraaf. Being the lead plane kinda makes us a big target, know what I mean?"

"Well, I'm only deputy leader this trip, so we'll be back a bit."

"Yeah, right. And when the lead gets knocked out, we move on up."

The interphone came alive with the voice of the pilot, Nick Mackay. "Pilot to bombardier, we're at ten thousand feet, let's pull the pins and get rigged for oxygen, DeGraaf. Five-minute oxygen checks. We'll make our run at twenty-eight thousand. Make it every three minutes if we get hit hard at that altitude."

DeGraaf eased his bulky flight suit through the passage from the nose section, climbed to the flight deck, passed the two pilots and the engineer, and entered the bomb bay. On both sides of a narrow catwalk that led to the aft of the airplane, two stacks of five-hundred-pound bombs, five to a side, rested peacefully in their racks.

He removed the safety pins from each bomb and examined the load. Wires were securely attached to each weapon. After the bombs fell, the wires popped loose, and the little propellers spun free, they would be fully armed. Satisfied, he returned to the nose section.

He took the oxygen hose from the panel on his right and plugged it into the facemask, then got on the interphone. "All stations, hook up your oxygen and report in."

He waited until every crew member confirmed their oxygen flow.

"Mack seems obsessed with oxygen," said Jones.

"*Ugly Duck* got hit hard yesterday. A bunch of guys got shot up. About eight minutes went by between oxygen checks. They found the ball turret unplugged. They pulled the gunner out dead. No wounds, just ran out of the good stuff, probably never knew he had a problem."

Barbara Jean reached an altitude of twenty-five thousand feet as it approached the coast of Holland. The sky above was clear blue. Miles below him, sunlight highlighted the beauty of the billowing cumulus clouds. Scanning the sky around the aircraft, DeGraaf witnessed a sight that surpassed his wildest boyhood dreams. Stretching for miles on both sides, an armada of hundreds of bombers, all bristling with machine guns, cruised serenely through the air, leaving their individual contrails.

Through the clouds below, Amsterdam appeared. All those Dutchmen would be starting their day, perhaps looking up at the contrails of hundreds of bombers five miles above them, maybe even cheering for the brave Americans who came to free them.

He turned around to see the navigator hunched over his charts. "Hey, Jonesie."

Jones looked up.

DeGraaf pointed toward the ground. "My dad grew up somewhere down there. Groningen, wherever that is. He even taught me to speak some Dutch."

"Let's hope you don't get a chance to test your language skills today." Jones returned to his charts.

When the strike force reached altitude over eastern Holland, Bombardment Groups peeled off to their assigned targets. In the smooth, clear air, the eighteen planes of Bombardment Group 351 were neatly arranged, proceeding farther east into Germany. With a strong tailwind, the Fortresses were racing toward their target at a ground speed of over 250 miles per hour.

In spite of their electrically heated and well-insulated flight suits, the minus-forty-degree air entered through open gun ports and circulated freely around the unheated cabin and managed to find its way to the crew.

DeGraaf checked his oxygen hose and spoke into the interphone. "Oxygen check. Report in, starting aft. Tail gunner, report."

A shout from the right waist gunner interrupted. "We have company! Fighters at three o'clock moving east."

DeGraaf leaned forward in his bubble and scanned the sky to his right. He shouted into his interphone. "They're banking left!" After a few seconds more, the wings of the fighters glinted in the sun. DeGraaf shouted again, this time shocked by the high pitch of his voice. "They're turning again! Prepare for a frontal attack."

With his thick gloves, DeGraaf pulled up his fifty-caliber machine gun and aimed it through a hole in the plexiglass. The navigator jumped to a position by his right shoulder and took over the machine gun in the chin position.

DeGraaf's heart pounded violently in his chest. He clamped his hands on the big gun to control his shaking. At a closing speed of over five hundred miles per hour, the Focke-Wulf fighter was quickly within range. When DeGraaf saw red flashes from its twenty-millimeter guns, he fired his weapon. The plane shuddered as the two guns in the nose were joined by the twin fifties in the top turret and the ball turret in the belly of the plane.

Although his gun was firing madly, DeGraaf felt helpless as the fighter bore down on him. The likelihood of death captured his mind. The Focke-Wulf then flipped over, and DeGraaf watched in awe as the belly of the fighter raced below him.

Jones released his grip on his gun. "That guy's crazy."

"Crazy like a fox. They told us in briefing they would do that. After they flip over, they pull up hard and get out of town. The Germans figure they have less exposure that way."

"Oxygen check and damage report," said DeGraaf over the interphone.

Responses were all positive until it came to the pilot. "We have a hole in the windshield big enough for my granddaddy's cane to slide through. The round hit the armor plate on the bulkhead behind us. Smitty got some cuts in top turret. He'll be okay. We have new vent holes in the walls and ceiling but—"

A shout from the left waist gunner, "Nine o'clock high! Coming in."

The airplane shuddered again as the top turret and left waist blasted their weapons. Three Focke-Wulf fighters raced toward the formation, all firing their twenty-millimeter cannons. Two flashed below the *Barbara Jean*, apparently undamaged. The third fell victim to fifty-caliber rounds from one of the many B-17s firing at it. Trailing fire and smoke, it went into a vertical dive.

For the next fifteen minutes, chaos reigned inside the Flying Fortress as shouts from crew members constantly advised the other men of incoming enemy planes. That noise was frequently overwhelmed by the sounds of the heavy machine guns. *Barbara Jean* kept flying, suffering multiple wounds but none fatal.

Lisa Mae, the lead ship for Bombardment Group 351, was not so lucky. DeGraaf watched in horror as cannon fire from two diving fighter planes shredded the waist section of the plane. The tail broke free, and the bomber rose, then fell to the side and plummeted toward the ground. The airplanes behind the stricken plane took hasty evasive action. Most avoided the wreckage. Two did not. They collided with each other, and both planes broke apart and fell.

The voice of the tail gunner came through the interphone. "I see chutes back there. Lots of chutes."

The deep voice of the pilot made DeGraaf's heart jump. "That makes you lead bombardier, DeGraaf. We're moving up front. Also, there's a cloud bank ahead. We are going under it for the bombing run. Intelligence says flak at the target will be light. We'll come in at twenty-two thousand feet."

Ten minutes later, the navigator looked up from his desk. "About thirty minutes from the initial point."

DeGraaf got on the interphone. "Crew, put on flak suits. When complete, give me an oxygen report."

With trembling hands, DeGraaf pulled on the heavy armored body covering and the steel helmet that protected his ears and neck. He snapped a parachute to his chest. Finally, he ensured that his oxygen hose was fixed to his face mask.

DeGraaf sat behind his Norden bombsight. He would need time to set up the device before reaching the initial point, or IP as they called it. That's the place they'd stop their zig-zagging and begin the bomb run. He entered altitude, airspeed, wind movement, temperature, everything relevant to making sure the ordnance fell on the target.

When the Norden was calibrated, DeGraaf and Jones peered through the glass bubble, searching the terrain for the IP.

Jones nudged DeGraaf. "There it is." He pointed at a bend in a river below. The pilot had approached the target perfectly.

DeGraaf conducted one last oxygen check with the crew. It would be the last until bombs away.

As the IP passed below, he got on the interphone. "Bombardier to pilot, level."

After a few seconds, the response came. "Level."

DeGraaf set the two gyroscopes in the bombsight to allow it to stay on target if the plane bounced around during the run. He pulled the lever to open the bomb bay doors.

"Bombardier to pilot. Prepared to take control."

"It's your airplane, DeGraff. You own the 351st."

"He sure knows how to relax a guy," mumbled the navigator.

A puff of black smoke appeared about a quarter mile ahead. With adrenaline pumping through his nineteen-year-old body, a wild euphoria filled DeGraaf's mind, giving him a mental clarity he had never experienced.

More puffs, closer. Then red flashes preceded those black clouds, close enough that bits of shrapnel peppered the fuselage like a hailstorm.

DeGraaf glanced back at the navigator. "I think intelligence was wrong. Anti-aircraft can reach us here."

He turned his attention to the bombsight and tried to tune out the chaos around them. The intensity of the flak bursts increased as they neared the target. *Barbara Jean* was frequently pummeled with the hailstorm of small pellets. The rotten egg smell of cordite penetrated his layers of protection. Some explosions were so close that he held his breath and waited for the plane to come apart. The obedient aircraft flew as straight and level as the flak would allow.

DeGraaf's earlier sense of euphoria was gone, replaced by fear approaching panic. As he peered through the scope, desperate for the target to appear, his mind wandered to sitting on the front porch on Lynch Street, watching his father water the flowers. Another flak explosion jolted him back to an unwelcome reality.

There it was. The target crept into his crosshairs, and he held it there. "Please, God," he muttered.

The airplane leaped upward, free of the weight of its bombs.

DeGraaf sat upright. "Bombs away." His knotted muscles relaxed.

The pilot came back. "Good work, DeGraaf. Let's go home." The airplane banked left.

DeGraaf reached down and pulled the lever to close the bomb bay doors. He looked outside and turned to his navigator. "We lost some planes. I'd say at least a half-dozen."

"And we have another ten minutes of flak."

A sharp explosion tilted the plane to the right. Number two engine, just feet from the nose section, trailed flames and smoke. Another blast jolted the bomber. DeGraaf looked out the right side. "They got number four." The outboard engine was smoking.

The plane shook violently. A shout from the flight deck commanded, "Feather both of them." The shaking ceased as both propellers came to rest, their edges set so they wouldn't catch the wind.

Barbara Jean, in spite of her gallant effort, slowed and descended. The fully capable Fortresses around them maintained their altitude and speed. The only positive element of this scenario was that the flak gunners continued to focus their attack on the intact formation above them. Soon, they were alone in the sky as the wounded airplane limped along toward England with two dead engines.

When they'd descended to ten thousand feet, the pilot came on the interphone. "We are going to hop the cumulus all the way over Holland if we can. Crew can shed the flak suits and oxygen. Everyone put on parachutes."

The navigator abandoned his charts and joined DeGraaf as he watched the plane move from cloud to cloud. "I have no idea where we are except over the Netherlands. We do have a big target, the ocean. Then I'll find England."

A shout from the interphone broke the peaceful ride. "We have company! Two fighters at three o'clock. Can't tell what they are."

DeGraaf leaned up to the plexiglass bubble and looked right. Two dots came into view, flying parallel to *Barbara Jean*. They banked left, separated slightly, and headed directly for the stricken bomber. When they were about a thousand yards away, *Barbara Jean* trembled as its multiple fifty-caliber guns desperately tried to stop the attackers.

At five hundred yards, one plane faltered and fell helplessly toward earth. The second continued its charge.

Multiple bullets pierced the fuselage all around DeGraaf. The glass bubble exploded, and the rushing wind knocked him to the floor beside Jonesie. He shook his friend without response. He pulled himself farther. Most of the navigator's head was missing.

Before his brain could grasp what had just happened, the plane began to tumble. DeGraaf managed to pull himself to the forward escape hatch, open it, and climb out of the plummeting aircraft.

As he whistled through the air, *Barbara Jean* and one separated wing tumbled madly to earth. No parachutes appeared.

DeGraaf grasped the ripcord D-ring. "Not too soon," he said to himself. "Can't be a target."

When he guessed he was under a thousand feet, he pulled the rip cord. He jerked when the parachute popped open, then drifted to a soft landing in a plowed field.

He swept up his chute and ran for the nearest ditch. Seeing that it was dry, he jumped in. About a quarter mile away, black smoke rose into the sky. Staring at the wreckage and knowing that his friends were gone, his strength abandoned him, and his chin sagged to his chest.

An hour later, the exhausted, depressed airman lay in the ditch, watching the sun edge toward the western horizon. German soldiers had come and gone. Could he move now? *Why did I leave my pistol home today?* Maybe after dark, he could find some good Dutch farmers.

A rattling sound came from somewhere up the road. He lifted his head enough to see through the tall grass. A girl on a bike. Alone. About his age. His heart jumped. The bike got closer. He strained to remember the Dutch his father taught him. Surprised by his squeaky voice, he called out. *"Helpen!"*

The rattling stopped. The girl leaned on one foot and scanned her surroundings.

"Helpen!" His voice was stronger this time. He waved his hand.

The girl laid her bike on the road and crept in his direction.

DeGraaf stood and continued in strained Dutch. "I'm an American. I need help."

He gasped as he looked into the muzzle of a Luger automatic pistol. His arms shot up toward the sky. He abandoned his Dutch and spoke in English. "Hey, take it easy. I'm unarmed."

"Let's go with English," the girl said. "I speak it well. Your Dutch is awful." She jabbed the Luger closer to him. "And if you are a German, you will be dead soon."

"I'm not German. I promise. Don't you know about the plane that went down over there?" He pointed in the direction of the crash.

She aimed the weapon at his nose. "I know. I also know that English-speaking Germans are real good at pretending to be Allied flyers and catching Resistance people. I lost a dear friend to German guns. I don't play games."

DeGraaf lowered his hands and frowned. His voice was strong. "Look, I lost friends too, okay? That plane over there is full of their bodies."

She lowered her aim from his nose to his chest. "Okay, let's try a little quiz. Name?"

"Richard DeGraaf. Lieutenant. Bombardier. Bombardment Group 351."

"You are well-briefed. So am I. Who won the 1941 world series?"

"Easy. The Yankees."

"Good boy. Who lost?"

"The Dodgers."

"Quickly now, where do the Dodgers play?" She pointed the gun at his nose again.

DeGraaf's heart pounded in his throat. His mind was a vacuum. "Um ... um." He blinked, swallowed. Then the words came. "It's Ebbets, Ebbets Field."

The girl lowered the gun and engaged the safety lock. "Welcome to the Netherlands, Richard. I am Jenny DeHaan. I believe you. However, you will need to convince some other people before you have a place to hide out. If you do that, we just may get you home."

"So, what do we do now?"

"We sit here until dark. Then we grope our way to my home. Hope you're hungry. Mama is a great cook."

CHAPTER THIRTY-FOUR

24 August 1943
Transit Camp Westerbork

Reinaar scanned the information on his clipboard and flipped to the second page. "This is a lot of new hospital admissions, even for a transport day." He placed the clipboard beside his typewriter and slid his chair up to the desk.

Francien, wearing her crisp nurse's uniform, looked over his shoulder. "Some of these names have a way of reappearing regularly on the Monday night admission list. Those names are probably also on the transport list and crossed off." She shrugged. "Not a problem. We have plenty of beds."

Reinaar turned and smiled at his wife. "Indeed. Not only plenty of beds but also plenty of doctors."

Francien patted his shoulder. "And plenty of nurses, dear. Also, I might add, the best nurses and doctors in the country."

"The occupiers have a very effective recruitment process. All the best Jewish medical people seem to end up right here in Westerbork."

"And their names never appear on the transport list, at least not yet," said Francien.

Reinaar nodded. "Nor have ours."

Francien kissed her husband on the cheek. "Need to run. Sick patients to see."

Reinaar glanced at his watch. "And I need to go to the ramp. Our Jewish Central Supervisor manages his transport list with great care, but I need to make sure he is up to date on all these new admissions. It will impact today's transport list."

Francien leaned over and whispered in Reinaar's ear. "I detest Klausman. A Jew with total control on who goes and who stays. The corruption disgusts me. Always happy to accept payment or services to keep people off the list. One day he will get his reward."

Reinaar frowned and scanned the room. "Let's discuss this elsewhere," he whispered. "And let's be glad we aren't on the train."

Francien nodded and left the room. Reinaar picked up his clipboard, walked out the front door, and headed south.

There it was. The ugly snake of a train had invaded the camp, as it did on most Tuesdays. The engine was very much alive. Smoke drifted from its stack, and steam hissed from various places as it waited patiently to do its work. Behind the engine, a string of cattle cars rested, silent, doors open, ready to gobble up whatever cargo came their way.

The loading process was well underway. Reinaar threaded his way through the crowd. Tension hung in the air like a toxic, invisible cloud. Many men wore suits and ties. Some, in spite of the August heat, wore overcoats. Many women also wore layers of clothing and dress shoes with heels. They all held a variety of personal items, often draped over their shoulders in bags. For every Jew standing beside the waiting train, both rich and poor, their entire personal wealth had been reduced to what they could carry.

Reinaar slowed and stopped when he approached the Abrams family, a father, mother, one toddler, and an infant in the mother's arms. He knew them well. Another businessman, a rich one, from The Hague. The father led the small boy by the hand. The infant's silent, pale face peeked out of a white blanket.

Reinaar, his mind churning with sadness and guilt, searched for words. He had been in their home, eaten with them, laughed with them. He had held that baby. Now they were doomed, and he was secure.

Finally, words came stumbling out. "Aaron, I'm sorry. I wish you well, my dear friend."

The man, his face etched with a deep frown, made only brief eye contact with Reinaar. He nodded and moved past without a word, following the mass of people toward the waiting train.

The authorities on the ramp, with calm, well-practiced efficiency, herded the deportees into the rail cars. A thousand people, pushed by an irresistible force and with no alternative, moved into the open-mouthed cattle carriers. When a car was fully loaded, a representative of the German Reich used chalk to record the number of Jews in the wagon, slid the doors closed, and slammed the latches in place, sealing the human contents to an unknown fate.

Reinaar proceeded toward the cluster of uniformed SS men and their OD assistants. He spotted Egburt Klausman, the top man in Jewish camp leadership. He was talking to the camp commandant. Reinaar carefully worked himself into a position where Klausman would see him and his clipboard.

As he stood and waited for an opportunity to speak, he noticed that the loading process was nearly complete. Although he felt a sense of urgency to speak to Klausman, his lowly position constrained him.

An SS captain approached and interrupted the discussion of the leaders. "Herr Commandant, I have a passenger count."

He looked to the young captain and nodded.

"Exactly 999 transportees."

Klausman's eyes widened. "Are you sure, Captain?"

A look of utter disdain flooded the young officer's face as he glared at the Jew. "The count is correct, Herr Commandant."

Beads of sweat formed on Klausman's forehead. His gaze settled on Reinaar, and he gestured for him to approach. He jerked the clipboard from Reinaar's hand and quickly scanned the pages. "The hospital admission list has grown since I last saw it."

The commandant turned a scornful look toward Reinaar, then back at Klausman. He slowly inhaled and exhaled while everyone nearby stood in silence. Looking at the cloudless blue sky, but clearly addressing Klausman, he spoke. "My orders are to transport 1001 Jews to Auschwitz. I will transport exactly that many Jews on this train today. We have a schedule to keep. The train will be leaving this place in a few minutes." He turned to Klausman and tapped the frightened man's chest with his baton. "If you do not reconcile these numbers, you will be on that train. You and someone in your family."

Color drained from Klausman's sweating face. His eyes darted around the platform and settled on Reinaar Demeester. "This man will go, and his wife. That will give us 1001."

The commandant shrugged. "Do what you must. In fifteen minutes, this train will depart."

Klausman pointed a trembling finger at Reinaar. "You. Get your wife from the hospital. Prepare to board the train." He summoned an OD man in his green coveralls, "Go with that man. Make very sure he is on the train in ten minutes, or I'll throw you inside."

Five minutes later, Reinaar Demeester assisted his tearful, trembling wife up the portable stairs into the one cattle car whose content number had been rubbed out and the door reopened. They carried no belongings. Francien wore her nurse's uniform. Her weak knees demanded her husband's full assistance. The silent passengers made room for them to enter. With Reinaar's arm wrapped around Francien's waist, they turned and faced the platform. In front of them, the heavy door rolled from left to right and thumped to a stop. The steel latch clanked shut. Black silence took command of the cattle car.

CHAPTER THIRTY-FIVE

August 1943
Auschwitz

Francien leaned her forehead into the rough boards lining the side of the cattle car. She slid her hand, using a light touch to avoid splinters, left to right until she found the gap between the wall and the sliding door. Finding it, she put her nose to the crack and inhaled the wisp of fresh air that managed to find its way into the car. She gathered her fading energy and drew in the precious air. The slight breeze whisked her cheek, brought a bit of clarity to her clouded mind, and pushed aside the foul, sickening environment she had endured for two—or was it three?—days since the train left Westerbork.

She felt the side-to-side swaying of her weak body as the chugging locomotive plied its way to some unknown destination, oblivious to the misery in the rolling boxes following behind. Her movement was limited by her husband's shoulder on the left and another body pressing her right side. The man's name lingered somewhere in the back of her mind but out of her reach.

In the dark, she explored Reinaar's side and grasped his rough hand. Her first words in hours left her mouth feeling dry and sore. "What day is this?"

"Thursday. Must be about midnight."

"I don't think I can endure the heat of another day. The water bucket has been empty since early Wednesday, and the waste bucket has overflowed." She shuddered. "And I think there are dead people in here."

Reinaar's voice had lost its deep power. "Perhaps we will stop today. There is a little breeze. Do you feel it?"

"Yes. It is a blessing. There must be a wind on our side of the train."

The metallic clicking of wheels on rails broke through the fog that lingered in Francien's exhausted brain. A slight change in the rhythm. "Reinaar, are we slowing?"

"I think so. Maybe stopping for fuel or water for the engine."

The thought of water gripped Francien and fed the inflammation in her dry mouth. "Maybe they will give us some."

"Perhaps."

The screech of brakes filled the car and stirred the lethargic group. A voice in the darkness echoed Francien's thoughts. "We are stopping. Pray that they will open the door."

The squeal of the brakes slowly diminished along with the pace of the clicking wheels. With a slight jerk, the bodies around her swayed as the train came to rest. Francien sensed the anticipation inside the wagon.

Light from outside pierced the slits in the wall. The steel bolt in front of Francien clanked open, and the large door slid along its track until it thumped into its stop. Cool, fresh air flooded the compartment. The drawn faces of her fellow prisoners blinked and squinted at the bright electric lights lining a concrete platform. Several people lay unmoving among the luggage that littered the floor of the car.

The eerie silence lasted only a few seconds. Large German shepherd dogs, barking and growling, strained at leashes held by men in SS uniforms. In contrast to the dogs, most of the men on the platform seemed calm, controlled, and well-organized. They went about a coordinated effort of managing the arrival of a thousand confused new arrivals. Their commands were authoritative, yet cold and flat. The message was consistent. "Leave your luggage in the cars. You will get it later. Everyone move along the platform."

The mass of people shuffled along, gravitating to their family members. Francien turned to her husband. "That foul smell. What is that? It's like the time the cook burned the chicken."

Without words, he gripped her hand and kept walking.

The next command was echoed by the SS spread along the platform. "Men to the right, women and children to the left."

Francien's hand remained clamped to Reinaar's. Family groups in front of her did the same until the leather truncheons began to fall. Aggressive blows to the heads of both men and women brought quick compliance.

An SS man moved toward the Demeesters, truncheon raised.

He released her hand. "See you later." They jumped apart. Francien joined the moving line of women and looked back to see Reinaar blending into the male group. Such a quick separation. No kiss. No hug. *How will I find him later?*

The two separate columns moved forward. As Francien neared the head of the queue, she witnessed a curious selection process conducted by a group of SS officers. The organized effort seemed to be routine, requiring little thought or discussion. The SS staff members acted at the direction of a man who seemed to be in command. With casual detachment, he examined new arrivals, a visual evaluation often lasting only a second or two. Then, with a lazy tilt of his baton, he directed the prisoner toward their left or right. The other members of the SS team then hurried the prisoner in that direction.

The selecting official directed all the elderly women, most middle-aged women, and women with children to the left. SS officers steered them toward a line of military trucks. The commander sent a few young, vigorous-looking women to the right. They formed a small, tense group who clustered together in wary silence.

Francien's gaze went from one group to the other. Why the difference? Where did she want to go? Little time to think. So much confusion. Her exhausted, clouded brain refused to help.

When her turn came, Francien stepped forward, stealing a glance at the officer's face. Young, tan, and smoothly shaven, displaying no emotion. She forced her stiff and tired body to stand erect. Jaw tight, she looked over the head of the SS examiner. In the distance, smoke billowed from several tall chimneys, capped with dancing flames. When the officer paused, Francien dropped her gaze, avoiding eye contact. He scanned her from head to foot. His calm eyes seemed to be focused on her nurse's uniform. Finally, he dipped his baton in the direction of the majority of women and shifted his gaze to the next woman in line.

With one last fruitless look at the line of men, she hurried to join the parade of women, all walking in the direction of waiting trucks. The SS men, some barking orders while others were casual and detached, herded the group into the waiting canvas-covered vehicles.

Francien climbed into the nearest truck and collapsed onto the wooden bench that lined the side of the truck bed.

A young woman holding an infant sat beside Francien and looked at her uniform. "Mrs. Demeester, I am surprised to see you. Were you not exempted?"

"Davida, I didn't know you were on this train. Reinaar and I were added at the very last minute." Francien touched the soft cheek of the sleeping baby. "I cared for baby Joseph in the hospital. I feared what might happen to him after they discharged him last week."

"Your fears were justified. They put us on the next train. I hope we can join my husband here. He was sent three weeks ago."

Reinaar moved to the middle of the group of men, as far as possible from the vicious dogs. The column crept ahead beside the empty train.

He turned toward the sound of hard wheels rolling behind him on the ramp. About a dozen handcarts on steel-rimmed wagon wheels approached the parked train. Thin figures wearing striped pajamas pushed these carts. They stopped at the open train cars, climbed aboard, and moved luggage from the train onto the portable baggage carriers.

Fearing a beating from the guards, Reinaar turned back toward the head of the slowly advancing line. A cart pulled up beside him. His jaw slackened at the sight of the figures unloading the train. In their drawn and expressionless faces and their dull, sunken eyes, Reinaar saw moving men who were not fully alive. Their striped uniforms, dirty and torn, seemed oddly comical but for the unearthly world that surrounded them.

A few men, similarly dressed but appearing to be much healthier, directed the work. Their behavior, the shouts, curses, and truncheon blows, mirrored the actions of the German soldiers.

The emaciated workers hurried about their task, seeming to ignore the abuse. When knocked to the ground, they pulled themselves up and continued their work.

As the group of new arrivals drew close to the head of the line where interviews and some kind of selection were taking place, Reinaar studied the process.

Just ahead of him in the queue, two companions, appearing to be father and son, approached the uniformed SS official. He turned his inexpressive gaze to the young teenager. "Age?"

The boy whispered a response.

The SS man glared. "What is your age, boy?"

"Thirteen, sir."

With an impatient grunt, the official waved the back of his hand toward the group to the left of the formation. With an anxious look at his father, the boy hurried off.

The father stepped forward. "That's my son."

The soldier shrugged. "Then go with him." The father hurried after the boy.

Reinaar forced his tired, clouded mind to process what he was seeing. What was the purpose of all this? What should he say?

The officer turned his attention to the next man, thin, stooped, and gray-haired.

With only a glance, the guard gestured with his thumb. The elderly gentleman moved to the expanding group on the left. That group was predominantly old men and young boys.

The man in front of Reinaar stepped forward.

"Age?"

"Fifty."

"Health?"

"Excellent."

"Occupation?"

"Merchant. Clothing store."

The examiner hesitated for only a moment. Without words, the lazy thumb tilted toward the man's left.

Reinaar approached, stood tall, lifted his chin, and fixed his gaze on the examiner's chest.

"Age?"

He lied with the most strength he could muster. "Thirty-nine."

"Health?"

"Excellent."

"Occupation?"

"Licensed electrician."

Silence as the officer paused. Reinaar stole a glance at the man's eyes as they scanned him up and down. Heart pounding, he looked at the German's hands. He was twisting the gold ring on his finger. Then his thumb eased up ... and tilted to the right.

Reinaar hurried to join the small group of fit-looking men clustered near the train's locomotive. The engineer looked down at him from the open locomotive window, then back at his watch.

About twenty minutes later, a line of military trucks appeared at the ramp. The larger group of men was loaded onto a caravan that followed the same road as the earlier trucks carrying the women.

Reinaar stood among a smaller group of about sixty or eighty men. Three trucks stopped nearby. The half-dozen remaining SS men, with shouts and truncheon blows, drove the prisoners to the vehicles. Reinaar gathered the energy that remained in his dehydrated and sleep-deprived body and climbed aboard. He sagged onto the wooden bench lining the side of the canvas-covered compartment, joining about twenty other silent arrivals and two armed guards. He sighed and peered out the open back of the truck.

The locomotive that had brought him to this place came alive. Belching smoke and steam, with emphatic chugs of gradually increasing frequency, it moved the long train away from the ramp. The glaring electric lights up and down the deserted platform suddenly went dark, waiting for the next incoming train.

Looking through the open back of the rumbling truck, Francien viewed a large, brightly lit camp consisting of perhaps hundreds of brick and wooden structures surrounded by dirt and mud. Tall electrified fences surrounded the place. Guards with guns peered down at the caravan from watchtowers. Barbed wire fences divided the camp into multiple sections.

The caravan of trucks rolled to a stop near the outer perimeter of the giant camp, beside a fenced enclosure that surrounded a solitary brick building. Flames flickered from the top of a tall chimney that protruded into the night sky.

The soldier who had accompanied them jumped off the truck. He beckoned to the attentive passengers. His voice was authoritative but calm. "*Alle raus.*" The young women assisted the older passengers and children to the ground. They joined the line of prisoners, all proceeding toward the entrance to a stairway that descended underground. The guard, more insistent this time and close to Francien's ear, jolted her. "Keep moving. You will appreciate a warm shower before you retire to your barracks."

While the women formed a long line, more trucks arrived and unloaded a group of men. Francien scanned the new arrivals, mostly elderly prisoners and young boys. No Reinaar. The tired, silent men joined the slowly moving line.

The stairs brought them to one large windowless room, empty except for benches that were scattered about. The wall held hundreds of bare clothing hooks.

The next instruction generated a stunned silence. "Everyone undress completely."

After a brief pause, while hundreds of people, old and young, men, women, and children, stared at each other, the commands became harsh and the truncheons came into play. One guard selected an old man, seemingly at random, and knocked him unconscious to the floor. "Everyone undress, now."

Francien held baby Joseph while Davida disrobed. The baby jerked awake and screamed. Francien put her cheek to the boy's face and whispered, "It's okay, sweetheart. It's okay."

The screaming continued. The disrobing process paused while nearby adults peered at the child. A middle-aged, overweight SS sergeant pushed his way through the crowd and jerked the child from Francien's arms. Holding a truncheon in his left hand, he used his right to hold the baby by the ankle. He strode up the stairs. The wail of the child and the screams of the mother filled the room.

A sharp gunshot echoed down the stairs and all around the room. The crying ceased.

With a groan, the child's mother fainted and collapsed to the floor. Francien, her breathing shallow and her eyes shifting between the unmoving woman and the approaching guards, attempted to unbutton her blouse, but her trembling fingers failed her. The guard splashed a pail of water on Davida's face. She blinked awake.

The SS man who had removed the child returned empty-handed, seemingly unaffected by what he had done. "Remember where you place your clothes so you can find them after your shower. Everyone move to the shower room."

Francien placed her clothes, along with Davida's, on a hook. With arms around each other, the women joined the naked group that moved to the end of the long changing room. From there, they made a right turn, through large metal doors, into another long, windowless room.

The room gradually filled with prisoners. Children gaped in awe at the naked adult bodies all around them. Adult faces were tight, mostly focused on the ceiling and its shower heads.

The metal door slammed shut. A small child's voice broke the silence in the totally dark room. "What now, Mama?"

A slight metallic clank came from the ceiling, along with rustling sounds of activity above them. Then, from the ceiling, a sound like hard grain falling into a pan, followed by the pan's lid closing.

In the darkness, total silence for a few seconds. Then isolated coughing. Francien's eyes and throat stung. Screaming and shouting erupted in the crowded room. She felt the rush of the crowd toward the entry door. Overcome with nausea, she bent and retched. Dizziness and muscle spasms forced her to the floor. Her coughing was replaced by an inability to breathe. Her pain faded away.

Sitting on the hard, wooden bench that lined the side of the truck, Reinaar closed his eyes and allowed his chin to sag onto his chest. The silent bodies on both sides jostled him slightly as the vehicle rumbled along the dark, uneven road. The steady sound of the engine drew his confused and clouded brain toward the haven of sleep.

He succeeded for only a short time. He jolted awake, confused. Bright lights pulled his blinking gaze out the open back of the truck. The vehicle had passed through an iron gate. Outside the electrified fence, men with rifles looked down on the caravan from watchtowers. The bright light illuminated the inside of the truck's compartment and allowed Reinaar to observe his fellow passengers. They gazed wide-eyed at their new surroundings. The two guards sat, expressionless, staring straight ahead.

The truck stopped, and the engine went silent, then the two guards sprang into action. They jumped to the ground, and the first one down shouted into the truck. *"Alle raus, schnell!"*

Reinaar joined the rush to the back of the truck. Without hesitation, he leaped to the dirt road. His weak body failed him, and he fell to his hands and knees. Seeing a pair of black boots heading his way, he scrambled to his feet. He joined the group that was moving into the nearby building.

A hostile welcome awaited them. Uniformed SS men, armed with truncheons, beat the arrivals for no apparent reason.

An SS sergeant called for order. "Halt."

Silence immediately settled over the room, and all eyes went to the sergeant. He produced a cloth bag and held it open with both hands. "You will deposit into this bag all of your personal possessions. This will be your one and only opportunity. I want everything. Money, jewelry, documents of any kind. If you hold anything back, you will be shot right here in this room."

Reinaar removed his wedding ring and noted the confused, anxious expressions around him.

One Dutchman stood up and translated the German's order into Dutch while he pulled items from his pockets.

The men clustered around the sergeant, dumping items into the bag and rechecking all their pockets.

The SS man closed the bag and nodded toward one corner of the room. "Now all your clothing. Pile it over there." He then pointed to an opposite corner. "Shoes there."

In only a couple of minutes, a pile of clothing in the corner displayed a wide variety of garments, from frayed work trousers to tailored suits.

Without comment, the SS men headed for the door of the building, several pulling out cigarettes as they walked. About eighty naked Dutchmen remained, all equal now. No evidence of wealth or position.

Reinaar leaned against a nearby wall, feeling faint. His knees trembled. After taking in no food or water for two days, his body was failing him. His mouth felt like sandpaper. The thoughts in his head were slow, muddy.

A group of thin men in striped uniforms rushed into the room and gathered the discarded clothing. Could these be the same people who collected the luggage from the railway platform? He edged over to the workers. Most of them went about their job without giving any attention to the new arrivals. One man, who had more weight and looked more alert than the others, made eye contact with Reinaar. He looked around, making sure he was not being observed, then looked back at Reinaar. "You are very lucky."

"Why do you say that?"

"You will live, for now."

"Did you unload the baggage from our train tonight?"

The man nodded. "I unload trains every night."

Reinaar's brain regained a bit of clarity. He looked into the man's eyes. "What happened to the other people from the train? My wife is in that group."

The man blinked and looked at the floor. "They are gone."

"Gone where?"

The man gathered up an armful of clothing and headed for the back door of the hut.

Reinaar called after him. "Gone where?"

The man stopped and turned back. "Up the chimney. They all went up the chimney."

In Reinaar's state of confused exhaustion, reality was somewhere out of reach. His mind pictured the fire-belching chimneys that he witnessed from the railroad platform. He recalled the feeling of Francien's hand when he left her, but he was unable to reconcile his confused, clouded thoughts. His dull brain was not capable of shock. Only vaguely aware of his own body, he stood and watched the man walk away.

CHAPTER THIRTY-SIX

September 1943
A farm near Nijkerk

Jenny knocked on the farmhouse door, stood back, and waited. This was her fourth such stop today. The door opened just enough for a frowning woman's face to appear at the edge. When her gaze met Jenny's, she pulled the door fully open and gestured for her to enter. "Oh, Greta. I am so glad to see you. I hope you have coupons. Since my husband died, it has been very difficult to get by, with the children and all."

"He was a brave man, Sophie. The Resistance misses him greatly. I'm glad I can help." Jenny went to the kitchen table and opened her satchel. She laid two textbooks and a Bible on the table and smiled at the woman. "If I get stopped, these things provide me with plenty of stories, like I am going to school or church." She then opened a hidden compartment at the bottom of the satchel, withdrew ration coupons, and handed them to her smiling host. "And now I have something extra." She pulled out a stack of currency. "Our people in England are now sending money to us."

Sophie watched Jenny count out some bills. "Oh, thank the Lord."

Two children entered the back door of the house. One immediately ran to Jenny and embraced her. "My friend Greta came for another visit." She turned to her young companion. "Greta helped me when those bad people took my mama and papa."

Jenny stroked the child's hair. "I am so glad to see you, Aniek. My goodness, how you have grown. Let's see. It's been about a year since we first met. That would make you about four now?"

The other girl spoke. "I'm four too."

"Wonderful. You are growing up together. I have a little surprise for you to share." Jenny reached into her satchel, then paused and studied the girls' faces until the suspense reached the optimum level. She pulled out a small paper sack and held it out.

Aniek snatched the bag and looked inside. "Ooh. Licorice."

"And your response is what?" asked Sophie.

The girls answered in unison. "Thank you." They trotted off to their bedroom.

After watching the girls' departure, Sophie turned to Jenny. "Bless you, Greta." She paused. "Or whatever your real name is. I pray for your safety every day."

"After the war, I will introduce myself properly, and we can talk more freely. I do need to run along. It's getting late." With a hug for Sophie and a promise to return, Jenny left the small farm and headed for Nijkerk.

Thirty minutes later, Jenny and her bicycle cast a long shadow as she rolled into Nijkerk. She leaned her bike against the police station and entered through the front door. Her childhood friend, Jake, looked up from the reception desk. "He's in his office, Jen. Go on back."

Jenny ruffled Jake's hair as she strolled past. She knocked three times on the closed door.

The deep bass voice responded. "*Kom binnen.*"

Jenny entered and shut the door. In his early fifties, the gray-haired captain's strong body still filled his tailored uniform. "Ah, Greta returns. I hope the satchel is lighter than when you left." He poured two cups of tea, handed one to Jenny, and they both took seats. "It is always a joy and no small relief when you return from a mission."

She took a careful sip and set her cup on the desk. "Sorry I'm getting back so late. I hope I didn't keep you."

"The police chief is always working. In fact, since the occupation, some of my best work is done in the dark of night." He winked. "I'm the only one in town who can break curfew. That gives me certain liberties."

"You have a risky job, Chief. I admire your courage. Sometimes, when I'm on a mission, I think my heart is going to break free and run away."

Atsma grinned. "Fear is good, Jen. Without it, people make bad mistakes."

He eased back in his chair, holding his teacup. "Let's look to the future a minute, Jen. I think this war is going to end before long. Do you think you will go back to university when it's all over?"

"Guess so. Right now, I try not to think too much about that. I just try to stay alive one day at a time and care for my kids." She leaned forward and whispered, "I know I can't ask too many questions, but my friend Jake at the front desk ... he's good, right?"

"Good as gold. You can trust Jake with your life. I do." He sipped his tea. "Our country has many heroes. The greatest of them don't seek recognition and probably won't get it. People like you and Jake out there. Their satisfaction comes from helping those in need." He lowered his voice. "And he is unattached right now."

"I'm not ready for romantic stuff right now. It's been only four months since I lost Marten. Seems like yesterday."

"I'm sorry, Jen. Sometimes I'm not very sensitive. Marten was a great man. Better than me, I think."

Jenny blinked tears away. She stood, set her satchel on the captain's desk, and pulled out the remaining ration coupons and cash. "I do enjoy watching our hosts' eyes light up when I pull out the money. They are heroes too."

"And your support allows them to practice their bravery." He pressed a button on the side of his desk.

Jake walked into the room. "Yes, sir."

The chief handed the coupons and cash to Jake. "Would you file this, please? Our courier has a little extra today."

"Yes, sir." With a quick glance and smile at Jenny, Jake closed the door behind him as he left.

Captain Atsma shifted in his chair. "A couple of things to tell you, Jenny. First, Richard DeGraaf is fully vetted with the Americans in England. In fact, British Military Intelligence has a man on the ground here making arrangements to evacuate him. MI-9 has alerted us that they will be at your door in the next few days. Make sure he is ready to go."

"Okay. We kind of hate to see him leave. He's a nice guy." Jenny blinked a couple of times. "What I mean is he's really helpful on the farm, and Joran loves him."

Atsma's eyes crinkled into his own kind of smile. "That's good. I sure hope he gets home okay. Now the second thing. The local NSB goons have been making some noise lately. As we get increasing numbers of young Dutchmen hiding from the German draft, the local collaborators are visiting people's homes at all hours, trying to find those *onderduikers* and any Jews. They hit the DeWitt family last night. Took them all away, along with a Jewish family they were hiding. We may never see any of them again. So please urge all your clients to be extra vigilant. This is no time to relax our security measures."

Jenny patted the pistol under her jacket. "One of these days, some NSB fool is going to get himself shot."

"Go easy on the cannon. If we take down one of them, the Germans will take a bunch of us. Our day will come. Be patient." Atsma looked at the clock on the wall. "Better run along, young lady. You're going to miss curfew."

"No problem. It's easy to hide on these quiet farm roads."

As Jenny rode out of Nijkerk, the setting sun announced its departure by painting the western clouds with shades of yellow and orange. When the fiery ball slid out of sight, it pulled the warm colors of the sunset and the rich palette of the Dutch countryside with it. The world faded to gray, then to the universal darkness of Holland under the Nazi blackout.

Thinking of the hot dinner waiting for her at the farm, Jenny walked her bicycle along the middle of the dark road, assisted only by a thin crescent moon and the multitude of stars. A chorus of crickets cheered her on.

A mile outside Nijkerk, Jenny approached the Baanders family farm, where she had placed the three-year-old Greenberg twins. Electric light escaped from one of the windows, illuminating a wagon parked outside.

"I don't believe this," she muttered.

She turned into the driveway and, fueled by adrenaline, strode toward the farmhouse. She approached the door and knocked sharply. Muffled sounds of activity seeped through the tight walls of the solid house. After half a minute, the door edged open, and light flooded out, exposing the face of a wide-eyed woman.

Jenny pushed her way in. "Hurry, Katryn. Close the door."

"Oh, it's you, Greta. You scared me half to death the way you rapped on the door."

Anger rose inside Jenny, warming her cheeks. "I meant to scare you. You have an uncovered window. You are lighting up your farm." She wagged a finger at Katryn's face. "The NSB is out prowling around, looking for onderduikers and Jews. You're inviting a raid."

Katryn gasped. "Oh my goodness!" She hurried to the children's room and quickly returned. "I am so sorry, Greta. The children pulled the curtain aside after I tucked them in. I secured it."

Jenny's relief and growing fatigue pushed aside her anger. Feeling tears rising, she hugged her trembling client. "I know it has been hard since Henk was taken to Germany." She paused as thoughts of Marten flashed in her mind. "And I must protect these children. I must."

"I did manage to get everyone hidden before I opened the door," said Katryn. "Jacob Kaufman and his wife are under the hay in the barn."

"Well, you do have the advantage that your barn is connected to the house." Jenny looked down at the table. "But if I was a Nazi or an NSB goon, I would now be dragging you out of here, probably along with the Jews in the barn."

"Why?"

Jenny pointed at the pipe resting in an ashtray, smoke curling from the bowl. "Unless you have taken up pipe smoking, there is a man close by. Even a stupid NSB collaborator would turn this place upside down until he found the people you are hiding. You absolutely must get rid of all traces of people who don't belong here."

Katryn's chin dropped toward her chest. Her shoulders sagged. "I wasn't thinking."

"I'm sorry I am being so harsh with you. You're among the bravest people in Holland. I will be back tomorrow with ration coupons and money to cover expenses. We'll talk more about how to stay safe."

With a firm hug, Jenny turned off the light, eased out the front door, and rode for home. Thirty minutes later, she opened the DeHaans' door and stepped into the darkened front room. "Hello. It's me."

Her mother's voice came from the kitchen. "Stew is waiting for you, dear."

She hurried to the room that had always been the hub of family activity. Mother turned from a sink filled with soapy water and dirty dishes and smiled at her daughter. "Stew is still hot, dear. Sit down. I'll bring you a bowl. You must be tired."

Joran and Richard DeGraaf sat opposite each other at the table, a Monopoly board between them. Joran grinned. "I'm winning, Jen."

"The kid is killing me," Richard said. "He owns both Boardwalk and Park Place. If I hit one of them again, it's game over for me."

Father, in his place at the end of the table, tapped the contents of his pipe into an ashtray. "We got a letter from Nicolaas today, Jenny. He works in a factory in Germany. The town hasn't been bombed since he arrived." He pushed the letter across the table, and Jenny read it while sipping her stew.

Richard let the die roll out of his hand, and it clattered across the game board. Five dots showed. Joran slapped his hands together. "That's it. He's a dead man. Go ahead, move that piece, loser."

Richard played along, moving his token slow enough for Joran to count each space. When he reached five, the piece came to rest on Boardwalk. He shrugged. "Well, it looks like I'm a bit short of funds, Joran. Do you think, maybe, you would be a friend and loan me some?"

"Doesn't work that way, flyboy."

"I'm afraid your victory will be bittersweet, young man," said Father. "Now you have time to complete your homework."

Joran shrugged. "Guess so." He turned his bright eyes to Richard. "Better luck next time, fella." He disappeared into his room.

Richard loaded the Monopoly game pieces into the box. "Great kid."

Mother dried her hands on a towel and joined the others at the table. "Joran has become like another son. I do worry about his parents. All we know is they left Westerbork on a train. That's the last we heard."

Jenny scraped the last of the stew from her bowl. "Well, Richard, it looks like your kitchen remodeling project is done. Let's have a look."

With Father on one end and Richard on the other, they lifted the table and moved it about four feet from its normal position, exposing the well-worn rug.

Jenny slid the rug across the wooden floor. "Well done. You created the perfect trapdoor. Very hard to see it. Where did a young flyer learn to do that?"

"My dad is a building contractor. He learned carpentry after he moved to Michigan from Holland. I think I started helping him when I was about eight." Richard slid a screwdriver into a crack between two floorboards and lifted the edge of the hinged trap door, exposing the hideaway beneath the kitchen. "It has only a dirt floor, but it's big enough for three people. Hiding down there is a lot better than crawling under the hay in the barn."

After restoring the kitchen to its normal state, they invited Joran to take a break and gathered at the table for coffee. Jenny took a sip of the hot brew and set her cup down. "I got some news about you today, Richard. You might not need that new cave of yours."

"Oh?"

"I got the word that British MI-9 has your escape plan in place. They have an agent on the ground who will come here to get you in the next couple of days. The path through Belgium seems solid right now. They eliminated a couple of collaborators in the chain."

Richard's eyes brightened. "That's good." His mild enthusiasm met blank faces around the table.

Joran seemed to voice the family's mood. "Wouldn't you be safer right here until the war is over? It can't last much longer."

Father, busy stuffing tobacco into his pipe, looked up with a twinkle in his eye. "I agree with Joran. Richard does eat quite a lot, but he's a hard worker. Definitely worth keeping around. America didn't seem to spoil him too much."

"The truth is that I'm incurably Dutch," said Richard. "My mom and dad are both Dutch, born in Groningen. And our neighborhood in Grand Rapids is mostly Dutch families." He looked at Joran. "I'll miss you guys, but I'm an airman. I need to get back to my unit if I can. Also, I want to see my brother, Lawrence. He's based in England too."

"There is something else I need to mention," said Jenny. "Captain Atsma had more news. He said the NSB people are causing problems. They raided the DeWitt family last night. Found their Jews and hauled everyone away. Everybody needs to be especially careful."

A sharp knock on the front door generated an immediate and well-rehearsed response. In less than fifteen seconds, the American airman was inside the hidden space under the kitchen and the table was back in its place. Joran hurried to his room, Mother went back to washing dishes, and Jenny sat at the kitchen table, pretending to read a book. Father moved through the darkened front room. In a deep, calm voice, he spoke through the closed door. "*Ja*."

"Albert, it is Klaas Atsma."

Jenny jumped up and joined her father at the door. He opened it to see Captain Atsma and a companion who was dressed in black. They hurried inside.

The stranger offered Father a quick handshake. "I'm Jack Holbrook. I'm here for Lieutenant DeGraaf."

Together, they opened the trapdoor in the kitchen. Holbrook extended a hand to help Richard climb up. "Greetings from London, Lieutenant DeGraaf. I'm Holbrook from MI-9. We are ready to move you. We had to eliminate some snags down in Antwerp, but we think the organization is clean now."

Richard turned a concerned look toward Captain Atsma, who nodded. "Holbrook is solid, Richard. Probably the best operative in the country. Sorry I couldn't give you more notice. We decided we should expedite the process since we have troublemakers prowling around right now."

Richard immediately looked at Joran who was standing in the background with a deep frown on his face. "Looks like I need to go, partner."

The frown remained. "Okay."

Richard hugged the boy. "After this lousy war is over, you and your family can move to Michigan if you want. You would like it there." He turned to Jenny. "Actually, I would love it if all the Demeesters and DeHaans moved there."

Holbrook, face sober, glanced at his watch. "We need to get going, DeGraaf."

When it was Jenny's turn for a goodbye hug, she pulled the airman to herself and held him close. With firm arms and shoulders, he did the same. It felt good, comforting somehow. She released him and stepped back. Their gaze locked for just a moment.

Richard inhaled and turned to Holbrook. "Okay, let's go." He followed the MI-9 man and the police chief out the front door.

CHAPTER THIRTY-SEVEN

3 June 1944
Auschwitz II - Birkenau

"*Antreten zum Appell.*" The order to form columns for the roll call sent a jolt through the body of Reinaar Demeester, prisoner number 202788. The jarring call echoed through the dimly lit building and prompted a rush of frail bodies clad in dirty striped uniforms.

On his way out of the block, he hurried past the man who gave the order, the chief of Block Twenty, the *blockälteste*, a non-Jew named Maslanka, who wielded unlimited power of life and death over his prisoners.

Reinaar sensed tension rising from all corners of Birkenau as the daily ordeal began. Roughly one thousand men, frail and gaunt, cringed as they ran past the block leader, most unscathed. Some events here were unscheduled and unpredictable: hangings, floggings, shootings, and selections for the gas chamber. But the *appells*, the roll calls, were as certain as the setting of the sun.

In spite of hunger, exhaustion, disease, and wounds, tens of thousands of prisoners, called häftlings in Birkenau, gathered in formations near their barracks for the daily ordeal of the appell. Roll call went on until the häftling count was reconciled. It could take minutes, hours, or all night, and was done in any kind of weather.

Reinaar stood near the rear of the group, looking at the backs of frail, starving men, all dressed in their striped uniforms, berets, and wooden clogs. The blockälteste and his helpers, with shouts, curses, and crushing blows of their cudgels, perfected the appearance of the formation until Maslanka was satisfied that they were prepared for the review of the SS. On the left flank of the group, the prisoners built a pile of bodies, häftlings who had lost their lonely battle with the Nazis' final solution.

Standing at attention, face forward, Reinaar scanned left and right, moving only his eyes. Formations were building at all neighboring barracks. All around those blocks, the mud of winter had become the hard dirt of summer. Not one blade of grass was visible anywhere inside the electric fences. Any emerging sprout would be quickly consumed by a starving häftling. Looking over the roofs of the multiple rows of prisoner huts, the chimneys of the four crematoria belched fire and smoke into the clear blue sky ... the fires of hell rebelling against the glory of creation.

A lazy breeze pulled the smoke containing the ashes of many thousands of human beings and scattered them across the green Polish countryside. Reinaar felt the ash on his face. Smelled it in his nostrils.

The appell had begun. He watched the SS lieutenant enter the gate of section BIId, the men's camp, and approach the first formation in the row of barracks.

Inspection of the first three blocks proceeded uneventfully. Reinaar felt just a tiny bit of relief each time the SS lieutenant shouted, *"Stimmt!"* The häftling count reported by the blockälteste matched the number recorded on the SS clipboard.

When the lieutenant strutted up to Block Twenty, Reinaar's body tensed.

The blockälteste barked the order, *"Stillstand! Mützen ab!"* Instantly, Reinaar and a thousand fellow häftlings yanked the caps from their heads and froze in place. Maslanka approached the SS man and snapped to attention. "Block Twenty reports a force of 1005 häftlings, 990 alive and fifteen dead."

The *Unterscharführer* studied his clipboard, frowned, and shouted words that pierced Reinaar's heart. "*Fehlt einer!*" The count was off by one. Reinaar, experienced and disciplined, maintained his absolutely rigid posture, looking straight ahead, jaw tight. One unfortunate häftling, standing in the front row, only feet from the SS man, jerked his head. The lieutenant, expressionless, turned to the man and slid his clipboard under his arm. He pulled out his Luger pistol, placed the muzzle on the prisoner's forehead, and paused for a couple of seconds while the man trembled. The Lugar jumped slightly, and the shot echoed around the silent yard. The häftling collapsed to the ground.

As far as Reinaar could see, not one person in the 989-man formation moved a muscle. They looked like frail marble statues covered with rags. While Maslanka and his assistants conducted a desperate search for the missing man, the Unterscharführer casually strolled along the grouping, occasionally stopping and examining a rigid häftling.

A spasm developed in Reinaar's right leg. As it claimed more territory, his tension grew, and a feeling of dizziness crept into his head. He stole a look at the SS man. His back was turned. He risked his life and allowed himself the luxury of blinking, clamping and unclamping his jaw, and taking weight off his spasmed leg. When the lieutenant turned back to the formation, Reinaar was rigid as a granite slab, feeling enormous relief.

After about ten minutes, the blockälteste returned, dragging a dead prisoner. They dumped the body on the pile of dead prisoners. Maslanka hurried to the lieutenant, and, in a breaking voice that betrayed his fear, amended his report to include the dead man. The lieutenant nodded and shouted "*Stimmt!*" He moved on to Block Nineteen, and the tension drained from Reinaar's body, leaving it just a bit weaker than before the appell.

Two hours later, the SS declared that the häftling count in section BIId was reconciled, concluding the appell. Except for the piles of dead beside each formation, thousands of häftlings had survived another day in the hell of Auschwitz-Birkenau.

Reinaar hurried to the barrack to collect his supper, a piece of black bread, this time with a thin coating of margarine. Holding his bowl under his chin to catch every falling crumb, he proceeded to eat. His desire to savor this bit of food was quickly overwhelmed by his ravenous hunger. In seconds, he was picking the crumbs from the bowl.

A kapo, one of the Jews assigned to oversee inmates, led a small group of prisoners into the hut. Their normal weight identified them as new arrivals. One of the healthy-looking men caught Reinaar's eye. He forced his brain, cloudy from exhaustion and hunger, to review the long list of acquaintances he had acquired over the years. *Jacob Baumann.* Yes, that was it. Factory owner in Budapest. He waited until the kapo left the small group standing in the barracks, confusion written on their faces. He approached Baumann. "Jacob?"

The man, expression blank, looked at him.

"Jacob, it is Reinaar Demeester from Holland, one of your best customers."

Recognition crept onto the man's face. "Yes, Reinaar. I recognize you now." He paused. "Please forgive me, but you have changed."

"I have not seen a mirror in many months, Jacob, but since all the häftlings in this hut look like twins, I assume I am as gruesome as they."

Baumann frowned. "Then I must expect that I will look the same before long."

"If you are blessed to live so long."

The man blinked, and he moved closer. "Please tell me more. I want to survive this place. I want to see my family again."

"Did they arrive with you?"

"Yes, my wife and two small children. They separated us on the train platform. When will I see them again?"

Without hesitation, Reinaar slipped into a lie. "Perhaps soon, Jacob."

They sat in the dirt outside the hut. A häftling shuffled past, cheeks hollow, eyes sunken and lifeless, his head bowed. Reinaar nodded at the man. "They call men like that Muselmann. They are beyond hope, dead men whose hearts still beat."

"Why? What caused that?"

"Starvation sickness, maybe other diseases besides. Most men who work outdoors soon fall victim. If he survives the night, he will probably be taken away tomorrow."

"And?"

Reinaar raised a thin finger and pointed at the billowing chimney nearby. "There."

Baumann followed his point. His head jerked, and he swung around with a hand to his face. "Please tell me how you have survived."

"I have been fortunate. When I was a young man, my father insisted that I expand my knowledge by developing a workplace skill. I studied to be an electrician. I even worked as an apprentice for a time. When I arrived at the Auschwitz complex, I was assigned to the Monowitz camp, where the Germans are developing an industrial operation. Living conditions are bad in that division of Auschwitz also, but because my skills were valuable, I escaped harsh treatment on the job."

"And you are back here in Birkenau. Why?"

"The kapo said people are needed in the *Kanada Kommando* because of the many new arrivals." He shrugged. "But I have been here a week, and I have been working outdoors, digging a large pit. That kind of job will turn me into a Muselmann."

"What is Kanada Kommando?"

"A work group that collects and organizes property that people bring to the camp."

"Yes, I saw them at the ramp when we arrived." Jacob scanned the bleak surroundings and the emaciated men around the hut. "Please tell me how I can live to see my family."

Reinaar paused and tried to organize his thoughts. "Please forgive my hesitation, Jacob. The weakness of my body has invaded my feeble brain. First, eat all you can. Every crumb. The food is terrible but essential. Next, conserve your energy. If they assign you to a strenuous labor kommando, work as slowly as you can. Exertion robs more energy than a mild beating."

A deep frown creased Jacob's plump face. "It seems that those steps will only delay the inevitable."

Reinaar scratched the dry skin on his soiled arm. "Much is out of our control. Sanitation here is very bad. There is much disease. Dysentery is common. We get typhus from the lice. Tuberculosis is spreading. The poorly fitting clogs cause sores that do not heal." He paused. "The Germans expect us all to die here, Jacob."

A Muselmann staggered past. A slab of bread dropped from his hand. Immediately, two prisoners dove for it, and a vicious fight resulted, ending when one man prevailed and gobbled the morsel.

"There you see it," Reinaar said. "Starvation in a group eventually turns men into savage beasts. Their humanity dies, and soon their bodies follow. Listen to what I say, Jacob. I think this is critical. Maintain your dignity. Live inside your conscious mind, your soul. Feed it with joyous memories and hopes for the future. You will find that your mind and your body are not the same thing. Your mind belongs to you."

He again studied Jacob's face, reached out with his bony hands, and grasped his companion's fleshy arms. "You notice I keep addressing you by name. That is part of building a human relationship. Having a friend in this awful place will help keep you alive." He sighed. "I am afraid that I have exhausted my meager storehouse of wisdom today. Perhaps we can talk more tomorrow, my friend."

The approach of a man wearing a kapo armband and carrying a clipboard ended their conversation. They jumped to their feet. The man looked at the prisoner number written on Reinaar's tattered uniform and referred to his clipboard. "Show me your arm."

Reinaar uncovered the tattoo on his left forearm and held it out for inspection.

"You are moving to the Kanada barracks. Let's go." He walked toward the door of the hut.

Reinaar had time only for a brief wave at his new friend before he hurried after the kapo.

Sometime before the sun rose over Auschwitz, the reveille gong jolted Reinaar from a shallow sleep. He lay still while the man lying beside him pulled himself off the wooden platform, allowing Reinaar to follow. On his way to the latrine, he scanned the area, his first good look since he arrived in the new section the previous night.

Kanada was different from the men's section of Birkenau. This area consisted of rows of huge warehouses. Trucks were parked outside, all filled with luggage items. The male häftlings wore regular striped uniforms but had leather shoes. The women wore civilian-type dresses. Apparently, they were allowed to enjoy some of the benefits of the riches looted from all the new arrivals.

Reinaar joined the line of prisoners waiting to receive the morning ration of ersatz coffee. After gulping it down, he observed his fellow häftlings until he found a man who seemed to have an alert mind. "I am Reinaar Demeester from Holland. I arrived last night."

The man offered a bony hand. "I am Augustyn Bukowski from Krakow."

Bukowski's bright eyes nurtured a sense of excitement that was buried deep in Reinaar's hunger-clouded brain. He grasped the man's hand. "Tell me about this place."

"We only have a few minutes, Reinaar. May I call you by your first name?"

"Yes, the sound of my name brings me joy. It is my last possession besides my memories."

"This is Kanada, named after the rich country in North America. As you can see, we sort out all the rags and riches brought here on the trains. Because of the flood of new prisoners, Jews from Hungary mostly, the workforce has expanded greatly, you among them. I estimate that we have almost two thousand workers here right now."

Reinaar looked around. "I have been in the Monowitz camp and the men's camp here in Birkenau. Things seem better in Kanada."

Augustyn nodded. "I only know Kanada. We are beaten sometimes. Some people have been flogged for stealing, but I have seen no hangings or shootings here." He shrugged. "Right now, we have value. They need our work."

Augustyn pointed at a brick building across the wire fence. "Our existence is infinitely better than what we witness over there. That is Crematory Four. Beyond it is Crematory Five."

"I worked in an area beyond those buildings yesterday," Reinaar said. "We dug a large pit. About fifty meters long and three meters deep. Perhaps they were just giving us work to wear us down."

Augustyn shook his head and frowned. "I fear their motives are more sinister."

The sound of a chugging locomotive interrupted their discussion.

"That train is pulling into the camp," said Augustyn. "We will be going to work soon."

"How many people are on each train?"

"Too many for me to count. Probably three thousand. Maybe more. Jews from Hungary, I think."

Kanada suddenly came alive. A squad of kapos appeared and, with their customary shouts and curses, drove the men into nearby trucks. They made the short drive to a rail siding that extended directly into the camp. Waiting there was a locomotive pulling a long line of boxcars like those that brought the Demeesters to this place.

Reinaar and the rest of the group from Kanada Kommando stood together on the ramp and waited beside the train. He counted thirty cattle cars, each closed and latched. He stood close enough to hear coughs and muffled conversation from inside the train.

The SS arrived in a short caravan of staff cars. One group of officers gathered at the end of the platform, near the front of the train. As the remainder of the SS detail, some accompanied by large dogs, proceeded down the platform, the laborers followed.

The SS men appeared calm and detached. It was just another day in this smelly, disease-filled place. Along the length of the train, the SS men snapped open door latches and slid open the large wagon doors, exposing a crowd of anxious, blinking faces.

Without giving the new arrivals a chance to study the scene on the ramp, the SS went into their well-practiced routine. The shouts were the same up and down the train. *"Alle heraus, schnell!"*

Passengers who understood German pushed toward the doors. The rest immediately clambered after them. The SS directed the arrivals to leave their luggage in place and move toward the end of the platform. Snarling, snapping dogs and occasional truncheon blows hastened compliance.

As the arrivals moved down the platform, the kapos ordered the Kanada Kommando workers to move all the luggage onto waiting trucks. Reinaar followed another häftling into an open wagon and tossed bags from the car onto the platform below. Two still bodies lay among the luggage. Reinaar's companion looked out the door at a kapo. "Two dead ones in here."

The kapo's dark brows pulled into a tight frown. "Throw them out, fool."

Without words, Reinaar and his partner took the bodies by hands and feet and dropped them onto the platform. He winced and looked away when he heard the impact.

Augustyn appeared in the crowd. He moved close to his new friend and joined him in the work of unloading the train. When the wagons were all empty, the locomotive came to life and backed the train out of the camp.

In a few minutes, the ramp was clear, and a caravan of loaded vehicles moved toward the western perimeter of Birkenau, to the warehouses in Kanada. The workers followed on foot. A shrieking train whistle announced the arrival of a second train. Another group of laborers rushed past, hurrying to receive another load of Birkenau arrivals.

Once inside the Kanada compound, they climbed into the trucks and tossed the bags to the ground. When the trucks were unloaded, a small army of women prisoners began the sorting process, and Reinaar and Augustyn moved to the side of the Kanada compound where they waited for further orders.

From that location, they had a clear view of Crematorium Four, its twin chimneys belching smoke. The smell filled Reinaar's nostrils and throat. His eyes teared. His coughing lungs refused to abide the assault. He turned to Augustyn. "This is very hard to endure. Before today, I knew what was happening, but to be witness to it ..."

He blinked, giving him a clear view of events across the wire. He watched, stunned. Uniformed men were ushering people into the lower end of the crematorium.

Softly, Augustyn spoke. "This is a place of evil, perhaps worse than hell itself. They go in like sheep. Thousands of them. They don't come out." He pointed to the south. Over the barracks roofs, the chimneys of two more crematoria were pouring out smoke. "Four killing machines. Gas chambers combined with ovens. The smoke you see is from those people you saw this morning. A trainload of Jews. Most will be ashes within two hours of arrival." Augustyn paused while he pondered. "I was angry at first, and I cried. Now I am empty."

Reinaar held his gaze on the spectacle at the crematories. "While we were returning from the ramp, I saw another train arriving. It seems like more people than the crematories can handle. Perhaps more will be admitted to the camp?"

"Perhaps." Augustyn laid a gentle hand on his shoulder. "But it looks like they have chosen to make use of that pit you dug yesterday." He pointed through a stand of trees to the north.

SS men were herding a line of people past the smoking chimneys of Crematorium Five in the direction of a huge pit. Men, women, and children. Only now, smoke was pouring from that pit.

Reinaar's hands trembled. "Oh, no. Are they ..."

Augustyn turned his back to the smoke and looked toward the eastern horizon. "You must know, Reinaar. Perhaps one of us will live to tell the world. I heard the Germans talking. They call those pits *Der Scheiterhaufen*, the pyre. They use them when the trains come too fast. Sometimes the ovens—they have forty-six—can't keep up with the arrivals. They must do something with all those people, so they shoot them and throw them into the burning trenches. Listen, you can hear screaming. Some are not yet dead when they fall into the flames."

Reinaar's already weakened legs failed him, and he sagged to the hardened dirt. "I thought nothing could be worse than the gas chambers. The Devil himself is right here among us. If death is the only escape, I welcome it."

Chapter Thirty-Eight

5 June 1944
Nijkerk

"Something big is going to happen soon." Captain Atsma, eyes bright, leaned forward in his creaking desk chair. "Our long wait is almost over." He beckoned for Jenny to enter his office. "Sit down, Jen."

She closed the police chief's door and hurried to a seat facing his desk. "I could use some good news."

"I got word from British MI-9 that invasion preparations are far along. They wouldn't give me details, of course, but I got the definite impression that it will happen very soon. American troops are crawling all over their country." Atsma slapped the top of his old desk. "Europe is about to be liberated."

Excitement raced through Jenny. She straightened in her chair. "I thought I would never hear those beautiful words. Do you think they will land on our beaches?"

"Who knows? Probably in France somewhere. Maybe here too."

Atsma pulled a map from his drawer, opened it, and spread it across his desk. "We have a role to play right now. The Allies want us to gather some vital information for them." He tapped a spot on the map near the city of Arnhem. "The Brits and the

Americans are interested in the Deelen airbase. That's the place the Germans call *Fliegerhorst Deelen.* I think it may be the largest German Luftwaffe base in the Netherlands, and it's right in our own neighborhood. For some reason, the Allies haven't hit it much. MI-9 told me they have a reconnaissance report from a couple of days ago that reports a large number of night fighters on the ground there. We need more information on what the Luftwaffe is doing. That's where you come in. You have family down that way, around Arnhem, right?"

"Right. My uncle Bert lives in Arnhem. I rode my bike there about a year ago. There is an airfield, but there wasn't much going on. I remember farms and a couple of small villages around it. Didn't seem like a big problem."

"The Brits now suspect the Germans might have camouflaged their operation. Do you think you could bike there with gifts, produce from the farm perhaps, for your relatives? Then you could just happen to ride past the airbase and have another look. If they are using camouflage to hide things, aerial pictures aren't good enough. The Germans also put in a rail line that has brought in a lot of material. We don't know why. We are hoping you can enlighten us. Their security probably won't be suspicious of a young woman riding past on a bike."

Jenny leaned forward and rested her arms on the captain's desk. "I have a suggestion. We have a full moon tonight, and it looks like the sky will be clear. I could go there tonight and get a really good look at the place."

"I don't know about that. There isn't much risk for you to ride past the place in daylight. But if they caught you at night ..."

Atsma leaned back in his chair and folded his arms. After pausing for half a minute, he rolled his chair tight to the desk. "A lot of lives are at stake. The Luftwaffe is a threat that must be contained. A hasty daylight pass of all that camouflage might not tell us enough. I'm going to let you go tonight." He pointed a finger at her. "But you be careful, young lady. If you're caught out after curfew, near an airbase on top of that, you could be shot on sight. I'll be sitting here worrying the whole time you are gone."

The chief went to his closet and pulled out a canvas backpack. "One of our Resistance men used this stuff on a night operation. It's a sabotage type of thing. The black clothes should fit you." He lifted some dynamite sticks from the bag and put them in his desk. "Won't need these."

He pulled out a long-barreled handgun and handed the weapon to Jenny. "You may be the first to get one of these in our country. It's a Welrod pistol. The Brits developed it. The fat barrel serves as a noise suppressor. They tell me it's as quiet as snapping your fingers. It shouldn't recoil much either. That place is bound to be heavily guarded. If you need to shoot somebody, you really don't want to bring the whole German army down on you."

He put the weapon in the backpack and withdrew a pistol. "I also want you to take this American forty-five automatic. If you are in really big trouble, this cannon could knock down a mule. Hold it with both hands."

Jenny blinked and swallowed a lump in her throat. Atsma frowned. "Forgive me for shocking you, but you need to recognize the danger. If that base is as important as I expect, it will be heavily guarded."

Atsma leaned back in his chair. "There is another side to this thing, Jenny. Your brother, Nic, along with thousands of other Dutchmen, is doing forced labor in Germany. With the war coming to Europe and on into Germany, those boys will be in greater danger. We need to do everything we can to hurt the German war machine."

Jenny stood and slid into the backpack. "You sure know how to motivate me, Chief. Now I'm eager to get going. This is for Nic."

"What have you heard from him?"

"Occasional letters get through. We don't know exactly where he is. It sounds like he gets moved around. The last one said he was sick but not to worry. We worry anyway."

Wearing all black and with her face smeared with coal dust, Jenny hid her bicycle in the woods a quarter-mile from the Fliegerhorst Deelen. She proceeded on foot through the woods. Progress was slow. She used moonlight to avoid noisy things like dry twigs and branches. Every few steps, she paused to scan and listen.

As she approached the edge of the woods, she stopped. A low humming sound in the western sky joined the chorus of crickets in the brush around her. The drone grew louder, deeper. "Aircraft engine," she whispered. A dark shape appeared and passed directly overhead, taking the engine noise with it. The moonlight revealed the silhouette of a twin-engine airplane.

In her mind, Jenny reviewed the pictures that Atsma had shown her. "Junkers eighty-eight night fighter," she mumbled. The plane throttled back and glided silently toward the ground. Dim runway lights came alive, just long enough for the plane to set down, then went dark. The plane slowed to a stop, and the engine came alive again. Under the light of the moon, it taxied away from the runway along what looked like a winding road. It soon disappeared into the darkness, pulling its sound with it. Quiet returned to the woods, except for the friendly crickets.

More airplanes approached. "More Junkers," she whispered. As they passed low overhead, Jenny studied the two twin-engine machines. *No, not Junkers. A different tail. Must be Messerschmitts.*

One plane glided to the airstrip while the second made a slow turn around the horizon and touched down like the first. For these planes, like the Junkers, the dim runway lights broke the blackout only momentarily to ensure safe landings. Both Messerschmitts taxied along the path of the earlier Junkers plane.

So much for the nice little farm village. This was definitely a much larger facility than she had suspected the last time she passed on her bike. But what else was going on here? She sat on a fallen log near the edge of an open field, then pulled a canteen from her backpack and sipped water while she watched.

After a few minutes, engine noises sounded from somewhere on the airfield. Multiple planes emerged in the moonlight. Jenny counted five. They lined up at the end of a runway. Dim lights along the airstrip came alive. The lead plane's engine quickly ran up to what must have been maximum power, and it surged down the strip. The next plane immediately pulled into position and followed the first. In half a minute, all five planes had departed, and the runway lights blinked off.

Jenny felt her forehead pull into a frown. Those guys were definitely not out for a joyride. *We need to shut this place down.*

The moonlight glinted off two gleaming railroad tracks that passed in front of Jenny. Staying near the edge of the woods, she followed them. As she edged ahead, constantly monitoring her surroundings, a large block-shaped object appeared ahead of her. She left the tracks and approached the structure carefully. As she reached the edge of the cleared area around the building, passing clouds blocked the moon, forcing her to stop in the almost total darkness.

Footsteps approached from Jenny's right. Her heart pulsed in her neck. A narrow flashlight beam bounced along a nearby path.

She eased the Welrod pistol from her pack, crouched low to the ground among some bushes, and waited. Two figures conversed in German as they walked. "I hate night guard duty," a young-sounding voice said. "I would rather be in the club drinking good German beer."

Guard number two sounded older. He scolded his companion. "I expect that you have not been on the Russian front. We are in heaven here, fool. Think about it. You are not getting shot. You sleep in a bed. And most of all, there are girls, hundreds of them, all around us. Have you ever seen so many beauties in one place? And they can't leave the air base."

Guard number one stopped to light a cigarette. As he drew from it, the little fireball burned bright and illuminated his young face. He exhaled loudly, and the smell drifted to Jenny, squatting in the brush only feet away. "I guess you're right, Horst. What are all those girls doing here?"

"They work in Diogenes, that big bunker over there." He seemed to be pointing toward the giant concrete structure behind them.

"What is that?"

"Don't know much about it. I heard they do something with the airplanes. Must be a big deal. It's a huge place."

"How do you know about it?"

Guard two lit a cigarette and started moving down the path, talking as he walked. "I know a girl who works in the place. We took a walk in the woods last night. She told me a little about it."

"What else happened in the woods?" Guard one's young voice sounded eager.

Guard two laughed and elbowed his companion. "I can't tell you that, kid."

Jenny remained frozen in place until the voices had faded and she was certain the men were gone. She replaced her gun in the pack, wanting to keep both hands free. The full moon reappeared through the breaks in the foliage above her, and she crept back to the path where she could walk quietly. She approached the building the soldiers had called Diogenes.

At the edge of the woods, she had a clear view. Seeing a sentry strolling along the sidewalk beside the structure, she went to her knees and peered through the thick brush. *It won't win any design awards.* The building appeared to be a plain, solid concrete block, about sixty meters long and nearly as wide. The area with windows indicated a three-story building.

Multiple female voices broke the quiet of the night and approached. The individual in the lead carried a flashlight. Jenny pulled back to avoid the bouncing flashlight beam and studied the voices, striving to extract usable intelligence. There was none. Except for the different language, the discussion sounded like a group of college girls in Utrecht heading for a school function. The laughter was the same. The only difference was these women talked about cute soldiers rather than cute college boys. After the woman with the flashlight passed, Jenny rose in the darkness and tried to estimate the size of the group. About fifty or sixty.

The group disappeared into the bunker and quiet returned. About five minutes later, a door in the side of the big concrete cube opened, and light spilled out, illuminating another group of women who were leaving.

Jenny ducked and listened. The casual tone of the conversation was like that of the first group. As they approached Jenny, a flight of several aircraft passed low overhead. The engine noise covered their voices. When quiet returned, one of the women spoke. "We sure kept our guys busy tonight. I hope they shot down a bunch of those nasty British bombers. I'm afraid they might drop one on us sometime."

Her companion answered, "And I hope our guys aren't too tired to party when they get back." The comment generated laughter in the group. The chattering faded as the crowd passed into the night.

Jenny stood. *That's enough. Time to go.* She studied the location of the full moon and calculated the direction back to her bicycle. Leaving the Diogenes bunker behind, she began her slow, methodical, and ever-vigilant trek through the woods. She reviewed the things she had witnessed. The urgency of her mission to help neutralize the Luftwaffe base at Deelen pushed her onward.

She jerked to a halt. Footsteps somewhere off to her right. A form was moving in her direction. She lowered herself to a crouch. Moonlight glinted off the figure's helmet. A rifle barrel extended above his shoulder. In the man's hand, the tight beam of a flashlight exposed a path only five meters ahead of Jenny. She eased to her knees and waited.

When the man was about twenty meters from her, a low-flying aircraft passed overhead, and the soldier stopped to watch the plane. Taking advantage of the noisy distraction, Jenny quickly opened her backpack and selected the Welrod pistol with its built-in silencer.

The man passed her close enough that the scent of cheap aftershave drifted down and tickled her nose. She held her breath and devoted all her energy to crushing the sneeze that grew inside her. She pinched her nose, but the sneeze overpowered her. When it broke loose, it was more of a grunt than a sneeze.

The man stopped and turned. He slid the weapon slowly from his shoulder and raised it into a firing position. Jenny watched the rifle barrel swing wildly in various directions.

Another sneeze grew inside her. She closed her eyes, gritted her teeth, and tightened every muscle in her body. The sneeze faded.

The soldier edged in Jenny's direction. She raised her pistol and aimed it at the man, who was now only about twenty feet away.

A rustling sound near Jenny froze both her and the man she was watching. For the first time, he spoke. The nervous, young voice reminded Jenny of her own brother. "*Was ist das?*"

Terror gripped her, and the Welrod trembled in her hand as she stared at the man, who was now aiming his rifle in her direction. Her thoughts raced. The mission must be completed. Many lives were at stake. One shot, and the man would be down. *Just go away. Please.* Those words demanded to come out of her. She restrained them.

The rustling sound returned. Jenny's heart jumped, then the subtle movement became an eruption in the bushes beside her. A rifle blast shattered the quiet of the night. A rabbit broke through the vegetation and ran past the soldier and into the brush on the opposite side of the path. "*Ein hase,*" he exclaimed.

As she inventoried her body for damage, relief flooded Jenny's mind. *Yes, it is a rabbit, and it saved my life, or yours.*

The young man shouldered his weapon and strode away.

Jenny, whose knees were still too weak to support her weight, offered a quick prayer of thanks, then sat and waited for her heart rate to return to normal. She opened her backpack to insert her pistol. The slight smell of spent gunpowder caught her attention. She sniffed the muzzle at the end of the sound suppressor. Her knees went weak again. "I must have fired when he did," she whispered. "Thank the Lord; I missed the guy."

About three o'clock the next morning, Jenny quietly walked her bike through the blacked-out streets of Nijkerk. Her backpack now bulged with the black outfit from the night operation. She had used the last of her canteen water to remove the coal dust from her face. The full moon was easing toward the western horizon, its work almost finished. She rested her bike against the wall at the back of the police station and knocked lightly on the door.

The door eased open, and Captain Atsma's face appeared. A bright smile replaced the deep frown. He beckoned for her to enter. "How did it go?"

"Whatever the Allies have done to that place, it wasn't enough. Based on what I saw, it is an extremely active Luftwaffe base. It must be very well camouflaged. And there is more. I saw a giant concrete bunker, and I heard the workers talking. Apparently, the place is a command center for Luftwaffe operations. It's probably hardened and might be immune from big bombs, but the Allies need to pound that place."

"Good work," Atsma said. "Sit down and draw me a map. I'll get it to MI-9. Then go home and get some sleep. You look pretty beat up."

Jenny grinned. "You might want to check a mirror, Captain. You look a bit worn down yourself." She handed her backpack to him. "I hope I won't need this stuff again."

"I trust you didn't need to use the guns."

"Well, I did fire the Welrod one time. Thankfully, I missed."

The captain's eyes widened. "Sit down, young lady. I want to hear the rest of this story."

CHAPTER THIRTY-NINE

17 January 1945
Auschwitz III-Monowitz
IG Farben Industrial Complex

Reinaar hugged himself, sliding his cold, stiff hands under the arms of his thin jacket. He looked up and met the steady gaze of his crew leader.

A heavy knit cap covered the kapo's forehead all the way to the deep wrinkle between his bushy eyebrows. He shoved his gloves deep into the pockets of his wool coat, squeezing his wooden cudgel under one arm. As the cloud of his warm breath rose in the frigid air, he nodded a silent command.

Reinaar exposed his bare hands and placed them on the large chunk of cold concrete. He and three fellow prisoners lifted the two-hundred-pound weight. Shuffling their wooden clogs across the icy concrete, they carried their burden a short distance and dropped it onto a pile of rubble.

The workers, all dressed only in their striped uniforms consisting of a threadbare jacket, shirt, undershorts, and trousers, turned their backs to the wind and bent at the waist, listening for further orders. Heavy snowflakes, falling from a dark, overcast sky, settled on their shoulders. Around them, other members of the twenty-man kommando groaned under their burdens, chunks of broken concrete courtesy of Allied bombers.

The wail of a distant siren brought all activity to a halt. With words formed with difficulty through red, stiff cheeks, the kapo gave the order that the prisoners longed to hear. "Work is finished. Form up for the march to the lager."

The men dropped their loads and hurried to establish a formation. At the command of the kapo, they set off, following their taskmaster. Walking into a wind that pierced his light uniform, Reinaar blinked large snowflakes from his eyes. While trying to avoid the slippery patches of ice, he used a sliding gait in an effort to keep the sores on both heels from rubbing on the rough wood of his clogs. The hunger, a constant presence, gnawed at him.

He scanned the largely silent Farben complex, or what was left of it. After thousands of prisoners had lost their lives in the building of this place, broken machines silently gathered snow amid the rubble.

The formation broke down into a sullen group, trudging along, leaning into the wind. The kapo, for the very first time, was conversing with men at the front of the group.

Reinaar exchanged glances with his fellow workers. Their surprised expressions reflected his puzzlement. Something was very different that day. The kapo had not beaten or even cursed anyone, and now he was calmly interacting with the workers. *Why the change?* It wasn't their surroundings. The IG Farben complex had been largely a pile of wreckage since the last Allied bombing on the day after Christmas. No, the difference was revealed by the sounds around them. What had been a distant rumble of artillery now had a sharp edge. The Russian guns were closer. Much closer. Liberation was coming. It was imminent, and everyone knew it, including the kapo. He would soon be just another vulnerable häftling.

Reinaar's weak body felt a slight rush of new energy. The evil of Auschwitz was about to rupture. But would his blood be part of the destruction?

As he walked, his tired mind tried to push aside his hunger and the cold. Yes, Auschwitz was doomed. Yet the tiny speck of hope deep inside him refused to grow. The Nazis clearly intended to kill every living Jew. They would never allow the hated Russians to rescue anyone. Surely the Germans had enough bullets to leave heaps of dead Jews as they ran away. What should he do? What could he do?

As they neared the gate to Auschwitz III, the kapo ordered the group into a neat formation. He halted the procession at the SS guard station and ordered, "*Mützen ab!*" The häftlings jerked the caps from their heads.

After the kapo reported the return of the twenty-man kommando, the SS officer, expressionless and silent, admitted the group to the camp with a casual wave of the back of his hand. Inside the gate, the kapo ordered the häftlings to await the roll call.

Evening roll call proceeded smoothly. No hangings. No floggings. No shootings. The SS seemed distracted, eager to finish the proceedings. As soon as the roll call was complete, the SS withdrew, leaving the blockältestes and kapos to manage the crowd of prisoners.

Reinaar went to his hut in Block Forty-Nine and joined the men crowded inside, out of the wind and snow. Their collective body heat served to raise the temperature in the drafty structure a few meager degrees.

He coughed. The man in front of him turned and glared. With another cough rising in him, he worked his way through the crowd and leaned on the wall of the hut. A series of coughs took control of him and left him dizzy. A feverish chill added to the cold that went deep into his frail body.

Aaron Mendel, a Jewish prisoner from Italy, approached him. "You are sick, my friend."

"It is coming on me just now." More coughs forced him to bend and brace his hands on his knees. He stood up and looked up at

Aaron. "I was relieved when they transferred me from Birkenau to Auschwitz III, back to my electrical work. But the bombing ended the indoor work, and I was assigned to work outdoors, clearing the rubble. Now I suffer."

"You must go to the medical unit. Perhaps they will give you medicine if they have any."

Reinaar nodded. "Perhaps. With the Russians coming, they have no need to save anything." He paused for a moment. "On the other hand, this is no time to reveal any weaknesses. If the SS evacuate this place, they will surely kill off the sick before they leave."

All conversation in the hut ceased as the blockälteste burst into the building. Nervous hyperactivity replaced his usual arrogant and aggressive manner. "Listen, everyone. The camp is to be evacuated tomorrow. Yes, you heard me right. Everyone able to walk will march out of Auschwitz." He glared at one nearby häftling. "Don't look at me that way. I know it's snowing. Yes, the freezing cold will pierce your flimsy rags. But think of it, you fools. Listen to what I say. You are leaving. No more selections. You have hope for the future. Sometime tomorrow we leave Auschwitz behind."

The prisoners stared in numb silence as the blockälteste strode into his room and closed the door.

That evening, the meal consisted of a double ration of bread with margarine. Reinaar licked the margarine from the first slice and slid it into his pocket. He split the second piece, ate half, and traded the rest for some rags to serve as padding for the sores on his feet.

After the mealtime, conversations sprang up among the idle häftlings. In a few, largely the newer and healthier prisoners, the small flicker of hope grew into a torch of enthusiasm. The others, weak, sick, and starving, sat with blank faces. Whatever hope remained in those human skeletons was only a tiny flicker deep in their souls. From months or years of unimaginable hardship, their hopes and dreams were limited to surviving the present day. They had learned to respond to circumstances by taking the path of least resistance.

Reinaar leaned his back against the wall of the hut. A draft of cold air penetrated his garb and chilled his feverish body. He forced his dull brain to process his situation. In a world of few choices, he had one. Should he attempt to take shelter in the infirmary? The prospect of marching in a Polish winter storm was grim. *But what about all those who are left behind in the infirmary?* His tired mind settled on the answer. His chances of survival on the road were poor, but his chances in Auschwitz were worse. The infirmary patients would die. Every last one. He made his decision. If able, he would leave this place. If he were to die, it would not be here.

The night passed slowly. His frequent coughs prevented any sleep.

January 18, 1945, was a day unlike any other in Reinaar's life in Konzentrationslager Auschwitz. No work kommandos. No beatings. The kapos seemed to know that they would soon join the ranks of prisoners, trying to somehow survive a march in the dead of winter to some unknown place. That destination was the subject of wild speculation among the thousands of prisoners. To Reinaar, the noon soup seemed to be a bit richer. He received another double portion of bread for dinner.

At six o'clock that evening, it happened. With the ring of a bell, the camp sprang to life. The giant searchlights lit up the area, exposing huge snowflakes that descended on the expectant faces of waiting häftlings. Hundreds of SS men rushed into the camp. Block by block, prisoners arranged themselves into formations. The camp gates swung open, and the mass exodus began. The prisoners in Block Forty-Nine watched as the formations of all the lower-numbered blocks passed them. More men than he could count. He guessed eight or nine thousand. And this was only one division of the Auschwitz complex. How many would be left when they reached their destination, wherever that was?

Finally, their turn came. The order to march. A horde of human skeletons left the hell of Auschwitz and entered a dark, freezing

Polish night. Reinaar Demeester, once one of the richest men in the Netherlands but now reduced to a sick skeleton of a man known only by a number, clung to dim memories of his precious family and previous life. His bowl, dangling from a strap around his neck, bounced on his chest as he marched. Did he need that burden? If they provided soup, he would. But would he survive that long? He tossed the bowl into the darkness.

Occasional shouts and curses erupted from the SS men who marched beside them. Reinaar ignored the abuse and marched in silence, conserving every ounce of precious energy.

When the occasional SS motorcycle passed, the headlight reflected off the millions of small snowflakes blowing in the wind.

Conscious of the pain of the draining sores on both heels, he tried to practice a sliding gait to reduce the pressure on his wounds. This effort became impossible when the road, snow-packed from the thousands of marchers ahead of him, turned to ice.

A marcher in front of him slipped on the ice. His legs thrashed in a vain attempt to avoid a fall, but he crashed to the ground with a grunt. Reinaar stumbled on the scrambling man but managed to recover. The cacophony of thousands of marching men was abruptly shattered by a sharp gunshot behind him. Was it the man who fell? Reinaar focused on the bodies immediately in front of him and continued to march.

The first hour passed without overwhelming difficulty. The pain in his feet grew, jolting him with each step. The freezing wind numbed his face and cut through his clothes, but his constant exertion seemed to push the cold away. Occasional rifle blasts shattered the air. Only the SS spoke. All the prisoners seemed to be engaged in their individual battles for survival.

After a couple of marchers dropped out, Reinaar found himself on the outside of the column. As he passed a slow SS man, he felt a heavy hand on his shoulder. *"Häftling, komm her."*

He jumped out of the formation, approached the man, pulled off his hat, and stood rigid.

The soldier removed his backpack and handed it to Reinaar. *"Sie tragen diese."*

He took the pack and slid his arms into the straps.

With a wave of his hand, the man motioned him to proceed.

Reinaar jumped into the stream of marchers, paying close attention to his new master, who marched beside him with a rifle hanging on his shoulder.

The added weight pulled on his back and knees. The sores on his feet shouted their pain. His pace slowed. Some men passed him. Angry voices behind him sent jolts of fear into him. *I will not survive if I carry this fool's pack.*

Hearing a commotion behind him, he looked back to see his SS master stop by a fallen marcher and unsling his rifle. Reinaar faced forward and continued to march. The sudden rifle blast jolted him. When he dared to take his eyes from the mass of marching feet in front of him, he ventured a quick glance to the rear. He saw only a mass of exhausted häftlings. The SS man, the owner of the burden that threatened his life, was nowhere in sight. The formation marched on.

After about ten minutes without the reappearance of the backpack's owner, Reinaar worked his way to his right, eventually reaching the opposite side of the formation. Quickly glancing around, he tossed the backpack into the ditch and hurried on, just another walking skeleton in a striped suit.

Night turned to day. The rising sun hid behind a thick wall of dark clouds. The snow continued, driven by a constant north wind that cut through his rags. A white blanket covered the nearby fields. Deep drifts gathered beside objects large enough to block the constant north wind.

Daylight revealed the extent of the evacuation. Ahead of him as far as he could see, thousands of people plodded forward. The once-tight formation had broken down.

The huge procession passed through several small Polish villages. The houses showed no sign of life. Had the people fled? Were they watching? *Someone must see and remember.*

The guards had changed. These were not the same people who strutted around Auschwitz in their nice uniforms and gleaming boots, shouting and killing with communal glee. They now seemed tired and cold, their pride or ambition gone. Their arrogant aggression toward camp prisoners was replaced by casual indifference toward the filthy creatures they were herding through the Polish winter. For the victims, the result was the same. The killing continued.

Reinaar carried no feelings whatever toward the SS. No hatred. No fear. In his mind, they were simply living creatures who took up space. His only goal was to keep moving ahead, desperately hoping his body would continue to function. Somewhere in the back of his mind, he knew that a bullet could end his life, but he felt no fear. While he still chose life, the thought of death offered some comfort.

As the day progressed, the life in his body continued to shrink. The pain in his feet was gone. In fact, all feeling below his knees had vanished. He stomped his foot. The sound of the clog striking ice rose, and he felt the vibration in his leg, but his foot seemed dead. The effort only succeeded in stirring up the monster that grew in his chest. He coughed violently and spat out the stuff that his lungs rejected.

In spite of his exhaustion, anger welled inside him. His body was failing him when he most needed it. Abandoning him when he had devoted every fiber of his being to care for it. This anger seemed like a stranger. He hadn't felt rage since Auschwitz had made the futility of it clear. And it seemed to energize him, but only in his mind. His thoughts were strong, determined. His memory was vivid, more lucid than when he languished in the camp. But his body was fading, losing its capacity to carry and nurture his conscious mind. It seemed like a sputtering engine that was running out of petrol. How much longer could his tormented and brutalized body continue?

A motorcycle approached from the rear of the formation and passed Reinaar, close enough that the heat from the exhaust gave him just a hint of warmth. The machine stopped alongside an SS guard. As Reinaar passed them, he got a second little dose of warm exhaust. The words he heard caused his tired eyes to widen. "*Wir bleiben stehen.*"

For the first time in hours, his cracked lips opened, and he echoed the German's words. "We are stopping to rest."

The SS directed the marchers off the road. Reinaar's group moved into a thinly wooded area. He hobbled to a young oak tree barely wide enough to partially shield his frail body from the unrelenting wind. He grasped it with both hands to keep from falling, then moved to the downwind side and slid down to a sitting position in the snow.

After glancing around for potential thieves, he pushed a numb hand into his pocket and pulled out his precious slab of frozen bread. He forced his stiff face to consume the morsel before it could be taken from him. He hoped this new fuel would somehow restore him. It did not.

The realization took root in Reinaar's mind that he lacked the strength to stand. With his unfeeling hand, he scooped snow and ate it. After a few minutes, this new hydration restored some clarity in his mind, but his body did not respond.

As the snow drifted around him, his body's sensations retreated toward his chest. His extremities no longer existed. With eyes closed, his chin drooped. His body gathered all its energy to generate a feeble cough.

His mind still lived, but sleep beckoned. *Can't sleep. Must not sleep.* Even that thought was hard to formulate.

From off in the distance somewhere, a harsh command reached him. "Form up to march."

Sleep—beautiful sleep—beckoned.

A nearby voice intruded. "Is this one dead?"

Reinaar felt a jolt on his chest. His lungs refused to cough.

A second voice joined in. "He's dead. Leave him."

Silence. His mind seemed to be floating, free of his body. Sleep summoned him.

CHAPTER FORTY

April 1945
Nijkerk

Karl Müller looked over the hood of the black sedan as he cruised along the road from Putten toward the Gestapo office in Utrecht. The warm sun on his face brought a bit of calm to the anxiety that churned inside him. Ernst Schmidt would be at the Utrecht office, awaiting his report. He contemplated how he would describe his unsuccessful mission. In spite of promising tips from NSB collaborators, he had learned nothing about any remaining Jews or any Dutch Resistance activity.

Approaching a farm wagon rolling in the opposite direction, Karl slowed the car. He studied the two men who sat high in the front seat. One man held the reins of the two large horses. They offered no greeting, no smile. Nothing but blank expressions. Karl expected this reaction. He had a car and petrol to fuel it. That made him a German or a collaborator. Should he stop and examine their load? Why waste time on such things now? The Canadians were closing in. How much longer before they reconquered all of Holland? Weeks? Days? It was time to run. But where?

Karl accelerated past the farm wagon and approached the next village. The sign said *Nijkerk*. Just another nondescript little Dutch hamlet. Although the sounds of big guns rumbled off to the south and the east, life in Nijkerk seemed fairly routine. He passed a brick schoolhouse where playing children drew his attention.

He jerked upright, gripped the wheel, and stopped the car in the middle of the road. That boy. The blond-headed kid in the playground crowd. He looked familiar somehow. The way he stood with his hands on his hips. *Could he be Joran?* Karl reached to his right, rolled down the dusty window, and studied the boy until the group entered the schoolhouse. He parked his car on one of the side streets and took a seat on a storefront bench where he could observe the building. A clock in the nearby store window read almost two forty-five. He waited.

After about fifteen minutes, children poured out of the school, most heading in Karl's direction. The blond-headed boy walked in a group of children on the opposite side of the street.

Karl turned his back and entered the store. Once inside, he watched the passing group through the window. Might be him. He looked about fourteen, maybe fifteen. About the right age. Hard to get a good look at him in that group of rowdy kids.

"May I help you, sir?" The friendly voice startled Karl. He turned and glared at the shopkeeper and strode out the door. Scanning the various groups of children in the area, he spotted the blond boy with three other students. Karl followed just close enough to keep Joran in sight as they left the village and entered farm country. When the boy turned into the DeHaan driveway, Karl returned to his waiting car and hurried toward Utrecht.

Karl Müller stopped at Ernst Schmidt's open office door. The colonel looked up from his cluttered desk. A nearly full wastebasket sat within arm's reach. He pointed at a chair. "Sit. Did you do any good out there today, Müller?"

Karl stiffened in the wooden chair and looked at his commander's forehead. "No, sir. I carefully followed procedure at both sites but found nothing. There was no evidence of occupants other than the family. I searched the houses and barns carefully. Nobody hiding. No weapons."

Schmidt shrugged. "All right. Maybe tomorrow."

"Colonel Schmidt, I did see something that was interesting."

The Nazi tossed a bulging folder into the waste can and looked up. "And?"

"When I went through Nijkerk, I saw a child that looked familiar. Do you remember the youngest son of the Demeester family, the blond-headed boy?"

Schmidt paused. "I think so. Little kid. About nine or ten. Weepy boy."

"I might have seen him; at least, he looked like him."

Schmidt frowned. "You don't sound too sure. This miserable country is full of blond-headed kids."

"Well, it's been about five years now, and I didn't get real close, but it might have been him. Something about the way he acted."

Schmidt waved at the pile of papers on his desk. "Look, Müller, I am really busy right now. The Allies are knocking at the door. It's time to make a new plan." He tossed another folder in the trash can. "Time to rewrite my history. I need to be righteous once again."

The colonel leaned forward and rested his arms on his cluttered desk. His eyes brightened. "Still, there might be more of that Demeester money out there. It could pay my way—our way—to a new life. Am I right, Müller?"

Karl blinked. "I could use some money, yes, sir."

"I want you to go out there and check this out. We need to act right away. The Canadians are getting close. Go out there tonight. I need to stay here. Lots of records that must be burned. If it is the Demeester kid, bring him back to me immediately. He is the key to any remaining money. Then we'll force information from the people hiding him. Can you find the place in the dark?"

"It's easy. It's on the road going east toward Barneveld, just outside town."

Schmidt dismissed Müller with a casual wave and turned his attention to his files.

In the light of a crescent moon, Jenny and her well-traveled bicycle rattled up the DeHaan driveway. Sturdy canvas bags hung on both sides of the rear wheel. They once carried school books. Now they held documents vital to the war effort and dangerous to the courier.

Jenny leaned her bike against the side of the house. Blackout curtains hid the life inside. She announced her arrival with three light knocks on the front door, followed by two more light knocks.

From inside, a quiet voice, "Jenny?"

"It's me."

The lock clicked, and the door swung open. Jenny gave Joran a quick hug. As she hurried to the kitchen, she jerked off her black cap and slid out of the black jacket. She dropped them on a chair.

Her mother, clearing the table, looked up, and her face softened. "Stew is still warm, Jen. Have a seat."

Jenny took a seat opposite her father. Wrinkles creased his forehead. "Going out again tonight?"

"We have a lot of information that needs to go to the Canadians. Mostly maps and drawings of German positions."

"Just you?"

"Afraid so." Jenny glanced at her mother, who stood at the sink with her back turned. She turned to her father and patted the bulging side pocket of her black men's slacks. *Just me and my pistol.*

Her mother brought Jenny a welcome bowl of stew and another for herself. "Albert, this child is taking years off my life. I will spend another long night in my rocker praying. That old chair won't survive the war."

Jenny paused with the spoon dipped in the stew. "I carry those prayers with me, Mama."

Karl Müller drove his car through the blacked-out village of Nijkerk and parked it a few hundred meters from the DeHaan farm. He followed his flashlight beam along the country road until he reached the entry gate, then switched off the light and, relying on the glow of the crescent moon, edged up the driveway. Crickets encouraged him but went silent as he approached. About fifty feet from the front door, he stopped and pulled the Luger from its holster. He inhaled deeply and strode toward the home's entrance—running the last couple of steps—and drove the heel of his boot into the door, just beside the handle. With a sharp crack, the frame splintered, and the door burst open.

It took only a few seconds to run through the darkened front room to the lighted kitchen. He burst into the room and swung the pistol toward the shocked occupants, all sitting silently at the kitchen table.

"Don't move. Nobody move, or I will shoot you where you sit."

Joran Demeester gasped. His heart pounded on his ribs. "Karl?"

Müller, his hands trembling, glared at him. "I was right. It is you. Now you belong to us. You are coming with me. You and all your family secrets."

The spoon in Aunt Emma's trembling hand clattered against her bowl.

Uncle Albert leaned forward and rested his arms on the table. "We know all about you, Karl. Joran has spoken of you often."

A bit of uncertainty seemed to capture Müller's face. "Told you what?"

"He told us that he missed you, that you were always good to him. He said you taught him some soccer moves, and that you even volunteered at one of the orphanages. The one that sheltered you as a child after the last war."

Karl seemed to gaze into empty space for a moment. He looked back at the family, eyes cold. "Well, things have changed. I came to this country when I was a child because we were starving in Germany. Then, under our Führer, Germany became powerful again. I joined a great cause."

Jenny leaned back in her chair and dropped her hands into her lap. "Your Führer is nothing but a—"

"Quiet, child," Uncle Albert said. His sun-wrinkled face and thick beard masked any expression. "Karl, the German cause is not going very well. Even now, the Allied guns are getting closer."

As if on cue, the rumble of distant artillery penetrated the walls of the farmhouse.

"There," Albert said. "You can hear the Canadian guns. You must look to the future, Karl. It is time for you to do what is right. Joran is a perfectly innocent child. If you take him away and harm comes to him, you will surely hang for it. You now have a choice. You can allow him to live, and we will testify for you. All you have to do is turn around and leave this house."

Karl swung his weapon toward Joran.

Joran shifted his gaze from the gun muzzle to the man's face. "We are friends, aren't we?"

Then a change. The glare faded, and a hint of kindness appeared in Karl's eyes. His face softened. The Luger drifted downward until it pointed at the kitchen floor.

A sharp explosion echoed through the house.

As a horrified Joran watched, the spark of life faded from Karl's eyes. His body went completely limp. He collapsed onto the kitchen floor, exposing a man standing behind him, in his Gestapo military uniform, holding a pistol at arm's length.

The man strolled around the kitchen, eyeing his captives, speaking in fluent Dutch as he walked. "The more I thought about it, the more I suspected that Müller could be right." He stopped and looked directly at Joran. "And here you are, young Demeester, alive and well. Müller was, in fact, quite correct."

The German resumed his pacing. "But my concerns grew that Müller would fail to complete his assignment." He nudged Karl's lifeless body with the toe of his gleaming black boot. "And he has confirmed my suspicions. He lost his resolve right there in front of me." He shrugged. "I had no choice but to kill him, of course."

Joran's hands trembled as the man's cold gaze rested on him. "You're him. The man who took our house."

The Nazi moved closer and rested a gloved hand on the boy's shoulder. "Well, well. The last living Demeester."

Joran gritted his teeth and looked down at the table.

The Nazi squeezed the shoulder. "That's right, the last one. Your brother, shot down in the street like a stray dog. And your parents. Off to Auschwitz never to return. Poof. Reduced to ashes, up the chimney, and out over the Polish countryside. I am glad you remember me, boy. I am Colonel Schmidt, and yes, I took your house, as well as everything else. At least what we could find."

Joran's strong body failed him. He grasped the edge of the table. The sound of Schmidt's voice faded.

The German scanned the group. "I am taking all of you with me. We will wring every bit of information from you. And just possibly, we will find the remainder of the Demeester fortune." He stopped, reached into his pocket, and produced a roll of adhesive tape. He tossed it on the table and turned the gun on Aunt Emma. "You. Use this tape, and tie the hands of everyone else. I am going to lay you creatures like cordwood into the back seat of my car. All except the boy. He goes in the trunk."

Emma extended her trembling right hand and grasped the tape, then dropped it on the table and pulled her arm back. She bowed her head and responded with a quavering voice, "I will not."

The German lowered his weapon and reached across the table toward the tape. "Foolish woman. You will do it or you will—"

A pistol appeared above the table in the steady hand of Jenny DeHaan.

Schmidt pivoted and swung his Luger toward her, firing as he turned.

An instant later, Jenny's gun responded with a sharp blast.

The German staggered backward, his weapon sending one more round into the ceiling as he collapsed to the floor.

Jenny rose and continued to aim her pistol at Schmidt as he thrashed for a few seconds, then lay still.

With her thumb, she uncocked her weapon and looked down at herself. "He missed me."

Nobody spoke for a long moment.

The body of Karl Müller lay in a contorted position, face down. Blood drained from a small bullet hole in the back of his head. Nearby, Colonel Ernst Schmidt lay on his back, the chest of his uniform soaked with blood. His boots, perfectly shined, rested on the hardwood with their toes tilted to either side. His lifeless eyes stared at the ceiling.

Jenny set her weapon on the table and pushed it to arm's length with a shaking hand. "That man was evil, Papa. Now he's dead. I killed him. I had to do it, didn't I?'

"Yes, sweetheart. You had to do it."

"They'll come for us now," she said quietly. "The Gestapo will kill us all."

Chapter Forty-One

The DeHaan Farm

As Jenny gazed at the two dead bodies on the kitchen floor, gunpowder fumes filled her nostrils and sent a shock wave through her. The image of Marten Demeester dying in the street, surrounded by that same awful smell, filled her mind and numbed her senses.

"Karl was going to let us go," Joran said. "I know it. I saw kindness in his eyes ... until that man shot him." Tears welled. "How can people be so bad, Uncle Albert?"

"I can only think that evil itself held that man in its grasp, Joran. Let's be thankful that Karl was able to embrace good at the end."

Jenny's gaze fell on the dead Gestapo colonel on the kitchen floor, and fear suddenly gripped her body and cleared her mind. "We need to get these bodies out of here. Now."

"Could we take them somewhere and make it look like they shot each other?" Joran asked. "We could leave their guns with them."

"No," Jenny said. "The Gestapo is too smart. They will see it as a killing by the Resistance. Then the retaliation will start. It will be bad. Really bad."

Joran stood and raised himself to his full fifteen-year-old height. "Bury them here. We have a big farm with a plowed field. I can dig a hole right now. By morning, they'll be gone." He paused. "I want a separate place for Karl."

"What about the cars?" Jenny's father said. "Since none of us know how to drive, we can use the horses to tow them behind the barn or—"

"No," Joran said. "I can drive."

Jenny stepped toward him. "What? When did you, I mean, how ..."

"When I was a boy, Karl would let me sit in his lap sometimes when he drove. Never if Mama or Papa were in the car, only Marten and me. I learned how to do everything, and now I can reach the pedals." He brushed off the tears with his sleeve. "I can do it."

Jenny glanced at her father, and he nodded. "Okay. Papa, you ride with him. Throw a couple of bikes in the car with you. Drive toward the Allied lines and park the car in a wooded area a few miles from here, then ride the bikes back and get the other vehicle. While you're gone, I'll start working on the graves, and Mama can clean up in here. We should have everything done by dawn."

Jenny's mother raised her hand. "Before we do anything more, there is something I must do right now. I must pray for forgiveness."

Jenny felt a mixture of love and puzzlement as she looked at her mother. "Forgiveness, Mama? For what?"

Her mother's voice took on an uncharacteristic firmness. "Listen to me. This is important. I am speaking for myself, but I think this applies to all of us." She pointed a finger at the lifeless body of the Gestapo officer. "That man was filled with evil. When I watched him kill Karl and abuse Joran, I hated him. Seeing him die on the kitchen floor pleased me—excited me." She looked around the room at her family. "Don't you see? The evil in that man got inside me. And later, guilt will come, and it will follow me. I want to be free of it. I must pray now. Perhaps you should too." She folded her hands and bowed her head.

Jenny noted that every head in the room was bowed. She did the same. The only sound in the old farmhouse was the clicking of the mantel clock in the front room.

330

Joran and Uncle Albert turned their bikes into the driveway and followed their flashlight beams to the farmhouse.

"I'll find Jenny," Joran said. "She'll need help burying those bodies."

"Good. I'll check on Emma. You'll have to work fast out there. Sun will be coming up soon. Come get me if you need me. Oh, and don't shine any lights out there."

Joran paused for a minute to allow his eyes to adjust to the darkness and edged into the pasture.

"Over here." Jenny's whispered shout echoed across the field. "Under the oak tree."

He followed Jenny's cues until he found her standing in a hole about a foot deep.

"I thought this would be a good spot for Karl. What do you think?'

"Perfect. He won't be close to the Nazi, will he?"

"No. Schmidt is already buried. No one will ever know where except me. I didn't have time to finish digging this one yet. Another hour and I'll be done."

Joran took the shovel from her. "Please, sit. I need to do this."

He scooped load after load of soft, dark soil from the hole, allowing the rhythm of the work to clear his mind. As he dug, the distant rumble of artillery sounded like thunder. Like a big storm was approaching. A storm bringing not rain, but freedom.

When he finished digging, they lowered the body gently into place, covered it with a sheet, and replaced the earth.

Joran stood and inhaled deeply. "Jenny, I feel like I should say a Jewish prayer, even though Karl was not Jewish. I attended one burial with my parents, and they said a prayer. I think they called it *Tziduk Hadin*. My father translated it for me. I only remember a little."

She rested an arm on his shoulders. "Just say what you remember."

Joran leaned on his shovel and closed his eyes. "The Lord has given and the Lord has taken. May the Name of the Lord be blessed."

He gazed at the grave for moment. "*Shalom, chaver.*"

"What does that mean?"

"Goodbye, friend."

Just after sunrise, Jenny and Joran returned to the farmhouse. They took seats in the clean kitchen. Her mother brought coffee. "I could fix some breakfast," she said. Nobody responded. "Maybe later."

Albert leaned a rifle in a corner. "I found this thing in the Gestapo car. The Resistance always needs these."

Mother got up and walked to her stove. "Hungry or not, you people are going to eat. You need your energy."

With little discussion, they consumed a large platter of hastily prepared eggs and a pot of coffee. Father pushed back his empty plate and raised a match to his packed pipe.

Jenny jolted the table as she jumped to her feet. "We still have a big problem."

Everyone looked to her for an explanation.

"It may not be over. Schmidt probably hurried over here on impulse to check on Karl, and he probably wanted to keep his search for the Demeester money a secret. But it is still possible that he left a note about where he was going. If he did, the Gestapo will be coming here—any minute."

Jenny's wide-eyed mother turned to her husband. "Oh, dear Lord, Albert. We could leave. We know lots of people who will hide us."

Jenny checked her watch. "No. The Gestapo could be on their way right now. They would catch us marching down the road."

Joran stood. "I'm not going to sit in here and wait to be caught or killed. I'm taking that rifle and hiding in the field."

Emma gasped. "No, Joran. Please stay."

The boy grabbed the gun, opened the back door, and responded without looking back. "I have to do this."

"Please stop him, Albert," Emma said. "He is the last of his family. He's my child now."

"I love him too, but he is no longer a child. His decisions are his own." He paused, then slowly nodded. "As are ours. Joran has lost much in this war, as have we all."

"Well, he's not going to fight alone," Jenny said. "If the Gestapo takes us away, none of us will survive. I'm going to take my pistol and hide in the bushes out front."

Father took his wife's hand. "I will stay inside with Emma." He paused for a moment. "And I will take Karl's gun."

Mother drew her lips into a thin line. "Then we will stand together. Albert, is there time to show me how to use that Nazi colonel's pistol?"

Joran selected a dry ditch where he could conceal himself and see anyone approaching on the road. He settled in the grass and examined the Karabiner rifle. The stock was scratched, and the metal showed rust, but the firing mechanism was fairly clean. "Good. Just like the others," Joran whispered to himself, remembering the captured rifles that Resistance fighters occasionally brought to the farm.

He grasped the bolt action and racked it smoothly to its rear position. A spent shell flipped out and landed in the grass. When he slid the bolt forward, the mechanism loaded a fresh cartridge. After inhaling deeply, he slid around in the grass until he had established a position where he could watch the farmhouse and the road. Jenny hid in the shrubbery at the front of the house, and he returned her wave.

Movement on the road caught his eye. A group of three uniformed Germans approached on foot from the east, still about five hundred meters distant. They carried rifles slung on their shoulders and trudged along, seemingly unconcerned about their surroundings. He watched them without raising his weapon.

When the group was about a hundred meters from Joran, he looked toward the house. Jenny gestured that she had seen the soldiers.

The sound of an approaching vehicle drew Joran's attention. The three soldiers stopped and turned toward the sound. They scrambled off the road and disappeared into the roadside ditch.

A black car came into view, moving fast, and leaving a cloud of dust.

Heart pounding violently in his chest, Joran raised himself onto his elbows and poked the muzzle of the rifle through the grass. Although the car was still out of range, he aimed the gun sights on the moving vehicle and tracked it as it neared.

When the car, a black sedan like Schmidt had driven, was almost in front of him, Joran put his index finger on the trigger and looked down the sights at the driver.

The car did not slow. The driver and passenger, wearing black fedoras, seemed to be studying the road ahead. They roared past the DeHaan driveway. Joran relaxed his aim. In a few seconds, the car was gone, quiet returned, and the dust settled.

Relieved, Joran started to get up and move toward the three hiding Germans but stopped and lowered himself to the ground. The Gestapo had shown no interest in the farm, but maybe they missed it. "They may be back," he whispered.

New sounds from the east. Different sounds. Multiple vehicles. Deep, roaring engines along with mechanical clanking sounds. Curiosity overcame Joran. He raised his head.

A military tank appeared, creeping along the dirt road with its big gun pointed forward. In the dust behind it, more vehicles followed. *Panzers?* The lead tank rumbled closer, still about four hundred meters away. *No. Something different.*

A jeep rolled past the creeping tank. It displayed a red flag. "No swastika," Joran mumbled. In one corner was a familiar design. A Union Jack. "Canadian. They're Canadian." He jumped to his feet.

He walked toward the road and stopped. The German soldiers who had hidden in the roadside ditch had not reappeared. He bent at the waist and crept ahead, weapon raised, mumbling to himself. "No more. They aren't going to attack our liberators. I'll kill them."

As he edged forward, he looked right. The procession stopped. The men in the jeep jumped out and aimed rifles directly at him. He pointed his rifle muzzle toward the sky. With his free hand extended high overhead, he made a slow wave and pointed toward the hidden Germans.

He plunged ahead in the tall grass, a mild breeze whisking his cheeks. He stopped short. Three soldiers lay on their bellies, each peering toward the approaching army.

"Freeze!" shouted Joran, surprised at the strong voice he generated. They all froze. "I really want to kill you all, like you killed my family. If you move, you will die right here in this ditch." Joran shifted his aim from one silent man to the next.

Hearing footsteps on the road, Joran looked up to see several approaching Canadians. He maintained his aim at the Germans until a gentle hand rested on his shoulder, and the liberators took control of the prisoners.

Tension drained from Joran's body. He took a close look at the Germans he had captured. They were shaking with fright, their smooth, unshaven faces dirty and pale. "They're just kids, like me."

The officer turned to his fellow soldiers. "Hey, this guy speaks perfect English." He shook Joran's hand. "Have you ever been to Canada, young man?"

"I've been to New York."

"Close enough." He pulled off his hat and put it on Joran's head. "You're a great soldier. You deserve this."

A few minutes later, a caravan of Canadian tanks and trucks ground to a halt on the road at the DeHaan driveway. A jeep rolled up to the farmhouse. The DeHaans stood in a group, smiling broadly and clapping their hands. In the front seat, Joran Demeester sat, wearing a Canadian captain's hat, slightly too large. He jumped out. "Look everyone, I have my own army."

CHAPTER FORTY-TWO

10 June 1945
The DeHaan Farm

Jenny scraped the last bit of whipped cream from her dessert plate and leaned back in her creaking kitchen chair. A light breeze whisked her cheek as cool spring air flowed through the open window of the farmhouse. She studied her family, all gathered around the kitchen table. A small wooden box, containing the collection of Nic's letters from Germany, held its prominent place in the center of the table. Words were absent at that moment, but sober and distant expressions spoke of their solemn thoughts. The love that had nurtured Jenny's soul during her entire life still lived there, yet the joy and peace that once filled the place seemed wounded and broken.

The presence of the two men who died in that room two months previous still lingered. And Nic was absent. His most recent letter from the Red Cross hospital said he was recovering, his strength returning. Every day young men were returning to Holland, but her brother had not been among them. She watched the road daily, a lump in her throat.

Shoving aside her somber thoughts, she looked at her father, who was pushing tobacco into the bowl of his pipe, the same old pipe Jenny remembered from her childhood. The war had deepened the lines on his sun-weathered face. "Looks like it's going to be a good year on the farm, Papa."

The comment seemed to add a small spark to her father's eyes. "No matter how harsh the winter, spring follows, Jen. True of a war too. Life goes on."

Her mother, clearing the dishes, directed a warm comment at her husband. "Your optimism is a blessing to me, Albert. Always has been."

He set his unlit pipe on the table, then retrieved his reading glasses and the old family Bible from the shelf and returned to his seat. "There's a verse somewhere in the New Testament where Paul talks about moving on. The preacher talked about that in his sermon a couple of weeks ago. Where is that?"

Joran looked up with a glint of humor on his face. "Can't help you on that one, Uncle Albert. My family always read from the other end of that book."

"I think it was somewhere in the book of Philippians," said Jenny.

He leaned over the Bible and flipped pages as he looked through his wire-rimmed spectacles. He stopped. "Here it is." He peered at his gathered flock over the top of his glasses. "Listen to this." He shifted the glasses on his nose and lifted the book. "'But one thing I do: Forgetting what is behind and straining toward what is ahead, I press on toward the goal.'"

He closed the Bible and placed his glasses on top. "There. Pretty good sermon for an old farmer, don't you think?"

Jenny's heart warmed at the sight of her lifelong hero. "You are exactly right, Papa. We need to move forward." She paused and looked down at the floor. "But it's hard with all the bad memories that hang all over our home—over our whole country."

Jenny swallowed hard. Now was the time. The war had changed many things, but not her hopes for a future. She shifted forward in her chair. "I've been thinking about what Richard said about moving to America."

The corners of her father's mouth turned up just a notch. "Oh?"

"He said there is a community of people just like us. A place to get a new start. Go to college even."

Her mother raised her eyebrows. "America is a long way, child." She winked. "Perhaps not so far if someone is waiting for you at the end of the journey."

Jenny's heart swelled. "Maybe Nic will go too. We could all go."

Mama wiped her hands on a towel and took her seat at the table. She paused for a few moments, attracting the attention of her family. She slowly shook her head. "No. This is my home. The only home I know. I will stay here." She turned the focus to her husband.

Father lit his pipe. He lowered it to the table. Smoke curled toward the ceiling as he looked at his wife. "Our roots are deep in the soil here. We will stay." He pointed at Jenny with the stem of his pipe. "If you go, young lady, I expect you to come visit us."

"Yes," her mother said. "And bring your children. I know you will have some."

Jenny rested a gentle hand on her mother's arm and looked into her moist eyes. "Don't worry, Mama. I will bring all my children to visit you. They will feel the same love that I have enjoyed."

She glanced at her father and back to her mother. "But I also have another commitment. I promised Marten that I would care for the children. I am not finished. I will never be finished. I might be a pediatrician, run an orphanage, become a teacher—whatever door opens to me."

As Joran observed this discussion, an ache grew deep inside. He rested his arms on the table and gazed down at his folded hands. The voices at the table faded, and his mind recalled happy days with his family. When he sensed quiet around him, he looked up. All eyes were watching him.

Jenny broke the silence. "I would like to bring you to America too, Joran. You are also my brother."

Her comments lifted Joran's mood just a little. "Maybe I could do that." He paused, and the dark thoughts returned. "The family of my birth is gone. Almost all of the Dutch Jews are gone, never to return. It feels like there is an emptiness in the Netherlands that can't be filled. I feel like a stranger in my homeland, except in this house."

Emma reached over and laid a gentle hand on Joran's arm. "Albert and I also consider you a full member of our family. You are welcome to live here as long as you wish."

"Thank you, Aunt Emma. But I will be a grown man soon. I must find my own path in life."

The sound of tires on gravel interrupted their conversation. Jenny went to the window. "It's a Red Cross car."

"Is it Nicolaas, Jenny?" asked her wide-eyed mother.

Jenny pressed her nose to the glass, turned back, disappointment written on her face. "No, not Nic, somebody else."

Joran stood. "I'll see who it is. Maybe they have news about Nic."

He opened the front door. A car with its bright red cross eased to a stop. The driver's door opened, and a uniformed nurse stepped out. She walked around to the side and helped the passenger step out. She handed a cane to the man. Tall and very thin, he leaned on his cane and raised himself.

Joran's knees trembled. He leaned on the doorframe for support. "Papa?"

Their eyes met. The man dropped his cane and moved toward Joran, first slowly, but accelerating until they met. Joran pulled the man's frail body to himself.

Reinaar Demeester whispered, "My son. Oh, my son." Joran sobbed and felt tears stream down his cheeks. He pulled back and looked into his father's tearful eyes.

Reinaar's voice was weak, but his inner strength went straight to Joran's heart. "In that place, I lost my tears. But now I have you, and my soul has come alive. My tears have returned." As they embraced in silence, a flood of happy childhood memories filled Joran's mind.

After several long slow breaths, he studied his father's eyes. "Mama?"

Reinaar shook his head slowly and pulled his son back to himself. They wept together.

The family came outside and gathered in silence.

The Red Cross nurse approached and laid a gentle hand on Reinaar's shoulder. "I must return now, Mr. Demeester. Is there anything more we can do for you?"

"No, child." He held her hand in both of his. "Your love has helped me survive. Bless you."

The nurse turned to Joran. "Your father is a strong and courageous man. He has endured incredible hardships." With a glance at the family, she continued. "The Red Cross found Mr. Demeester mostly covered by snow, barely alive. His recovery was slow, and he lost parts of his feet to frostbite, but he is now doing well. Unfortunately, due to the loss of our communication and transportation systems, it took us a while to find you."

While Joran and his father embraced, the nurse approached the DeHaans. "I have an update on your son. The British freed the workers at Lübeck and brought Nicolaas to us. He was quite sick and malnourished, but we think he will be ready to come home in a week or two."

As the Red Cross car departed, Reinaar extended a slightly trembling hand to Albert. "I am Reinaar Demeester. You must be Albert DeHaan. You and your family risked your lives to look after my son. I owe you more than I could ever repay."

Albert gave the hand a gentle shake. "Joran was a blessing to us."

After introducing Reinaar to his wife, Albert led the group into the front room. Joran assisted his father to a seat on the couch.

Reinaar looked around the room. "You have a lovely home, Mrs. DeHaan."

"This house is filled with love, Father," said Joran.

"I can feel it. After being in a place with no love, my heart is warmed when I am surrounded by it. Tell me, son, after living in two different families, are you now Jewish or Christian?"

Joran thought for a moment. "Perhaps both, Father."

A gentle smile graced Reinaar's deeply lined face. "That's nice." He paused. "Joran, would you do something for me?"

"I would do anything in this world for you, Father."

He pointed at the cello that was resting in the corner. "When I was in that place, I sometimes shut out the evil around me and listened in my mind to your cello. Would you play again for me?"

Sitting close to his father, Joran poured his heart and soul into the instrument. Reinaar sat, head bowed and eyes closed. When the music eased to a gentle end, the bow seemed to have a life of its own as it rose from the instrument in Joran's gentle hand. Joran opened his eyes, inhaled, and straightened in his chair.

After a long moment, Reinaar raised his head and looked into his son's eyes. "That was beautiful. It fills some of the emptiness in me."

"What else can I do for you, Father?"

"Your presence and your voice are all I desire right now."

"What should we do? Where should we go?"

Reinaar gazed straight ahead while he rubbed one frail hand with the other. "Holland holds too many painful memories. I would like to go, but I am no longer a rich man."

"Our homes have been badly damaged, Father, but there is still some money that Jenny and I buried in the pasture. We could move somewhere."

Reinaar turned to Joran, and his eyes brightened. "Sometimes in the camps, I would dream of a small house in a quiet place. Somewhere we might find peace and perhaps a place where hope might be reborn. I think, son, that I would like to go home to Jerusalem."

Printed in Great Britain
by Amazon